Valerie Anand was born in London and grew up in Kent and Surrey; she attempted her first work of fiction at the age of six. In her twenties she became a journalist and wrote several short stories, before her first novel, *Gildenford*, was published. She is now a full-time writer and lives with her husband in Surrey.

Crown of Roses

Valerie Anand

HEADLINE

First published in 1989
by HEADLINE BOOK PUBLISHING PLC

First published in paperback in 1990
by HEADLINE BOOK PUBLISHING PLC

10 9 8 7 6 5 4 3 2

ISBN 0 7472 3344 6

Typeset in 10/11½ pt English Times
by Colset Private Limited, Singapore

Printed and bound in Great Britain by
HarperCollins Manufacturing, Glasgow

HEADLINE BOOK PUBLISHING PLC
Headline House
79 Great Titchfield Street
London W1P 7FN

Dedication

This book is for Anne, Alan, Shirley, Roy and all the other members of the Richard III Society Croydon Group, in whose company I visited so many of the sites mentioned.

It is also dedicated, with great affection, to Eileen who was there when it all began in September 1952, and to the memory of Paddy, whose steady encouragement I so much valued.

Note On Detail

I should perhaps note that because of the complexity of the material, I have taken the liberty of simplifying some of the details. I have for example amalgamated the two Stanley brothers, William and Thomas, into one. I have also very much simplified the reasons why Warwick had his former brother-in-law John Tiptoft executed. For these and other bits of artistic streamlining, I hope Ricardian experts will forgive me.

Acknowledgements

In order to write this book, I have consulted so many works over so many years that to list them all would be impossible, but foremost among them were:

The Battle of Bosworth by Michael Bennett (1985, Alan Sutton, Dursley, Glos)

This Sun of York by Mary Clive (1973, Macmillan, London)

The Princes in the Tower by Elizabeth Jenkins (1978, Hamish Hamilton, London)

Richard the Third (1950), *Warwick the Kingmaker* (1957) and *Louis XI* (1971) all by Paul Murray Kendall (George Allen & Unwin, London, Sydney and Boston)

A Town Grammar School Through Six Centuries by John Lawson (1963, Hull University Press)

Richard the Third by Charles Ross (1981, Eyre Methuen, London)

Daughter of Time by Josephine Tey (1951, Peter Davies, London)

The Mystery of the Princes by Audrey Williamson (1978, Alan Sutton).

Contemporary works consulted included *The Paston Letters* (1924, Ed. John Warrington), the works of Sir Thomas More, and Dominic Mancini's *Usurpation of Richard III* (1936, translated by C.A.J. Armstrong).

I am especially indebted to the Richard III Society and their superb library, from which I borrowed many out-of-print works, and to the University of Hull Library which provided *A Town Grammar School*, a book containing much valuable information on Bishop John Alcock.

DESCENDANTS OF EDWARD III

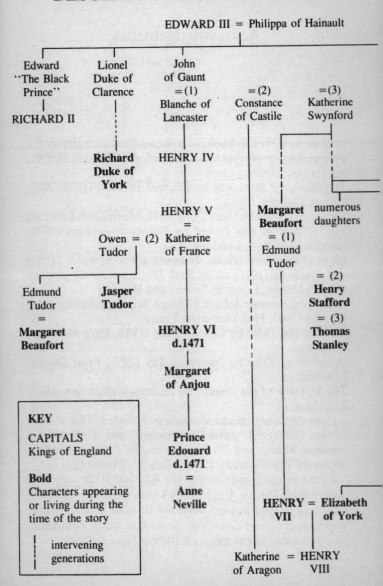

EDWARD III = Philippa of Hainault

Edward "The Black Prince"

RICHARD II

Lionel Duke of Clarence

Richard Duke of York

John of Gaunt
= (1) Blanche of Lancaster

HENRY IV

HENRY V

Owen = (2) Katherine Tudor of France

Edmund Tudor = Margaret Beaufort

Jasper Tudor

HENRY VI d.1471

Margaret of Anjou

Prince Edouard d.1471 = Anne Neville

= (2) Constance of Castile

= (3) Katherine Swynford

Margaret Beaufort
= (1) Edmund Tudor
= (2) Henry Stafford
= (3) Thomas Stanley

numerous daughters

HENRY VII = Elizabeth of York

Katherine of Aragon = HENRY VIII

KEY

CAPITALS
Kings of England

Bold
Characters appearing or living during the time of the story

┆ intervening generations

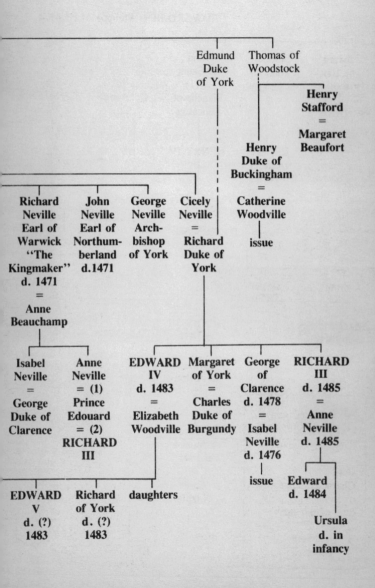

Principal Historical Characters

Plantagenets and Woodvilles

Richard Plantagenet, Duke of York (deceased before story opens)
Cicely Neville, Duchess of York, his wife
His children:
    King Edward IV
    George Plantagenet, Duke of Clarence
    Richard Plantagenet, Duke of Gloucester
    (later Richard III)
    Margaret of York (later Duchess of Burgundy)
Bess Woodville (formerly Lady Grey), wife to Edward IV
Her sons by Sir John Grey:
    Thomas Grey (later Marquis of Dorset)
    Sir Richard Grey
Her children by King Edward:
    Elizabeth of York
    Edward Prince of Wales
    Richard of York
    younger daughters
Sir Anthony Woodville, brother of Bess
Catherine Woodville, Duchess of Buckingham, their sister
Harry Stafford, Duke of Buckingham

The Nevilles

Richard Neville, Earl of Warwick
Countess Anne, his wife

Their daughters:
   Isabel Neville (later Duchess of Clarence)
   Anne Neville (later wife successively to Prince Edouard
   and Richard of Gloucester)
Edward, the son of Anne and Richard
Warwick's brothers:
   George Neville, Archbishop of York
   John Neville, Earl of Northumberland for a time
Warwick's brothers-in-law:
   William Lord Hastings
   Thomas Lord Stanley
   John Tiptoft, Earl of Worcester
   John de Vere, Earl of Oxford

The House of Lancaster

King Henry VI (deposed)
Margaret of Anjou, his wife
Prince Edouard, their son
Margaret Beaufort (Countess of Richmond), widow of
Edmund Tudor, later Lady Stanley
Henry Tudor, her son
Jasper Tudor, his uncle

Prelates

John Alcock, successively Bishop of Rochester, Worcester
and Ely
Cardinal Thomas Bourchier, Archbishop of Canterbury
John Morton, later Bishop of Ely and then Archbishop of
Canterbury
Thomas Rotherham, Archbishop of York (succeeding
George Neville)
Robert Stillington, Bishop of Bath and Wells

Crown of Roses

Prologue

February 1466

The infant Princess Elizabeth of York had been christened in a brand new font installed for the occasion in St Stephen's Chapel at the Palace of Westminster. George Neville, Chancellor of the Realm and Archbishop of York and a cousin, if remotely, of the baby, had baptised her. His brother Richard Neville, Earl of Warwick and the eldest of the three Neville brothers, was godfather. Holding the child in his arms during the ceremony, Warwick had been seen to study her tiny face with a somewhat grim expression on his own, as if wondering whether she would grow up to resemble her mother.

Now, four days later, the royal mother, Edward the Fourth's controversial, low-bred Queen, had been churched. Priests and choristers led the procession. After them came sixty lords and sixty ladies and forty-two royal minstrels playing appropriate music.

On the heels of the minstrels came the Queen herself, walking under a canopy borne by two dukes all the way from the Palace of Westminster to the Abbey and back.

At the Palace, four great halls floored with marble and glittering with leaf of gold and silver had been set with tables to accommodate between them a giant banquet. Even so, they did not accommodate the Queen, who dined separately in a fifth chamber, attended by her threescore ladies and waited on in person by her mother and her husband's sister, their humble respect a measure of her exalted rank.

'I have never seen such an exhibition in my life,' said Richard of Warwick disgustedly later, to his other brother John Neville of Northumberland, and to his young cousins. He was an exceedingly handsome man, his blue eyes and amber hair so intense in colour, his height so commanding and his personality so powerful that to look at him could give one an almost physical shock. When he was angry, as he was now, the shock was very nearly an assault.

'Her mother,' said Warwick, 'who is a countess however obscure, and the Lady Margaret who is not only your sister –' momentarily, he turned his wrathful azure gaze full on to his cousins ' – but, even more to the point, is the King's sister too, had to kneel whenever Bess Woodville deigned to speak to them and she deigned to speak to them only to ask for wine or fingerbowls. When I paid my respects she made it clear that I was honoured because she exchanged a few stilted phrases with me!'

The elder of the two cousins, George of Clarence, was eighteen, fair as an angel. His cap and doublet of heavenly blue had been chosen to match his eyes and the doublet was padded at the shoulders and slashed with gold satin. He said fastidiously: 'Her mother is supposed to be a witch. Like mother like daughter, if you ask me. The daughter's put a spell on brother Ned all right. All sweetness and modesty when she's with him, and God help us all, he thinks that's what she's really like. She makes our sister curtsy to her every five minutes and Ned beams indulgently on his darling Bess's delight in her new position. She pushes all her ghastly relatives into high office and Ned says how charming it is of her not to forget her family now that she herself has such advancement. It makes me want to puke.'

John Neville would have been as handsome as Warwick except that a childhood attack of smallpox had dimmed his good looks. Perhaps because of this, he was of a more thoughtful temperament than either of his brothers. 'She may have been just the widow of a knight at one time,' he said, 'but she's Ned's consort now. We must just make the best of it.'

The younger cousin, Dickon of Gloucester, had not yet spoken. At thirteen, he was expected to listen more than talk, and besides, he was self-effacing by inclination. He was small and dark, having missed the Neville looks, and he was conscious of it. But he possessed, nevertheless, all their nervous energy and depth of feeling.

Now he contributed to the conversation for the first time. His voice was low but contained so much suppressed violence that the others turned sharply to listen.

'I've admired Ned all my life,' he said. 'He avenged our father when Margaret of Anjou killed him and put his head on a spike over the gate of York city. He won the battle at Towton. He knows how to make men love him. He made me love him. When you and I were small, George, and we were living in lodgings in the City and Ned was at court with Father, he found time every day, every single day, to come to see us. I thought he was wonderful. And now I've seen him just . . . just bewitched, George is right, there's no other way to put it, by a woman who's nothing. He hardly sees us any more. He only sees her and he can't see through her. She only wanted to marry him to get the crown on her head. She stole the crown. She stole Ned. *I hate her*!'

Such events as the churching, which drew lords and prelates together from all over the land, were opportunities, not to be let slip, for conducting business. Noble foregathered with noble to arrange tournaments and marriages, to lay plans to promote or block the appointment of this man or that to crucial positions, and to use the said plans skilfully as bribes or threats to obtain royal audiences, better dowered daughters-in-law or new and remunerative appointments of their own. The bishops did much the same thing except that few of them needed to arrange children's marriages, although even this was not unknown.

On this occasion, Archbishop Neville of York and his

counterpart of Canterbury, the conscientious and apolitical Cardinal Thomas Bourchier, had seized the chance of summoning senior clergy to confer on a financial agenda ranging from the propriety of raising loans on usurious terms for major cathedral repairs, down to the widespread public laxity over paying tithes. At half past ten on the morning after the churching ceremony, Dr Stillington, Bishop of Bath and Wells, and his old friend and former pupil Dr John Alcock, Dean of St Stephen's, with whom he had been staying, set out for Archbishop Neville's house to attend the conference.

The distance was too short for horses to be worthwhile but the temperature had plummeted during the night. Heavily wrapped against the weather, velvet-capped tonsure bent into the February wind, Stillington attempted to distract them both from their discomfort by discussing yesterday's events all over again.

'It's done now,' he said glumly, unconsciously echoing Northumberland. 'And there's a child and there'll be more. Oh yes, undoubtedly there will be more. King Edward is uxorious. But he has made such a fool of Warwick. Warwick was halfway through most delicate negotiations to get a French princess for the King, when Edward suddenly declared that he was married already, in secret, to a commoner! A widow,' said Stillington disapprovingly, 'five years older than he is and with two children by her first husband, and far too many relatives.'

'Ah yes,' Dr Alcock smiled. 'You should hear Clarence on that subject.'

'I've heard him already.' Holding his cap in place. Stillington looked up at his companion. Short and rotund, he was inclined to embonpoint and had to look up at very nearly everybody, but with Alcock he noticed it more. For one thing, Alcock was a big man, sixteen and a half stone in weight and eight inches taller than Stillington. For another, Alcock's stature was more than just physical. Stillington valued, even loved, his ex-pupil but he was never quite at

4

ease with him. He was a bishop and Alcock was not, but every time Stillington looked up into Alcock's fresh-skinned Yorkshireman's face, with the round blue eyes which seemed ingenuous until you saw their intelligence, he became aware that Alcock was his intellectual superior and by a wide margin at that.

'I detest secret marriages!' Stillington said now, suddenly angry. 'They always make trouble.' He sounded as though he had a personal grievance about it. 'If a marriage can't be open in the first place, something's wrong with it.'

'Or with the people the parties are afraid to tell,' said Alcock mildly. It was one of his disconcerting remarks. He had always been prone to them – it was as though, Still-ington thought, he were secretly questioning the fundamen-tal rules of society. 'There's nothing so terrible in the King's marriage,' Alcock said, 'except for the damage it's done to Warwick's schemes and Warwick's sense of his own impor-tance. Bess Woodville – or Grey, her first husband's name was Grey, was it not? – is virtuous, at least.'

'Oh that, yes,' said Stillington. 'The marriage came about, so it's said, because she refused to be the King's mistress. He held a dagger to her throat and she went on refusing even then. But I daresay she knew he didn't mean it. She was playing for high stakes, anyway. I suppose she thought the crown was worth the risk.'

'I wonder if she still thinks so,' remarked Alcock.

'Can you doubt it? She was wallowing in it yesterday! I never saw such curtsying! And oh, how she enjoyed the processions and the ambassadors paying their respects!'

'That's your reading of her, is it? That she is proud, ambitious?'

'Why, yes. Is it not yours?'

'I don't know her well enough to be sure, but on the whole – no,' said Alcock. 'I think the virtue was genuine and the desire to marry Edward, the man not the king, was genuine and that the crown was a temptation which came after those things. I also think that she may be finding it

5

heavier than she expected. Sometimes, when I've been with them – King Edward and his wife – I've caught a look on her face as though she was wondering whether something she had said or done were the right thing. I'm inclined to feel sorry for her.'

'Ah.' They turned into the Archbishop's gatehouse and out of the wind. 'Well, yes, there I could agree with you,' said Stillington unexpectedly. 'She's a target for intrigue,' he explained, as Alcock glanced at him questioningly.

'Not a very good one, I should have said,' Alcock observed. 'Not while she remains virtuous and I fancy she will . . .'

He broke off. They were emerging from the shelter of the gatehouse, having considerably outdistanced their attendants. Coming in the opposite direction, and sidling to pass them, was a gap-toothed individual whose sombre, travel-marked garments were like a parody of their own decent dark clothes, and whose bearing had the air of manufactured confidence which instantly marks the salesman of questionable goods. But as he edged by, his slate-coloured eyes met Alcock's directly, and without guile. Alcock half-turned his head to watch him disappear into the shadow of the gatehouse.

'A pardoner,' said Stillington with distaste. 'I've seen him before. He's been peddling his odious wares, I suppose, to the Archbishop's servants under their master's very nose. They would sooner spend their wages on his forged pardons than go properly to confront their sins at confession, and perform their penances. The Pope should act. No doubt that man claims that all his pardons have a Papal seal, when the truth is that they were sealed by his unhallowed hands in some grimy garret by the Thames!'

'If there were no customers, there would be no pardoners,' said Alcock tranquilly. 'Like whores. Men like those pardoners can be useful. They travel widely and without question. They enter households of every kind and most have a way with them which means that people talk to them.

6

Pardoners, jugglers, peddlers, travelling minstrels; always be careful what you say in the hearing of such men, Dr Stillington. You never know to whom they may report it.'

'I've heard that the King uses them as his eyes and ears,' Stillington said. 'You know all about it, I expect. You see so much of the King these days.' He could not quite keep the envy out of his voice. 'Tell me,' he added confidentially as they sauntered across the wide courtyard, loitering to let their attendants catch up, 'I've heard Clarence talk about the Queen, as I said – but is it true that the one who hates her most is Dickon?'

'Most? I wouldn't go as far as that, but he has always hero-worshipped Edward so much. He practises constantly with sword and bow, you know, trying to match the King's skill . . .'

'Yes, and I once heard him say that he was glad Edward had hazel eyes like his instead of the Neville blue,' Stillington agreed. 'It was touching, even a little pathetic, if you know what I mean.'

'Yes, I do, and now I think that his brother has disappointed him by behaving in a way that Dickon thinks isn't kingly, by marrying a woman of insufficient breeding. He's jealous. And he's been listening to Warwick, who has indeed been made to look foolish. Dickon has been under Warwick's influence for too long – he's been Warwick's ward for years, after all. I think Warwick is responsible for the way Dickon tries to imitate the Nevilles instead of being himself. He's an able boy and good-looking in his own right, but he doesn't know it yet. I hope that now the King has brought his brothers to court – they were too far away from the centre of things, up there in Middleham – he may persuade them both to accept Bess.'

'Does the King know how much they detest her?'

'Oh yes,' said Alcock, 'he knows.'

Alcock himself had informed him. Peter the Pardoner was not at the moment hovering round the houses of the great merely in order to sell pardons to their servants. He was here to gossip with the servants about their employers' affairs, to eavesdrop on the exalted as they passed through public rooms and courtyards. His glance as he passed Alcock in the gatehouse arch had been a salute, agent to controller.

King Edward had strong family feelings but he knew the simple value of keeping oneself informed. He had made sure that he knew exactly what every member of his family, what every one of his lords, thought of the Queen, and how intensely. Pardoners, peddlers, jugglers, minstrels: they did indeed make excellent informants and Alcock had a gift for finding good recruits and managing them.

At times, he was ashamed of this. He used his skill only in the service of the realm and the lawful King. He used it with scrupulous honesty, editing nothing, but his conscience frequently protested, as much on account of the honesty as in spite of it. He had not liked reporting to the King Dickon's overheard opinion of Queen Bess.

All men suffered their temptations. Some celibate priests spent their whole lives racked by longing for sex. Alcock admired women from a distance, without undue difficulty. His weakness, his temptation, was intrigue.

PART ONE
NEVILLE VERSUS WOODVILLE
1466–1469

Chapter One

Petronel: The Summons

Late summer 1466

'Marriage,' said my mother, 'is a transaction. Girls of your age often harbour romantic notions; they're natural but they're childish. When you go to church tomorrow, you will enter into a bargain. Your husband will house, feed and clothe you and if need be, defend you with his sword. On your side, you will keep the house, food and clothing I have just mentioned in good order; you will be a hostess to his guests and the mother of his children. The children are important. Make sure he has them, and especially that he has a son, as soon as possible.'

'Yes, Mother,' I said, wondering how, precisely, one was supposed to control this process. I wished she would stop lecturing me. I clasped my hands tightly in the lap of the green dress which she had lent me. It didn't suit me, and it didn't fit either. I was not to wear any of my trousseau wardrobe until after the ceremony but none of my old clothes were suitable to wear meanwhile.

'We have done very well for you,' said my mother now, still in that slightly hectoring tone. 'You will have social standing and mix with the best society in Yorkshire. You're a very lucky girl.'

'Yes, Mother.' From the hall below the solar where we were sitting came a snatch of song, my half-brother Tom in a zestful if untuneful rendering of a love lyric. Outside, the wind chased shadows across the cornfields of our Sussex manor of Faldene and across the bronze-green slopes of the downs which ringed our valley. The first migrating

11

swallows had gone. Soon I too would go, but I would journey northwards, not south.

My mother looked at my face and seemed to realise that she had been speaking to me as though I were at fault, although I had neither said nor done anything amiss. She attempted a friendlier, more woman-to-woman tone. 'Were you surprised to be summoned home without warning, Petronel? You must have wondered why.'

'*Her brow so brown, her eye so dark, with lovely face she on me smiled,*' carolled Tom from below.

'Yes, I did, of course. But Aunt Eleanor – Mother Abbess – thought perhaps you wished to see me at home just once more before I took my vows. She said that girls' parents sometimes did.'

I used the word 'home', but as I said it I thought that I had used it wrongly. My mother would regard Faldene as home, certainly, but I didn't. My home was five miles away in Withysham Abbey and its abbess, Aunt Eleanor, was more of a mother to me than my own had ever been.

Even now, I could not bring myself to believe that I would never see either Aunt Eleanor or Withysham again.

My mother came from Suffolk, where her parents had a small manor. She had been three times wed. As a girl she had been a beauty in an ash-fair, ice-cool way and since she was also adequately dowered, there had been several contenders for the hand of Mistress Joan. The two chief suitors were a young man from a neighbouring manor, and an older one, John Grinstead, who hailed from Sussex.

The young suitor had come into a good inheritance early and my mother's parents settled for him. Three weeks after the wedding, one of the outbreaks of plague which have regularly scoured the country since the century before this, killed her husband. She was allowed six months to mourn him and to ensure that no child she might bear had a dubious paternity, and then she was married to John Grinstead. As it chanced, there was no child from her first husband

12

and, after three years as Mistress Grinstead, none from her second either. Then Tom was born. Shortly after that, Master Grinstead died and very soon, my mother married his neighbour, William Faldene. She already knew him well since Grinstead manor marched with Faldene and the families often visited each other. It was a fact, recognised in our household but never discussed, that Tom looked much more like a Faldene than a Grinstead. He was dark, not over-tall, and had the same thick eyebrows as my father and all us Faldene children.

Those eyebrows were a source of anguish to my sisters, of whom I had three − not that I knew them well, for they had all been betrothed young and sent off to grow up in their future in-laws' homes. My young brother Simon had been sent away too, as the custom is, to be trained in someone else's household. Only Tom stayed at Faldene, presumably because from his point of view, Faldene was not his father's house. I myself, at the age of eleven, had been despatched to Withysham Abbey. I was no worse-looking than my sisters, but my father wanted one of us to go to Withysham because of a Faldene tradition.

The Faldenes had a long ancestry. They could trace it back to the Norman lord who had been given the manor after the Conquest. It was said that even then, Withysham had a link with Faldene, and that the abbess of the time was related to the Saxon who had the manor before the Normans came. Certainly it was true that as far back as anyone knew, it had been not a rule, exactly, but a custom that one girl in each generation of Faldenes should enter the abbey. The tradition had only been broken when there was no daughter but only sons, or once when the daughter concerned had died young, before she could take vows. It was because of this tradition that we knew so much about our own family. The abbey had kept a chronicle and we figured in the records with some frequency, for Faldene had furnished Withysham with several abbesses, some of them distinguished, and also presented it with valuable gifts in the form of land, new building, treasures and monetary donations.

My mother, who although dainty to look at was actually very brisk and practical, took a somewhat cynical view of the Faldene love of tradition and family history. She always maintained that it was because my father had made an over-generous gift to Withysham on one occasion and thereby put himself in straitened circumstances, that he behaved as he did over the Eynesby affair.

I didn't know all the details then and don't even now, but that hardly matters. Lionel Eynesby, of Eynesby in Yorkshire, had married a lady who was in some way connected to the Faldenes. She had brought him a second parcel of land in Yorkshire, a place called Bouldershawe. It was valuable, because it consisted mainly of first-class sheep pasture, and a flock of very fine sheep went with it.

But there was a dispute over whether or not she really had the right to inherit it. She had few close relatives. In a world where sickness carries off so many, we could have done without civil war, but civil war there had been, over many years. The house of Lancaster, represented by King Henry the Sixth, who was said to be simple-minded, and his queen, Margaret of Anjou, who was said to be plenty of things although not that, fought against the house of York, represented by the Duke of York and his sons, for the right to wield the sceptre.

Mistress Eynesby's family had suffered casualties and her rival for Bouldershawe was therefore not a close kinsman, but instead, was my father. There was one lawsuit after another.

And then, in 1459, came the time when the old Duke Richard, his sons and his supporters and his nephew-in-law the great Earl of Warwick, were besieged in Ludlow Castle and barely managed to escape. Many of their lesser supporters in fact did not escape but were seized along with the castle when the besiegers got in. Among them was Lionel Eynesby, who was one of Warwick's men.

Like many others, he bought himself out. Eynesby he succeeded in keeping, but he paid a money ransom and handed over Bouldershawe. That it was the subject of a dispute didn't worry the Bitch of Anjou. The moment it was out of Lionel Eynesby's hands, however, my father put in a claim for it and because the Faldenes had remained neutral throughout the conflict, and possibly because the Lancastrian officials who considered the claim grasped the fact that this would upset Lionel even more than simply losing the land had done, the Faldene claim was allowed. There was a payment, which was deferred so that Faldene could pay it out of Bouldershawe's own profits. My father did very well from the transaction.

The war was over in 1462. The Bitch was in exile, King Henry was in the Tower, the old Duke of York was dead and his son Edward was King. The moment peace was restored Lionel Eynesby began on a new round of litigation, but this time with an extra edge of bitterness because he considered that my father had taken advantage of his misfortune.

By this time, he was a childless widower. He had built up his own manor of Eynesby, which was close to the Earl of Warwick's Yorkshire castle at Middleham, into something of considerable value by then ('While he had the chance, he stocked it with sheep from Bouldershawe,' my father said). Every summer he and the nephew who was his only heir, would ride down to London with the wool train after the mid-summer shearing and invest a sizeable proportion of the wool profits in hiring lawyers.

And every summer therefore, of necessity, my father too would hasten to London and hire lawyers of his own to wrangle with Master Eynesby's. Sometimes the matter would get as far as a court hearing, which invariably ended in adjournment. Sometimes matters never even reached that point. Lionel Eynesby and my father never met face to face except across a courtroom and their exchanges then, according to Tom who sometimes went to London too, were extremely acid.

15

Whatever course the business took, my father was rarely free to come home until October and this pattern was well established before I went to Withysham.

And so, when in August 1466 I was so unexpectedly called home, I was surprised to be told that my father was there, and utterly amazed when I learned that Lionel Eynesby and his nephew Geoffrey had accompanied him, as guests.

Walter, our steward, fetched me from Withysham. He knew no more than me what it was about, he told me, when I was summoned to see him in the guest parlour. He stood respectfully in the middle of the floor, not quite at ease in this atmosphere of holiness and femininity. He held his cap in his hand and scratched his short grey hair worriedly when I questioned him. 'No, mistress, nothing's wrong that I know of, they're all in good health. Your father's come home and brought guests, but you're to come at once, he says. He gave me a letter for your Lady Abbess. I've got a pack pony for your things and a pillion saddle on my nag.'

The pillion saddle was necessary. Nuns rarely require much skill in horsemanship and having been destined for the abbey since I was small, I had ridden very little. I jolted behind Walter on the five-mile journey home along the track which skirted the downs, passing through the pastures and woodlands to the north of them. Faldene looked just the same as ever, I thought, as we entered the courtyard: a long, two-storey house with doves from our dovecot flying about it in the sun, though it did seem to be in need of a few repairs. The plaster was flaking between the struts of the timber frame, and the thatch was untidy. But I hadn't time to stare for long, for my mother hurried out to meet us as soon as she heard the hooves.

'There you are! Down you come, Petra. I wish you could ride properly; we'll have to do something about that. Walter, get someone to bring Mistress Petronel's baggage up to my solar as quickly as possible. No, no, Petra, not

16

that way.' She caught my arm and steered me away from the hall entrance towards a side door to the solar staircase. 'Your father is in the hall with the Eynesbys.'

'The *Eynesbys*?' I cast a reproachful look at Walter.

'Aye, your dad's guests. I said there were guests.'

'But the *Eynesbys*!'

'Petra, come along!' said my mother, and towed me away.

She hurried me up the stairs and into the solar. 'Stand there in the light.' She stood back and regarded me with dispassionate appraisal. 'You can't meet the Eynesbys till you're fit to be seen. Religion is all very well but girls with your colouring always look terrible in black.'

'Mother, has Lionel Eynesby really come here to Faldene?'

'Yes, and his nephew with him. Come into the bedchamber. I'll see what I can find for you.'

'But why does it matter if . . .?'

'Don't argue, Petra.' She hustled me through the door into the adjoining chamber. I sat down on my parents' bed while my mother, having put her head out of the further door and shouted for her maid, Bet, came back and began hunting through a clothes press. 'Take off that dreadful serge affair,' she said over her shoulder. 'Jesu, how you've grown. Nothing that you had before you went away will fit you now. Still, those were dull gowns too. With a little luck, you can wear some of mine. A little stitching and a few pins should be enough to make them fit you . . .'

My mother, as I have said, was ash-fair. She had the kind of blue eyes which looked as though there were a layer of transparent glass over the iris, and a perfect, wild rose skin. My father, however, was dark, with grey-green eyes and a swarthy skin. Most of his children took decisively after him but I was an amalgam of my parents. I had his eyes and eyebrows, but for the rest, my hair was an indeterminate mid-brown and my skin, though fine and dry, a little sallow in tone. Before I went to Withysham, I had been too young

17

to give much thought to my appearance, and once there, I was in a world where vanity and mirrors were discouraged.

I therefore remained passively amazed while my mother and Bet, who had now appeared, experimented in rapid succession with dresses of bright blue, dark green, light green, violet and ash-grey, flung up their hands in despair at the effect of them all, when held against me, and finally settled on a blue 'which will have to do though it's too harsh a shade for you,' said my mother. I was told to put it on and then take it off again so that Bet could make some adjustments. When I was finally dressed in it, I was made to sit on a stool while Bet brushed my hair and put it into a silver net. 'And look out my cornelian necklace for her,' said my mother. 'And then come and help me. I must get myself ready too. I must look elegant. This is an important occasion.'

While my mother was dressing, I sat once more on the edge of the bed to wait. I had made one or two more attempts to ask questions but my mother merely said: 'Just do as you're told, Petra,' and clearly wasn't going to provide any more satisfactory answers. When, down in the hall, Walter struck the gong which summoned the household to dinner, I followed my mother downstairs obediently, holding my skirts, which were still over-long, clear of the ground and still completely at a loss as to the reason why I was wearing them.

I felt in fact as though I had been caught up in a gale. That morning, I had woken in the novices' dortoir at Withysham, thinking that before me lay another day of choir and prayer, the study of Latin with the novice mistress, and a little work in the kitchen, slicing beans with meticulous care 'for perfection even in the humblest task is a way of praising God.'

By noon, I was being handed up on to Walter's pillion, and bidding goodbye to Aunt Eleanor. She knew no more than Walter or me what it was all about. She had told me that my father's letter merely required her to send me back with the steward. She said: 'I pray we shall soon see you here again. You have been happy with us at Withysham, have you not, Petronel?'

'Yes, Mother Abbess, I have,' I said. She had given me a parting blessing, but now she reached up a hand to me and let me cling to it for a moment. She was a tall woman with a dignified air but I had long ago sensed the warmth beneath that austere appearance. I was as much in awe of her as any other novice, but I loved her too.

I think that she had sensed that our parting would be lengthy. That extended hand was unusual and it left me with a sense of uneasiness. Entering the hall at Faldene in my borrowed and uncomfortable fine clothes, I felt that uneasiness deepen.

For years, even before I went to Withysham, I had been encouraged, even compelled, to adopt nunlike attitudes. I had been given sober clothes to wear and discouraged from any kind of conspicuous behaviour. Now all these precepts had been unceremoniously thrown away. I had been dressed to be looked at. And there was more: to my amazement I was led to a seat beside my father at the dinner table, and now he was introducing me formally to our guests the Eynesbys, and in a voice which said quite plainly: 'Here's my daughter Petronel. Look at her, look carefully, admire her!'

I think I understood then, that I was not to return to Withysham.

In the eye of memory I can see the hall of Faldene as it was that day; the long, well-scrubbed trestle table up the middle where the household servants, including the men from the stable-yard and the home farm, dined; and the low dais placed cross-wise at the top where, draped with a white cloth, was the family table at which my father and Tom and our guests were already seated.

Our household was not large. My father claimed that his original Norman ancestor had been a knight, but we were yeoman farmers with no pretensions to gentility. No more than twenty people normally sat down to dinner in our house, and all, including my parents, worked hard.

Today, the long centre table was crowded with extra people, strangers who must have come with the Eynesbys. Yet my mother had not, as she usually did, helped our cook Mattie with the meal. On the contrary, she did not even glance towards the kitchen door as she took her place. She was wearing pale violet, a difficult shade, but on her it appeared charming. She smelt of lemon verbena and wore, I remember, a necklace of amethysts and green agate. I heard my father murmur: 'Joan, you look very beautiful,' to her, and once the introductions were over, despite the way I had been put forward, the Eynesbys looked more at her than at me.

Therefore, I was able to study them for a while, unobserved.

I did this with caution, feeling that I might be rebuked at any moment. At Withysham, we were supposed to keep our eyes lowered, but curiosity was too strong for that now. I wanted to examine these people who had been for so long our enemies and were now so strangely translated into guests.

No one had ever described, in my hearing, what they looked like. My father spoke of them often enough but his remarks mostly concerned their characters, and consisted of adjectives such as cunning, avaricious and obstinate. I did not know what such people might be expected to look like.

Lionel Eynesby was in fact a tall thin man wearing good clothes in quiet colours. He was middle-aged and his scanty hair had lost its colour except for a sandy trace on top. He had a long nose in a narrow face and eyes set a little close. His accent as he greeted me had been northern, but not the extreme form of it which can make wayfarers from the north as incomprehensible as foreigners in the southern counties. When he spoke or smiled, he showed that several of his teeth were missing, and the survivors were mostly stained with brown. He was not especially prepossessing but he didn't resemble anyone's enemy.

Nor did his nephew.

I know quite well that here, memory plays me false. The human body does not radiate light. Aunt Eleanor had told me that even saints don't really have visible haloes. But in the dim hall – for though the afternoon was still bright, our greenish window glass cut out much of the light – Sir Geoffrey Silbeck appeared to illuminate the air around him. He was under thirty, and if at fourteen I did not call that young, I nevertheless knew that here was a man in his prime. He was all broadness and good cheer, all blue and gold; crinkly amber-golden hair and splendid blue doublet with shoulders padded in the extreme of fashion, even though Sir Geoffrey's shoulders needed no such enhancement. A gold ring set with turquoises adorned his right hand. Only his eyes were an unexpected hazel. He saw me looking at him, and smiled. I was at once overcome with hopeless shyness.

Fortunately, I was not expected to talk. The meal began and I pretended great interest in the food. This ceased to be pretence almost at once, for when I actually looked at the table arrangements, they startled me.

The to-do my mother had made over our clothes, and her desertion of Mattie, had told me that this was a special occasion, but the appearance of the table drove it home.

Normally, we ate solid fare off pewter and earthenware and turned wood, helping ourselves even when guests were present, and we only had flowers on the board on Sundays.

Today, the silver was out and burnished, and although it was a Tuesday, a vase of the late-blooming crimson roses which my mother cultivated stood in the middle of the cloth. In addition, Mattie's two maidservants had been called from the kitchen, put into clean aprons, and were handing the food, and the food itself was positively elaborate.

Only at Christmas or harvest dinners could I recall seeing trout and a huge mutton pasty both on the table at once, and as well as these, there were capons, a sweet junket, and a remarkable confection of marchpane which must have used up immense and costly quantities of sugar and almonds. It had Mattie in a fuss. She brought it in herself and set it down with a worried 'Hope it's all it should be, Ma'am,' to my mother, who frowned and said repressively, 'I'm sure it is. That will *do*, Mattie.'

Whereupon Tom, seated opposite me, kicked me under the table and made a *what's going on?* face at me. I made an *I don't know* face back.

Gradually, however, I began to realise that if we were setting out to make an impression, so was Lionel Eynesby. He was doing most of the talking and his theme was the Earl of Warwick. I knew, of course, that he was one of Warwick's followers and had served him in the field, but to listen to Master Eynesby now you would have thought that Warwick could not conduct his life from day to day without him.

'. . . I spend a certain amount of time each year in his household, ye know, mostly when he's at Middleham. That's his smaller castle. It's nobbut half a day's ride from Eynesby. But I attend on him at Warwick Castle too, now and again. I act for him in certain matters, overseeing his shepherds and buying and selling sheep and wool for him. I bring his wool down to London and negotiate prices with the wool merchants. There are big flocks on the Middleham estate and I see to it that that side of the estate is run as it should be. I've had a lifetime's experience of sheep and he finds me useful. I'm honoured that he puts so much faith in me. I reckon it's as great an honour as having "Sir" before one's name. Isn't that so, Geoffrey? Geoffrey's his man too. Got his knighthood on the field at Towton, when Edward made himself King. Defended his lord when Warwick had slipped and fallen, and Warwick recommended him. But I trained Geoffrey in arms, I taught him all a knight should know. I always had hopes of him. Did I not, Geoffrey?'

'You did, Uncle,' said Sir Geoffrey. His voice was pleasant, deep and melodious. It was also a little cool. I suddenly wondered if Lionel Eynesby had been a hard taskmaster.

'I've heard,' said my mother, 'that the Earl of Warwick's hospitality is famous.'

'Aye, so it is. I've been present at some of his banquets,' said Master Eynesby. 'I was at Warwick Castle the time he gave a sixty-course dinner for a party of visiting Bohemian envoys. It caused a great stir, although there's no denying,' said Eynesby with, unexpectedly, a tinge of disapproval in his voice, 'that it was mightily wasteful. But there,' he checked himself before he had actually ventured a criticism of Warwick, 'my lord is so very wealthy that it hardly signifies. There were roast meats enough to sink a fleet of ships, believe me, and fancy custards enough to float one. No one could taste more than a fraction of the dishes offered, and most of the leftovers were distributed afterwards to the poor.'

Tom caught my eye again and on a very small scale, mimed nausea. I wasn't sure whether this was on account of Warwick's banquets, Lionel Eynesby's sycophancy or both, but I was obliged to swallow a giggle.

My father, who was jovial when among other adults, although to us children he always seemed remote, said: 'I heard in London that the object of that feast was to outshine the one the King gave to the same envoys, which had a mere fifty courses. They must have been very plump Bohemians by the time they sailed for home.' Gratefully, feeling that I had been given permission to laugh, I joined in the merriment that this provoked. My mother said that the earl must be a very powerful lord indeed if he could vie with the King.

'From what I heard in the City,' said Father, 'Warwick wants nothing more than to vie with the King just now. They've been at loggerheads ever since the King's marriage.'

23

The talk became political. I lost the thread after a time. Some of the topics were familiar to me, of course. I knew about the King's unpopular wife, and about poor simple ex-king Henry in the Tower of London, and I knew that his ferocious queen had been exiled to her old home in Anjou, amid general relief. Even blind Sister Edith in Withysham, over ninety and apt to say, first thing every morning, that she hoped God would take her home today, knew all that.

But some names were strange. Who was the person to whom Lionel Eynesby kept casually referring by the nickname of Dickon, and who was the one called Clarence? They were obviously important, since Warwick had invited them to marry his daughters, according to Master Eynesby. Dickon appeared to be especially in demand, for he had also been invited to marry a French princess. The French wanted a connection with the English royal house. Balked of Edward himself, said Master Eynesby, they were trying for other members of his family. Sir Geoffrey agreed.

'But the King will never consent to the French marriage,' said Eynesby, with the air of one deep in royal counsels. Tom caught my eye again and grinned. 'Such an alliance could harm relations with Burgundy. The Burgundians helped King Edward's family during their bad times, when the Anjou woman was in power. King Edward wouldn't have settled for a French princess for himself, even if he'd never set eyes on Bess Woodville.'

'Did Dickon of Gloucester want to settle for one?' my father enquired, 'or for the Warwick marriage? I take it nothing is going to come of either suggestion.'

'No, nowt,' said Master Eynesby in his northern voice. 'Dickon's a good lad, though he's nowt but a lad yet. Folk still call him just Dickon instead of Gloucester. In a few years' time I daresay they'll take to saying Gloucester, the way they call George of Clarence, Clarence, but not yet. Still, as I was saying, lad or not, he showed his loyalty. The King said no to both offers, and Dickon stood by the King's wishes, and that was in spite of all my lord of Warwick's coaxing. Warwick made so much of Dickon at one time – earlier, this was – that they say the King came near to having Dickon arrested.'

'Things are as bad as that between Warwick and the King, then?' said my father.

'Aye, I'm afraid they are. And Clarence is still playing with the notion of accepting one of Warwick's girls, and that's not helping.'

'If it came to a clash, in arms,' said my father suddenly, 'which side would you support, Master Eynesby? You're one of Warwick's employees, after all. And both of you –' he glanced towards Sir Geoffrey ' – have served him on the field.'

Lionel Eynesby said, 'I reckon I'd stay out of it if I could,' and Sir Geoffrey said, 'It would depend on the exact circumstances,' at the same moment.

'They'd need to be pretty peculiar circumstances to make it right to take the field against the King, lad,' said Eynesby repressively. He looked at my father. 'But it was right to raise the matter. It was something you might have wondered about too late, otherwise.' He caught a glimpse of my face and added: 'There's a young lass there wanting to ask a question. What's puzzling you, Petronel, lass?'

'Ask a question if you wish, Petra,' said my mother. Her voice was encouraging but her slight frown warned me to sit up straight, speak up clearly and ask something sensible, for the love of God.

Everyone was looking at me. My parents were visibly waiting for me to speak, to perform, as though I were a dancing bear and they its proprietors. Timidly, stammering, I said: 'I only w. . .wondered who Dickon and Clarence were?'

Lionel Eynesby's grey brows rose. 'You've not heard the names before?'

I shook my head. My father said drily: 'News does filter into convents in the end but they're never up to date. As I told you, Petra has spent the last two or three years in

25

Withysham Abbey. Dickon of Gloucester, Petra, is the King's youngest brother. George of Clarence is the brother in between. They're persons of some eminence and no doubt we shall hear much more of them in the future.'

'Petronel certainly will. She'll likely meet them,' said Lionel Eynesby astonishingly, and smiled his gap-toothed smile at me. Sir Geoffrey smiled too, his own teeth white and flawless. My parents beamed.

I began to understand, or so I thought.

I faced them in the solar the next morning, my face shiny from the scrubbing my mother had made me give it, my hair loose, which made me feel half-dressed, and another of her gowns – this one was violet – threatening to trip me up at every step.

Both my parents were there, and Lionel Eynesby, and a secretary. I remembered seeing him at table the previous day, seated close to the dais as befitted an upper servant. He was now seated at a table in the corner, where my father sometimes did his farm accounts. My father said: 'Don't be alarmed at this summons, Petra. This is a happy day for you and for us all. You know of the long-standing dispute between Faldene and Eynesby. I'm glad to tell you that it's to be resolved at last, and through you.'

'You're a very fortunate girl,' added my mother, in a quelling tone, as though she expected me to argue about it.

Master Eynesby, clearing his throat, said, 'Forgive me, but there's such a thing as making sure. It's a way we have up north. Before we put any signatures to that contract Master Secretary has ready over there, I must ask once more. Petronel's turned fourteen and she's been at Withysham Abbey since she was eleven, and it was first intended she should take a nun's vows. Can you confirm for absolute certain, Master Faldene, that she's not done so?'

'You may speak for yourself, Petronel,' said my father.

'Mother Abbess said I shouldn't take vows until next year, Master Eynesby,' I said. I felt as though a fierce light were playing on me. 'I'm – I was – only a novice. I'm not bound in any way.'

'Of course she isn't bound,' said my father rather indignantly, or we shouldn't be here like this. What do you take me for?'

'I understood,' said Master Eynesby calmly, 'that there was a tradition . . .'

'That one daughter in each generation in our family enters Withysham? Yes, there is, but that tradition's been broken before and can be again, and Petra's still free to change course.'

'And you can confirm that she's of an age now for child-bearing?'

I grew hot. A few specks drifted before my eyes as though I were about to faint. I had in fact started a course that morning. Hitherto, it had been simply a tiresome phenomenon, something that happened to girls as they grew up. But now, as I listened to my mother saying calmly that yes, she had enquired of her sister-in-law the Abbess of Withysham, and I had reached maidenhood a year since, and that the Faldene family had a good record of fertility, I understood that this was to do with men as well as women, to do with children and with all that part of life I had thought would never concern me. It was going to concern me after all. Me and . . .

Geoffrey Silbeck of the broad smile and the wide, stylish shoulders? Was that why he had come to Faldene with his uncle? The thought had been hovering in my mind since dinner the day before. Now it settled, and I almost gasped aloud.

I had spent more than two years in Withysham, preparing for a life as a nun and I had been happy. I had loved my Aunt Eleanor and found astonishing satisfaction in the rhythmic days which began with the singing of Lauds at daybreak and closed with the candlelit Matins deep in the

27

night, the days that were balanced throughout between the singing of the Office and the hours of study and manual toil. I had not felt put-upon, being sent to the abbey. I had felt privileged. As well as Aunt Eleanor, there was the unseen person of Christ to love, whose presence pervaded every stone and every blade of grass within the abbey walls, in whose name everything, even the simplest or more mundane tasks, was performed, whose life and personality were more marvellous than those of any man. Aunt Eleanor had said I had a vocation. She had once told me that she had a great ambition that Withysham should one day found a daughter house. Though the abbey was not quite, as yet, well-off enough for that, she hoped it would come in her lifetime. 'And if it does,' she said, looking at me with grave kindness, 'it would need a prioress. How splendid if the Faldene family could furnish one, as they have so often provided abbesses like myself.'

Now, within a few hours, Aunt Eleanor and Withysham, and even the image of Christ, had begun to slip away, to grow small and grey and distant. A wild excitement shot through me. I had to grip my hands tightly together over my bunchy violet skirt.

'The business of children's important,' Lionel Eynesby said. 'My family's short of bairns. It seems satisfactory, right enough. All right, Master Faldene, call my nephew in. Are you ready, Master Secretary?'

At the desk, the secretary unstoppered an inkpot and adjusted the parchment which was lying unrolled before him, weighted at its corners. My father opened the door and Sir Geoffrey, who must have been waiting in the parlour adjoining, came in.

'There you are, lad,' said Eynesby heartily. 'Master Faldene here reckoned you should have been here at the start, but I said to him, let's get all the questions sorted first. He'll be happy with what makes me happy, I said. He's like my son to me, I told him.'

Sir Geoffrey, this morning, was jaunty in peacock

colours, as effulgent now as in the dim hall the day before. He gave me a kindly good morning and went to stand beside his uncle. My heart had begun to pound. At the desk, the secretary coughed, and then read out the contract.

In Withysham, I had of course occasionally glimpsed the possibilities of another kind of life. One of my fellow novices had once smuggled in a copy of the *Canterbury Tales*, written in the last century by a man called Chaucer. All the girls had sighed over Chaucer's perfect gentle knight. Last night, in bed, I had thought romantically to myself that Sir Geoffrey Silbeck could well have been the pattern for him.

Then I began to take in the details of the contract.

It was a complex document. My dowry, for instance, included a sum of money and some jewellery and silver plate, and all of this was carefully itemised. But the main clauses concerned Bouldershawe, the disputed Yorkshire estate. The rights to its revenues were to be held in trust by my husband for our eldest son or else for division among our daughters. If I died without issue ('God forfend!' said Lionel Eynesby piously), and before my husband, then the rights in Bouldershawe passed to him and whoever he named as his heirs. Only if I outlived him did they revert to me.

And Bouldershawe was the cornerstone of the contract, and it was with Lionel Eynesby that my father was in dispute over it. Sir Geoffrey's interest in the matter was at one remove. He was at the moment his uncle's heir and if Lionel Eynesby had children, Geoffrey would be cut out.

'But he's got his own place and connections in his own right and he's already doing well with tournament prizes. He's not going to end up a pauper, are you, lad?' said Master Eynesby heartily. 'He's never quarrelled with my right to have a family of my own. So I brought him along to witness my signature and be my best man in church, and make it clear to my bride and her kin that there's no trouble over it in my family; she'll be made welcome.'

Lionel Eynesby considered that my father had robbed

him of Bouldershawe and in some fashion or other, he meant to get it back. I listened in silence as the contract details were read, and knew before my bridegroom's name was spoken that my excitement must be put away, that my dreams were just that, dreams, doomed to vanish at daybreak. There would be no perfect gentle knight for me. There would be no Aunt Eleanor and no Withysham either. I was to marry, not Sir Geoffrey, but Lionel Eynesby.

Walter was called in to witness my father's signature to the contract. My mother began to talk to me, telling me that when I was mistress of Eynesby, I would meet important people, attend on the Countess of Warwick, would have to grace my position, be courteous to those above me, set an example to inferiors, be this, remember that . . .

I hardly listened. I was to go to Yorkshire, more than a hundred miles away, with Lionel Eynesby? That middle-aged stranger with the faded hair and the eroded teeth? I was to be *his* wife, have *his* children? There must be some mistake.

There was no mistake. The signatures were placed, sanded. There was a mutual shaking of hands between my father and the Eynesbys. As for me . . .

I knew what was expected of me. Every girl knows that from infancy. I gathered up my bulky violet skirts, rearranged my feet inside their perilous hem and went down into a curtsy. I said I was most honoured and I thanked my parents for the wise and loving arrangements they had made for me. I would be very happy, I said untruthfully, to be Lionel Eynesby's wife.

They all kissed me in turn. Lionel's breath was noisome. Geoffrey's was sweet.

I think it was then, knowing no more of him than that he had a handsome face and broad shoulders and courtly manners, that I first began to fall in love with my future husband's nephew.

Chapter Two

Petronel: Departure

Autumn 1466

We had five weeks to prepare. Invitations had to be sent out
to relatives and neighbours and Walter was despatched to
London in haste to fetch fresh supplies of luxuries such as
sugar, saffron, almonds and pepper. My father had
brought some of these commodities when he came back
from the City, but not enough. 'Well, I didn't want
Eynesby to think I was counting my chickens while they
were still in the egg,' I heard him say to my mother.

He had, however, brought back a couple of rolls of good
cloth, in russet, which suited me, and off-white, which
could be dyed. In addition, my mother had some lengths of
white silk and brocade put by, which could also be converted into colours that looked well on me, such as tawny
and rose and apple-green. Mother and Bet and I spent most
of those five weeks stitching.

The new gowns seemed elaborate to me, and some of
them had trains, which I was sure I would never learn to
manage. 'Nonsense, they're the fashion, and you'll be
going among fashionable people,' said my mother firmly.
'You'll have to attend on the Countess of Warwick, as you
know. You'll just have to practise.'

Meanwhile, the old black woollen twill gowns which I
had worn at Withysham were ruthlessly cut up for dusters,
and I wore my mother's dresses, tacked to fit, and listened
every day to her concentrated instruction course on my
future duties. Two themes kept reappearing. I must have
children and I must remember that I would be mixing with

31

the kind of people my parents never even expected to be in the same room with; I must not let my family down, or Lionel Eynesby either.

I wanted to cry out: 'But how am I to do all this? How can I be sure I have babies? What am I supposed to *do* to please people like the Warwicks? But I had gathered by now that my father had humbled himself to Lionel Eynesby to arrange this match and end the litigation over Bouldershawe, which was costing us so much that we couldn't afford to repair the thatch. He needed a way to surrender Bouldershawe without losing face and I had provided it.

I was raw and young but simply because of this, I was capable of learning how to acquit myself as Mistress Eynesby, my father had said to Lionel, and I would give him a chance of getting an heir. On that basis, with Bouldershawe thrown in, Lionel had accepted the deal.

In any case, I could remember my sister Philippa, sent away to her betrothed husband's home when she was only nine, bursting into tears on her last day at home and saying she was afraid to go to strangers: what if they didn't like her? And she was told to do as she was bid and say her prayers and she would have nothing to fear.

If I voiced my misgivings, I would be condemned as selfish, and I would certainly not be heeded. So I said, 'Yes mother,' to everything and at least avoided censure.

We saw little of Lionel Eynesby or Sir Geoffrey. They had gone to stay with friends a few miles off, making formal calls only now and then. 'The bridegroom shouldn't stay in the house of the bride,' said Lionel waggishly when they left. I was sorry, not because I wanted Lionel's company but because I wanted to see more of Sir Geoffrey. The one thing that made me feel happier about the future was the knowledge that he would be part of it. I was too ignorant, at fourteen, to understand what a dangerous state of affairs this was.

Their absence made the preparations seem oddly unreal.

On my wedding morning, I was congratulated on my poise. 'I think Withysham taught you a great deal,' said my mother, but my calmness was really due to the fact that from the day of my betrothal, I had been expecting to wake up soon and find myself safely back in the dortoir at Withysham, and I had somehow gone on expecting this, all through the lectures from my mother, and the feverish stitching and even the letter from Aunt Eleanor. She had written, mildly regretting 'certain wishes you know I harboured concerning the daughter house I long to see founded', but assuring me that my father knew what was best, that nothing could separate me from the love of God, whether I stayed in the world or not, and wishing me happiness.

So, still in a semi-trance, I let myself be dressed in the pale pink brocade which my mother thought suitable for the ceremony, and I walked with my father out of our main gate and through the short street of cottages and up the hill to St Mary's church where Lionel Eynesby and his companions were waiting with our priest. In the church porch we made our vows and my small hand was placed in his bony one.

Then we all walked back to the house and there was a feast at which I drank unwatered wine for the first time in my life, whereupon the feeling that I was in a dream intensified, because I became quite tipsy.

I had to be given milk with water, to stop me from giggling and get me sober enough to lead the dancing with Lionel. But no one rebuked me. My father roared with laughter and told Lionel that this was another Faldene tradition and was thought to be lucky. 'They say that when my Norman ancestor married his lady, they drank freely at the feast and conceived their son at once.'

'May it be an omen, then,' said Lionel, good-humouredly steadying me as he steered us on to the floor.

It was a long, noisy, successful celebration. My mother was complimented on the excellence and variety of the dishes, at which she graciously shook her head and called Mattie to be toasted in her own homemade elderberry wine. Walter, who like me had had too much of it, climbed on a table and made a prolonged and incomprehensible speech which I think was meant to express congratulations to the bride and groom. Then, amid shrieks of laughter and improper jokes, I was led away to the best bedchamber, which my parents had yielded for the night, and Lionel was pushed in after me. There was a playful scuffle when Sir Geoffrey pretended he was trying to force his way in to join us. Lionel thrust him out, shut and bolted the door, and my marriage night had begun.

I was still under the influence of the wine and my feeling of detachment from reality had persisted. In the events of the night, I was more a spectator than a participant. Lionel did not talk. He just undressed and got into the bed and I did the same. Then I lay there while my husband, like a big friendly dog with bad breath, climbed all over me. There were candles in the room which he hadn't blown out and by their light I saw what I had not noticed before, that my bridegroom's eyes were indeterminate in colour, like stone or water. I also observed that his ears had gone red, and that he seemed to be in some way angry, or ashamed.

Presently, he muttered what might have been an oath, slid away from me and sat on the edge of the bed with his back to me, doing something out of sight. I lay and looked at the knobbly spine of his back. Then he came back to me and there was more bad breath and, at length, a central and invasive pain.

But it was not violent, only tiresome, and like everything else that night, apparently at a distance. I was conscious of being flooded with a warm wetness and then he rolled on to his side, nuzzled his nose into my shoulder, said, 'Thanks, lass,' and went to sleep. I blew the candles out myself, thinking that Bet and Mother and I had spent endless hours, day after day, making my new clothes, that contracts had been signed and witnessed, and that the priest had been

called upon to conduct a marriage ceremony in full vest-
ments, and my father had given a feast so costly that the
roof repairs would still have to wait, just for the sake of
this. Extraordinary. In fact, absurd.

Next day I left Sussex, as far as I knew, for ever.

It was a fair-sized cavalcade which assembled that morning. We had three laden pack mules with two men in charge
of them. Because there was always the risk of robbery on
the road, we had in addition four men-at-arms for protection. All of these were part of Lionel's household. We
also had Sir Geoffrey and a young squire called Giles who
was his personal attendant, the secretary, Master Hardynge, who doubled as Lionel's own personal servant,
and Kat.

Kat was one of the numerous daughters of our neighbour
at a nearby farm called Westwater. Once its owners had
been Faldene tenants; now all that was long ago but something of the old relationship still lingered. Bet was a
Westwater girl originally and now that I was married and
going away we looked to Westwater again to provide a maid
for me. Kat was sixteen, plump, cheerful and according to
my mother, trustworthy in all respects.

'But remember, Petronel,' said my mother, neatly abol-
ishing any ideas I might have of treating Kat as a friend and
companion, 'you are responsible for her behaviour and
well-being. Always set her a good example and make sure
she attends Mass regularly. In due course, see she has the
chance of a suitable marriage.'

Kat was to travel on Master Hardynge's pillion while I
was to ride behind Lionel.

Pillion riding over long distances can be hard on a horse
but Lionel had very sturdy animals. On one of his visits
before the marriage, he had told us that there was a monastery not far from Eynesby, a place called Jervaulx Abbey,
where the monks bred destriers but had also, of late years,
kept an Araby stallion. 'Geoffrey keeps a few Flemish

mares at Silbeck; he's got good pasture there,' Lionel had said. 'He uses the Jervaulx sires to breed a few destriers on his own account, but most years now, he sends one of the heavy mares to the Araby stallion instead. The result's a good sort of cob, intelligent and short in the back. My nags'll make nothing of the double weight, rest assured.'

I came out of the house into the sunny late September weather and there was Lionel, already in the saddle, with the pillion awaiting me behind him. That was when the sense of unreality left me at last and in a panic, I knew that it was true, I was married to the man up there on the grey cob, and I was about to be wrenched away from everything that was loved and familiar and I couldn't bear it. My father was beside me, holding out a hand to help me mount, and I turned to him, the tears spilling down my face. He pulled me towards him and hugged me, but presently he put me back from him and glancing up, I saw that Lionel was fiddling with his horse's mane and averting his gaze from me. His ears had gone red, which I now knew for a sign of displeasure or embarrassment. I must not annoy him, I was his wife now. I wiped the back of my hand across my eyes.

'Come on,' said my father. 'Up you get.'

He spoke briskly but his face was anxious, as though, too late, he had doubts about these arrangements he had made for me. He had said 'up you get' but he didn't move to assist me and my mother, seeing the two of us stand there as though we had taken root, came up and detached me. She pulled me aside. 'Now, Petra, what's the matter?'

In a whisper, I blurted out: 'I wish I were going back to Withysham!'

'Nonsense!' She held my shoulders and shook me gently. 'You're married now. You must forget Withysham, and don't chatter about it to Master Eynesby. He won't want to hear about it. Better pretend you didn't like it there and much prefer Eynesby. Now, remember all I've told you, especially about children. All men want sons and they blame their wives if the boys don't appear. Master

Eynesby's first wife disappointed him, I believe.' She glanced quickly towards Lionel but he was now talking to someone on the far side of his horse. Very softly, so that only I could possibly hear, my mother said, 'See you have children but remember that no one must ever question their paternity. Now you must say goodbye.'

I knew that she was giving me both covert information and covert advice, and also that it was of a nature which would have horrified Aunt Eleanor. She would have told me not to listen. I wondered how many others beside myself had noticed Tom's surprising resemblance to the wrong father. But there was no time to ask questions. Tom had come up to us and it was he who finally put me up into the saddle. Others crowded round to say farewell: Walter, Mattie, Bet. 'Safe journey! You'll see London and York on your way, mistress. Every joy to you . . .'

'Look after her, Master Eynesby,' said my father, last of all.

'Aye, I will. Right, then,' said Lionel and turned the cob's head towards the gate. I couldn't speak. I managed a stiff smile, with lower lip taut, and as we went out of the courtyard, I waved.

The young are resilient and easily distracted by novelty. Once we were out of sight of home and I was irrevocably committed to the future, my spirits rose somewhat. The weather was clear and warm without the heat of summer or the flies which pester riders and horses alike. Lionel talked to me as we went, asking if I had seen London before, which I had not, and describing it to me. Sir Geoffrey led us all in singsongs, ably seconded by his squire Giles. Everyone joined in, including Lionel and even Master Hardynge. Geoffrey did not ride close or talk to me very much, but I felt happier because he was there.

Before we reached London, we passed a night in a hostelry. I was by then growing curious to see the city and was thinking about it so much that I did not even mind Lionel's ritual lovemaking. It was soon over, anyway. I had begun already to regard it in the light of a minor inconvenience once every twenty-four hours.

The second day was cloudy and I was stiff from the first day's riding. So was Kat and she complained about it. Lionel heard her. 'It wears off,' he told her brusquely. I did not complain, since this would obviously displease him, but asked him to tell me more about London instead.

We were to make a stay of a few days because Lionel wished to raise a loan from a contact there. 'I'll be in for some expenses now I'm wed, improvements to the house and so forth,' he said. 'My sister Alison, Sir Geoffrey's mother, looks after it when I'm away and you'll find it in good order, right enough. I've written her, so she knows to redd it up for a bride. But there'll be more to do. You'll want new hangings and so on, new furniture, maybe, and those London lawyers eat other men's cash for breakfast.'

It occurred to me that Lionel had possibly been quite as glad to settle the Bouldershawe quarrel as my father was.

'I'd not thought of getting married when I left home last,' he said, 'so you'll find shortcomings, but we'll put them right, even if it means a bit of debt.'

He was trying to please me and I was touched. I wondered what his sister, Alison, was like, and if she would be glad or sorry about my arrival. He had mentioned her before, but only as someone living away at Geoffrey's home, Silbeck. It seemed that she was more closely concerned with Eynesby than I had thought. Once more, I began to feel nervous. I would have to take charge of my husband's household, and what if this Alison criticised me to Lionel?

I was worrying about this as we rode into the outskirts of London. Then I forgot it again, in my amazement.

I had never seen a city before. I could never have imagined buildings packed so closely together or crowds so dense and varied. The jostling streets, the meanness of the poor quarters and the magnificence of the great houses, dazed, stimulated and shocked me, all at once. At home, our labourers' cottages at least had a square of garden each, and did people who were not actually royalty, live in those enormous crenellated places? The noise was incredible: stallholders shouting their wares, the mounted escorts of the wealthy shouting for way for their masters through the carts and pedestrians, horses whinnying, dogs barking, church bells ringing, the rumble of cartwheels. The smells were incredible, too. Shops of a kind were clustered together, so that one street smelt of leather and the next of spices, another of offal, another of fruit. While beneath them all like a continuous theme, was the smell of rottenness bred by close-packed humanity, of excrement and refuse.

I exclaimed at everything and had plenty of opportunity as it was some distance to the house which Lionel had bespoken in advance by messenger. It was ready for us, a two-storey hired lodging by the river, with a landing stage attached. Once we were installed, Sir Geoffrey and Giles went off on some expedition of their own, and Lionel took me and Kat out to see the sights, and to shop.

He gave me some money and I bought clogs to protect my shoes and Kat's from the dirty footways, and gloves for myself from a strident street trader in a fetid lane so hemmed between higgledy-piggledy tenements that the sun never touched its trampled surface. I gave alms out of pity to a one-legged beggar who said he'd been crippled fighting for the king at Towton, in the north, in the battle that put King Edward on the throne.

I did not give alms to any other beggars, however, because I sensed that for some reason, my first essay in charity had not met with Lionel's approval. From the moment we had entered London, indeed, I had been aware that I was in some way incurring his displeasure although I did not know why.

He said nothing, however, and we went back to our lodgings to find that its resident servants had prepared a good dinner for us. Lionel was rather quiet all that evening, but the events of the night were as before. Next day, we went to meet the acquaintance from whom Lionel hoped to raise his loan.

'Dress with care,' he told me. 'Something fashionable.'

A light rain had begun, but the hired barge which took us to our destination by the river had an awning to protect us. Sir Geoffrey came with us and so did Master Hardynge, Giles and Kat. I think they were there to lend an air of consequence.

Lionel seemed to be himself again and approved my choice of gown. The barge brought us to a house on the south bank of the Thames. It was one of the splendid crenellated residences which had so impressed me the day before. Its owner, Master Halford, and his wife came out to greet us.

In the Halfords' house, I made a heady discovery; that marriage confers status. As Lionel's wife, I was treated with a consideration I could not have imagined, one short week earlier. I marvelled at it, relaxing into it, almost purring, as Master Halford, who was a much-befurred merchant somewhat younger than Lionel, asked after my health with the courtesy of one adult to another and his wife sent for warm water so that I could wash my hands, and a maid carefully took my wrap.

The water was rose-scented, and my seat at dinner, for which we were asked to stay, was at the high table beside Lionel. Over dinner, Master Halford asked me how I liked London and I replied enthusiastically, telling him about the sights we had seen on the way to his house, about the width of the shining river and the massiveness of the Tower walls. 'They look as though they were built by giants!' Everyone laughed and Master Halford called for more wine for me. I was careful not to take too much, remembering what it had done to me at my wedding feast. I had already noticed that Lionel had once more become silent, at least towards me, although I couldn't understand why this should be. I had gathered that he and Master Halford enjoyed each other's company and that the loan had presented no difficulties; on the face of it, Lionel should have been cheerful. I must be doing something wrong, I supposed, but what?

In the barge on the way home Lionel, his ears red with annoyance, told me.

He was tired, he said, of being embarrassed by my childish behaviour. 'I'm weary to death of all this daft oohing and aahing over what's nowt but commonplace. The Thames is the Thames as everyone knows and of course it's wide. The Tower was built the way any castle is built, by putting one stone on top of another! I held my tongue at the time, we were guests at Master Halford's table, but I'd best make it plain before there's any more of it. We're stopping at Warwick Castle before we get to Yorkshire and if my lord and lady are there, I'll not have you making a fool of yourself. And in future, don't waste the money I give you on whining beggars. That one yesterday had his left leg bent at the knee and the foot strapped up behind him. Were you blind?'

They all heard: Geoffrey, Giles, Kat, Master Hardynge, even the boatman. I wanted to cry with mortification except that when Lionel saw the tears in my eyes he stared at me so angrily that I held them back for fear of worse rebuke. I sat upright in the boat, looking out across the water with eyes too blurred to see it, my hands clasped tight to stop them from shaking. When we landed, Geoffrey helped me out and tried to say something kind, but I wouldn't look at him. I ran straight indoors from the landing stage, up to our chamber and to bed at once, shutting out even Kat. Lionel did not come until it was dark. He said nothing more and the night was . . . as usual.

In the morning, everyone behaved as though nothing had happened and so did I but inside myself, I was different. The day before, I had been spontaneous, answering to my surroundings as the harpstring answers the minstrel. Now I tested every remark against Lionel's likely opinion before venturing to make it. I lost interest in London and was glad when we set out again.

The warm weather had gone for good. We rode through cold rain and blustery winds which tore leaves from the trees before they had even begun to change colour. No one, not even Geoffrey, felt inclined for singsongs. I thought of Withysham often, but I did not speak of it.

We stayed two nights at wayside inns, and on the third day came in sight of Warwick Castle. At the sight of it, notwithstanding Lionel's lecture, I nearly fell off the pillion.

It stood upon a hilltop, its huge, buttressed walls as vast and inhospitable-looking as the Tower of London itself. It stared down at us and I stared back, past Lionel's shoulder, and longed yet again for Withysham, or for Faldene or for any of the lodgings we had stayed in on the journey; for something, anyhow, of reasonable size and friendly aspect. Just in time, I remembered not to say so.

I sat very still and very quiet as we followed the road uphill to the main gate. The gate was open but there was a guard to ask our business. The gatekeepers seemed to recognise both Lionel and Geoffrey, however, and waved us through. We rode through an arched entrance which was almost a tunnel, where the horses' hooves echoed, and into a courtyard with stables.

What happened next was remarkable. It was as though some powerful piece of machinery, such as a watermill, had started up. We were the grain. Grooms appeared to take the horses as we dismounted. A boy led the mules and muleteers away and a sergeant with pike and helmet took charge of our armed escort. A liveried page, conjured it seemed out of the air by the noise of our arrival, showed us through another arch and into an astounding inner court, if such a small word can be used of such a huge place. Laid with turf, it was as big as a meadow, but all round, instead of a fence or a hedge, were frowning walls and towers and hundreds on hundreds of overlooking windows. The rain had ceased that morning, and people in clothes of intimidating elegance were strolling on the paths that ringed and crossed the turf.

We were taken in at a door, up some narrow stairs and into a square chamber. There were four pallets on the floor, each big enough for two or three people, and an inner door leading to another room where there was a bed with hangings. 'Ladies' attendants share a room on the floor above,' said the page, addressing Kat. 'It's just up the stairs. The privy house is at the foot of them. The usual receptacles are in the rooms.'

'Thank you. We require some water for washing,' said Master Hardynge.

Humphrey Hardynge was one of the most completely self-contained human beings I have ever met. I never came to know him, never learned anything of his background, his tastes or ambitions. In all the years we spent in the same house, I never heard Master Hardynge say that he was tired or had a headache. When he finally died, it was in the most discreet fashion possible, by simply passing away one night in his sleep. Where Lionel went, Master Hardynge went and it was he, always, who either in person or by messenger arranged our accommodation, meals and transport, smoothing the way for his master. He was a human version of the ox-drawn roller that my father used for flattening newly gravelled paths. He scarcely even laid claim to a name of his own, for Lionel usually addressed him as Master Secretary. No doubt he was used to places like Warwick Castle but I am sure he would have maintained the same air of competent authority if asked to see to his employer's comfort in a Byzantine palace, or in hell.

The page responded to that air of authority. The page was no older than I was, but he was sophisticated in his green and white satin, with the Warwick badge of the bear and ragged staff embroidered on one shoulder, and he struck me as likely to be impertinent. I wouldn't have dared give him orders. But he said 'Certainly, sir,' most respectfully to Master Secretary, and withdrew. The water came in five minutes.

When we had washed and our baggage had been brought in, Lionel told me to change; we were going outside. I took a look through the leaded window at the ladies sauntering below and searched for something suitable to wear. My most elaborate dresses now seemed absurdly plain. I settled on a deep rose brocade with a train, made Kat brush and shake it and donned it with her help.

'Aye, that'll do,' Lionel said, glancing at me, 'come along. But no gawping. Kat, you'll attend your mistress.'

Geoffrey joined us as we made our way out. The sun had reappeared and the late afternoon was mild although the air was damp. Long shadows lay across the turf; dinner might begin in daylight but it would end by candlelight. At one side of the great court a group of minstrels was playing to a casual crowd, and near the door to what I surmised was the great hall, half a dozen ladies were admiring a small dog and persuading it to beg for titbits. I took Lionel's arm, Geoffrey walked on his other side and Kat, after looking hastily round to see what other ladies' maids were doing, picked up my train. We joined the strollers.

We took a path across the green. It brought us to the other side just in time to encounter a man and a woman as they emerged from a door.

I did not need Lionel's prod, or even the example of the bowing and curtsying people round me, to tell me that here were the lord and lady of Warwick. I went instantly down, placing one foot with precision behind the other, unable to remember what if anything I should be doing with the infernal train and obliged to trust it to Kat's probably panic-stricken hands. I did not know how long I ought to stay down but the Countess of Warwick solved that by putting out a hand to raise me. I came to my feet and the Warwicks both smiled at me from what seemed an immense height while Lionel explained that I was his wife.

In truth, though Warwick himself was tall, the Lady Anne was only the same height as myself, but she had such presence and so had he that to my awed vision they were both like giants.

Listening to Lionel's conversation with them, I gathered that he had informed them of his nuptials, as a courtesy, and that he had been overwhelmed by the generosity of their gift (what gift?) and that he would be bringing his new wife to Middleham in due course. He hoped I would find favour with her ladyship and would prove to be of service . . .

'Why shouldn't she?' said the countess, cutting him short. 'He told us your name was Petronel, child. A form of Petronella, is it not? A good saint's name.' Her dark, observant eyes scanned me from head to foot. 'Petronel is a pretty variant, and your wife has a pretty face, Master Eynesby. I wish my daughters had complexions as good.'

'I have freckles sometimes,' I said, taking courage, and beside me I felt Lionel stiffen in case my temerity failed to meet with approval.

It didn't fail. 'So has Warwick,' said his lady with amusement.

I looked up at the earl, who was grinning, and saw that it was true, although the freckles which were strewn across his dignified aquiline features were subtle; his skin might have been dusted with gold.

'So you're in good company,' said the countess. 'I shall hope to see you at Middleham. My elder daughter Isabel is of an age now to have her own ladies. Perhaps you will be one of them.' She glanced towards Geoffrey, to whom Warwick was now talking. 'We're pleased to see you looking well, Sir Geoffrey. You've had no more trouble with your cough?'

'No, my lady, the summer weather cured it.' There was no subservience in Geoffrey's voice; unlike his uncle, he seemed at ease with the Warwicks and they with him.

They moved on. Kat, who had let go of my train in order

45

to make her own curtsy and since no one had given her permission to stand up again, had stayed down, now rose and rubbed her knees rather inelegantly before picking up her burden again. Lionel frowned at her and said to me: 'You got away with it and I won't say you were wrong. She took to you. But watch your manners, don't be pert. Now it's time to go indoors.'

'I didn't know Sir Geoffrey had been ill,' I said, when we were back in our quarters, once more washing, this time in preparation for dinner.

'He gets a cough and a cold most winters, and with him it lasts till spring,' said Lionel. 'It was gracious of Lady Warwick to ask about it. He's strong enough otherwise. There's the trumpet for dinner.'

We dined – placed modestly near the salt – in a wide and beautifully proportioned hall with windows overlooking a tumbling river, but I can't remember what we ate, for I was plagued throughout the meal by a persistent and bewildering desire to pass water, in spite of having relieved myself before we went in. I was glad when dinner was over and I could get to a privy. When I did, the business hurt.

I told Kat, who consulted one of the other maids in the room where they all slept, and they brought me a posset to drink which they said might help. It didn't seem to make any difference, although it tasted foul, as medicine should. When Lionel embarked on his nightly ritual (which he observed religiously although even I, uninformed as I was, knew by now that he found it an effort), I cried out in pain. It was like being assaulted with a saw.

He withdrew, somewhat sulkily, and I managed to fall asleep, but in the morning things were as bad as ever and to my alarm there was blood in my water. I drank more possets, holding my nose to conquer my revulsion, and rested that day in our room.

Lionel let me alone that night and was, I suppose, considerate in a grumpy fashion. I felt a little better next day and when Lionel asked if I could travel, I said I could. Later I wished I hadn't, for the weather was overcast and wet again and a cold wind was blowing, which seemed to eat into me. My symptoms worsened anew and I recall little of the second half of that journey north. My memory is all blurred over by a haze of physical malaise.

Lionel did not try to make love to me again while we were travelling, and I was thankful. At the end of the second day after leaving Warwick Castle, we arrived in York. It was like London but even noisier, for innumerable church bells all seemed to be ringing at once. Every church seemed to be either having a bellringers' practice or announcing a marriage or tolling for a death. But I had long since lost the desire to comment even on the most surprising things. I was by now entirely taken up by my ailment, and I was in a state of continual struggle with myself, taking secret oaths not to ask to dismount until we'd passed that tree, or the next milestone, or were over the brow of the hill.

The other members of the party knew by now that I was ill and at York, where we stayed with some more merchant friends of Lionel's, someone – and I think it was Geoffrey – apparently managed to convince Lionel that my sickness was genuine and not some form of feminine difficultness. He sent me to share Kat's pallet that night and in the morning said quite kindly that I should rest at Eynesby that evening, when the travelling would be over. I was glad. I only wanted to lie down, preferably for ever.

We bore north-west from York. The weather was still wet and judging from the swollen state of the streams we encountered, there had been heavier downpours here than we had experienced on our journey. As we rode, the moorlands rose around us. Ill as I felt, I noticed them, for they were so very different from the downland and forest to which I was accustomed. These hills towered, with fretted crests and crag-strewn flanks, and instead of the grass and woodland of the south, there was heather which turned the land sombre purple where it was in bloom, and dark brown where it was not. I thought it bleak and cheerless.

We came on Eynesby suddenly, as we reached the brow of an upland track. At first sight, I took it for a small village but Lionel pointed and said: 'That's Eynesby. Those buildings there are the dairy and the bakehouse,' and then I saw that the central structure was a gabled house. There was indeed a village of some kind but it was in the distance, beyond a great spread of fields and grazing land stretching up a broad vale between those dominating hills.

A river ran through the vale between us and Eynesby, and the path led us down to it. It was running high, its waters swirling and noisy and brown with silt. There was a low stone bridge, but instead of riding on to it, Lionel pulled up and swore. Craning my neck from behind him I saw that halfway across the bridge ended in jagged, broken stonework. Fallen masonry lay tumbled in the water. Lionel's ears turned red. 'That's my new bridge!' he roared at Geoffrey above the thunder of the river.

'I was against using Nicholas Hawes at the time!' Geoffrey shouted back. 'He's too cheap and his reputation with his guild isn't all it might be, either. He should have built higher with thicker piers!'

'It was a plain masons' job I wanted, not fancy architecture!' Lionel snapped. 'Even a cheap workman shouldn't have made this much mess of it. One spate and down it goes! All right for you to sit there grinning, my lad. If it was your bridge, you'd have Master Hawes out of business as quick as lightning. Though not any quicker than I'll be doing. I'll have him for this. Master Secretary,' he twisted round in his saddle, 'when we get home, if ever we do, look out all Hawes's bills and the copy of the instructions I dictated for him, and send him word to attend on me. Assuming he can get to me across *that*. If the ford's no good either we'll be sleeping the night at Silbeck, Geoffrey.'

'And serve me right for saying I told you so?' shouted Geoffrey cheerfully. 'Silbeck's on this side of the river,' he added by way of explanation to me, 'but the ford's usually fit to use. Let's see! I'll come with you so far.'

How much longer? I thought as we turned downstream and away from the gabled house. How much longer before I could ease myself as I so desperately needed to do, and find a bed to hide in till I was better?

We jolted on for nearly half a mile before we came to the ford. My bladder throbbed and ached. At the ford, the river spread out over a wide, pebbly expanse and became shallow. It was still swift and didn't strike me as being quite shallow enough but Lionel said: 'Aye, we'll manage, just about. Come with us, Geoffrey? Your mother'll likely be at Eynesby to meet us.'

'Yes, I'll come on with you,' said Geoffrey, and since the mules showed signs of balking at the water, he rode on to lead the way.

The ford was passable, just. I raised my feet and pulled up my skirt hems to keep them clear of the water, but even so I was badly splashed. Once over the river we took an uphill track across pastures where sheep were grazing, towards the stout wooden fence which circled the house. Within it, the path wound among outbuildings, and then there was a little timbered gatehouse where the gate stood open, and beyond that a paved yard where a holly tree grew in one round bed of earth, and the house proper was in front of us.

It was smaller than Master Halford's had been, but it was much, much bigger than Faldene. It had in fact been built, as Faldene never was, to withstand attack, for times in the north had always been wilder than in the south. Eynesby was like a small castle with a manorhouse perched on top, the timber and plaster and the mullioned windows beginning at first-floor level, while the lower walls were made of aggressive-looking stone with arrow-slit windows. The lower level, clearly, was just used for cellarage. Steps led up to a little hall porch and people were hurrying down them to greet us. A steward, dignified of bearing but with a thin worried face, came at once to Lionel, and there was a groom to help me dismount. Hands whisked the baggage

49

off the mules and our animals were led away. On a smaller scale, it was like the polished reception at Warwick, except that here people wore brown fustian instead of livery and they spoke broad Yorkshire. But at Faldene, arriving guests sometimes had to sit on their horses in the courtyard and shout for attention. Lionel clearly took his standards from his lord.

Lionel dismounted and took my arm, turning me towards the house. At the foot of the steps, Geoffrey was embracing someone, lovingly if a little awkwardly, since he still had his horse's reins looped round his arm. He stepped back as Lionel led me up.

'Petronel, this is my sister Alison Silbeck. Mistress Alison, you'll call her. Her husband wasn't a knight. Alison, my wife, Petronel.'

She was spare and businesslike, dressed in brown. She was nearly as tall as Geoffrey but otherwise there was not much resemblance. She looked more like Lionel, with the same narrow face, the same long jaw and nose. Her lightish hair was faded and her skin peeling from exposure to the weather. Lionel was saying: 'You'll stop on a week or two and give Petronel some help in managing the place? She's young, as you see!'

'Time'll cure that,' said Alison, offering me a pinched smile as I took her hand. My own hand I knew was cold and shaky, for I felt not only unwell but self-conscious. Her colourless eyes, which were also very like Lionel's, seemed to be appraising me dubiously, though her voice was amiable enough as she said, addressing me directly: 'Aye, I can stay, but tha shouldna find it hard. Eynesby has oiled hinges. I should know. I oiled them mysen.'

She was prepared to do her duty by me, evidently, whether she liked me or not. I thought of the novice mistress at Withysham, so competent in all she did and so determined that others should be competent too, but never happier than when asked for advice. I had better ask Alison's advice often, I thought, though I'd be well advised not to ask the same question twice.

'I shall be glad of your help,' I said timidly. She let my hand go and Lionel marshalled us all indoors, except for Geoffrey, who went off to look after his horse. He preferred to do this himself where possible, I had noticed.

I was thankful to be under cover at last. My bladder throbbed wretchedly and I wanted to ask for the privy but felt embarrassed. The hall into which we had come seemed to be as full of people as the courtyard. Indeed, many of those who had met us outside had come in with us.

I found myself being presented to a stream of men and women and trying, through a fog of discomfort, to say the right things. The worried-looking steward was called John; a burly, swarthy man in a white apron was Ralph the cook. A woman called Chrissy, sonsy and amiable and plump, was the steward's wife. I thought I might ask her for the help I needed but I wasn't quick enough and found myself being led on to greet a couple of menservants instead. I looked for Alison but she had disappeared. So had Kat.

I smiled, made polite answers, admired the hall as Lionel evidently expected. It was spacious, with a modern hearth set in one wall, glazed windows, and some hangings in painted leather depicting scenes of war and feasting. 'Those are the Earl of Warwick's gift, that I thanked him for when we met him. They've not been hung in the best place to my mind though I'll leave that to you to say. That staircase there is new; that was put in last year. I'm proud of it.'

It was indeed a fine staircase, far more handsome than anything at Faldene. It was made of some golden-toned wood which glowed agreeably, and now squeaked musically underfoot as Alison came hurrying down. 'I've just taken thy maid up to thy chamber with a pannier of clothes off the mules. I've told her where to get hot water and . . .'

'Alison,' I said, 'I mean, Mistress Alison . . . I . . . can you help me? It's just that . . .'

'Well, then, I forgot. Alison,' said Lionel, 'take Petronel to the privy and look after her, she's got some kind of

51

illness. She's been off that horse three times since we set off this morning and I told her to drink nowt at breakfast.'

Alison took charge of me. In the privy, too worn out by now to pretend any more or care whether or not my new sister-in-law despised me, bludgeoned with new things and new places and faces and mistily aware that this house, so much bigger than Faldene, was to be my responsibility and that I had not been trained for it, seared by the pain of passing water and terrified by the blood in it, I began to cry helplessly.

'Oh, that,' said Alison in a commonsense way which brought instant comfort to my fears. 'That's nowt.' Her accent was far more marked than Lionel's. 'Tha's new-wed, it often happens. I'll make it plain to Lionel. If he leaves thee alone a week or two and tha drinks all the water tha can swallow – drink nowt at breakfast, indeed! – it'll pass. Water's the cure, lass and we've good pure well water here.' She stayed with me, brisk but reassuring and I clung to her hand in anguish, thankful to have her there, thankful that someone at last could tell me what was wrong.

I was ill for days after that. I don't know when Geoffrey went away to Silbeck across the valley, and at the time I didn't care.

Chapter Three

The Plantagenets: Diagram of Power

June 1467

John Alcock had been born in the city of Hull, in a tall, galleried house overlooking the Humber. The river, grey-coloured and muddy and full of commercial vessels, provided a workaday view, but the house itself was pervaded with smells which were not workaday at all. His father William Alcock was a merchant catering for the luxury trade. He imported silks, perfumes and spices and often brought samples home. Over the years, the oak beams and the walnut furniture had absorbed the scent of jasmine and musk, cinnamon, nutmeg and ginger, and whenever the house was warm, breathed them back into the air.

As a result, to the day he died, grey muddy rivers and the scent of exotic perfume or spice, would for John Alcock bring back precisely the same memory. They spelt security.

His home had been secure both financially and emotionally. William Alcock and Joanna his wife and their frequent guests wore fur-trimmed clothes and gold ornaments as a matter of course, and when at dinner the conversation turned as it so often did on money, people talked in easy voices and mentioned large sums, or the purchase of a house or a warehouse or a fully-found ship, casually and without awe. The household was well-off enough to take such things for granted.

The emotional solidity was less obvious outwardly but went as deep. William and Joanna came from Yorkshire merchant families of long-standing acquaintance. They had been accustomed to meet each other socially long before the day when their parents proposed that their marriage should seal a joint business venture. They had consented willingly, since they were already at home with each other, and after the marriage, acquaintanceship matured quietly into love.

John Alcock could remember the quality of that love. His father had died when he was not quite six, but nevertheless, John knew that he had never heard his parents quarrel, and that he had fallen asleep many times to the sound of their voices in tranquil, companionable talk. And he could remember the whiteness of his mother's face after his father's death, and the sound of her sobbing.

But the disaster had not shaken his sense of security. He could recall the conclave at which relatives from both sides of the family had discussed the future. His elder brother Thomas, just on nine years old, had been treated with a special courtesy, as his father's heir, and been seated among the adults. John himself had sat in a corner of the inglenook with his baby brother Robert and while Robert sucked his thumb, John had listened and tried to make sense of what was happening, and considering his age, succeeded fairly well.

At least he had grasped that his elders were united in wanting the three of them brought up just as they would have been if their father had lived. His mother and one of his paternal uncles were to control the business until Thomas was of age, and they would all stay in the house as before.

Later – much later – he had learned that in the years that followed his mother had turned down more than one persuasive offer of marriage, fearing to disturb her sons' home by introducing a stepfather, or to risk any of the business getting into hands which might not do their best for Thomas. Later still, he had understood that on her part this was a sacrifice.

Meanwhile, he and his brothers had attended the Hull grammar school as their father had intended. It was not a

54

particularly good school but its master was conscientious and at least wise enough to know his own limitations. When he saw that John was capable of learning more than the school could teach him, he said so frankly. John had been forthwith despatched to study at a more renowned institution in York, attached to St Mary's Abbey.

St Mary's was his first journey away from the safe, ordered world of his home and he had thought at first that he would die of bewilderment and homesickness. What had saved him had been the studies. The school did not teach only Latin and Greek, but also offered a grounding in logic, rhetoric and the sciences. As new intellectual horizons opened before him, he reached for them, and in reaching forgot to be unhappy. He learned the pleasures of asking questions and solving problems. Already too stout to be physically agile, he discovered that mental agility could compensate.

Then had come the question of his future.

John Alcock had wanted to be a schoolmaster. He had already on occasion helped out by teaching the younger boys and had enjoyed it, but in successive interviews with the principal master, the abbot of St Mary's and finally a bishop, he had been induced to aim higher. A mind as alert as his, they said, should go in for the study of law. He should also, of course, enter the priesthood since most lawyers were drawn from the clergy. The church and the law should be his twin professions and between them they would open the way to the highest posts open to any commoner. If he liked teaching, well, opportunities would come. If his career prospered, men would come to him for training.

There had followed three years of studying law at Bruges, and five years more at Cambridge University, working towards his ordination and his doctorate, with Robert Stillington as his tutor. After that, polished and travelled, still glad to visit his family in Hull when he could, but immune now to the pangs of home-longing and even – just a little

– inclined to patronise his less sophisticated brothers, he had become a practising lawyer in London, had obtained at length a court post, and been finally made Dean of St Stephen's.

That meant less law and more ministry, but this suited him. The frustrated teacher in him was demanding an outlet and the ecclesiastical duties of preaching and advising appealed to him.

He had been hearing confessions when a minstrel lately returned from a continental journey chose to use the privacy of the confessional to whisper what he had heard while he was playing for the household of the exiled Margaret of Anjou. He wanted to sell his information, said the minstrel, but didn't know how to go about it. Could Alcock . . .?

Living and working in the south, Alcock had not seen first hand what Margaret of Anjou and her mercenaries had done in the north, but he had heard about it. When her husband King Henry the Sixth had fallen mad, Margaret his wife had fought his kinsman Duke Richard of York for the right to act as Protector of the Realm. In the course of this, she had slain the duke himself and one of his sons and treated the duke's dead body with ignominy. Further, she had not only permitted but actually instructed her men to burn and pillage freely, in order to terrify the population into obeying her.

The duke's eldest son, now Edward the Fourth, had put a stop to that. With Warwick's assistance he had driven her out, put King Henry into honourable confinement in the Tower of London, and taken control of the country. But now, apparently, Margaret from her exile in France was attempting to gather money and adherents for a new attack and had been in secret contact with certain lords who had fought, or whose fathers had fought, on her side before.

Alcock carried his news to the King, seeking a personal interview. 'I can't vouch for the truth of it,' he said, 'but if it's true . . .'

'Pay the minstrel,' said Edward. 'Not too much, but pay

him. I shall proceed as though the report were true. If it proves to be so, you can pay the minstrel more.'

Edward had a couple of the lords watched whom the minstrel had named, and messengers waylaid just after leaving their houses. The rumour was proven, the conspiracy ended, and Alcock duly presented the minstrel with a second purse of silver. He also despatched him back to France with orders to find out anything else which might be of interest.

'You have a talent for this sort of thing, I think,' said Edward when Alcock explained this. 'I suggest that you find a few more people who'd like to be paid retainers for gathering information. I've learned by experience,' he added, 'that one can never have too much of it.'

With that, John Alcock found himself embarked upon a third career, that of King's unofficial intelligencer, and was slightly shocked at himself for enjoying it.

What he enjoyed was the exercise of subtlety, the teasing out of a coherent background meaning from a welter of bits and pieces: two men seen walking together here, a snippet of talk overheard there. Something mischievous in him also enjoyed knowing more about the great – in some cases, the pompous – than they would have liked him to know. The news that was brought to him was often decidedly indiscriminate. His informants were not always required to gather news on specific subjects, merely to gather news of any kind, and from their reports Alcock discovered not only rumours about political manoeuvres but also the fact that a particular bishop couldn't keep his hands off the maidservants and that a noble knight of great dignity was terrified of mice.

The same mischievous streak also caused him to be amused by the absurdities into which his new calling occasionally led him. His agents were not always people with whom he would naturally consort. Meetings were sometimes arranged, of necessity, under extraordinary or even ridiculous circumstances. He had had reports made to him in a beggar's whine, to the accompaniment of inappropriate gestures of appeal; had been fetched at midnight to the bedsides of allegedly dying men, and found himself instead receiving a report in a lumber room or a shed or, once, in a freezing cold privy.

But the tendency to be shocked was always there and surfaced occasionally like a shark's fin through otherwise calm waters. Its origins lay in his upbringing, which had been not only loving and solvent, but also respectable. The merchant community from which he sprang drove hard bargains but also kept them and they did not plot each other's deaths. As a boy, he had supposed that the whole world was like that.

Only after he had come to court had he realised that, after all, the rest of the world was not necessarily the same, that there were men who would unhesitatingly send their enemies to the block if they got the chance, that not all men and women regarded marriage vows as sacrosanct, and that he was now in the midst of such intriguing for power and money that the shrewd business ploys of his own community looked by comparison like innocent games for children.

The things that were said of Bess Woodville were an example. No one – except apparently Alcock himself – believed for a moment that she had withheld her favours from the King before marriage merely out of virtue. Like Stillington, the court took it for granted that she had been playing first and foremost for the crown.

Once in a while, John Alcock would find himself detesting his surroundings, wishing he had held out against his mentors all those years ago and insisted on being a schoolmaster instead. At these times, he would even harbour wild thoughts of abandoning his career and retiring to run a school after all.

And once in a while, he would startle someone by actually saying so.

'There are times when I truly wish,' Alcock said, 'that I were my own second cousin.'

Dr Stillington, standing beside him in the minstrels'

gallery above a marble-floored hall in Westminster, looking down on the crowd below, said: 'You envy him? Who is he?'

'Not all the time, just some of it. He's no one in particular. He's Yorkshire-born like you and me.' The hall was garlanded with white roses, the insignia of York. A rope of roses was threaded through the balustrade of the gallery. Alcock gently flicked one with a forefinger. 'He's a chantry priest and a schoolmaster in a little north-country town, teaching the rules of Latin grammar, and a little arithmetic to the sons of burgesses and yeoman farmers. He's also one of the happiest men I know, and in that world down there –' Alcock nodded towards the well-dressed and noble gathering below '– he'd be lost. He knows that and he's impressed by me because I know my way about it, but of the two of us, he may be the better man.'

'I'll never understand you, John.' In the presence of his former pupil, Stillington held on to his dignity and his ten years' seniority by addressing Alcock by his first name. 'You have had a fine career. You might have a bishopric one day. You've made your way in the face of competition, without ever compromising your reputation. No one's ever accused you of bribery or sycophancy. But you say you'd rather be a schoolmaster!'

'Teaching interests me. One of the things I'd like to do one day is found a good grammar school at Hull, where I come from. The one there now is very badly funded and I hear that it may even be closed when the present master retires. I do some tutoring now because I like it; I'd have been happy as a schoolmaster. As for making my way at court, thank you for saying I've never compromised my good name. But if I've never greased palms or paid fulsome compliments to people with remunerative posts to bestow, I've made sure I know the right people and I've made sure I've been seen being efficient, resourceful and all the rest, at the right moments and in the right places. I'm no saint. The dividing line is very narrow, Dr Stillington, and I'm not as sure as you are that I've never stepped across it.'

'You're too hard on yourself. You're spoken of as a pillar of integrity,' said Stillington, and then remarked, 'I see that Dickon of Gloucester isn't here yet. That won't please the King. Did he find the archery butts at Greenwich too beguiling to leave, I wonder?'

'I doubt it,' said Alcock. 'Dickon is one of the people who make me feel I ought never to have come to court. I was once obliged – it was my duty – to let the King know of certain opinions held by Dickon. In fact he knew them already because Dickon had already let them be seen, but it wasn't a nice position to be in. Fond of archery he may be, but I doubt if he's lingering at Greenwich even for that. It's the Queen's house now and he only lodges there under protest.'

Stillington glanced round but the minstrels had withdrawn for refreshments and the two of them were alone. He rested his elbows on the carved oak balustrade alongside Alcock.

'He still detests the Queen then?'

'Regrettably, yes. He's solidly loyal to his brother, but he avoids his sister-in-law as much as he can and when they do meet, is just barely civil.'

'Nevertheless,' said Stillington, 'I know he was invited today and he ought to be here. If the butts haven't kept him . . .'

Quick, firm footsteps on the stair at the end of the gallery made them look round. Dickon of Gloucester had appeared. 'My lord,' said Stillington nervously, 'we were just wondering where you were.'

'I was delayed coming up the river,' said Dickon. 'My boat had to wait and backwater while two ships flying French and Burgundian flags wrangled over right of way. It's a *piquant* situation, having embassies from both of them here at the same time.' Like all his family, Dickon spoke perfect French and he gave the word *piquant* its correct pronunciation. He also put it into audible inverted commas. His clipped voice was overlaid with the broad vowels of the north of England where he had spent so much of his boyhood. Alcock knew that he thought of himself as a north-countryman. When he used French terms, he did it as though he were laughing at his own pretensions. 'France and Burgundy,' he said now, 'are in a permanent state of near-war, and by the way those two captains have taken the rivalry to heart, it could be real war at five minutes' notice.'

Since February 1466, well over a year ago, when he had come to court and attended the christening of the King's first child, Dickon had grown up. Last winter, he had gone with Warwick and John Neville to York to represent the King in an official enquiry into an outbreak of rioting in the city. The responsibility, Alcock thought, must have speeded up the maturing process. Dickon held himself better now, and spoke with a new assurance. The grey shadow of an incipient moustache gave a new masculinity to his young face. He had been puny as a child but he had left that behind with childhood itself. The continual hard practice with sword and bow to which he subjected himself had given his shoulders and arms a muscular development unusual in one of his otherwise slight build.

He still wore the quiet colours he had worn as a boy but now they looked like a considered and personal choice, whose purpose was to enhance their wearer and not to conceal him. His brown doublet and cap were of a sumptuous velvet, their colour rich and the pleating of the doublet generous. The tunic beneath, showing through the doublet's slashed sleeves, was a glowing magenta, embroidered with the golden broom flowers, the *planta genesta*, which had been the emblem of the Plantagenets long before the wars with Lancaster began and the protagonists took red and white roses as their badges.

He was a young man now and he looked to be more of a Richard of Gloucester than a Dickon, although he still answered to his nickname.

'What brings you up here, my lord?' Stillington asked.

'Should you not be joining the King downstairs?'

'Presently,' said Dickon. 'I wasn't late on purpose, but I'd have liked to be. I didn't want to come today, I don't enjoy these tricky diplomatic situations. I'm too apt to come out with something blunt. Two rival ambassadors at court and both attending the same function may be Ned's idea of sport but it isn't mine. I came up for a hawk's eye view of what was going on before I ventured into it.'

Alcock's attention had returned to the scene below. 'The King's idea of sport?' he said with amusement. 'You may be right. Look.'

The gathering in the hall was what King Edward the Fourth liked to describe as informal, which meant that there was no set programme, no sitting down in orderly fashion to dine or watch an entertainment. People might sit or stroll at will and refreshments were handed round on trays. Invitations were technically without obligation. 'Come if you wish but there's no compulsion, and wear what you please,' was the way Edward phrased them.

No one who valued their position at court ever failed to arrive and they wore their best clothes because otherwise, the ushers might not let them in.

King Edward, mantled despite the June heat in blue velvet with ermine trimmings, and not unnaturally rather red in the face, was the central figure in the throng. The rival ambassadors were both with him. He had draped a heavy arm round each pair of rigid diplomatic shoulders and even from the gallery, it could be seen that his eyes were dancing with mischief as he genially compelled his captives into polite conversation.

'I wish I were back in Yorkshire,' said Dickon in heartfelt tones. 'People there say what they mean and they don't waste time talking to people they don't like – or let anyone make them, either.'

'You can't conduct diplomatic life like that,' Alcock said mildly. 'A king has to talk to ambassadors and listen to them, too, whether or not he likes them, and ambassadors have to treat each other with courtesy. So must many others who wouldn't normally be drawn to one another. No one can go about baring all his thoughts and opinions, any more than he can with his body naked.'

'Very true,' put in Stillington. 'A little pretence is as essential as clothing. And both Dr Alcock and I *are* Yorkshiremen.'

'But why must there be pretence? What's wrong with honesty?'

'Well, it can hurt people's feelings, for one thing. But also . . .' Alcock's shrewd blue eyes were amused. 'You are observant, my lord, but are you observant enough? You look down into that crowd and you see people pretending, as you put it. But if you looked harder, you would see the reasons too.'

'How do you mean?'

Alcock beckoned and Dickon came to his side. All three of them stood leaning over the balustrade. 'All the interests, all the men of power and influence that make up the realm of England,' said Alcock, 'are represented down there. Looking at them from above, as we're doing now, they're like a diagram, or a map. The important people are the cities and boroughs, the less important are their dependent hamlets. Instead of roads – well, you can see quite clearly if you watch, who is dependent on whom, who is linked to what other. And when your fortune is bound to someone else's, my lord, it is irrelevant whether you like him or not. You've too much to lose to risk offending him, and there may be others – family, friends, tenants – whose fortunes are in turn linked to yours. You can't let them down. Examine this scene with care. You may learn something.'

In silence, the three of them stared down, contemplating the political scenery of England.

Alcock was right. The capital city on the living map was of course the King, but there were others who ran him close, and from all of them there stretched out lines of power, so definite as to be almost luminous, to touch those whose prosperity they ruled.

The Queen, Bess Woodville, had the special advantage of being seated on a dais. Her own court was grouped about her. Almost every well-groomed head in that cluster bore a title, lay or ecclesiastical, and almost every one of them was a relative of hers who owed his position to her.

In Bess's case, the charge of pretence could hardly be made to stick. Few of her circle were there out of pure self-interest. The Woodvilles had been a family united by affection long before Bess acquired any influence whatsoever. Her brother Sir Anthony, leaning over the back of her chair to talk to her, was known to be fond and protective of his sister. He was a noticeable figure for his clothes were not only expensive but also fantastic.

'I don't dislike Sir Anthony as much as I do some of the other Woodvilles,' Dickon remarked in an undertone. 'He's cultured and knightly and he's taught me some useful swordsmanship. But the way he dresses! One green leg and one violet, I ask you! And those curly-toed shoes! It's ridiculous to have toes that length. And that doublet is so short you can see all his assets. He's worse than my brother Clarence.'

'Harry Buckingham is something of a fashion-plate, too,' said Alcock.

There were three young boys in the group, aged from nine to thirteen. Born Bess Woodville, the Queen had once been the wife of the knight Sir John Grey, and the two younger lads, seated on stools beside her canopied throne, were Thomas and Richard Grey, the sons of that union.

However, the third and eldest of the boys, pinkly sullen and clearly longing to be somewhere else – and certainly not guilty of pretence, for the quite evident reason that it would have choked him – was a different proposition. Harry Buckingham was a duke in his own right and shared a common royal ancestor with the King, and was a reluctant rung on the Woodville climb to eminence. He had been made to marry the Queen's younger sister.

'But she's a *nobody*!' he had said fastidiously.

'*Somebody* and *nobody* are titles in the King's gift,' he had been warned. 'Of course, if you want to be nobody yourself . . .'

He had obeyed but not, by the look of him, forgiven. His wife was fifteen and he should by now have been trying to get to know her in preparation for their bedding next year. He never spent a moment in her company if he could help it. She too was on the dais, standing close to her sister. Harry Buckingham had placed himself as far away from her as he could, his profile averted from her, his carefully posed attitude and the magnificence of his azure and ivory satins a declaration of his own personal rank.

'One could look on the Woodvilles as a raw, newly-built town, a scar on a landscape where no town was before,' Alcock remarked. 'But across there . . .'

The eye, scanning across the room, passed over several lesser power groupings: the King's brother Clarence (exotically clad) in conversation with Cardinal Bourchier of Canterbury; some City merchants positioned strategically near Edward, no doubt in expectation of being asked for yet another loan; a cluster of influentially bred and married ladies. But Richard Neville, tall, tawny-headed and gem-studded, aquiline profile outlined against the crimson wallhangings beyond him, stood out as much as the Queen although he had no dais. He was surrounded by a bevy of lords.

The three in the gallery knew them all. There were no upstarts here; they were all from established families. The man with the crude, intelligent face, and the inches that matched Warwick's own, was John Tiptoft of Worcester. He was a much travelled man who had served when young in Italy and also in central Europe, where his brain and his sword had been at the command of a count of horrific reputation. He was highly cultured and possessed the casual brutality of an earthquake. He could spend a morning in a sunlit study, writing verse in Italian, and then stroll out, rhyme and metaphor still dancing in his head, to supervise the savage mutilation of a poacher. He was not much liked even by people who had no reason to be afraid of him, and most people were afraid of him whether they had reason or not.

The handsome, ebullient young man beside him was William Lord Hastings, and the short thin one whose facial lines suggested that he made a habit of sucking lemons was Thomas Lord Stanley. Hastings was a cheerful soul, a fine hand with a sword and highly attractive to women. Stanley preferred to use his tongue as a weapon but usually lost contests of words with his wife.

The three had nothing outwardly in common but they were in animated conversation with Warwick and it was Warwick who united and, like a golden eagle among falcons, dominated them. All three were now, or in the past had been, his brothers-in-law. They were beholden to Richard Neville, and they formed his power network, though not all of it, for the six Neville sisters all made a habit of good political marriages.

'A formidable bond of womb and wedlock,' Alcock murmured. 'You know, I can see a sound practical reason why the King, passion apart, might have wished to marry a lady whose kin could act as a political counterweight. Can't you, my lord of Gloucester?' Dickon looked once more towards the Queen and scowled. 'You're homesick for Middleham, I expect,' said Alcock kindly.

Dickon sighed and his face relaxed. 'Yes, I am. I've lost touch with the friends I had there. I went back last winter, for a while, but they were mostly gone. My particular friend Francis has been sent away to finish his training in some other household and God knows when I'll see him again, if I ever do. Nothing has been the same since Ned married.'

Stillington gave him a sharp glance. Alcock said firmly: 'Your brother's marriage has nothing to do with your leaving Middleham. It was time for you to come to court and learn how to be useful to your brother. And you *are* learning. You went north in the winter to be part of a commission of enquiry, did you not?'

'Yes.' Dickon's face lit up. 'It was very interesting.'

'But there was nothing mysterious about the affray you were enquiring into, surely?' said Stillington. 'It was just one of the regular squabbles, wasn't it, between the people who approve of a Neville as lord of Northumberland and those who want to reinstate the old Percy family?'

'Yes, but amidst the general uproar a lot of men were pursing private feuds,' said Dickon. 'It was like . . . like a window on the life of the city.' His tone was animated. 'One man assaulted another who'd called him a thieving Scot two years ago. The Scots have raided over the border so often that up there, you can be fined for calling a man Scottish. I didn't know that before. And some fishermen ganged up on someone who'd put an illegal fish-garth in the Ouse and depleted their catch. They threw him into his own garth. We spent two whole days, after the main enquiry, hearing the cases arising. It was fascinating.'

'But you couldn't have borne your part, if you hadn't had a few months seasoning down here at your brother's despised court,' said Alcock. 'And,' he added, 'King Edward has seen you. He's signalling.'

Edward had looked up, caught sight of them and was making imperious gestures. 'I must go,' said Dickon.

They went down together. In the hall, the heat was intense and aromatic. The marble floor was free of rushes and some of the windows were open but warm spicy smells rose from the trays of meat pasties which were being handed round, and the crowd reeked of sweat and perfume.

Some of the patterns had changed. Warwick had detached himself from his past and present in-laws and was talking with a group of ladies, which included the King's sister Margaret. Cardinal Bourchier and Clarence had got together with Hastings, but Edward was still with his ambassadors. Alcock, Dickon and Stillington ploughed through a group of lesser persons engaged in a name-dropping contest, avoided the City merchants and reached him.

'We'd all but given you up,' Edward said candidly to Dickon. 'Where on earth have you been? Though I'm glad to find you in such learned company.' He turned to the ambassadors. 'Allow me to present my brother, Richard of Gloucester. He has been avoiding the court or you'd have met him before. This is Dr Robert Stillington, Bishop of Bath and Wells, and Dr John Alcock, Dean of St Stephen's. We have been discussing tournaments,' said King Edward urbanely.

'The English are gifted at the arts of war,' said the French ambassador. The word 'Agincourt' flickered through all their minds but was not spoken. 'I had hoped to see some feats of arms in London but no tournaments are taking place just now, alas, and soon I must be gone. My lord of Warwick is to accompany me on a return visit to King Louis.'

'I had heard of the plan,' said Dickon civilly.

They had all heard of it and been slightly surprised by it. It seemed a pointed, even rude, arrangement to make while the Burgundian was still on the premises, and the Frenchman's open reference to it was hardly courteous either, in his rival's presence.

But the latter's smile was all good humour. 'For so long,' he said, 'we have been hoping to organise a friendly match between English and Burgundian champions but as yet nothing has come of it.' His French was courtly, his tone gracious and his dark eyes rested joyously on the faces of the new arrivals to the group, as though inviting them to share a secret jest.

Edward's hazel eyes were narrowed and full of cryptic laughter too. Alcock's senses pricked. He saw that Stillington remained oblivious but that Dickon too had recognised the signs of something in the air. He met the King's eyes and read a wordless warning: *no questions now*.

'We should pay our respects to the Queen,' said Alcock smoothly, and drew Stillington away. If Edward wished to explain the joke, he would do so in his own good time. Meanwhile, Stillington couldn't be trusted not to ask a tactless question.

A few moments later, Alcock wished he had risked it.

The party on the Queen's dais opened up to admit them. Bess was gorgeously dressed in gold tissue and white satin and Alcock saw that she was happy with her kinfolk round her, sufficiently at ease to be informal. He and Stillington knelt, kissed her well-tended white hand, engaged in a little trivial conversation and withdrew. They found themselves once again in the midst of the name-dropping group, who were drifting past the dais, apparently making for an open window and its promise of a cool breeze. Alcock knew none of them, and realised too – at first with amusement – that most of the names they were bandying about to impress each other belonged to people who were not present. He and Stillington paused to let them pass, and at that moment there fell one of those near-silences which occur fortuitously in gatherings. The nearby merchants had stopped talking in order to investigate a tray of refreshments which was being offered to them, and on the dais Sir Anthony had paused in mid-sentence to choose the perfect word. Into the momentary quiet a voice, as anonymous as the unknown faces, and not identifiable as belonging to any one of them in particular, said disastrously: '. . . don't know if you were there when the Earl of Desmond made that joke about the King's Grey mare . . .'

The little group, too engrossed with itself even to notice its proximity to the dais, moved on. Alcock and Stillington stood transfixed. As naturally as possible, they changed direction and turned to bring Bess into view again. Perhaps, after all, she hadn't heard.

But she had. They all had. Anthony Woodville had started talking feverishly, pointing out that the minstrels were coming back into the gallery. Catherine Buckingham was biting her lips and Harry Buckingham, his head turned away from the Queen, was smiling. Bess herself sat bolt upright, gazing into space, taking no notice of Anthony. Her face was always pale but now it was like white marble, and in her white and gold lap her hands clutched each other so tightly that her fingertips had turned mauve under the pressure.

For a moment, Alcock felt the court around him not as a diagram of power, but as a sea full of hidden rocks and invisible, perilous currents. Once again, on a surge of revulsion, he wanted to be elsewhere. He also wanted to rush up on to the dais and reassure Bess, tell her that while she remained the King's true wife, no one could harm her.

But he could not do that. He must not even appear to have heard. Stillington, who was now mopping his brow and saying how hot it was, had evidently reached the same conclusion. Dickon came out of the crowd and made towards them. Alcock turned to him thankfully as to a distraction.

Dickon caught his sleeve and drew him aside. 'The King wishes us to join him in his chamber. There is something private to discuss. Presently, when he and the Queen withdraw.'

Chapter Four

The Plantagenets: Undercurrents

June 1467

-

The informal reception was still in progress when Alcock
left the hall, but Edward and the Queen had taken their
leave and no one, not even Warwick, would follow them
uninvited. The gathering which assembled in their private
quarters, therefore, was handpicked. At first sight, it suggested a family party. Then, looking again, Alcock saw that
it was not. There was no Neville present, neither Warwick
nor any other, and as well as himself, there was another
outsider; one of the merchants who had been near Edward
in the hall was standing by the window, gazing out at the
river.

Alcock knew him, for he was a frequent and prominent
visitor to the court. This man had the accent and the
swarthy skin of a Portuguese, and the dark eyes sunk
behind high, jutting cheekbones, the strong white teeth and
black moustache of an archetypal bandit. He bore the
unlikely name of Edward Brampton. He was a naturalised
Englishman, a Portuguese-born Jew who had converted to
Christianity, probably for the sake of trading advantage
when dealing with a largely Christian world. He was very
wealthy. And for King Edward, who had sponsored both
his conversion and his naturalisation, and whose name he
had taken at his baptism, he was reportedly willing to do
anything.

The King himself, tall frame relaxed on a cushioned settle, was watching benignly while his Bess poured wine for
him with her own hands. In private with the King's family,

71

as when she was with her own kin, Bess did not demand ceremonial. Her sister-in-law Margaret, who had knelt to her at the churching banquet, was now comfortably sharing another settle with Clarence. Anthony Woodville was perched in a window seat, shapely violet and green legs crossed and extravagantly pointed shoes gently swinging. For the purposes of this occasion, Woodvilles were evidently welcome when Nevilles were not. Bess handed the goblet to her husband, looked reproachfully at Dickon who had come in with Alcock, and said: 'Oh, Dickon! You did not pay your respects in the hall just now.' Her tone was faintly bantering and also nervous. She was still too pale.

Dickon could not have overheard that appalling remark in the hall, but he should have noticed the nervous symptoms now. He did not. He bristled visibly instead.

'I am sorry, madam. I was ashamed of coming late.'

'It was partly my fault,' said Alcock, firmly and cheerfully. 'I met him when he arrived and kept him by me. Do forgive me.' He smiled at her and she smiled back, aware that celibate though he was, he admired her and meant kindly by her, and that although he probably had heard that horrible joke, he would never repeat or refer to it.

Not for the first time, Alcock was annoyed by Dickon. It was perfectly possible, even likely, that Bess, once she knew she had attached the King, had been tempted by the prospect of the crown. But if so, she was finding the weight of it heavy now. Couldn't Dickon see how intimidated she was by the disapproval of her husband's clan of coruscating Nevilles, and by that of Dickon himself?

Evidently not. Dickon was perhaps still too young and unimaginative to make that leap into someone else's mind.

Alcock himself could only admire her dignity, and if occasionally he knew that he was also moved by that self-contained beauty with its mysterious aura of promise, well, although he was less troubled by sex than some, any celibate living out in the world must file women under some heading or other. Some churchmen put them uncompromisingly under Sin and Temptation. Alcock was able to class them with sunrises and children, as objects of beauty to be admired and beings in need of protection, to be guarded. It was easy to think of Bess in that way. Furthermore, it was probably accurate.

'There's wine for everyone,' Edward said, 'and you may all be seated. We're in conference. Dickon, if you spent more time at Westminster with me and less planting arrows with dull regularity in pockmarked targets, you wouldn't have to apologise for being late and you'd need fewer things explained to you.'

Dickon flushed but held his tongue on the subject of French and Burgundian skippers, and busied himself, as the youngest present, at the wine jugs. Edward waited until everyone had been served and then said: 'I called you here, Dickon, to tell what I had thought to tell you before today's reception. I took the opportunity of calling Alcock in too, because you have a good mind, Dr Alcock, and I'd value your advice. I take it that you and Dickon were both aware of . . . undercurrents today? Involving those two ambassadors?'

'Yes,' said Alcock.

'Ever played chess with yourself?' Edward asked. 'Either of you? Right hand against left? It's been like that with the ambassadors. The object being to despatch the Frenchman and Warwick safely to Louis in a glow of goodwill – Warwick's taking a suite of two hundred and a couple of pedigree mastiffs because I understand that Louis likes animals more than he likes most men – while I get to grips with a Burgundian treaty that really means something. Their ambassador knows all about it, of course!' Edward threw back his head and let out a shout of laughter. 'He's been impersonating a cheerful loser. He could earn his bread as a player, that man. The fact is that Burgundy is offering to lift restrictions on the import of our woollen cloth and that's a concession worth a fortune each year to our merchants. In return, the duke wants Margaret's hand for his son.'

Margaret smiled. Edward caught Anthony Woodville's eye. 'You can tell the rest,' he said maliciously, 'since most of the rest is your fault.'

Anthony's slightly protuberant eyes were rueful. 'The negotiations began as a quiet exchange of messages through unobtrusive couriers,' he said, 'but one fears that they will soon become all too public, and at the wrong moment. I'm afraid it *was* my idea that one of the messages should suggest that by way of demonstrating our friendly attitude to Burgundy we should forthwith arrange the tournament which has been vaguely under discussion for so long. Whereupon . . .'

'Whereupon,' interrupted Edward, taking over the narrative after all, 'Burgundy replied that their champion would leave for England within a month, bringing full treaty proposals and a formal offer from the young heir, Charles, for Margaret's hand.' He brushed imaginary sweat off his forehead. 'We then had the task of getting Warwick, who is against any alliance with Burgundy, and the Frenchman, out of the way in time. On no account must they find out till the agreements are all signed. They'll try to wreck the scheme if they do. Once we have a *fait accompli*, let them do their worst! We'd intended holding the tourney after the signing, not as an appetiser to it. The French ambassador suspects something – he was probing today. The sooner that French fleet sails, the happier I'll be. And that, Alcock, is the problem I need to solve. The fleet was to sail tomorrow but Warwick has delayed departure because some of those he wants to include in his suite can't arrive in time. I've been tormenting my brains, trying to think of a reason for insisting that he goes tomorrow, without them. We have precise details now of the Burgundian champion's plans. He's coming with a fleet of his own and unless Warwick leaves promptly, the new Burgundian fleet and the French ships will meet in the Thames. I'd rather they didn't.'

'No, it wouldn't be at all a good idea,' said Dickon with

feeling. 'But if we try to make Warwick hurry, he'll know something's afoot.'

'The alternative,' said Edward, 'is to send a fast vessel to intercept the Burgundians and keep them out of the Thames until it's clear. But I'm not willing to create the impression that I'm afraid of Warwick. The champion they're sending is a natural son of the duke and he'll report back to his father. The ambassador knows the situation, of course, but he's discreet. I'm not afraid of Warwick, as it happens,' he added, 'but I prefer to avoid unpleasantness and I don't want the treaty jeopardised.'

Alcock said slowly: 'Ships can be delayed for many reasons. Is the Burgundian fleet not putting in at Dover for the normal clearances before entering the country? Have you waived that requirement for them, sire?'

'No, as a matter of fact I haven't.'

Alcock was still thinking, and aware that he was taking pleasure in his own ingenuity and – a little – hoping that Bess Woodville would be impressed by it. 'Then,' he said, 'a fast horseman should set out for Dover at once and inform the Constable of Dover Castle that when the Burgundians arrive, he has invited them to dine. He can feast and fete them and there would be no harm in it if he let them know that the French ambassador is about to leave your court. No need to mention my lord of Warwick. The Burgundians will merely regard it as tact on your part if you wish to keep them apart. They will co-operate and you will acquire a reputation for both hospitality and diplomacy.'

'Humph!' Suddenly Edward laughed, 'Well, put like that . . . yes. Yes, I think it should work. Thank you, Dr Alcock. Do you know, it was Bess here who said to me, this morning, that I should have you in. She knew you'd find the answer.'

Bess Woodville gave Alcock a smile, very nearly her usual serene one. Alcock smiled back once more, attempting to put reassurance and approval into it. Dickon turned away. Bess noticed and the smile wavered.

Privately, Alcock sighed. He would have a quiet word with Dickon soon, but he feared it would do little good. If Dickon had heard that joke, he would have agreed with it.

It had been a filthy jest, he thought angrily, and all the worse for its subtlety, for the neat packaging of so much meaning in so few words. *The King's Grey mare*. Just the ex-Lady Grey, in fact, a regular and reliable ride, and disposable to another owner, perhaps, once the King grew tired of her! But Bess was Edward's wife. She ought to be respected as a wife. Alcock noticed that she was once more enceinte. Perhaps it would be a son this time. King Edward needed a healthy male heir, Bess Woodville would feel more sure of her position then and the country would feel safer too. Perhaps even Dickon would soften.

'The tournament will cost something to put on,' Clarence remarked.

Edward Brampton, who had continued to gaze out of the window throughout, with the air of being in the gathering but not entirely of it, significantly turned.

'Oh, I see,' said Clarence.

'Master Brampton will arrange a loan,' said Edward, 'and the City guilds will provide pageantry from their own resources. They welcome the opportunity.'

'I suppose it will be a spectacle,' said Dickon. 'Though sometimes I think tournaments are just – playing at war. Who will the English champion be?'

'It would serve you right if I said it should be you,' said Edward. 'I know you disapprove of them. In fact . . .'

Clarence was making jabbing gestures with his thumb. Anthony Woodville grinned, raising his goblet.

An inevitable choice, of course, thought Alcock. The honour was bound to go to a Woodville. Well, the well-bred, well-mannered Anthony was an accomplished knight and would perform the task well. Pop eyes and all.

'I would like to know,' said Margaret, alone with her brothers, her small and carefully manicured hands clasped in the damask folds of her skirt, 'a little more about this Charles of Burgundy. Warwick met him once and didn't like him. He told me so.'

'He was rude to Warwick,' said Edward cheerfully, 'but you're not Warwick and he won't be rude to you, my love. He's in his thirties, intelligent, courageous and respectable. He has a daughter by his first marriage, and Mary is said to be a charming child. Charles is musical like his father but he doesn't drink like his father. He's altogether estimable.'

There was admittedly a slight fading of enthusiasm on Edward's part as he recounted Charles of Burgundy's virtues. Edward drank a good deal himself and there were whispers that he was not as faithful to his Bess as an altogether estimable man should be.

Margaret nodded thoughtfully. 'The treaty is worthwhile, I realise that,' she said.

When a princess formed part of such a deal, she was lucky if the bridegroom were both respectable and fairly young and Margaret knew it.

'We shouldn't hand you over to anyone we didn't think would make you a good husband,' George of Clarence assured her.

Edward nodded. 'Not for any amount of treaties. My Council wouldn't let us! You will have to appear before the Council and tell them in your own words that you are willing for this match, before they'll allow it to proceed.'

'I know. It was only that Warwick said . . .'

'Meg, I'm sure you can trust Ned's judgement,' Dickon said earnestly.

Margaret nodded again, considered, and then sat up straight and looked at them directly. 'I will do as you ask. I will tell the Council so.' She was elegant in dress and given to cultivating her dignity but she was still young enough to lapse on occasion. She now allowed herself the indulgence of a giggle. '*Whatever* will Warwick say?'

'Warwick,' said Edward with positive pleasure, 'will be furious!'

'Edward,' said Bess Woodville, 'who is the Earl of Desmond?'

'Desmond?' Their attendants had been dismissed and the curtains of the great bed drawn round them. Edward, alone with his wife, whose body was not the less attractive because it now included the bulge of their second child, was not willing to give his attention to anything else. 'He's an Irish lord,' he said dismissively. 'His name's James Fitzgerald. He doesn't come to England often and he's not here now. Why?'

'I overheard something . . .' Bess's voice trembled. In the darkness, she felt his hand brush over her hair.

'Tell me,' Edward said.

When she had finished, he laughed. 'Just jealousy,' he said. 'They all think the same. If I wanted to marry a subject instead of a foreign princess, why couldn't it have been their sister or their daughter? Forget it, darling. How beautifully smooth your hair is. I can't see it in the dark but do you know, if I'd never seen it, if I were blind, I would know its colour by the feel of it. It feels smooth and bright and cool. My very fingers know it's silver-gilt. Come here. That's right.'

She hadn't explained herself well, Bess thought in despair and something near to panic, as she lay in his large and demanding embrace and yielded to him apparently with her usual sweetness. He didn't understand. Afraid to anger him, she had spoken too mildly, showing her hurt but not her fear. She was so very much afraid that one day one of these people who hated her, who thought themselves so superior to her, would succeed in undermining Edward's love so that he would set her aside. But if she said that, he would think she didn't trust him. The undermining process might begin at that moment! And she must not show anger, either. No lady should ever show anger openly, her mother had said. Men hated it. They only loved women who were always gentle, always softly-spoken.

She must do something about the Earl of Desmond. If she didn't, then the word would go round – just as that ugly jest was obviously going round – that they could say what they liked and nothing would happen to them. She would be defenceless before them and they would slander her as they liked. She repressed a shiver, thinking how very much they would like it: Dickon, Clarence, Warwick . . . Warwick might well be the most dangerous, because he was the eldest and so very powerful. Whenever he looked at her, he made her feel like a rabbit before a bird of prey.

She didn't want to be so vulnerable. She had tried not to be. She had sheltered behind public ceremony, grateful for the estate that Edward had bestowed on her, and claiming every bit of respect due to her. Or trying to. Dickon had ignored her today and what had she been able to do about that? Nothing.

If this next child were a son she would feel better, but what if the baby were only a girl?

Edward was a man, strong, a warrior who had won battles. She couldn't expect him to understand how dangerous to her mere words could be. She must deal with Desmond herself, somehow.

She had no idea how, but she didn't know the members of the court very well as yet. Perhaps, somewhere among their number, was somebody who would help her . . .

'If you withdrew your support from King Edward and placed it instead behind your poor incarcerated ex-king Henry, you would assuredly find the Lancastrian house willing for you to make what treaties you wished with me, for England's good. But you will not do so because Edward is your cousin and was your protégé. Edward in turn insists on keeping faith with Burgundy out of gratitude for past favours. Ah, these personal loyalties,' sighed the man who had none, stroking the wrinkled forehead of the mastiff by his side.

The chief guest chamber of the Franciscan friary adjoining

Rouen Palace was lofty and well-lit, furnished for secular guests of rank. Richard of Warwick had rank, and looked it. Louis the Eleventh, ruler of France, who daily came padding on sandalled feet along the gallery which linked palace to friary, for private talk with his visitor, more closely resembled one of the friars. Grey robe, rope girdle, bare toes poking out of sandals: what a garb for a king! Warwick thought disapprovingly. Even Louis' person was unimpressive. He had neither inches nor beauty, except for the deep-set dark eyes which reminded one of the fabled jewel in the head of a toad. There were liver spots on the back of the hand which caressed the dog.

The mastiff was one of the animals Warwick had brought. It had hitherto been used only to its handler but it had taken to Louis. Animals generally did. No human being, not even his parents, had ever loved Louis and in turn he loved no human being. He had sired children on his self-effacing second wife (the first had died young, bullied out of existence by Louis and his court for failing to produce any offspring). Warwick did not think Louis knew what was meant by making love. His only knowledge of affection came from the brute creation, which seemed to respond to him. He should have been pathetic, this grey, unprepossessing man whose life had been so barren.

So it was odd that the lord of Warwick, with his gold-freckled Neville skin, his powerful physique and his even more powerful personality; Warwick, family man and earl with, well, almost the status of a king, should feel outclassed in Louis' presence and impelled to earn his admiration.

'These personal loyalties,' said Louis, 'are like the figures of a dance. One takes a partner – York, let us say, or Burgundy. The partners go forward a pace or two, hand in hand. Then they bow and take new partners – Lancaster, perhaps, or France. The dance goes on. One must move towards tomorrow, not remain handfasted to yesterday.'

'There's a middle way,' said Warwick. 'For me to

abandon King Edward would be a personal betrayal, but if Edward abandoned Burgundy – well, Burgundy is a place rather than a man. And whatever he owed to the old duke, when young Charles inherits, Edward will be no more in debt to him than you are. For Edward to let go of Burgundy would not, I think, count as a betrayal.'

'Ah, but can you convince Edward of that?' asked Louis, gently.

Let a man be encrusted with gems. Let the populace cheer him as he rides by. *But what can you actually do?* enquired Louis' lustrous eyes, searching Warwick's face. *How much real power have you? Who rules England – you or King Edward?*

'I shall convince him,' said Warwick grimly.

Chapter Five

Petronel: Season of Festivity

Christmas 1466

'Now there's no call to look so panicky,' said Alison. 'Tha's been taught to read and write and keep accounts, hasn't tha? The rest is commonsense. Look over what we ordered last year and who we asked and then do the same again. Most years are alike. Happen we'll be asked to Middleham for part of the time if my lord's there, or you will. I don't leave home much. My lord's away south at the moment and my Geoffrey with him. About Eynesby's own Christmas feast. The Scropes of Masham are always asked . . .'

'The . . .?'

'The Scropes. Surely tha's heard of them? They're a local family, gentry. Lionel makes a point of standing well with them; they're titled and they've got influence. They accept – because he's got Warwick's ear and his hospitality's good. They'll likely ask thee back later in t'year. Tha'd best put the Bouldershawe tenants on the list this year; they're Lionel's people now since thee brought the place into the family. Happen he'll tak thee to see Bouldershawe soon. The Abbot of Jervaulx is another one tha mun ask . . .'

I was sitting beside her in the hall at Eynesby. The fire crackled brightly in the hearth but the hall, which went right up to the roof (though there were upper rooms and attics over the parlour and kitchen at each end), was still very cold. Outside the hills were dark against an iron sky. Shakily, I pushed away the strands of hair which escaped my indoor cap and kept getting into my eyes. I was still weak from my illness and I was tired, too. Last night, Lionel, having asked civilly if I were now free from symptoms, had tried to perform his marital duties, failed, and then woken me up twice during the night in order to try again.

He had finally succeeded at his fourth attempt, at dawn. I didn't feel as though I had slept at all.

Yet now, when I had in any case been up and about for only a few days and had barely begun to grasp my duties as mistress of Eynesby, I had been faced with the task of organising Christmas. I must apparently conjure into being feasts and entertainments to please aristocratic guests. I must issue invitations and give orders and be hostess to people with titles and influence. I hadn't the faintest idea how to begin and it felt presumptuous even to try.

It was all very well for Alison to talk about common sense; she had been running Eynesby as well as Silbeck for years. She could take the Scropes in her stride just as she did everything connected with either house, or with the land that accompanied them. Looking after noble guests, or advising the head shepherd about buying a new ram in Lionel's absence: it was all one to Alison.

But I had been educated for Withysham, for singing the Office and working in kitchen or linen room or garden under the closest supervision. I had never given orders. I had studied, but did not know how to use what I had learned. I stared at the lists and tallies on the table before me, and wanted to run away.

The most nerve-racking thing about my new responsibilities was that they mattered. 'Well, well, an over-salted soup isn't the end of the world,' the nun in charge of the cooking had once said to me at Withysham. But here at Eynesby, I already knew, an over-salted soup could lower Lionel's value and prospects of advancement if it were served to the wrong guest, while wrong instructions to a shepherd could mean sheep miles away when they were needed at hand for shearing or slaughter, could mean time and money lost. I was part now of the face which Lionel presented to a demanding and critical world and I must make sure it was all it should be, or his comments would be blistering. Even in the short time since I had begun to shoulder my duties, I had found that out.

But there were so many things to do and even quite everyday orders had to be given to people who were older and far more knowledgeable about their work than I was. Going to the kitchen to discuss the meals for the day was an ordeal because I was terrified of Ralph the cook. Alison said he had a hard life; the dinners he produced had to match the best in the county but he was short-handed because 'Lionel doesna hold with feeding more mouths than he need, which is right, but I don't say he doesna tak it too far at times,' said Alison. I couldn't, however, feel sorry for Ralph because he made it so plain that he considered me to be a childish and uniformed intruder whose orders were just one more cross to be borne and to my intense embarrassment he did not hesitate to show this in front of his subordinates.

Another alarming task was adding up the weekly accounts and making them come to a figure which was both accurate and acceptable to Lionel. I feared that these two things were going to be incompatible more often than not. And as if all this were not enough, Alison had said that I really must make some sort of effort to learn about the sheep properly.

I wasn't quite without support. Alison was there and though brusque, was for the time being willing to be leant on. John Steward was prepared to answer questions and Chrissy his wife was kind.

But Alison wouldn't be there always, John Steward was forever harassed (like Ralph, he was short-handed), and Chrissy wouldn't take decisions. Her usual answer when asked for advice was: 'Tha mun ask Master Eynesby.' Or Mistress Alison, or John.

Alison's instructions on the subject of the Christmas feast continued to flow. 'Tha needn't trouble thysen about minstrels and mummers. Lionel arranges for them.' That was a relief. 'But tha'll need to give Ralph a list o' dishes for the feasting and tell him how many there'll be at table. He doesna read or write but he'll remember what tha tells him.'

'Won't he know what to do if he just knows how many and which days?'

'Happen he would but that's not the way,' said Alison severely. 'Tha's been doing too much of that; I've heard thee. "Do as thee thinks best, Ralph, I'm sure it'll be very nice." Christmas matters, hinny, it's important to Lionel. Tha mun know what's wanted and tell thy people because if owt's not to his liking, he'll be down on thee hard and tha doesna want Ralph or summun saying they did their best but t'mistress didn't tell them this, that or t'other.'

Would it be much better, I wondered, if the mistress did tell them this, that or the other, and turned out to have told them wrong? I thought about going into the kitchen and laying down the law to Ralph, and quailed.

Alison was still briskly talking. 'Now, decorations. Tell Chrissy to tak her two little lasses out the week before Christmas and fetch home some holly and ivy. Plenty hereabouts. Chrissy likes seeing to that. And have a few pallets put in t'loft right up under t'roof in case anyone falls sick while the house is crowded. All the proper chambers upstairs'll be full with guests and their servants and if owt's catching, whoever's caught it is best put well away from the rest of us.'

'What if it snows? Will people come then?' I asked. The weather looked as though snow might be imminent. If only it were heavy enough, I thought, perhaps the Scropes and the Abbot of Jervaulx might not be able to reach us.

Alison dashed my hopes of reprieve by blizzard. 'Aye, it snows early in these parts, but folk get about – short distances, any road. We're used to it,' she informed me.

The hall door banged and Chrissy came in with her two

small daughters, all flushed and windswept from walking a mile and a half each way to Eynesby village and back. I hadn't been there yet but understood it to be a fairly big place, bearing the name of Eynesby but containing houses and plots owned by Silbeck and by Middleham direct, as well as by ourselves. It had a yearly fair which was quite famous and it contained a number of useful tradesmen. We bought our candles from the chandler there and when we wanted cloth woven from the wool of our own sheep, all the weaving, fulling and dyeing could be carried out in Eynesby village.

It also had a church, and it was to the churchyard that Chrissy had been with her girls. They came in looking cheery as usual but their errand had been sad. As well as her two living children, Chrissy had four buried in Eynesby churchyard and every now and then, she and Betsy and Anna went to put wildflowers or evergreens on the graves. But they seemed nevertheless to accept the graves in a robust fashion. Chrissy evidently regarded them as simply part of motherhood, like wiping the survivors' noses, and the survivors took their example from her. I wondered sometimes if I would one day have to bear the same sorrow and whether I would put as good a face on it.

But before one could lose children, one must first conceive them. Chrissy and the girls greeted us, said they meant to have something hot to eat and drink, asked if they could bring us some as well and on being told yes, went off to the kitchen. Chrissy was not in the least afraid of Ralph.

And Alison, as though Chrissy and her expedition had set her mind travelling the same paths as mine, said: 'She's got two that's healthy, any road. Any news yet of thee? Tha had time before tha fell ill.'

I shook my head. 'I . . . I'm sorry,' I said.

'Aye, well, tha's young yet but I hope thee'll kindle quick. Lionel wants sons. Drink good ale and don't eat green apples.'

'I pray, too,' I told her.

When I had finished in the hall, I went to our chapel.

Eynesby had one of its own, close to the house. We worshipped there most of the time, rather than go all the way to St Matthew's in Eynesby village. We also had a chaplain of our own. He was another member of the household who had been kind to me.

Father Edmond (Lionel of course always called him Father Chaplain) was proud of his chapel. He cared for it meticulously and from his own not particularly generous pay had squeezed out the wherewithal to buy statuettes and relics to adorn it. I especially liked the image of the Virgin and Child which stood in a niche to one side, with a little altar of its own for candles and floral offerings. The image was a simple affair of painted plaster, only three feet high, but the Virgin had a young, vulnerable expression which appealed to me, perhaps because that was how I felt myself.

It was to her that I was going now. Father Edmond was not there and I took advantage of the chance to say a very private prayer to Our Lady, out loud. I prayed to have a baby soon, and promised to light a candle at the Virgin's altar every day as proof of my faith in her. And I begged for help in organising Eynesby's dreadful Christmas revels.

I felt better after that. The act of praying reminded me of Aunt Eleanor, and Withysham. It was a comfort.

The expected snow came, but it quickly thawed, to be followed by a heavy mist which rolled down from the hills and reduced visibility to a few feet. A carter with barrels of salted fish on board, coming from York, drove blindly on to the broken bridge. He tried to back to safety but the horse was frightened and backed crookedly so that the cart fell through a gap in the damaged parapet. The driver cut the traces in time to save the horse, and then he jumped clear, but the cart was smashed and four barrels burst open on the boulders under the bridge.

Two days later, returning to the hall after one of my

alarming interviews with Ralph, I found a small man with a red face standing in front of Lionel while Lionel told him in a voice of deadly calm that he had a simple choice before him. He could return the money spent on the bridge, compensate the carter and leave York, or find himself brought to court on a charge of incompetent workmanship, with the risk of ending up in the stocks and the near certainty of ejection from his guild.

'But I'll be destitute! Floodwaters like we had could have brought down any bridge, rolling great boulders downstream the way they did! This isna justice!'

'A good many bridges survived,' said Lionel coldly. 'Properly built ones, that is.'

'I did the best job I could for the money thee were willing to pay. Beat me down, didn't thee? I'd have been makkin a loss, if I'd used more stone. I'll pay thee and the carter, but why should I leave York?'

'Haven't I just told you?' said Lionel. His voice was still dreadfully level and more frightening than if he had been shouting.

And the little man was frightened. He was also resentful. He was holding his cap in his hands and twisting it into the likeness of a rope and I could see the strength of anger going into that twist. 'Tha won't pay for decent stonework but tha'll take Warwick's name in vain with the guild. Tha'll put work their way if they give thee what tha wants, and steer it elsewhere if they don't. Benefit of the doubt, I won't get.'

'There'll be no doubt in the matter,' said Lionel. 'You're not in good standing with the guild as it is.'

This, evidently, was Nicholas Hawes who had built the fallen bridge. Lionel, busy every day since our return with a number of matters to do with Eynesby and Bouldershawe, had put off 'dealing with Hawes', as he put it. Now the reckoning had come.

'I'm not unreasonable,' said Lionel. 'You have till the end of February to leave York. The money for myself and the carter, I expect to be paid before Christmas. You may go.'

'But . . .'

Lionel turned away and caught sight of me. 'Oh, there you are. I have something for you. Come with me.' He spoke as though Nicholas Hawes were not there and I saw that as far as Lionel was concerned, he wasn't. Nicholas Hawes, to Lionel, was finished. I went slowly across the hall to my husband. I caught Hawes's eye by accident but didn't acknowledge him beyond that. I didn't know how. I think he took my expressionless glance to mean condemnation. The crimson in his face deepened and his eyes, already shiny with anger and panic, flashed hatred at me. I was glad when Lionel led the way upstairs.

We had the big upper chamber at the south end of the house. It was a fine room, hung with good tapestries. In addition to the big bed, it contained a locked chest with a flat top, which we sometimes used as a seat. This, Lionel unlocked. From it he took a roll of sanguine silk, embroidered with green and gold flowers. 'I bought this in London. It's to make a gown for Christmas.'

'It's magnificent!' I fingered the strong, gleaming material with pleasure. 'Thank you very much.' Thank goodness, at least I could sew well. 'You'll like the gown I make, I promise.'

'Aye, I'm sure of that. Though it's not the gown I most want to see you make. There's another roll of material in there, finer still, enough to make a gown with plenty of room in it. That I'll give you when you've good news for me. Chrissy tells me there's none yet.'

One of Chrissy's regular tasks was boiling the linen. I had had to give her stained garments that week.

'No,' I said. 'I'm sorry. But we haven't been married very long yet.'

'Long enough, lass, and I hope you'll have something to tell me soon. Now you'd better find that girl of yours and get her to help you with stitching this. Give her something to do. She gossips and sits about too much,' said Lionel.

He spoke, in fact, quite amiably and not as though he really disapproved of Kat, but as I stood there with the rust-coloured silk in my hands, a bolt of fear went through me.

I was such a long way from home and even if I had been only a mile away from Faldene, I was now Lionel's wife which meant, virtually, his property. I depended on him for everything I ate or wore. He could use me how he chose and I would have no redress.

I was afraid of failing him. Downstairs, at that moment, I could hear John Steward on his master's behalf, ordering Nicholas Hawes out. To go where? To do what, for the rest of his life?

Down there in the hall I had just seen how Lionel dealt with people who failed him.

When I think of those first days at Eynesby, I see myself in a series of pictures, like the little illustrations which adorn the margins of illuminated manuscripts. I seem, always, to be looking down on my fourteen-year-old self from above.

I see myself lying under Lionel on the feather bed in our chamber, arms and legs and resigned face with closed eyes, sticking out from under his pale, bony body.

I see myself kneeling, palms pressed together, before the Virgin's image in the chapel, where, as I had promised, a candle now burned always.

I see myself, busy and housewifely, keys at belt, seated at the table in the hall, doing the accounts with Alison, or standing stiffly, determined not to show my inward quaking, in the kitchen in front of Ralph. And I see myself, dressed in sanguine silk embroidered with green and gold, my hair braided with gold cord and drawn through an improbable headdress of wire and linen, welcoming the Scropes at the door as the Christmas feast began.

By some means or other – mainly because Alison had helped so much – the organising had been done. Since I was now more afraid of Lionel than I was of Ralph, I had nerved myself to tell Ralph quite firmly that he must serve a certain ginger-flavoured sauce with the meat when the Scropes came because it was Lord Thomas Scrope's favourite. The extra supplies we needed had come in time, and I did not think any items had been forgotten.

In addition, we were not to go to Middleham until March, to my relief. My lord of Warwick would not be there for Christmas. This lifted away some of the nervousness I had felt, and besides, the first two days of the feast, which we had spent privately, had gone well even though Alison was not there to watch over me. Her son Geoffrey had returned home and they had been feasting their own household at Silbeck across the valley.

They would join us today. Silbeck had beautiful pastureland but the house, though sunny and attractive, facing south across the vale from a snug position under a hillside called White Screes, was small. Its main room was barely eighteen feet long and Eynesby therefore hosted the Christmas gatherings on behalf of both.

More snow had fallen but though the hilltops were white and wreathed with cloud, there was only a crisp layer over the valley floor, through which horses could crunch without difficulty. Our guests began arriving early: the Grimsdales from Bouldershawe, the Hornes who rented a farm from Lionel, on the far side of the village; the Abbot of Jervaulx. His was a Cistercian monastery in which silence was observed for most of the time but he used to obtain a dispensation for Yuletide socialising. 'And he uses it,' Alison had told me. 'Talks more than all the rest put together, like a dammed-up river being let loose.' Jervaulx was wealthy , with wide lands in the valley of the River Ure, and he rode in not only on a fine white mare, but with silver buckles to his saddlery, and trappings of blue and silver to protect his mount from the cold wind.

Alison and Geoffrey came next. I was astonished at my own pleasure in seeing Geoffrey again. I had not seen him since the day of my own arrival at Eynesby, and I felt as though I had been missing him all these weeks, although while I was living through them, I had been too harried and nervous to think about him.

I had little time to think about him even now, for the Scropes arrived almost immediately after, riding up in the company of the FitzHughs, another notable local family. They made a big crowd of horsemen and -women, bundled in fur wrappings, with bells on the horses' bridles. The escort of servants seemed enormous. I did a hasty head-count while everyone was dismounting and realised that there were indeed far more than had come last year, according to Alison's records. I must remember to warn Ralph, I thought, as I welcomed the guests, was congratulated by Lady Elizabeth Scrope on the charm of my gown, and led the way inside.

The minstrels Lionel had engaged had arrived from York on Christmas Eve, glad of employment away from the city, they told us. There had been political riots in York that December; we had been luckier than we knew when the food supplies we had ordered from there had reached us on time. The minstrels were in their places and playing, and we brought our guests into a room full of music. 'A delightful welcome,' said Lady Scrope. She was younger than I had expected, and less intimidating.

I looked round the hall, searching for flaws. The evergreen decorations were still fresh, and the fire was bright, with logs piled ready to replenish it. The feel of the hall was right, homely and friendly, with no sign of the agonising which had gone to make it so. Alison, helping Chrissy to fill goblets, caught my eye and gave me a glance of approval.

I wanted to go out to the kitchen, both to speak to Ralph about the extra numbers and to inspect the progress of dinner, but Lionel caught me as I was going out of the door. 'Where are you off to? You shouldn't leave your guests.'

'I just wanted to tell Ralph . . .'

'Send Chrissy. That silk gown's not to be taken into all

that steam and heat.' The Eynesby kitchen was a stone cavern built on to the hall, with two huge hearths, tables down the middle, and oak beams above from which mutton and pork hams hung to cure. It was indeed hot and steamy. So I fetched Chrissy, who was by now gossiping with a friend from the Scrope retinue, listed my messages for Ralph '. . . at least fifteen more people than we expected, and make sure that the ginger sauce is in the making . . .' and concentrated on my task as hostess. We had singing, dancing, conversation, an interlude in the solar listening to music while the tables were prepared, and then we filed back into the hall for dinner.

As we took our places, I found Geoffrey on my right. 'Arranging all this must have been a formidable task,' he said. 'I congratulate you.'

'I'd have been lost without your mother.'

'Ah, my mother's a good teacher. Wait till next year. You'll find you can do it all yourself then. The food smells appetising.'

Father Edmond recited grace and then a procession came in from the kitchen, bearing the first course and singing a carol as they came. John Steward, carrying his wand of office, led the way. My befurred, bevelveted, bejewelled guests were all smiling. 'I must admit,' I said to Geoffrey, 'that I've been much afraid that something would go wrong, but . . .'

'Mistress,' said one of the servers, tugging at my sleeve and whispering in my ear, 'we've not enough meat for them below the salt and Master Cook, he says he can't send in more without you tell him. He says it'll be taking from what's to be served for supper. Can you come?'

On my other side, Lionel was talking to Thomas Scrope. I attempted to slip from my place without attracting his attention but failed. He broke off his conversation and turned. 'Where are you going *now*, Petronel?'

'Master Cook wants some instructions,' I said.

There was now an audible murmur in the hall from the

hungry people below the salt, and from a ripple of disturbance higher up the table where generous souls were passing what would have been their second helpings down to the less fortunate.

'What kind of instructions?' Lionel shot a glance down the table and took in what was happening. 'Surely you told Ralph there were extra mouths to feed? Didn't you?'

It wasn't fair. I had been going to the kitchen to do precisely that, and he had stopped me. So I had told Chrissy to do it for me but I had also asked her to check on several other things at the same time, and Chrissy, in holiday mood and full of the excitement of reunion with friends, had obviously forgotten one of my messages. The most important message, of course. It would be! I couldn't defend myself without accusing either Lionel or Chrissy. I dared not do the first and didn't like to do the second. I began to stumble an apology, saying there had been so much to do, but I would soon have it put right. Lionel's ears had gone red. Lady Scrope and Lady FitzHugh were whispering together and everyone in the hall seemed to be staring at me. I had been caught out; the little girl who had tried to play the chatelaine and been so proud of her pitiful attempt. I wanted to fade into the tapestry or alternatively, see them all struck dead. 'I'll speak to Master Cook now,' I said tremblingly. I would have to tell him to serve the capons and mutton he had intended for a cold collation just before bedtime, and order him to prepare more food for supper. He would say: 'Well, mistress, it's very inconvenient. If only I'd been told. It'll mean . . .'

I looked once, hopefully, at Alison, but all she said was: 'Well, thee mun learn these things. Off with thee now to t'kitchen.'

'And I suppose,' said Geoffrey, rising to his feet, 'that that brute Ralph's in charge of it, making difficulties over everything. It's a bit hard, Mother, sending Petronel into the lists against him. Ralph always was a bully. He needs a clout round the ear every morning and a boot up his backside on Sundays. Attention all!' He clapped his hands. 'More meat is about to be served!' He grinned at me. 'Sit down, Aunt Petronel, leave this to me.' He disappeared towards the kitchen. He was back almost at once, laughing. Further dishes of meat appeared as if by magic. From outside came the agitated clucking of poultry. Ralph had sent someone out to wring the necks of a few more hens. Geoffrey resumed his place. His shoulder pressed mine as he sat down. He was so near that I could feel his warmth.

'Thank you,' I whispered.

Across me, he said: 'Uncle, Aunt Petronel has done wonders, you know. And it's her first Christmas here. She was quite right to arrange the food so that there wouldn't be too much to spare. You know you always insist on no waste.' Lionel's whole face, not just his ears, now went scarlet, but Geoffrey merely smiled at him and for the first time, I saw my husband subside in defeat. 'Will you allow me to partner Aunt Petronel when the dancing begins again?' Geoffrey asked politely.

Lionel muttered an assent. Geoffrey nudged me. 'Don't bite your lip any more. It's all right. Enjoy your dinner, you deserve it.'

And with that – although to outward appearance I remained sitting on my bench, upright and proper, very much Mistress Petronel of Eynesby – within myself I was changed, and the change was as complete and fundamental as that for which we hope at the Resurrection.

I knew now that I was in love with Sir Geoffrey Silbeck, that he had replaced for me the abstract Christ of Withysham, that if only he were where I could see him, then Lionel, Ralph, Eynesby, could all be borne, and that if he were not, nothing else in the world had any sweetness to offer me.

Outwardly Petronel dined, made conversation, applauded the minstrels, laughed at the antics of the comic tumblers who had come with the minstrels to amuse us.

Inwardly Petronel cast herself at Geoffrey's feet in a passion of abasement, gratitude and adoration.

I was very humble in my love, and very secretive. Glorious, golden knights like Geoffrey might be kind to plain, solemn fourteen-year-olds, but they didn't fall in love with them. Added to which, of course, was the awkward fact that this particular plain and solemn fourteen-year-old was Geoffrey's aunt by marriage.

So it was enough that he should smile at me sometimes, enough that I should dance with him at the Christmas feast and my hand be briefly held in his. One of the bleakest things about Eynesby had been the fact that there was no one there whom I could love. Now I had Geoffrey. The hall was hallowed by his presence; the whole valley was filled with light because it was his home. I cuddled the thought of him to me, a private and beautiful talisman.

It made me selfish. Alison's prediction that someone might fall ill over Christmas, was fulfilled. Two people did. One was Kat and the other was Geoffrey himself. They both caught bronchial colds. Neither was gravely ill, however, and I was actually glad of Geoffrey's illness. It kept him under my roof for a whole extra week.

He didn't, of course, retire to a pallet in the attic. He had been put in one of the guestchambers when he arrived, and there he stayed. His squire Giles, and Alison, ran his errands, but as hostess I had the right – and the joy – of visiting my ailing guest. I went to see him daily, asking how he did, sending him clean bedlinen, mulled wine and horehound possets. He croaked his thanks for every small service and apologised for the trouble he was giving, but it was no trouble. To serve him, at that time, was all I asked of life.

I looked after Kat too, of course. They recovered almost together. It was mid-January by then. Kat returned to her duties and Geoffrey went home to Silbeck and then away to London to rejoin Warwick, who was in the south to report to the King – so Geoffrey told us – on the enquiry into the riots in York.

The sky seemed to darken when he left. But he said at his leave-taking: 'I shall see you all in March. I'll be there at Middleham when you come.'

Chapter Six

Petronel: Middleham

March 1467

Before we set out for Middleham, Lionel gave me careful instructions about the way in which I must conduct myself there. I must be dignified and restrained. I must not gawp. I must not gossip with pages or maidservants. I must use such and such forms of address to such and such people. I must memorise this or that badge or shield blazon so that I would know who certain people were at once. He might not be with me often as he would be much involved with the business of Warwick's flocks and wool sales. I would be among the countess's ladies. He hoped I could be trusted not to let him down.

I hoped so, too. I had been excited at first, because I knew that Geoffrey would be at Middleham, but long before we set off my joy at the thought of seeing him again had been drowned in my alarm.

I had seen Middleham Castle from a distance already. During a mild spell in February, Lionel had taken me about the district. I had learned by then to manage a quiet horse. Our first expedition had been up the valley to where a narrower vale ran into it from the south. Half an hour's jogging through this, along the side of our river's rocky upper reaches, brought us to where the hills opened out again, and there was Bouldershawe. I was interested to see this place which had caused so much litigation and was the means, after all, of bringing me here. We were given ale and black pudding by the Grimsdales in a grim stone farmhouse, crenellated like a miniature castle and circled by a stone wall.

It was set, however, amid the kind of rolling, well-drained pasture which I was learning to recognise as ideal for sheep. The white-faced flocks which grazed there had longer, thicker wool than our Eynesby sheep; I could see why Lionel coveted them. The Grimsdales paid some of their rent in wool, and Lionel expected a healthy profit on it the next year.

Two days later we set out again and this time went north, on a track across the moorlands, until we saw a hill ahead of us, crowned by a castle. It was much smaller than Warwick Castle, however, and at first sight I found it reassuring. When the day came for us to go there, I wished that Lionel had let me remain reassured. I was more likely to make mistakes if I was nervous. And I did so want a free mind to think of Geoffrey.

When we arrived, and rode in through the gatehouse, I thought the place undeniably attractive. The day was fine, though cold, and the thin sunshine found unexpected gleams of golden-brown in the dark stonework. The proportions of arch and tower and doorway were manageable, almost friendly, compared to Warwick, just as I had thought. It looked like a place in which people of ordinary human size might actually live.

The front courtyard was full of colour and bustle. Others, like ourselves, were arriving to pay respects or take up duties or conduct business, now that my lord of Warwick had come to Yorkshire. Grooms were leading horses to the stables or carrying saddlery; baggage panniers were piled in heaps along one wall, each heap with one of its owner's servants standing over it, waiting to be told where to take it. People stood in groups, greeting each other. A page in the green and white livery that I recognised came to meet us as we dismounted. Our horses were led away and we were taken to a room in a tower. It was a quarter the size of our chamber at Eynesby and was at the top of a precipitous and narrow stone stair, but the hangings were fine and the ewer and basin were of silver.

We were sent for again very soon and fetched to the hall. Our tower was part of a separate building and we had therefore to cross a courtyard to get there. It is an odd thing, but castles and abbeys, all places of importance, are much less comfortable on the whole than manor houses. In even the best of them, one usually has to go out of doors to get from one place to another. In winter it's cold and, should it be raining, you get wet. I have even heard of a man who was struck by lightning on his way to breakfast in a castle!

Middleham, although so pleasant in so many ways, now showed itself a prime offender in this. The great hall, the solar and the audience chamber were all in one big central building with the kitchen and cellars beneath, but everything else, brewhouse and bakery, guests' lodgings and estate office, was away across one or other of the open courtyards.

In the hall, we found a fire roaring in an old-fashioned central hearth and the Warwicks holding an impromptu reception for the latest arrivals. They were not seated, but strolling about, their attendants following them. They were wearing what I now began to realise were their everyday clothes, which meant that my lady's quilted turquoise satin had no train, and that none of the rings on my lord's fingers were worth more than a smallish manor. My own dress had a train – I had become quite good at coping with it by now – but I immediately felt dowdy.

They welcomed us amiably, however, and my lady at once said to Lionel: 'Sir Geoffrey is about the castle somewhere. You'll be glad to know that he's kept his health since he rejoined us. Did Mistress Alison receive the preserved fruit I sent to her? One misses fruit so much at this season. It was quinces, from a manor of ours in the West Country.'

I listened to this domestic, not to say familial, monologue in astonishment. I remembered the Warwicks asking after Geoffrey's health at our first encounter. Did they take this kindly, personal interest in all the members of their household? How did they keep it up? They must have hundreds in their employ.

Lionel was assuring the countess that Alison had indeed received the quinces and had charged him to express thanks on her behalf. The earl drew him aside and I heard the word 'sheep' and then something about Burgundian export duties. Warwick sounded annoyed. The countess smiled at me and said: 'Business has taken over, you notice. I'm glad to see you, Mistress Eynesby. At Warwick you struck me as quiet and sensible and the sort of person I want for my daughter Isabel's household. I mentioned it to you then, I think? Would you be willing to attend on her while you're here?'

'Yes, Lady Anne, of course. I should be honoured.'

'It will really be a matter of attending both my daughters. They are together so much that they can scarcely not share their ladies. That will change when Isabel marries, of course, but there's no formal betrothal yet – although there are hopes of a fine match for her.' Lady Anne smiled and then put a finger to her lips, as though warning me not to reveal a secret. I wondered if she meant one of the King's brothers. When Lionel came to Faldene, he had mentioned something of the sort over the dinner table, I remembered. Lady Anne meanwhile was continuing: 'You would have the usual rate of pay when on duty but you would be on duty only when you're here with your husband. That's the arrangement I generally make with married ladies whose husbands are not a permanent part of our ménage.'

'I should be very happy, Lady Anne.' I hesitated. 'I suppose I must ask Master Eynesby but . . .'

The countess laughed. 'He won't quarrel with anything we ask either of him or you, and he'll like your salary,' she said drily, and I saw that she knew Lionel well and had his measure. But I was puzzled. She spoke as though we were relatives rather than retainers. Relatives of a humbler social station than her own, of course, but still members of her family. I couldn't understand this and didn't know what to do with it. She had tapped the arm of one of her attendant ladies. 'Fetch my daughters,' she said.

We were six weeks at Middleham and after all, despite all Lionel's strictures and misgivings, the visit was a delight to me.

For one thing, I saw Geoffrey often. I sat near him at dinner each day and he frequently came to the solar to talk briefly with the ladies of the household. This alone would have cheered me, even if other things had gone badly, but they did not. As Lionel had expected, I spent most of my time among the women while he was preoccupied with business. I saw little of him, which was frankly no hardship. And then there were the Warwick daughters.

I don't know what I had expected them to be like, but I think I had imagined them as rather proud and remote, and probably older than me. Although Isabel's mother always spoke of her as though she were quite mature, she was much the same age as myself, while Anne, the younger sister, was not yet eleven. The little bevy of attendants which I now joined were nearly all quite young as well; sixteen or seventeen on average. We formed a group of girls with much in common, firstly because we were young, but also because we all came of families who owned land, be it much or little, and because we were all well-educated. Until now I had not known how much I had missed the companionship of Withysham where I had also been one of a group of my own age, and where we had the stimulation of our studies. Kat couldn't read or write and had never been a companion to me in the same way. Here, I felt at home.

Isabel and Anne were our leaders, of course. I liked them both straight away, although they were very different from each other. Anne was a formal, mousey child and very self-sufficient. She would brush and hang up her own gowns, bath her own dogs, and fetch and carry for herself. She was little trouble to her ladies. Her only fault was a tendency to be sharp of tongue.

Isabel on the other hand was fair, pretty if a little plump, and dreadfully indolent. But no one minded this because she always said please and thank you and never spoke unkindly. If upset, she would sulk silently for a while and then forget whatever it was.

Since I was officially one of her attendants, I noticed her personality more keenly. She used to exasperate and amuse her ladies, both at once. When Isabel moved from one place to another, the book she had been reading, the needlework she had been doing, was invariably left behind, dropped on the floor as often as not. When she came in from outdoors, the cloak she had thrown round her in order to cross the cold bailey would just slip from her shoulders and land in a heap. Pins fell out of her head-dress, brooches undid themselves. 'Her ladies don't so much attend her as scavenge after her,' one of the other girls said to me once, but she was laughing as she spoke. None of us really objected. We made it a joke, and Isabel laughed too.

We had a senior lady in charge of us, naturally. One of the things that united us young ones into a giggling coterie, all differences of rank forgotten, was the fun of outwitting Mistress Ankaret Twynyhoe.

Ankaret Twynyhoe was over forty, wife of a West Country man of some standing who was one of the earl's attendant gentlemen. As a matter of fact, we all quite liked Ankaret. She reminded me a little of Aunt Eleanor. She had the same warmth beneath an austere exterior. But she was always watching us, to check us if our gossip became too spicy, to see that we went to Mass and behaved ourselves when there, to restrain us from flirting with the young men of the household. She was also apt to lecture us on the seriousness of life, and she worried about Isabel. The world was a hard place, she said, and Isabel wasn't prepared for it. She said this to Isabel herself, many times, but it had little effect.

'I'm Warwick's daughter,' Isabel said serenely on one

104

occasion, 'and when I'm married, I shall be the King's sister-in-law.' Less discreet than her mother, Isabel was quite open about the fact that her prospective bridegroom was the King's brother Clarence. The King himself was apparently against the match still, and there was another hitch in that the parties were cousins, which would mean obtaining a Papal dispensation. However, Isabel waved these difficulties away and treated the matter as settled. 'Why should the world be hard for me?' she asked. 'I'm one of the lucky ones. I know I'm lucky and I'm grateful for it. But it's true, isn't it? I am fortunate.'

But I myself had begun to know that although one might expect, might certainly hope for, happy interludes, the world was indeed a hard place. Like Ankaret, I found myself becoming a little fearful for Isabel.

Long before we went back to Eynesby, I had become very fond of her indeed.

To leave Middleham meant leaving both Isabel and Geoffrey. The Warwicks were about to set out for London and Geoffrey was going too. It was a good thing for him, for he had been coughing again and the milder air of the south would probably benefit him. I rode away with Lionel, disconsolate, feeling that I had parted from everyone I cared for.

I had another reason for feeling low spirited. One of my duties at Middleham had been to share Isabel's bedchamber on occasion. We had a rota for it. At Middleham, therefore, one night out of four, I had escaped Lionel's embraces. Now I must be with him every night, without remittance.

He was pleased with me for winning a good opinion at Middleham. Isabel and the countess had both said they hoped I would soon come again, and they had given me parting gifts. They included, I recall, a fine set of bed-hangings. Since Lionel had raised a loan to cover any household improvements I wished to make, I had somehow felt that I was expected to suggest some. New bedhangings were on my list. The gift from Middleham provided them, however, for nothing, and there was no doubt that Lionel found this satisfactory.

All the same, when a few weeks after our return a courier came from Geoffrey in London and Lionel sought me out to discuss the message he brought, his first words were: 'Tell me, Petronel, is there owt to stop you undertaking a long ride? To London?'

'No, I think not,' I said sadly. Lionel had not mentioned the matter of children for a long time but I knew it was never far from his thoughts.

He sighed. 'I'm a fair man, I hope. You can't command these things. And you did well at Middleham, my girl, very well. So here's a treat for you. Tell me, Petronel, have ye ever seen a tournament?'

Chapter Seven

Petronel: Tournament

Summer 1467

The Tournament of Smithfield in that summer of 1467, held to celebrate the betrothal of the King's sister Margaret of York to the son of the Duke of Burgundy, was the first tournament I had ever seen. It was also the last I ever saw so how it compared in splendour to other such occasions, I cannot tell. It seemed magnificent enough to me.

We reached London on the ninth of June, in a heatwave. London smelt. I still thought the moorlands of Yorkshire bleak and forbidding, but nevertheless I had become used to the strong, fresh winds of the north, and on the hills round Eynesby there were grassy pastures – our sheep-runs – which were vividly green in spring and studded with small wildflowers. I liked the swift play of cloud and sunshine across them, and the sparkling rush of our cold, clean, boulder-dotted river. In London, suddenly, the skies were closed in by buildings and though the streets were festooned overhead with banners in honour of Burgundy, they were also malodorous underfoot with twice the usual amount of horse-droppings. There had been two processions a day for the past week, according to Geoffrey.

Geoffrey met us at our lodgings. He had arranged these for us and also our seats at the tournament itself. Although he was one of Warwick's household, he had not accompanied the earl on his state visit to France. And although those Nevilles who were still in England were ignoring the tournament, Geoffrey meant to take part.

'But – should he?' I asked Lionel. There was no secret

about the fact that betrothal and tournament alike had been organised behind Warwick's back. All London was laughing over it.

'He was invited,' said Lionel, 'by Sir Anthony Woodville, the English champion. He knows Sir Anthony. The suggestion likely came from the King in the first place, though. I fancy there's a quiet move afoot to draw Warwick's adherents to the King's side now. Geoffrey thought it over before he sent word to me that he was to ride in the lists, but he said he couldn't see how he could be accused of owt simply for riding in a public display. It doesn't commit him to anything and there's always the chance of winning a good purse. Geoffrey's not one to pass up an opportunity like that and, being fair to him, I wouldn't think Warwick would expect it.'

I nodded. It was all part of the curious relationship which Geoffrey had with so many noble folk; on easy terms with any he met privately, but officially almost ignored. The King, knowing he would be an ornament to the lists, had thought it worthwhile to whistle him up through a proxy. But Warwick, going abroad on state business, had left him behind.

I was no longer surprised by all this, however. I knew more about Geoffrey by this time.

'It's time thee were told,' Alison had said abruptly. It was before we set out for London. She had ridden over from Silbeck and we were sitting out in the capricious sunshine of early summer, using the bright light for the purposes of needlework. We were making baby clothes for Chrissy, who would have another child in July. 'And one day we'll be readying them for thee,' Alison had said as we settled down. 'No sign yet?'

'No,' I said shortly.

'Well, well, these things canna be ordered. But Lionel'd be that glad.'

I didn't answer. We stitched in silence for a while and

then Alison suddenly raised her head and said those unexpected words. 'It's time thee were told.'

'About what?'

'About Geoffrey. Lionel's funny about it. They're all funny. It's known, it's acknowledged, it makes a difference how he's treated, but somehow or other they never speak of it, though the dear knows it's all long gone and over. Geoffrey's twenty-five now and his father dead these many years.'

'Yes, when did you lose your husband?' I asked, trying to pull a strand of sense out of these odd remarks.

'Ten or twelve years but I'm not talking about him.' Alison bit off a length of silk. 'Geoffrey's not my husband's child.'

I must have stared at her, for she seemed to realise that she was confusing me. 'I'd ha' thought Lionel would have told thee *something*,' she said. 'Thee's family now. I'd best start at the beginning, I can see that. It all goes back to me and Lionel oursen. We're brother and sister but not whole blood. Lionel's my half-brother. Our mother was married twice.'

That was a common enough state of affairs. My own mother had been married three times. I said: 'Yes?'

'Mam's first husband was nothing much when she wed him,' Alison said. 'Nor was she. He was a mercenary soldier and she was the daughter of another. He followed Henry the Fifth to war in France and my mother went too. He fought at Agincourt, and that's where things started changing. There was mighty slaughter at Agincourt and there's pickings to be had on a battlefield when it's all over, if a man's not too squeamish to tak advantage.' Her colourless eyes, so like Lionel's, rested on mine with an expression which was half defensive and half instructive. 'Poor men have to make the best of what comes their way. He took a sword from a dead Frenchman. There was jewels in the hilt which he prised out and sold. But he got summat else at Agincourt as well as jewels. He got a wound. He died a couple of months later and left my mother with me – I was a year old, then –and the money he got for the stones.

'So back she come to England and married again. I don't know how it was fixed up, whether she found the man herself or someone arranged things for her, but this time she did better. Her second husband was a landless knight though not landless for long. With the money she brought him, they bought Eynesby.'

'And he was Lionel's father?'

'Aye, that's it. Well, Lionel's been a good brother to me, but my stepfather didn't care for me and he didn't want to have to provide for me. He put up with me till my mother died, when I was only ten. Inside of three weeks, he'd got rid of me into service.'

'Oh, Alison,' I said. I used her first name. She had asked me to stop calling her Mistress Alison. We were sisters, she had said.

She smiled grimly at my sympathetic tone. 'Oh, Alison, indeed! *Poor* Alison, that's how I thought of it. My mother'd been having me taught to read and write by the parish priest; she said I'd marry better and have a chance of coming up in the world. And then, all of a sudden . . . but it could ha' been worse. As he said to me himself, it was *good* service. He'd been a household knight with the Neville family before he married and the place he found for me was with Cecily Neville when she married the old Duke of York, the King's father. I was one of the new servants she had when she was a bride. I was in the linen room,' said Alison, 'washing and mending and doling linen out to the chambermaids.'

'And you travelled with her?' Somehow I had always thought of Alison as belonging only to the valley.

But no. 'Aye, sometimes. Great performance, it was. We used to be like an army on the march. You'll see the sort of thing for yourself one of these days, if you spend much time with the Warwicks. When the household's on the move, it's a great column of riders, mules, chariots, shouting and dust

110

or mud according to the weather. Hours and hours on the roads, till you're so sick and tired you could fall out of the saddle, and then when you get there, if you're a servant, there's work to do before you get a bite to eat, let alone any sleep. I used to hate it. May I never travel out of my own country again. But that was going to be my life until I died, I reckoned. I'd no portion and my looks were nowt to speak of. I wasn't ugly but I wasn't bonny either, just middling and I was stuck all the time among the womenfolk. I thought I'd trail round after the Yorks, washing and mending, till I was too old and infirm to travel any more, and then I'd be dumped at one of their houses among the caretaker staff and in the end there'd be a pension, if I was lucky. I'd ha' seen a lot of places and never lived a day of life that was living,' said Alison, startling me. She had struck me as practical and unimaginative but the bitterness in her voice came from depths that were neither. 'And then,' she said, 'in 1441 it was, the February, at a manorhouse in a place called Hatfield – down in the south, that is – Cecily Neville was brought to bed of a child, and had a bad time of it.'

She was silent for a moment. I waited. 'Mostly,' said Alison at length, 'she had no bother at all with her bairns but that one damn near killed her. It was a boy and he didn't live long. He was weakly from the start and that was likely because of the bad confinement. He was born wrong end first and he took forty-eight long, long hours about it. Not that I was in the birth chamber, mind, but I had to take in cloths and clean sheets and so I saw some of it.

'And,' she said pensively, her eyes now distant, 'the poor duke, her husband . . .'

And as we sat there, stitching in the sun, she almost made me see him. A short, dark, wiry man – 'vital' Alison called him – waiting and worrying through the hours, growing first irritable and then angry with the friends who tried to keep him company and offer him cheerful platitudes. Continually sending for news, turning away when the women

111

came to say there was no news yet because they couldn't hide the anxiety in their eyes and he couldn't bear to see it.

Cecily's labour had started in the evening. It went on all night, all the next day and the night after. It was during the following afternoon that the duke, brushing aside the friends who tried to restrain him, had marched out of the hall and gone up the tower stairs towards Cecily's chamber. 'Not to go inside. That's no place for a man and they wouldn't have let him, any road,' said Alison, 'but just to stand outside the door; to be near her. He thought somehow she'd know he was near and it would help her. Well, he went too near. He went right up outside the door and he heard her screaming. It's a funny thing. Men'll go to war and do things in battle that we can't stand to think of, but when it comes to giving life instead of taking it, the bravest of them will panic, likely as not. *He* panicked, and he ran for cover.'

Not, I gathered, back to the hall where he would have had to face the eyes of his friends. He couldn't endure their eyes, however kind and understanding they might be. He bolted in search of solitude and blundered through a door into, of all places, the linen room where Alison was counting mended sheets.

'He just came through the door and he was crying. I said to him, whatever is the matter? – as if I didn't know! – and I pushed him down on to a stool we had in there. He was in such a state. I don't think he knew rightly where he was or who I was. I didn't matter, any road. I wasn't one of his friends or a woman of his station, not someone he had to keep up a front with. He started blurting it all out, that Cecily was dying, and it was all his fault, he'd given her just too many children, and what he'd heard in that room would drive him mad. He'd had no sleep the previous night and not much the night before that. He looked terrible. I didn't know what to do. I patted his shoulder and he put his hand up and clutched mine and then somehow or other I was holding him and he was holding me and things began to happen inside me and it must have been that way with him too . . . I was twenty-seven,' said Alison, 'and I'd never had a man or any hope of one but I'd looked at them and especially I'd looked at him. He had it, that thing that draws women. He'd pass thee in the hall and it'd be all tha could do not to turn thy head and stare after him. I didn't try to stop owt that he did. I held him and tried to comfort him and he burrowed into me as if he wanted to hide from the world. I don't remember how it ended or anything; I don't remember him going away. The child upstairs was born just before sunset and my lady came through. That would have been the end of it, except that a few weeks later I realised . . . well, guess what.'

'Geoffrey,' I said, seized with envy because Alison had quickened with such ease. Just the once, and there she was, with child. While I must tolerate the wretched business over and over and all to no avail, even after months.

She was nodding. 'The household was just packing up to go to Rouen. The duke had been appointed there. I had to seek him out and tell him. He was very correct,' she said simply. 'He found me a husband. Alan Bold his name was, though I don't use Bold as my name now. The duke gave me Silbeck for my dower, 'Nigh to where your brother is,' he said to me, 'lucky the place is vacant.' After Alan died, I took to using Silbeck as a name, same as Lionel uses Eynesby. It was Lionel's notion; he said it makes it sound like we belong. The way your people at Faldene do, that have been on their land since time out of mind. I never had any complaint of Alan except that the childer he gave me never throve. He was kind to me and maybe it's good that he died himself before the last of the bairns went, so he never knew he left no descendants. I don't know how the duke went about it, but when Geoffrey was seven, Lionel – his dad was dead too by then so he was master at Eynesby – told me he knew about Geoffrey's parentage and understood the boy's father wanted him educated properly. Lionel was educated fair himself; reading and writing and reckoning, and trained in weapons too. He took over Geoffrey's training and eventually Geoffrey joined the Earl of Warwick's household. Later he distinguished himself so well, he could be knighted and no one 'ud remark on it. But he'd ha' been knighted any road. The Warwicks know who he is. So does the King. So there you are,' said Alison. 'If folk seem funny with Geoffrey now and then, that's why. Wrong side of the blanket, maybe, but he's half-brother to the King.'

We both sat quietly for a while, and then I asked: 'Alison, you and Geoffrey – didn't you mind me coming here? I mean – Sir Geoffrey expected one day that Eynesby would be his. And it was bought with your mother's money. You must have wanted Geoffrey to have it.'

'Aye, I'll not say there wasn't a bit of feeling like that to start with.' Alison studied her needlework. A thread had snagged on her rough fingers. 'Not me so much, but Geoffrey told me afterwards that when he went with Lionel to Faldene to see you, he was putting a good face on it but at heart – well, no, he wasna pleased. It was you yourself that set that to rights. Till he got to Faldene, he hadn't pictured thee, I fancy. "But when I saw her," he said to me "she took me right aback." Such a sweet thing, he said, and so young; maybe harder done by in this marriage than I am, that's what he said. "It won't be easy for her, being wed to a man my uncle's age." Those were his very words. I shouldna have told thee that, maybe, but it's been true enough, I reckon. It's not been easy for thee, has it?'

'It . . . I . . . not always,' I said.

'But thee's done well and we've taken to thee. And we're fair-minded folk up here in the north. Lionel's got a right to wed if he wants. We've nowt to complain about and I'd have said as much to Geoffrey if I'd needed to. He's got Silbeck and a fair future as a knight.' She looked up from her work and gave me one of her wintry smiles. I think Alison had had a hard life, and it had made her wary of showing goodwill too openly. When she smiled, it was like sunshine trying to make its way through cloud. 'So don't go thinking you're not welcome. You just forget about all that, hinny, and give Lionel that baby if tha canst.'

'I'm trying!' I said. 'I light a candle in our chapel every day when we're at home.'

'Now, don't fret,' said Alison, quite kindly. 'Think of summat else and then it'll happen.'

'How can I think of something else when you and Lionel keep on asking? I'm frightened sometimes that I won't ever conceive and then Lionel will blame me. I'm scared every month, when I realise that once again I'm not . . . He was angry that his first wife didn't have a child, wasn't he?'

'Aye,' Alison said. 'I'll not mention it again, hinny. I didn't know tha was so upset. If it's any help, I'll tell thee this. Barrenness can happen to a man as well as a woman though most men don't believe it. Lionel's not been a monk since his first wife died. There was a woman in York and he'd have wed her fast enough if she'd quickened but she didna. Keep on lighting thy candles but if nowt happens, I said, don't fret. Only I hope it does,' finished Alison, 'for both thy sakes, lass.'

Well, here at the tournament, I decided, I wouldn't fret. It was a glorious day and I had sensed from the moment we set out that this was a grand occasion; I ought to appreciate being in the midst of it and should do it justice by enjoying it. I was wearing my second-best gown, of apple-green satin embroidered with pink and silver, and I knew I looked well and nothing at all like the plain childish Petronel who had first arrived at Eynesby. Also, when we reached the tournament field, I realised that Geoffrey had provided us with excellent seats.

We were near the foot of one of the two immense stands which had been built facing each other across a broad stretch of grass. It was a dusty summer that year but the grass was dazzling green. It must have been watered throughout the hot weather and when we arrived – we came early – perspiring groundsmen had been rolling it. But they had gone now and all round us, the scenery was filling up with people.

It was extremely noisy. Stallholders had set up their pitches round the ground wherever there was room and they were shouting their wares: 'Ale a pint a penny!' 'Hot pies and sweetmeats!' 'Flemish linen a shilling an ell!' The bet-takers were bawling odds; one, close to us, had twinkling eyes like bright small fish in a net of fine lines.

The usual beggars haunted the crowd. One approached whining just then and I can see in memory the skinny out-stretched palm and the professional pathos of his expression. Lionel, unimpressed, knocked the pleading hand away and the man went off to find easier prospects.

There was no sign yet of the contestants but there were billowing white pavilions at either end of the ground and the two biggest were flying English and Burgundian banners respectively. No doubt the champions and the other knights who would take part were all arming in their tents. There was an atmosphere of intense expectation.

The stand we were in was for contestants' guests and for City families. The one opposite was for the court. It was filling now and as it did so, it became like a vast window of stained glass, patterned in rich hues. Trumpeters announced the arrival of the royal party and as they took their seats a mighty banner with a great rayed sun on it rippled out from the top of their stand.

'That's the Sun in Splendour,' said Lionel, nudging me. 'The King adopted it after a great victory, when a portent, a triple sun, was seen in the sky.'

I knew this already but nodded dutifully. Edward himself (Geoffrey's half-brother; how extraordinary!) was a distant figure in purple. The glittering lady in white and gold at his side must be his controversial Queen, Bess Woodville. A small figure in dark blue had a banner with a white boar on it, draped over the parapet in front of him.

'Dickon of Gloucester, that is,' said Lionel instructively.

'He and Clarence used to be at Middleham, one time. If they come there again, you'll meet them.'

Last of all into the stand opposite were a group of prelates, mostly in sober dress, though one or two bishops were in full robes. I was a little surprised that they should attend such a worldly function, but Lionel said: 'Oh, they'll have blessed the weapons. They're men of the world, my lass, not nuns.'

On the field, something was now happening. Heralds were riding out ahead of a column of drummers, who tapped their drums softly as they marched. They were followed by a parade of contestants, who circled the green while the heralds called out their names and the details of their victories at other tourneys.

The parade was led by the two major champions and their seconds. The champions' chargers wore scalloped mantling and arched massive necks against the bit. 'There's our man – Sir Anthony Woodville,' Lionel said. 'The Burgundian's name is similar, he's called Antoine. He's a natural son of the duke. They're more open about these things than we are.' The seconds rode before their principals, carrying their weapons. They were bareheaded, and one of Sir Anthony Woodville's had the fairest hair I had ever seen on a man, so pale that when he passed close to us, I saw that where it had been newly cut, the ends glittered as though sprinkled with salt. 'Who is that?' I asked.

'Clarence, the King's middle brother.'

Isabel's betrothed, I thought, and then forgot him, for the other knights were now riding past, and there among them was Geoffrey.

He had met us at our lodgings two days before but he had not stayed long and we hadn't seen him since. Usually, when we met, I had to be careful to keep my eyes from following him too much. I knew what Alison meant when she said of Geoffrey's father that it was all one could do not to turn one's head and stare after him. But today Geoffrey was officially on show and I could look at him all I liked.

No one would remark on it. I watched in silent adoration until he rode off the field again. The first tilt would be between the English and Burgundian champions and the field was being cleared for them.

There were more formalities first. The two champions rode side by side to face the royal stand and salute the King. Only then did they wheel and trot majestically away to take up their positions at either end of the field, a hundred yards apart. The drums began to roll, a low and curiously disturbing sound. The whole bright scene – emerald grass, the crowded, vivid stands, the brilliantly caparisoned horses, even the banners which flew from the pavilions – became still. The very breeze seemed to be holding its breath. The seconds placed the helms on their principals' heads and handed them their weapons. Sir Anthony Woodville and Antoine of Burgundy took their lances in hand. The Chief Herald, positioned to one side, rose in his stirrups and raised a gauntleted hand. There was another still, tense pause.

I can remember that tension yet. Perhaps it was because we all knew that these men represented not only themselves but their lands and rulers. One could almost feel the tight determination behind the two silvery casings of new, ceremonial plate armour and the blunt snouts of the helmets. But for me, it was more than that. Little Petronel, sitting with tightly clasped hands, was for the first time beholding that world of power and chivalry to which Geoffrey belonged, and even, to a degree, my husband. I was for the first time dimly understanding why it mattered so much that when Lionel entertained the Scropes and the Fitz-Hughs, he should do it well.

And I was also understanding, with sadness, how very remote from me Geoffrey really was. Not only was he Lionel's nephew, he was knight and King's kinsman too. Now I saw what that meant.

The herald's arm dropped. '*Laissez les allez!*' The horses were surging forward before he had finished the sentence.

118

They went straight from a standstill into a gallop, the lovely rolled turf flying in fragments from the eight enormous hooves. The lances rose, were levelled each at the adversary's helmet . . .

And missed. In an anticlimax which unwound the tension with a great collective sigh from the audience, the destriers thundered harmlessly past each other as though their riders had merely wished to exchange ends. The seconds cantered out to consult with the heralds. It was announced that the parties would run another course, wearing lighter armour and using dulled swords instead of lances. There was a wait while the armour was changed. Master Secretary, who was as usual one of our party, fetched ale and meat pies from a vendor. Just as we began on them, the tournament resumed.

It was a somewhat brief resumption. Once more the signal was given and the two immense horses hurtled towards each other. They should have met flank to flank but at the last moment, the Burgundian's big grey veered sharply and rammed his forehead into the other's shoulder. Sir Anthony's horse staggered. The grey whinnied, reared and toppled over backwards. Antoine of Burgundy fell from the saddle, arms and legs whirling ridiculously in the air as though he were a tin toy thrown aside by a bad-tempered child. He hit the ground and the horse fell on top of him. Heralds and seconds rushed to help him. The horse was pulled clear. It seemed to be dead, neck flaccid and nostrils dripping blood. Antoine, however, was assisted to his feet and appeared to be unhurt. 'Whatever is the matter with you?' said Lionel rather irritably, and I found that I was crying.

I was crying, foolishly, for the horse, struck dead at the zenith of its prime and suddenly cast out from this splendid and beautiful world. I was also crying (but I could not even explain this to myself, still less to Lionel) because I too felt that there was a world of splendour from which I had been excluded and a terrible sense, almost of bereavement, had

119

swept over me. I turned my sobs to coughing and pretended I had choked on the meat pie. Out on the field some Burgundian supporters were shouting and pointing at Sir Anthony.

Sir Anthony, however, dismounted before the advancing heralds reached him. He lifted his horse's ornate red and gold mantling. Innocently displayed beneath were the girth, the saddleflaps and the charger's sweat-streaked chestnut hide. There was no unlawful armour and no spikes. The shouting died down. The heralds announced that the two champions would fight again tomorrow. Antoine marched away to his pavilion and the Chief Herald, for the benefit of the spectators, rode round the perimeter repeating Antoine's parting words, which had been that the following morning, Sir Anthony, who had only fought a beast today, would find himself fighting a man. There were cheers and laughter.

'There'll be some open contests now,' said Lionel. 'We'll see Geoffrey.'

Until I actually saw the two champions ride at each other, I had thought of the tournament as sport, entertainment. That was certainly how the cheerful, noisy crowd saw it. Half London seemed to be here, family parties and groups of friends, all intent on a day out in the sunshine.

But those lances wavering within inches of the champions' helms, the collision and the violently dead horse, had suddenly shown me that tournaments had their dangers.

So that when in due course Geoffrey and his adversary tore towards each other with the weight of their bodies behind their lances, and in a manner so fierce and businesslike that they gripped all the crowd's attention even though the celebrities had left the field, I found that now, when I was once more free to stare at Geoffrey all I liked, I could hardly bear to watch at all.

But I made myself watch, and at once saw something which distracted me. 'Sir Geoffrey – he's left-handed!' I exclaimed.

A lad whom my father had taken into the household at one time to educate along with Tom and partner him in arms practice, had been left-handed. He had been compelled, with exhortation first and later on with thrashing, to eat, write and fight right-handed like everybody else. I had supposed right-handedness to be obligatory.

'So is Alison, though she was taught to use her right hand when she was young,' said Lionel. 'And so was her father, so her mother told her.' He seemed to realise that I now knew most of the family history. 'But I trained Geoffrey and I didn't correct it and later, when he went to Warwick's household, it was too late for them to try correcting it and they didn't try. It has advantages though not many men have the sense to realise it.' He watched attentively as the two jousters, having failed to unhorse each other at the first attempt, prepared to charge again. 'It puts an opponent off,' he said, 'and most men use lighter armour on the right-hand side of their bodies because they think they're less vulnerable there and it saves weight. And then they meet Geoffrey and . . . good lad, well done!' Lionel shouted, leaping to his feet as Geoffrey took his adversary clean in the chest and swept him out of the saddle. 'He's won prizes enough to justify my methods, since he became a knight,' said Lionel with satisfaction. 'Some people said I was out of my wits but they were wrong.'

Jaunty and confident, Geoffrey came to us before the day was over. He was to fight again on the morrow, he said. He leant a hand on the bench-back, stooping to speak to us. I said impulsively: 'I am glad to see you safe, Sir Geoffrey. I was afraid for you. It looked so dangerous.'

'That's part of the sport. And why so formal, Aunt Petronel? I should call you aunt, but you need not address your nephew as sir. You are looking very beautiful today, Aunt Petronel. Is she not, Uncle?' He smiled, first at Lionel and then at me, and suddenly I saw that the smile was not that of a god looking down on a dull and childish mortal, but, after all, that of a man face to face with a woman who attracted him.

121

A jolt went through me, that same stab of loss which had made me weep when the horse was killed. For the first time the image truly came into my mind, of Geoffrey as a lover, of his body above mine instead of Lionel's. My whole body seemed to move towards him, and within me a voice that only I could hear, cried: 'If only they had given me to Geoffrey instead!' I looked away in confusion, but Geoffrey said: 'Aunt Petronel!' and made me look back at him. 'I'd like to wear a lady's favour tomorrow,' he said. 'Uncle Lionel, would you allow – would Aunt Petronel allow – me to carry hers?'

'Aye, you may give him your favour,' Lionel said indulgently. 'No harm in it; it's just a knightly custom. He's paid you a compliment.'

In my baggage, I had the gloves I had bought from a street trader when I first passed through London. They were of fair quality, soft leather with a pattern of beads on the back.

So next day, when we met at Smithfield, I gave the right-hand glove to him (touching his fingers, not quite accidentally, as I did so). He fixed it to his helmet crest with a strand of silk. And I took my place beside Lionel again, to see his nephew, Sir Geoffrey Silbeck, my beloved, do battle in my name.

On this second day of the tournament, the lesser bouts came first, occupying the morning. Geoffrey's turn came near the end. He was fighting in a sword contest on horseback, against a new opponent, a Sir William Somebody – I didn't catch the name. Geoffrey pranced out, his horse's mantling lifting in the breeze and the animal's strong neck tightly arched, mouth foaming round the powerful curb which was the only way of controlling these furious destriers one-handed. The opponents met. Geoffrey's horse shied. Geoffrey spurred it back but it shied again. Geoffrey lunged with the sword, making us all gasp as we thought at first that it was aimed at his opponent's horse, which was illegal.

Then we saw that his target was the mantling, not the horse. Sir William Whoever-he-was hewed at him but had to reach across his own body while Geoffrey had the advantage of using the hand nearest his foe. His blade-tip flipped the mantling up and there beneath it was another mantling covered in sharp steel studs. The sun caught them and they flashed. The crowd bellowed disapproval. Sir Anthony Woodville had been clear of this kind of dice-loading, but others were evidently less nice.

Geoffrey wrenched his horse away, thrust up his visor and shouted for the heralds, but they were already riding up. The crowd continued to boo. Heralds and knights conferred with violent gesticulations.

It was clear to me that Geoffrey, although behaving with scrupulous correctness, was furious. His gestures said it, and the way he sat with his right hand on his hip. Presently it was announced that Sir William had been disqualified and that an enquiry would be held later to decide upon a penalty.

'He'll be banned from tournament riding for years if not for ever,' Lionel told me.

The Chief Herald announced that Sir Geoffrey Silbeck had wanted to fight it out but that such a duel would not be in keeping with the friendly spirit of the tournament which was an 'act of pleasaunce'. Geoffrey was declared the winner and received a prize purse from the Queen's hands. He rode a victory circuit at a slow canter and then came to a halt in front of us.

He held out the purse to me on the end of his lance. I didn't know what to do.

'He's carrying your favour. Take the purse and keep it till he asks you for it,' said Lionel. I lifted the purse from the lance-tip. My hands quivered and I felt suffocatingly hot. From under his raised visor, Geoffrey was staring at me intently. The pupils of his eyes seemed enlarged and as they met mine I could have sworn there was an audible *snick*, like a latch clicking home. A sweet aching began within me and I sat back, heart thumping, head full of improbable imaginings, clutching the prize purse in my lap.

He joined us later, divested of his armour and clad in the loose shirt and comfortable old hose which tired knights always don when the fighting is over. Our eyes met again. I said something calm and formal. I was very much Lionel Eynesby's wife, being gracious to his nephew. And meanwhile, the air between wife and nephew hummed and sparkled with silent messages.

It was real. I knew it. It was unbelievable but it was true. God had stooped to my humble person and looked on me with favour. Geoffrey desired me as I desired him. I was dizzy with it.

Yet beneath my exultation, there was fear. Simply because this was suddenly no dream or fantasy, there was fear. Prim little Petronel stood, miraculously, on the edge of deadly opportunity, glamorous and dangerous as this tournament itself. If Geoffrey asked and I said yes, what would happen next would be irrevocable.

I paid remarkably little attention to the second bout between England and Burgundy. It was a hard-fought contest which had the King himself on his feet and shouting at one point and I believe it ended in a draw. I was too busy with my thoughts to notice and in any case, before it was finished, we had an interruption.

It came just as the battle on the trampled grass was reaching its climax. A beggar came working his way round the edge of the field, pestering the people in the lower rows of the stands. He was a small man with a red face and an erratic gait. He was less ragged than the average beggar but quite as importunate. When he caught sight of us, he changed direction. He clambered through the people in the tier below us, shoving his way between a burgher family and an indignant man who was watching the fight with stiff concentration and clenched fists. He seemed oblivious to their angry demands to know who he thought he was pushing. He arrived in front of Geoffrey, blocking Geoffrey's view. He had the authentic beggar's stance, knees bent, elbow clamped to his side, shoulder almost in his ear, palm upturned. But the palm, though filthy, had not the thinness of very long privation. He gave off a powerful reek of ale. He whined: 'Alms from Eynesby, I crave alms from Eynesby, tha's bloody ruined me!' and with that burst into tears.

I recognised him then. It was that inefficient mason of York, who built bridges that fell down. Nicholas Hawes.

Lionel recognised him too. 'Hawes, you're drunk! Be off with you or I'll have you handed to the constable!'

'Yes, take yourself off!' Master Secretary came to his feet. 'What do you mean, we've ruined you? You ruined yourself, my friend, with your incompetence and sharp dealing, though it seems you've still the wherewithal to buy ale!'

'Alms!' repeated Hawes in a desperate voice and shook an imploring palm once again, and principally at Geoffrey.

He was maudlin and repulsive. Geoffrey, however, said with a frown: 'What's all this? What're you thrusting your hand under my nose for, Hawes? It wasn't my bridge that collapsed. Explain yourself. And sit down, people can't see past you.' He pointed to the planking at his feet. 'Now then!'

Hawes sank to the planking. He said, snivelling: 'I backed Sir William to win against thee. I saw him arming t'horse, through a crack in t'fencing and . . .'

'You saw him putting illegal armour on his horse and backed him to win instead of reporting it?' demanded Lionel.

'I didn't know it were illegal. How'd a poor man like me know all these knightly rules? I saw him arming and I reckoned he'd win. The odds were good, I'd have made a bit. A poor man's got to make a living the best way he can, when he's driven from his right livelihood . . .'

He went on and on, in his broad Yorkshire voice, slurred with the drink, saying all over again that he was ruined, that he'd put all he had on the bet and now he'd have to live by begging and it was all Geoffrey's doing. First Lionel, now Geoffrey; between them they'd finished him. Still crouched on the planking at Geoffrey's feet and looking ridiculous, he pointed a wobbly and accusing finger at uncle and nephew impartially. He continued to draw considerable attention, half-irritated and half-inquisitive, from those around us.

Lionel said coldly, checking the outburst: 'If you gamble on a charlatan and he's found out, blame yourself. As for driving you out of your livelihood, if you fail your customers, what else do you expect? Now will you be quiet and leave or do we call the constable? I've half a mind to call him, any road.'

Hawes, beginning to see that his drunken outpourings had put him in jeopardy, fell silent and began to shake. 'This much is true, anyway,' said Geoffrey. 'Hawes had to leave York without speaking up for himself. Are you truly destitute now, Hawes? Tell me the truth.'

Hawes nodded, a hopeful glimmer in his eyes. Geoffrey turned to me. 'The purse,' he said.

I hesitated, not because I did not approve of his open-handedness but out of habit, because I was used to seeking Lionel's approval for everything I did. Hawes, as in the hall at Eynesby, misunderstood and glared at me. 'Go on,' said Lionel brusquely. 'It's Geoffrey's purse, lass.' I handed it over.

Geoffrey promptly gave the whole of it to Hawes. 'Take it and start your life again in some honest manner. Try . . . oh, go on pilgrimage, something of that kind, find grace to begin again respectably, and to keep to it.' In Geoffrey's tone disgust was audibly mingled with the generosity. 'And now be off.'

'Ye're a fool, nephew,' said Lionel as Hawes departed, clutching his booty to his chest as though he feared that Geoffrey might change his mind and snatch it back. 'If that bridge had been yours, maybe you'd not have been so big-hearted.'

'Probably not,' said Geoffrey with a grin. 'I pay my debts, Uncle, and if I ever come across Sir William Hawick in suitable circumstances for doing him an injury, do him one I will.'

'Sir William Hawick?' I asked.

'Aye, the fellow who tried to cheat in the lists today,' said Lionel.

'He'll be banned from competing but to my mind it isn't enough,' said Geoffrey. 'He could have ruined my horse, or killed him, and destriers cost money. But as for Hawes – well, Aunt Petronel, what do you say about it?'

'I thought it very kind of you,' I said truthfully.

Lionel snorted. 'You've thrown your prize money away, nephew. I hope you won't have to sell your clothes to pay for your lodgings. You'll need your best outfit tonight.'

'Ah yes,' said Geoffrey, 'Sir Anthony Woodville's feast.'

At the close of the previous day, Sir Anthony Woodville had announced that all the tournament competitors and their guests were bidden to a feast at his London house this evening. We were to go as Geoffrey's guests. We returned to our lodgings first to change, and I doffed my second-best green satin for my first-best gown, the sanguine silk which Lionel had given me for Christmas and on which Lady Scrope had complimented me.

Kat and Chrissy and I had made it to the latest fashion, with a v-neck so wide that it was almost off the shoulder, and a waistline dropped to the hips. Studying myself in the mirror now I saw that, yes, I looked better in it than I had at Christmas. I had acquired poise since then. Middleham had done that for me. I wondered if there would be dancing at the feast and whether Geoffrey would partner me. There would be no harm in that, I thought, and when we danced I could hold his hand. That – just that – would be paradise, would be enough.

We dined first, in a huge hall with a gleaming floor paved chequerboard style in black and white, with double doors open to the green and gold June evening. The company was exalted; Lionel pointed out to me the great personages at the top table. They even included King Edward and Queen Bess, seated under a canopy of crimson embroidered with gold fleur-de-lis and white York roses.

They left when the banquet was over, and as the shadows lengthened and the first lamps were lit, a quiet but well-drilled army of servants appeared to push back the tables and rearrange the benches round the sides of the room. Minstrels struck up a dance measure. I trod a set with Lionel but when the second set was called, I saw with thudding pulses that Geoffrey was coming towards me.

'I won a race to dance with you,' said Geoffrey as we took our places. 'Sir Anthony Woodville had the same intention. I heard him say so. He's with Lionel now, probably asking permission to lead you out next time, since I beat him to it just now.'

'Sir Anthony, the English champion?'

'The King's brother-in-law,' said Geoffrey, with good-humoured mockery. 'Yes! Why do you sound so surprised?' The set had begun. We took three paces apart and then returned to each other. 'Dear little Petronel,' said my nephew by marriage, dispensing with the 'Aunt' as we paraded forward hand in hand, 'you think you are of no account, as you did when you first came to Eynesby, don't you?'

Something impish in me made me say: 'When I first came to Eynesby and threw you out of your inheritance.'

His eyebrows rose. 'Does that trouble you? It was hardly your fault. Forget it, my lass, I always knew my uncle might re-marry. He's within his rights, I'm not his son. As for you, since you've been married you've changed and I don't think you know how much. You carry yourself differently and there is a different expression in your eyes. Why shouldn't Anthony Woodville want to dance with you? When he does, you must behave very graciously, as though you were conferring a favour on him. Because you will be. You have become beautiful, Petronel.'

We crossed hands and whirled. I had now learned the steps of the popular dances and I could acquit myself adequately. I didn't know how to answer him. We paraded down the set once more. 'Petronel,' said Geoffrey, 'if I were to ask you a favour myself, another favour – not a glove this time – I wonder what you would say to me?'

'That would depend on what the – er – favour was,' I said.

His hand tightened on mine and at once I knew, with hammering heart and spinning head, halfway between horror and hope, what his answer to that would be. But I did not know, had not the faintest idea, what I would say to him.

The figure of the dance compelled him to release me and move away, but it brought us together again in a moment, near enough for him to speak into my ear. 'When we go back to the north, if I were to arrange it so that we could be alone together for a while, would you agree? You know what I mean. You must know.'

Confused, I muddled my steps over the next phase of the dance, though it was one I knew well. Chrissy had taught it to me first, but since then I had practised it often enough at Middleham. Indeed, it was a favourite of mine, for it was accompanied by a delightful, yearning melody. 'I am so sorry,' I stammered, as I bumped into my neighbour.

Unobtrusively, Geoffrey put me right, turning me with his hands on my shoulders. As he did so, as if by chance his left hand brushed my breast.

Now that the moment was here, it seemed that despite his intoxicating nearness, despite the longing music and the melting warmth of the summer night, I was still the Petronel whom Aunt Eleanor had instructed in moral behaviour and filled with grave warnings of purgatory and hell, and exhorted to practise all the virtues, chief among which was chastity.

And I was still afraid of Lionel.

I desired Geoffrey. I hungered and thirsted for him. But I said the words that Aunt Eleanor would have had me say, the words that would keep me safe. 'Dear Geoffrey, I'm sorry, but I'm your Uncle Lionel's wife. Please, never speak of this again.'

'As you wish,' he said lightly. He smiled. 'But I shall for ever be my lady's loyal servant. That is the correct thing to say, I believe?' And with that he was again the perfect nephew, courteously leading out his aunt, and presently, smiling, returning her to her seat when the set was over.

Sir Anthony Woodville was waiting for me. I danced with him next and then, to my own surprise, with George Duke of Clarence. When we went back to our lodgings, Lionel was very pleased with me. I had been a credit to him, he said.

More than you know, I said to myself as I yielded to his unromantic lovemaking.

I wondered how it would be with Geoffrey. In the night, lying beside Lionel, I wondered how it would be if the dark sleeping body so near me were one I loved, so that its warm presence meant comfort and security and the need to snuggle close. I lay still, clenching my teeth to keep myself from weeping, not this time for an animal's uncompleted life, but for my own.

The tournament ended sooner than expected, for on the third day came the news that the old Duke of Burgundy was dead. Antoine must go home to attend his father's obsequies, leaving sport and business alike unfinished. The betrothal of Margaret of York to Charles, who was now the Duke of Burgundy, was announced, but out of respect for Burgundy's mourning there were no public rejoicings.

130

Lionel attended to some business to do with the wool sales, was satisfied with the contribution made by Bouldershawe, bought me an amethyst ring on the strength of it, and we went home. Geoffrey did not come with us.

We saw nothing of him, all the rest of that year.

Chapter Eight

Petronel: Two Unknown Children

1468–9

When the Earl of Warwick was not at Middleham but had left his family there, the countess used his audience chamber as a parlour, because it faced south. She liked to spend part of each day there with her daughters and the other ladies, sewing or listening to music, or practising the newest dances.

In February, when there was little sunshine to speak of, the room wasn't actually much brighter than the north-facing official parlour, but it was made cosy with hangings and good braziers. It was a pleasant place.

We went to Middleham early in the February of 1468, our second visit since we returned from London. I was glad to be there, happy to be once more with Isabel ('Dear, scatter-brained Isabel,' as Ankaret Twynyhoe used to say so often when retrieving the objects which Isabel so casually left about), and as usual exhilarated by the atmosphere of the castle. I had learned a great deal from the earlier visits and from our trip to London. I was aware now of the political world, knew who the personalities were and what their rivalries were about. I had heard of the Earl of Warwick's fury when he discovered that Margaret of York had been betrothed to Burgundy behind his back; I had come to understand the depth of the Neville dislike for the Queen and her clan of thrusting Woodvilles. I made a conscious effort to remember what I had learned and when at Eynesby I could now bear my part in the dinner-table conversation of Lionel's sophisticated guests.

If only I had succeeded in starting a baby, Lionel would have found no fault in me. But although I had indeed won his approval in many ways – at Sir Anthony's feast, at Middleham where I had made a place for myself, and when I proved myself to be well-informed at dinner – none of these could quite outweigh my one great failure. His disappointment showed itself every now and then, in a tone, a frown, an undeserved criticism, and I was still secretly gnawed by a fear of him. I went on lighting candles regularly to the Virgin, but my monthly bleeding continued with an equal regularity.

And, of course, although I had sent him away myself, I thought of Geoffrey constantly, daydreamed about him, wondered what I should say to him when we met again, wished I had answered him differently, was thankful I had not. Sometimes I wanted to sing and dance for the sheer joy of being alive and in love; sometimes I knew with a bleakness so intense that I did not even want to cry, that my life was real and harsh, and had no room in it for Geoffrey or for love – unless I had a child, for I supposed I would be permitted to love that.

Yes, I was very glad indeed to be at Middleham. There I had distraction, and was not in charge of the household and so could not be rebuked for any shortcomings.

The talking point that February was a new dance which had been created in honour of Margaret of York's forthcoming marriage. The wedding was going forward and Warwick had made his peace with the King over it. The Lady Margaret herself had begged him to, Isabel told me, and he had at last complied for he was fond of his cousin Margaret, and she of him.

The dance was pretty. The dancers made patterns, couples linking up with other couples in fours and sixes to form spoked wheels or crosses, hands joined at the centre of the formation. It was complex in the way that one figure changed to the next, but Isabel, although she could never control her belongings, could remember the most intricate dance steps with perfect ease. A week after my arrival, on a cold morning when the castle was wrapped in mist, she appointed herself our instructress. We pushed the furniture out of the way and Ankaret, who was a good musician, played the harp for us.

'Only,' said Isabel after our first attempt, 'I think the music is too slow. I haven't heard yet what tune they're using in London, but we could try it to *Lovely Joan*; that's a little more sprightly. You know it, don't you, Ankaret?'

One doesn't learn everything all at once, of course. I had picked up a great deal about current affairs but I hadn't till now discovered the name of the tune to which I had danced, with Geoffrey as my partner, at Sir Anthony Woodville's feast. When Ankaret began to play it, it brought back the memory of him so vividly that for a moment the Middleham hangings and the drifting mist beyond the windows vanished and I was again in Sir Anthony's hall on that June evening, with my hand in that warm male grasp. It was so real and heart-stopping that I once more muddled my steps. I came back to the Middleham solar to find myself standing with hand outstretched into an empty space in the midst of my fellow-dancers, and Isabel saying: 'No, no Petra, it's six skips before we join hands in the centre, not four. You know that. You were thinking of something else, I can tell by your face.'

She spoke laughingly, teasing me, meaning no harm. I pulled myself together, smiled, said: 'I'm so sorry. Can we try the figure again?' and turned to put myself into position, taking the hand of my partner Anne Neville and facing forwards, towards the door. Just as a page came hurrying through it, followed, unbelievably, as though *Lovely Joan* had conjured him from nowhere, by Geoffrey.

My face went hot at once, as though I had been caught in some misdoing. But no one was looking at me. They were all gazing silently at Geoffrey. He was dressed for hard riding; boots and stout brown hose and a quilted doublet, and his clothes were splashed with mud and dewed with mist. His face was graver than I had ever seen it. He did not glance towards the dancers; he did not even see me. He went straight to where the countess was sitting beside Ankaret to watch our endeavours, and knelt before her.

Seeing his expression, she had gone pale. She leant forward and spoke to him. I heard him say: 'No, no, ma'am, the Earl of Warwick is in good health.' She sat back in relief but then Geoffrey spoke again, too quietly for the rest of us to hear except for Ankaret, and I saw the horror on both their faces. She reached out a hand to Ankaret as if for support and Ankaret, leaving her harp, went to her.

'I can't believe it!' Ankaret said. She had placed a hand on the countess's shoulder. She spoke loud enough for us to hear this time. 'Not that the Queen ordered that! It's impossible!'

'Is it?' said the countess grimly. 'Did I not always say that Bess Woodville has the pride of Lucifer? Has not my husband always said the same? She'd do murder for her pride's sake. We've always known it.'

'But . . . children!' said Ankaret.

They became aware of our questioning faces. 'Tell them, Ankaret,' said the countess. Mistress Twynyhoe came and drew us all aside.

'There is nothing for us to be alarmed about but the news is very sad and . . . and tragic. Have any of you heard of the Earl of Desmond?'

'Oh yes, he's an Irish lord. George has told me.' Isabel always behaved as though she owned the Duke of Clarence, though the King had still not given his consent to their marriage and as far as I knew, there was as yet no dispensation from Rome, either. 'He was the one who made that joke about the Queen, calling her the King's Grey mare. George thought that was very funny.'

'The Queen didn't,' said Ankaret sternly. 'She heard the joke, Isabel, but she didn't laugh. And now Desmond is dead. He was taken from his house in Ireland and executed on what seems to have been an invented charge of treason.

Two of his young sons, one aged thirteen and the other less than eight, were beheaded with him. And the rumour is that it was done on Bess Woodville's orders. She was taking her revenge. The younger boy,' said Ankaret, staring hard at Isabel, 'apparently didn't quite understand what the block and the axe meant. He asked the executioner to be careful of the boil on his neck, because it was sore.'

My stomach clenched and grew cold. Isabel, who a moment ago had been almost ready to giggle, said: 'Oh, how horrible!' and her eyes filled.

'But surely,' said Anne, 'surely the Queen didn't order that the boys be killed as well?'

The countess and Geoffrey came over to us. Geoffrey, catching sight of me, acknowledged me with a bow. 'I did not know you would be here, Aunt Petronel. I came to my lady as Warwick's courier.'

The countess said to Anne: 'But they were killed, and on her behalf.'

Timidly, I said: 'My husband has some acquaintance with the Scropes and Lady Elizabeth Scrope attended the Queen at her last lying-in. She told us that the Queen loves children.'

I had reason to remember that last visit of the Scropes in some detail. 'I hope you may one day attend Petronel's lying-in,' Lionel had said to Lady Elizabeth, and then been irritable with me for a week.

'Lady Elizabeth,' said the Countess of Warwick sharply, 'is one of those tender-hearted women who always believe the best of everyone. Oh, I suppose the Queen's orders could have been exceeded, but according to Sir Geoffrey here, whose information comes from Warwick and is assuredly correct, it was John Tiptoft who carried those orders out. Unless she gave him very precise instructions on what he was and was not to do, she should have known he would go to extremes. Tiptoft is capable of anything. If you keep a savage dog, you have a duty to control it.'

'The King is angry, so my lord says,' Geoffrey told us,

'but there is nothing that he can do. There are hopes of a prince, nowadays.' The Queen's two children so far by King Edward had both been daughters.

'Those Woodvilles . . .' The countess looked at Ankaret, 'Ankaret, although you don't say so aloud, I know you think our dislike of the Woodvilles is pure prejudice. Believe me, it's more than that and this is the proof of it. Even if she did not mean the children to die, what of the grown man? To take a man's life for a mere joke . . .!'

Looking back, it seems to me that the death of the Desmonds was a turning point, the crucial thing which afterwards so burned in Warwick's mind that just over a year later, he went to war to rid the land of Woodvilles.

He did not, of course, put it that way when calling up his men. There had been some disturbances in the northern counties and although they were not near us, the news had reached us and sounded worrying enough to make us put the house into some sort of state of defence. That Warwick should summon his adherents to help him put the trouble down was natural.

Lionel, who was shrewd, said that he had a feeling about it all; he did not propose to answer the call or to send any men and he recommended Geoffrey not to do so either.

But Geoffrey, who had after all encountered criticism for taking part in the tournament at Smithfield, said he would respond to the summons. There was a little disagreement between him and Lionel over it, but in the end, Lionel helped him check his armour.

As for me, I found it hard to utter the conventional messages of well-wishing and offers of prayers for a safe return.

I had seen little of Geoffrey in all that time and when we did meet, he had been unfailingly courteous and unfailingly remote. My heart still somersaulted for love of him every time I set eyes on him, and he was going to war. And war was more dangerous than tournaments were, and tournaments were bad enough.

The violence never did reach Eynesby. In all the years I lived there with Lionel, war passed it by and now, of course, it is safer than ever before in its history.

Then, as now, those who lived there had to depend on news arriving from a distance, and we had to bear long passages of time during which no news came at all.

I took to lighting two candles in our chapel every day. One was for the child I had still not conceived, but the other was for Geoffrey.

Chapter Nine

The Plantagenets : King in Jeopardy

1469

Anne Neville, the younger daughter of the Earl of Warwick, was frightened. It was a frightening sensation, as well as a strange one, to find herself disapproving of her own father.

As a young child she had virtually worshipped her glittering, swashbuckling, recklessly generous sire. At the age of nine she had quelled the pretensions of her cousins George and Dickon when they boasted of 'our brother, King Edward,' by telling them smugly that her father's servants could regale any friend of theirs, any day, with as much roast meat as could be skewered on a dagger. 'I never heard that the King does that,' she said proudly.

'I should hope not. Ned rules England, not an almshouse,' retorted Dickon, an implied criticism of Warwick which had kept her haughtily refusing to speak to him for one whole day.

But now, she had begun to criticise Warwick for herself. Even at the age of thirteen, she was fairly sure that he shouldn't have fomented a rebellion.

She had first experienced a sense of alienation from her personal deity two years before. Her father had been expected home from a state visit to France. She and Isabel, waiting for him at Warwick Castle with their mother, were excited. Warwick's homecomings were like effulgent sunrises. Father, surrounded by noisy retainers like a private dawn chorus, would burst into whichever of their castles or houses the family chanced to be inhabiting at the time, summoning it to life. If this time their mother did not seem to share their eager anticipation, the daughters had been too full of it themselves to notice.

But their mother was right, for this time the earl did not arrive like a sunrise. He arrived like a thunderclap and a sizzle of vicious forked lightning. His retainers followed him in respectful silence as he strode into the great hall. He did not acknowledge his children's welcoming exclamations. He demanded food and drink and clean clothes, cast himself into a chair, shouted for someone to remove his boots, and smacked the head of a page who was clumsy in doing so. His wife stood stiffly, awaiting but wisely not requesting her customary kiss of greeting. He did not acknowledge her, either.

A second page came running and dealt with his master's boots. His footwear changed, Warwick shot restlessly to his feet. He paced about the hall. In his right hand he still gripped his riding gloves, and when words suddenly broke out of him, he slashed with the gloves to emphasise his remarks.

'Tricked, by God!' he bellowed, at the countess, their daughters, his men, impartially. 'Steered out of the way like a pockmarked girl being pushed into a nunnery!' The gloves descended, overturning a small chess table with inlaid squares of rose quartz and ivory. 'While Edward,' Warwick thundered, 'gets cuddly with the Burgundian!'

His countess very nearly smiled at the muddled figures of speech, at the staggering vision of the ultra-masculine Edward the Fourth cuddling Antoine of Burgundy, who was middle-aged and bearded. But she stopped the smile in time, and Anne saw her do it. This was serious, then. The countess said cautiously: 'The marriage is not until next year. Perhaps it may never take place at all. Political climates can change . . .'

'Oh, it'll take place,' Warwick assured her. 'Both Edward and the Burgundians are delighted with the arrangement, and as for Lady Margaret, she's choosing patterns for her wedding gown and asking for a portrait of Duke Charles!' The gloves bisected the air again and an alabaster statuette of St Thomas a'Becket fell from a wall niche to shatter on the floor. Anne saw her mother glance at it and decide to ignore it.

'How did the King greet you when you came home?' the countess asked.

'He was friendly. Why not? He's having his own way , isn't he?' said Warwick, through clenched teeth.

'*You want your own way, madam!*' Anne's mother had said to her long ago, when Anne was having a childish tantrum. In memory she saw herself lying on the floor, banging it with her fists, because the adults had crossed her. She looked at her father, overturning furniture and smashing ornaments because the King had crossed him. Not the King, but her father, was in a passion to get his own way, said a cold, mature little voice inside her.

But that time, two years ago, the voice had faded away. Because that time, her father had listened in the end to the counsels of others, including Dickon of Gloucester and Warwick's brother John Neville of Northumberland, and above all Margaret of York herself. She had wanted him in the escort which, the following year, took her to the coast to embark her for Burgundy and marriage. Warwick consented, if in a growling fashion. The Lady Margaret rode pillion behind him on the first stage of her wedding journey, and the quarrel was mended.

Or almost. There were occasional reminders. The news of the deaths of Desmond and his sons set the air humming again with hatred of the Woodvilles. 'Another crime to be laid at their door,' Warwick had said grimly, in Anne's hearing, when next they saw him, and her mother had agreed.

But please God, said Anne to herself, let it not be my father who decides to bring it home to them. She was old enough by then to grasp that to quarrel with the Woodvilles

143

was to quarrel with the King, and that the King was a dangerous enemy.

But when she silently framed that prayer, God had not been listening.

'Isabel, Anne, it's time to leave. Put up your hoods. It's raining.' The Countess of Warwick beckoned impatiently to Ankaret. 'See to them!' she said, and swept out ahead.

Isabel caught Anne's hands and swung her, dancing them in round Warwick Castle's hall. Her blue cloak flew out round her. 'Oh, Anne, isn't it thrilling! I'm to marry George of Clarence at last!'

'Not unless you hurry,' said Anne, detaching herself. 'If we don't go now, we may not get to Calais in time for the ceremony.'

Their mother, irascible with nerves and considerably less dignified than usual – if the King's spies learned what was afoot they would indeed not get to Calais in time for the ceremony, or at all – reappeared in the doorway. '*Will* you come?'

Obediently, chivvied by Ankaret, they went out to her.

The Countess of Warwick had longed to bear sons, but all her male children had died. Only these two girls had lived and when she surveyed them she could hardly believe that she and Warwick had produced such offspring. They were good girls, of course, dutiful and obedient, but . . .

But how in the name of all the saints had she and Richard, great lady and great earl as they were, brought forth a careless, sentimental child like Isabel, eternally strewing her small belongings about like May blossom in a breeze, laughing or crying at the least provocation, and still an emotional infant even now that she had one foot in the marriage chamber? In looks Isabel resembled her fair-haired father, but the muscles round her mouth had a softness which his lacked and after a pregnancy or two, she would get fat. While Anne . . .

Small mousey Anne was like neither of her parents to

look at, and yet she had a disconcerting pride which was all her own. She had a habit of sitting, prim as a prioress (and considerably primmer than some), small feet together, hands clasped, while the big grey eyes that dominated her triangular little face watched, judicially, the antics of her elders.

Antics? Had she, the countess wondered, picked that word out of her younger daughter's righteous little mind?

Yes, it was true that Warwick was now in stealthy rebellion against the King, that it was he who had set in motion the rising now gathering momentum in Yorkshire, and had mustered men, not to put down, but to support it. And it was true that he was marrying Isabel to the King's brother Clarence against what were now Edward's express orders, slipping across to Calais in order to do so. It was also true that she, Warwick's own wife, privately considered these things unwise.

But her husband had been provoked. The Woodvilles and their works were enough to drive anyone to extremes. The Earl of Warwick was not to be judged and found wanting by little girls of thirteen.

'Mount and be quick about it!' said the countess fiercely to her daughters.

'Will Father meet us in Calais?' asked Anne, complying. 'Where is he now?'

'Patrolling the Channel with his fleet. There has been some trouble with dispossessed Lancastrian exiles raiding our coasts from France. George of Clarence is with him. They will be at Calais when we arrive, yes.'

'They have to be there for the wedding, silly!' Isabel cried. She mounted blithely, without help. 'Oh, Anne, how wonderful it is! At last! George will have the dispensation from Rome with him – it's come through, Father's message said. I wish Petronel could be here to share it all. Her husband wouldn't let her; wasn't that unkind?'

'It was probably very wise,' snapped her mother unexpectedly. 'As for being in love, you know nothing about it.

145

What a seasoned wife feels for her husband has nothing to do with the vapourings of a greensick girl! Don't make such a fool of yourself, Isabel. Now, let us set off!'

Isabel, unaccustomed to such sharp rebukes and taken aback by this one, stared at her mother and her mouth began to droop. As the sisters' horses bumped together in the passage to the outer courtyard, Anne whispered: 'Mother meant that if George were a hunchback with leprosy, you'd still have to marry him because Father wants to marry us into the King's family, to help him elbow the Woodvilles out of it!' She observed with satisfaction that Isabel's easy tears were glinting in her eyes. 'You're just a pawn,' said Anne derisively. 'We're all just pieces on a chessboard. What if you are in love? I don't suppose George is.'

Being nasty to Isabel helped her pretend that she was not afraid. She wasn't supposed to know that the marriage was proceeding in direct defiance of the King and she wasn't supposed to know that her father was the moving spirit behind the growing disturbance in the north. But there was no privacy to speak of in Warwick Castle; she had heard the adults talking. The risk they were all now taking made her insides shake.

Isabel snuffled and spurred her horse on ahead. 'You'll be a pawn too, one day,' she said vindictively, over her shoulder.

'You were right, Brampton,' said King Edward grimly. 'So was Alcock. He warned me before I left London but I thought he was making too much of small rumours. I was sure it was just another north-country rising, just one more chapter in the squabble between the Percys and John Neville over Northumberland. I was mistaken.'

The July dusk was descending on Nottingham Castle and the massive Norman hall was full of shadows. There was no fire. There were only four men in the hall and when they spoke, their voices echoed.

146

They were not alone in the fortress, of course. The castle had a standing garrison and they had brought more men in with them when they rode in headlong, seeking the castle's shelter. On the walls, outlined against the afterglow, they could see the heads of the sentries who were watching for the foe whose whereabouts no one yet knew. There was a full complement of servants, too, although Dickon of Gloucester, who had just been to the kitchens to demand food, wine and lights, said he had found them 'cowering round a table, listening to the second cook's atrocity tales about the Bitch of Anjou and how her men used to treat the people in the castles that held out too long. I put a stop to it. We're not fighting the Bitch now, anyway.'

For the time being, since the tapers hadn't yet come, the four stood together under a narrow window where a shaft of sunset-tinged light slid over the deep, sloping sill to illumine the unpleasant document spread out on a small table below. King Edward, his friends Edward Brampton and John Howard and his brother Dickon, regarded it with loathing. 'You and Alcock,' said the King to Brampton, 'are both gifted intelligence gatherers. You should work together. When all this is over, I shall set that up.' He glanced towards Dickon. 'Thank you for dealing with the nonsense in the kitchen. I don't suppose the Nevilles would behave as badly as the Bitch, even if they got the chance. It's the treachery that is so shameful. What made you so sure, Brampton?'

The half-light did nothing to render Edward Brampton's brigand face more confidence-inspiring than usual. 'I was born,' he said, in the accent which was so very southern European, 'Duarte Brandeo, not only a Portuguese, my lord, but a Jew. My race has lived on sufferance in other people's countries for centuries. We know by instinct when danger threatens and from what quarter. But I did see evidence too. When we set out for the north, we called, did we not, upon the Archbishop of York who was staying on one of his southern manors? We asked him for extra men but he made excuses, and he is Warwick's brother. Was that not evidence enough?'

King Edward sighed. 'I think I half-believed you, yes. I said as much to Dickon here and he agreed. I didn't want to believe you, I imagine. But now . . .' he flicked the blackletter proclamation with a disgusted forefinger '. . . now, we *know*.'

'It's a piece of filth.' John Howard was a tall and deep-chested man whose voice sounded as though it were filtering through gravel. He was not only a long-standing York supporter but a personal friend, and he combined the wondrous virtues of integrity, battlefield experience and the advantage (which Edward had once remarked was nearly an achievement) of not being one of Warwick's brothers-in-law, either past or present. 'How did it get into your hands, my lord? I was half an hour behind you, getting here. All I had was an urgent message to round up my men and follow you in as fast as our horses could gallop. I've not yet heard the details.'

Despite the gravity of the moment, Edward grinned. 'The last time Dickon here went to Yorkshire, which he does at every conceivable opportunity, he met a girl, Katherine. She's the daughter of a York bullion merchant. Tell Howard all about it, Dickon.'

Dickon was also grinning. 'I dined at her father's hall and saw her. So I had myself introduced and, well . . . I called again next day and would you believe it, her father asked me outright if I were interested in her. I said I was and that I thought Katherine was interested in me. I half-expected him to throw me out but it can be mighty useful, being Ned's brother. He behaved as though I'd conferred an honour on him. He lit our way to the best bedchamber . . .'

'What, personally?' said John Howard.

'Personally. And showed us in and went out *backwards*. My first *affaire*,' said Dickon with amusement, 'began with the two of us clinging to each other in uncontrollable giggles. When Archbishop Neville behaved so oddly, I did

148

think it was worth making some enquiries, so I sent off a courier to Katherine's father asking him to find out what he could. He took this off a church door after dark, pushed it inside the courier's shirt and despatched him back to me on a fresh horse.'

'I'm going to give your Katherine's father a knighthood,' said Edward. 'Although I never thought I'd be grateful to be sent a thing like this. Dear saints, look at it! It accuses my lady the Queen and her family of being, between them, guilty of about every excess and impropriety known to humankind – from your face when you read it, Dickon, I fancy it shocked even you to your soul and you don't like any of the Woodvilles except maybe Anthony. I know that, so you needn't look embarrassed. It then has the impertinence to claim that I am under the influence of these outrageous persons . . .'

'I may dislike the Woodvilles,' said Dickon, 'but that makes no difference to my loyalty to you, Ned. What makes me sick when I look at this – thing – is that whoever wrote it claims that he is loyal to you as well. I don't like hypocrisy, either!'

The proclamation did indeed claim loyalty. Having finished its lengthy and imaginative smearing of the Woodville family, it called men to arms on the King's behalf, to free him from the pernicious power of his in-laws.

'What a poor thing I sound,' remarked Edward. 'Will I go down in history as Edward the Henpecked, I wonder?'

The document closed by giving with proud carelessness the pedigree of its instigator. He bore the rustic-sounding title of Robin of Redesdale, but added further credentials.

'He's not precisely hiding his light under a bushel, is he?' said Dickon sourly. 'Warwick's cousin by marriage!'

'I'm not the only one with objectionable in-laws,' Edward commented. 'Warwick's connections by marriage remind me of a smallpox rash. Too many, too repulsive and too bloody noticeable. Howard –you won't have heard this either yet – the word of mouth news the courier brought back says that this Redesdale is now marching south with a bigger force than ours. Hence my order to take cover in this castle. The damned, obstinate fool. Warwick, I mean. God, he could have had anything and everything from me but the throne itself, and to do him justice he's never wanted that. But because I won't marry where he chooses or sign treaties where he points, he must brood and sulk and then go to war.'

John Howard's notions of honesty could on occasion be devastating. 'Was it only that?'

'You mean Desmond?' Edward too could be blunt. 'Bess never ordered the boys' deaths. She sent Tiptoft to deal with Desmond and she didn't know him as the rest of us do. The boys' deaths appalled her when she heard. As for Desmond himself – well, I was angry at first when I heard what she'd done but I understand why she did it. It's time you understood as well, Dickon.' He glanced sharply at his younger brother. 'You thought it was pride, didn't you? That she believed she'd been insulted. It wasn't that. It was fear. She felt unsafe, hearing herself called a Grey mare. She felt that her position as my wife and my queen was not being recognised and that I might catch that attitude myself if it were to grow. She's very conscious that she hasn't yet given me a son. It is a pity she has given Warwick such a pretext to attack her and her family. I fear he is acting in a glow of righteousness.'

He leant on his fists, frowning down at the proclamation. 'At the moment,' he said, 'Warwick is with a fleet of ships in the English Channel, supposedly guarding it in case the Anjou woman decides that now, while I'm occupied in the north, is the moment to mount an invasion. It's possible. There have been a few Lancastrian sorties from the continent recently. But I fancy Warwick will be reappearing soon to join up with Redesdale. My brother Clarence,' he added, 'is with him, and since he has not apparently left him or sent me any word, we can only conclude he has thrown his lot in with Warwick. It wouldn't surprise me. He has persisted in staying betrothed to the elder Warwick girl, and he detests my wife.'

No one answered. A kitchen boy appeared at last, carrying a taper, and went round the hall lighting candles and torches.

'I'll send to Devon and Pembroke for help,' Edward said. 'Their earls are loyal. I shall also send for Will Hastings. I believe he's sound even if he is yet another of Warwick's confounded brothers-in-law. We have one Neville with us, by the way. Northumberland is standing by me. His messenger was here when I arrived, Howard. You'll have noticed that there are no Woodvilles here. I sent them all home. They're the target and I don't want them exposed.'

Dickon picked up the proclamation, between finger and thumb. 'What shall we do with this?' he enquired.

'That? Oh, burn it,' said Edward.

The Earl of Pembroke was six feet tall, with thighs like Norman pillars. The Earl of Devon was a little larger. At the moment, heads lowered and faces congested, they resembled quarrelling bulls. Their principal officers, whose lower-level wrangle the two earls had just taken over, stood mutely by in the main street of Banbury town, Oxfordshire, and awaited the outcome.

'I'm well aware that we're on the same errand,' Pembroke rumbled, 'but there are not enough billets in Banbury for your men and mine, and mine were here first. Why can't your men camp overnight in the open? It's July.'

You pompous idiot, said the Earl of Devon's expression. 'For the fourth time, my orders are to combine forces with you to relieve Nottingham. At the very least, half of your men and half of mine should sleep under cover tonight.'

'I doubt if I could get half my men to agree.'

'Ah, the temperamental Welsh, of course.' Devon's voice was almost silky. 'But they're not beyond your control, surely?'

They stared inimically at each other. In the background, there was the sound of scuffling. Three Devonshire archers had tried to assert their right to beds in Banbury by marching into a cottage already requisitioned by four Welsh pikemen. A knot of men now pummelled each other in the doorway. 'That's right!' a large woman shouted from across the street. 'Fight one another! Go on! That'll help the King no end, that will!'

'Put a stop to that!' Devon shouted at his nearest officers. 'You, madam, mind your tongue. If you were a man . . .'

'I'd be in the army and pointing my spear at the enemy!'

She was not young but she was as hefty as a wrestler. Several neighbours, moreover, were drifting towards her with the air of being about to give her moral support. Devon turned his back.

The city of Nottingham was shut fast and waiting. The northern leader Redesdale was said to be marching south to cut the King off from London and any support it might send. Redesdale might well approach Banbury. Already, some of its folk were piling belongings on to barrows, ready to flee. Others were barricading their houses. The spectacle of those who ought to defend them, quarrelling among themselves, was creating visible resentment.

'With the temper these townsfolk are in,' said Pembroke bluntly, 'I don't advise trying to wedge both sets of men in. It would end with doors slammed in our faces and then we'd have to uphold the King's authority by turning on a townful of loyal subjects. In the name of the King, my lord, I must ask you to withdraw peaceably outside the town. It is only for one night. In the morning we will march on together, in amity, I hope.'

His pikemen were already blocking the way to the town centre. Devon, faced with the alternatives of giving way or telling his archers to shoot at their own allies, turned magenta with mortification. 'I wouldn't ask my men to share quarters with your Welsh savages. We shall with-

152

draw. Well back, rest assured of that. In the morning, we'll march after you but not, by God, beside you. If you run into Redesdale while we're still ten miles behind, I wish you good luck!'

'I don't believe it,' said Edward flatly. He dropped his horse's reins on its neck as though they represented a surrendered sanity. 'I can't believe it.' He looked blankly at the people in front of him.

Their spokesman was a weary fugitive soldier whose left hand was wrapped in stained bandaging and whose padded jacket was slashed in half a dozen places so that the tow stuffing showed. 'It's God's truth, sire.' He spoke with a Welsh accent.

'But they were on the same side!' Edward shouted. 'My side!' He turned to William Hastings and Dickon, who rode beside him. 'Can you believe it?' he demanded.

Hastings shook his head, but in despair, not in refusal to believe in disaster. The ebullient young man whose cheerful nature had been evident to John Alcock at the court reception two years before, had made a swift and loyal response to Edward's summons. Brother-in-law to Warwick or not, he had erupted into Nottingham Castle with a well-arrayed force – though not, because of shortage of time, an overlarge one – saying: 'What are you sitting here behind a locked door for then? I had to sound my horn for ten minutes before I was let across the drawbridge. Good God, let's go and find this miserable Redesdale and eat him spit-roasted for dinner!'

But now he stared speechlessly at his mount's ears and his shoulders had an uncharacteristic sag. They had depended on Pembroke and Devon to make the spit-roasting of Redesdale possible.

'I was with Pembroke,' the soldier said, 'but Devon would only march behind us, after the squabble at Banbury. So when we ran into Redesdale, we had no archers. Christ, what we could have done with Devon's archers! Redesdale chewed us to bits. I was knocked out and left for dead, or there's dead I'd be by now in earnest. Pembroke was taken, I saw it happen. Redesdale's been burning villages, making himself felt. He's got Northampton now. Warwick's landed; must be somewhere behind us. The dear Lord knows how Devon's men fared. There were folk fleeing ahead of Warwick . . .'

The track stretched away south, a ribbon of dust between its wide borders of grass, parched for lack of rain. The road was dotted with refugees. There were two more soldiers dragging a small cart on which a third lay in teeth-clenched misery, his right leg splinted. An old woman clutched the halter of a goat and beside her stood a girl heavy with child and carrying another on her back. A peasant family were clustered round a handcart piled with brass pots, old rugs, an ironbound chest, half a huge cheese and a cask of something. Above them all, the sky throbbed with heat. The man with the splinted leg was asking for water. 'Give him some,' said Edward, gesturing to a retainer with a leather water-bottle hanging at his saddle.

'There's a village a mile back,' said Dickon. 'It's called Olney. The well there is good. You'll find water, and a church for sanctuary.'

A few faces brightened at the prospect of rest and water. Others became shut in, as though the sight of the King had at first raised hopes which by now had been disappointed. Some, who had put down burdens, picked them up, ready to plod on.

'And us, sire?' said Hastings, waking from his reverie.

Edward looked round. Dickon, Brampton, Hastings, Howard, all sat on their horses, watching him. Beyond them were the men they had mustered between them. Even with Hastings's contribution, it was a small force compared to the full-scale army which, by all accounts, Redesdale had commanded. And Warwick must have another. 'There's no point in throwing all your lives away,' Edward said. 'We disband.'

'I won't leave you,' said Dickon.

'You'll have the goodness to do as you're told. I'm not

154

sending you away to kick your heels. You've raised one loan for me already, for which I'm grateful as I know you dislike taking on debts. I am commissioning you to raise more, if you can. I also require you to ride to intercept Northumberland who is supposed to be on his way to me, and prevent him from coming any further until the two of you are certain you have a big enough force mustered to outnumber the foe. The rest of you can go with Dickon or go home.'

'But what of your own life, sire?' said John Howard. 'Where will you take shelter?'

'Nowhere,' said Edward. 'We,' he added pointedly, 'are an anointed King. It ought to count for something. Also, Warwick and this Redesdale person claim that they're loyal to me and only wish to rescue me from my relations, like a maiden from a dragon.' Startlingly, across the King's face there now spread a broad smile. He looked like a genial lion. 'We can't win this contest by force of arms,' he said. 'Or not yet, anyway. Meanwhile, let us see what brazenness can do.'

Chapter Ten

The Plantagenets: The Insouciant Knight

1469

'But this,' said King Edward, 'is quite delightful.' He sat, goblet in hand, in a carved chair in the great hall of Warwick Castle, and smiled graciously into the faces of two of his Neville cousins, and his brother Clarence. The smiles which they returned were considerably less gracious.

It was, after all, Warwick's own hall and the chair in which Edward sat was Warwick's own chair. But on stepping across the threshold Edward – without reference to Warwick, and still less to Clarence or Archbishop Neville of York or any of the curtsying ladies who, surprisingly, had accompanied Warwick back to England – had beckoned a page, ordered wine and commandeered the chair belonging to the master of the house. With the latter, he had worked a mysterious alchemy, turning it by sheer force of will into a throne.

Ever since Archbishop Neville and his men had arrived at last, but in support of the wrong side, and accosted Edward at Olney, he had insisted on behaving as though he were being escorted to Warwick as an honoured guest instead of a prisoner. He was now the only person in the hall who was seated. The others remained standing in his presence, tacitly awaiting his permission to sit down. He had not given that permission and they did not know what to do about it. He beamed at them.

'I very much regret, Warwick, that your good kinsman Redesdale could not leave Northampton to join us. What a blessing it is to have good, loyal relatives.' It was the nearest he had yet come to admitting that Warwick could not himself be so classified and he contrived to give even this barbed remark a sincere face value. Warwick's mouth tightened but Edward had given him no opening for a retort.

'And I believe,' said Edward smoothly, 'that I must congratulate my brother of Clarence. How is married life, George?'

'All that I hoped,' said Clarence warily. He was gorgeously dressed as ever. Edward observed with regret that he had gone to extremes about it. His elongated toes now outdid Sir Anthony Woodville's by at least two inches, and he had adopted the parti-coloured style, in crimson and gold. This was tasteless, for they were the royal colours.

'You must not think me oblivious to the feelings of young lovers,' Edward assured him. 'The marriage of the King's brother is important and I confess I had different plans for both you and your bride. But what's done is done and . . .'

'My lord,' said Warwick, 'I think you may be under a misapprehension. I want to assure you that despite all appearances to the contrary, you are in the company of your most devoted servants. We only . . .'

'I married for love myself,' said Edward reminiscently, 'so who am I to scold you, Clarence? Isabel, my dear, come and give your new brother a kiss and forgive him his grouchy objections to your wedding. I rejoice to see you so ecstatic in your love.'

Isabel, whose love match had so far proved far from ecstatic, since her bridegroom's embraces were both perfunctory and rough, in addition to which, he snored, came forward to plant a polite little kiss on Edward's stubbly jawline. He had had no chance to shave within the last day or two. In the background, hands gripped too tightly in front of them, eyes wary, stood Isabel's mother and her sister Anne. Ankaret Twynyhoe, still Isabel's faithful senior lady, waited quietly behind her mistress. Her hands too were knotted.

'Whatever appearances may suggest,' said Warwick

158

insistently, 'we all wish you to know that we are your most faithful subjects. We have acted only to protect your best interests, sire, and those of your realm.'

'I want a bath,' said Edward plaintively. 'Campaigning in hot weather makes one smell. And I need a hot meal.'

'Dinner is being prepared,' said Warwick. The high table was already covered with a white cloth and platters were being set out. He signalled to a maidservant and she brought some spiced cakes to them. She was a plump girl with a ginger plait escaping from her linen headdress. 'Darling,' said Edward immediately, reaching out with a long arm to draw her to him, 'could you arrange a bath for me after dinner? You can scrub my back.' The maidservant shrieked dutifully, eyed Edward's superb physique with candid admiration, curtsyed and said: 'It 'ud be a pleasure, sir.' Warwick looked furious, Isabel smothered a giggle and the rest of the ladies looked scandalised. Clarence guffawed.

'Out!' said Warwick to the maid. She glanced from him to Edward as if uncertain which of them to obey. Edward grinned. Warwick, seizing hold of the situation before it escaped him altogether, barked: 'Go and order the bath as the King tells you!' She went, with a mischievous glance over her shoulder at Edward, who raised his goblet in salute.

'I want to explain,' said Warwick harshly, 'that with the welfare of the kingdom at heart, we have in custody certain members of the Woodville family, who accompanied you from London, sire, but left you before you reached Nottingham. We intend to execute them for treason. The same applies to the Earl of Devon, who resisted our attempt to purge the government of this country, and has also been taken prisoner. Pembroke, guilty of a similar offence, has already been dealt with. I must make it plain to you why this purge was necessary.'

'Continue,' said Edward. At the word 'execute' the roguishness had smoothed out of his face, leaving behind it a high-cheekboned mask.

'There is no animus against yourself, sire, or against your

159

queen, whatever you may have heard to the contrary. Few women, other than such unnatural females as the Anjou tigress, are a force in the affairs of state. But their male relatives may be such a force. The Woodville family to which you have allied yourself by marriage is fundamentally Lancastrian in loyalty. If such men acquire too much power – and they have been setting out to acquire power – they become a menace. It is likely that the Queen was, shall we say, ill-advised by her male relatives over a matter not so long ago concerning the Earl of Desmond. One wonders what their motive could have been. To use the Queen's natural anger at a discourteous joke, to bring the royal house into disrepute, perhaps? A likely enough thing for a gang of Lancastrians to wish.'

'Hardly,' said Edward, 'while their kinswoman remains a Yorkist queen. And they gave no advice concerning Desmond.' A small sigh of exasperation escaped him. 'I explained all this to Dickon, not long ago. Now it seems I must explain it to you. The Queen acted on her own account. Hastily and unwisely, I agree, and with results that she herself never foresaw and which have since caused her the most intense grief and remorse. She saw in that jest a veiled recommendation to me to set her aside. I couldn't if I wanted to, and I don't. Our marriage was legal. But the Queen is a woman and she is a creature of emotion. She was afraid and struck in what she thought was self-defence. I too didn't understand at first but I do now. You are not yourself quite innocent of the Desmond deaths, my dear cousin. You underestimate the effect of your own haughty looks!'

'Indeed?' said Warwick coldly. He was wearing armour but not, while indoors and technically at an amicable meeting, his helmet. With his crest of amber hair and his aquiline profile, he was more than ever like an eagle. He was seeking a chance to pounce. 'But even so, my lord,' he said,' the Queen's relations are self-seekers and have loyalties which are dangerous to you. We believe that at heart you know this. For the very love you owe your gentle Queen . . .'

'You will kindly,' said Edward, 'speak of our wife with courtesy.'

'Is it discourteous to call her gentle?'

'In that tone of voice, yes.'

'Forgive me, sire. But I repeat. For the very love you owe her, you should deal with the danger to your throne which is inherent in her family. At the same time, we clearly see that you cannot do so in person – again on account of that love, for they *are* her family. That is why we have acted on your behalf – out of loyalty to yourself, not out of treachery.'

'I wonder if even you believe that?' said Edward. 'Am I to sign the death warrants, then?'

'Certainly not. We have accepted full responsibility.'

The tables were laid now. Food was being placed on them. Edward, however, rose and turned away from it. 'Excuse us, cousin. We will dine in our chamber tonight. We find our appetite is smaller than we thought. We will have the bath we asked for later, but after all, not with the young lady as attendant. Will someone tell her, and tell her why? Grief for kinsmen, she will understand. I wouldn't have her feel slighted. And George . . .' he turned to Clarence '. . . come with us. As your brother, we wish to speak to you privately.'

'Now tell me,' said Edward, dropping formality, 'am I also on the list for execution? And if so, why? And may I have the services of a priest and a clerk? I wish to make my confession and my will.'

George of Clarence gasped. 'There's no question of such a thing, Ned! Didn't Archbishop Neville bring you a white Jervaulx stallion with red and gold caparisons to ride on to Warwick? You are our King!'

'Yes, I found my stately mount heartening at the time,' said Edward. 'It gave me the courage to carry this through. But I notice a change in the atmosphere now.' He walked across the chamber to the narrow window and considered as much of the evening as he could see. 'This room, for instance,' he said.

The room was fittingly furnished, certainly. There was a down mattress on the bed and cloth-of-gold arras round the bedstead. Woven huntsmen and hounds pursued an antlered hart round the walls on exquisite tapestries. But the size of the chamber would have been suitable for a senior steward and a man's shoulders would never go through the slim windows, and there had been guards outside the door. Edward swung round with his back to the light and stared hard at Clarence.

'The very suggestion is an insult,' said Clarence. 'People would say I had connived at murdering you to get the throne!' His voice, higher-pitched than Edward's, was outraged.

'They would, wouldn't they?' said Edward maliciously. 'You'd inherit all my debts too. I've a lot of debts, Clarence. The London merchants are willing to lend and so are some of the Continental bankers, and I use them. In addition, those who didn't care for your methods might decide to rise in favour of poor old Lancastrian Henry. You'd have Margaret of Anjou back here in five minutes. What makes you suppose you would inherit my throne, anyway?'

'You brought the subject up. I didn't.' George sat down on the bed. His hair was the very pale yellow of a newly hatched chick. 'But I suppose I'm next in line.'

'Are you? I've three healthy, legitimate daughters and for all you know, the Queen is carrying my son now. If I die, for any reason at all, you could find yourself with two sets of rivals. Lancastrian Henry, and my offspring, each with a crowd of wealthy and well-armed supporters.'

'There's no question of your death!' shouted Clarence. 'You're the King! You're my brother! How many more times?'

Edward studied him, marvelling at the phenomenon of

162

brotherhood. Himself and George and Dickon. Born of the same parents yet so individual that at times they were strangers to each other. Above all, it seemed that there was a stranger inside Clarence. Unlike Dickon, he was never content to follow. Yet he had none of the attributes of a leader, and he did not realise it.

'So this is purely a move against the Woodville clan, is it? Based on personal dislike, I take it. Neither you nor Warwick can seriously believe that even if they were once Lancastrians, they'd want to dispossess their kinswoman. Do remember, George, that the Queen is a Woodville.'

'Is she?' asked Clarence.

'And just what,' said Edward, 'do you mean by that?'

There was a silence.

'Well?' said Edward.

'You'd better know. I mean, you'd better know that I know. But I haven't told Warwick or anyone else either. Warwick dislikes and distrusts the Woodvilles, that's all. But it does make them even more of a menace, doesn't it? I mean, if they found out . . .'

'Found out *what*?' demanded Edward.

'About Mistress Butler,' said Clarence. There was another pause.

'May I ask,' said Edward at length, 'where you got your information?'

'Bishop Stillington.' Clarence rose and began to pace nervously about. 'I don't mean that he blabbed! Or only to Almighty God. I overheard him at his prayers one day. The matter seemed to be on his mind.'

There was a seat by the window. Edward sat down on it. Strangely, it was an act of aggression. It was Edward who was dominant, Clarence who flinched. It was as if Edward had said: *I may be your prisoner but I am so strong that I can sit while you loom over me and still remain your King.*

Despite the heavy walls of Warwick Castle all round him and the boots of the guards outside, it did not sound in the least ridiculous when he said aloud: 'I am your brother,

Clarence, as you keep reminding me. I recognise the claims of that relationship. But if you ever speak again, by word of mouth or in writing, of Mistress Butler, I will have your head for it.'

'My lord is preparing for a confirmation ceremony just now,' said Stillington's steward doubtfully to John Alcock.

'He'll be pleased to see me, I promise. I'm bringing good news. Perhaps you would ask him if he can spare me a moment?'

The bishop's palace at Bath was a dignified building. Once, the town had been a Roman spa and the remnants of Roman masonry were everywhere, built into nearly every edifice of note. They were in the crypt of the cathedral and the foundations of the palace, imparting strong and orderly lines to the buildings which had risen upon them. It was a great pity, thought Alcock, not for the first time, that the organisation of Stillington's household did not match its architecture. Stillington's servants never seemed to be completely under his control. The steward did not, as he should have done, say: 'Please wait, sir,' and send in a page with wine to make the visitor feel welcome while the proper enquiries were made. Instead, he said: 'If you'll come this way, sir . . .' and led Alcock straight to the bishop's sanctum. It had an outer chamber where a secretary was working, and the secretary went to make the enquiries, but within earshot of Alcock.

Dreadful! thought Alcock, *Suppose he hadn't wanted to see me?* But when the secretary came back and repeated what Alcock had already heard, that Stillington would gladly welcome him, he went through to the inner room, feeling not contempt but affection.

For even in his bishop's robes, with his crook in his hand, Stillington was always indubitably Stillington, a short round man with a face like a worried apple; intelligent enough to know the limits of his intellect; generous enough not to be jealous of the pupil who had outstripped him;

conscientious in his duties to the point of pain.

He was in fact remarkably like Alcock's own father. Alcock's father had been a burgher of the city of Hull instead of a bishop, and he had been a couple of inches taller than Stillington, but in temperament the two of them were almost twins.

'Dr Alcock! What brings you here? I have a confirmation service in half an hour, a group of young people from prominent Bath families. Is there news?'

'There is. The rising's over.'

'Over? But – Warwick? Clarence?'

'They've made peace. The family is united again, brothers and cousins arm in arm in the utmost affection, the peace of the realm assured. At a cost,' said Alcock. 'Before this happy state of affairs was reached, there were deaths. The Earls of Pembroke and Devon, the Queen's father and one of her brothers have all been beheaded by Warwick and his adherents.'

'*What?*'

'But nothing will be done about it because if the King were to retaliate, the country would be plunged back into civil war. He is not prepared to countenance that.'

'It won't be the end of it. The . . . the Queen may see matters differently.' Stillington's face was appalled. 'And she has influence with her husband.'

'Perhaps, but the Nevilles have a new link with the royal house now.'

'Clarence and Warwick's daughter? Yes, that may prove a good thing.' Stillington, faintly, preened himself. 'I helped to bring that about, you know. I helped them to obtain the Papal dispensation by advising Clarence on how best to go about it.' He thought it over and the look of satisfaction faded. 'But if the quarrel does come to a head after all, it will be a quarrel between very close relatives indeed now. That will make it very bitter. Perhaps it was unwise to encourage that marriage after all. I wish I'd asked your advice before I involved myself.'

'It never struck me as a particularly desirable marriage,' Alcock said mildly, 'but of course, I didn't foresee that Warwick would set about wiping out the King's in-laws and his major supporters! My opinion might not have been so very valuable.'

'I'm quite sure it would have been. You're much wiser than I am. It seems unbelievable to me now that I ever corrected your logic. Those days at Cambridge seem a long way off now.' Stillington sounded anguished. He was in fact thinking of another occasion when he had acted without advice, and he was wishing with all his heart that he could roll back time and eradicate that stupid, stupid deed. He had been overborne and used by a stronger personality. Stillington sometimes felt as though the world were entirely peopled by personalities stronger than himself, and Edward of York had more charisma than most.

But he did not speak of his secret to Alcock. The only safety lay in keeping it a secret, from everyone, for ever.

'My young people will be assembling,' he said. 'Would you care to attend the service?'

'With pleasure. I find confirmation services very touching. The young can be so earnest. They're like pilgrims setting out on a great journey.' Alcock was willing to change the subject, especially to a matter which appealed to him as much as this. 'They can be almost frightening,' he said unexpectedly.

'The young? Frightening?'

'So hopeful and so innocent. They have no idea what the world can do to them. I've seen it happen, Dr Stillington. I've taught young lads with promising minds, seen them begin to understand, to reach . . . and then along comes a plague or a fever, or there's an outbreak of war which unfortunately they're old enough to go to, and that's the end of it. All that promise, all that yearning intellect, just snuffed out. Girls, too. I've taught girls – I did a little private tutoring towards the end of my student days, to make a little money. Girls don't go to war, but if they survive their

166

childish illnesses and avoid the plague, they get married and die in childbirth. It's a dangerous world. We never know what God has waiting for us. The church is the only haven for those who desire an intellectual life and even then – sickness doesn't respect monasteries, or nunneries either.'

'Women on the whole aren't intellectual,' said Stillington as they moved together out into the anteroom.

'No?' Alcock was amused. 'Have you not met Lady Margaret Beaufort?'

'Lady . . .? Oh yes. Of course. She married into the Buckingham family, did she not? She's the Duke of Buckingham's aunt by marriage.'

'She's more than that,' said Alcock. 'She shares a great grandfather with that poor wan ex-king who's still living in the Tower of London, which makes her a carrier of the Lancastrian bloodline. But that's by the way. What I meant was that she has the keenest brain of any human being I've ever met, male or female. I know of few people more learned.'

'She has no children, of course,' said Stillington. 'She is coming to mind now. I've come across her at court and she stayed here once when travelling to her Devon estate. What struck me most about her was her piety. She'd have made an excellent abbess. I didn't know she was the intellectual marvel you describe. Perhaps childlessness makes a difference.'

'Possibly.' They made their way down the steps to the door which led into the cathedral. 'It must be difficult to concentrate on Latin translations when suffering from morning sickness. But she does have one child, though not by her present husband. She was married when she was only about twelve or thirteen to Edmund Tudor, and had a son by him. He didn't live to see the child.'

'Oh yes, Tudor.' Stillington paused on the stairs to shake a disapproving head. 'The offspring of another of those clandestine marriages. He was the son of Henry the Fifth's widow by that Welsh minstrel, was he not? A thoroughly scandalous business, even if the two of them were married.'

'It gave the gossip-mongers a feast,' Alcock agreed.

It certainly had, rocking the court and the country with pleasurable outrage. The Welsh minstrel, Owen Tudor, had lost his head for his presumption. But his children were legitimate and the fury of the hardheaded and status-conscious establishment had been checked by the inevitable undertow of 'Yes, but isn't it romantic?' from wives who would have liked more romantic marriages, daughters who hoped for them and aged nurses who seemed to have an inbuilt instinct to encourage such subversive longings. At any rate, the elder son, Edmund, had been given the Lady Margaret Beaufort, descendant of kings, as a bride.

'Come to think of it,' said Alcock, as they continued down to the door, 'she was nearly one of the minds lost through death in childbed. She's said to have been so badly injured by having a baby at such a young age that she has never been able to have another. It's said to be a wonder that she survived, or that the child did.'

'Where's the child now?'

'Being fostered by his father's family, I believe. How did we get on to the subject of young Henry Tudor? Oh yes, his mother's intellect. Women have it, just as much as men. They have less chance to use it, that's all. Well, here I must leave you.' Just inside the cathedral, Alcock stopped. 'You will have your preparations to make. I will join the worshippers. I will pray for your young people.'

His prayer, when he knelt to make it among the families of those to be confirmed this day, was genuine and anxious. He prayed that those who were to become full members of the church in the course of this service should be kept safe and as good Christians should live their lives out to their natural span. He was afraid that some of them would not. To Alcock, despite the present outbreak of peace, the future looked alarming.

*   *   *

168

In John Neville of Northumberland's fortress at Alnwick, the news of the peace was greeted with relief, and the details of how it had been reached with hilarity.

'Not,' said Dickon, surveying the piled bedrolls of the men whom he, John Neville, Will Hastings and Edward Brampton had mustered between them, 'that we couldn't have rescued Ned ourselves. But . . .'

'The people of London have done it for us.' Brampton had brought the news, along with his contingent of men, who were not now required but had declined to disband until, as their captains had put it, 'we're quite sure that all's settled down and as it should be.'

'Warwick never had a chance,' Brampton said. 'He has held everyone too lightly; the people of England, and all of us. That he should have you and Hastings in his very fingers and let you slip! I can hardly believe it, but it makes me laugh. And now the Londoners!'

Dickon, who on hearing Brampton's report had thrown himself into a settle to sprawl, ankle on knee and a soldierly fustian-clad arm behind his head, recapitulated between snorts of mirth. 'The fact is that Warwick and my idiot brother Clarence could hardly run a farm, let alone a country! Uproars in East Anglia, local squabbles turning into local wars just because people can get away with it, risings on the Scottish border. And when Warwick and Clarence send to London for troops, the Londoners won't let them have any without the King's authority! I should have guessed it would happen when the people I asked to loan me money sent more than I had asked for. Most people want Ned in the saddle – so, in the saddle he is! The rising must be dealt with by *his* troops, answering *his* call or there'll be no troops at all. So here we are, with Ned in command again, and he's sending us word by you that we're all to join him to escort him in state to London with Warwick and Clarence in attendance. I wonder if he's forgiven them for taking him prisoner, or did he just pretend throughout that he hadn't noticed?'

'Whichever it is,' said Brampton, 'we are all to go to London in love and friendship.' He exposed his splendid teeth in the bandit smile which instantly made people think of concealed weaponry and ransom demands. 'But for how long, all this sweetness and affection, I wonder? There are dead men to account for. And if there are fewer Woodvilles now, there are enough left to keep Warwick in mind of how he was insulted by the King's marriage.'

'I know.' Dickon sobered. He shifted on the settle, bringing both feet to the floor. He fiddled with a ring. 'I don't trust Warwick to be circumspect,' he said. 'God knows I have never liked Bess. I've tried, because Ned asked me to and John Alcock said I should as well, but I've never succeeded, and when the Desmonds were killed I saw why. Oh, I know she never meant the boys to die.' He had seen their faces, watching him, and answered the question no one had asked aloud. 'She just blundered. But that is the point. She's not great enough, not wise enough, to be fit as a queen, but just because she's small, of little account,' said Dickon disdainfully, 'she isn't worth going to war about. But does Warwick see that? Will he ever see it? I know him, you see,' Dickon added simply. 'I know him very well.'

They nodded, silently. Dickon was eighteen years old but he had spoken as though he were ten years older than that at least. They recognised the authority in his voice.

'I wonder,' said John Neville grimly. 'Yes, Dickon. I wonder about Warwick, very much.'

In a country house in Devon a woman knelt at a prie-dieu in her chamber and prayed as earnestly as Stillington or Alcock had ever done. As Stillington had said, Margaret Beaufort was pious.

She was praying for her son.

He was being fostered far away and she, sharing her second husband's life, scarcely ever saw him. Nor did she attempt to do so. That might have reminded people of his existence and that, in his mother's view, could have been unwise.

170

She never told anyone but God of the dreams she harboured for her son Henry. To do so would have been not only dangerous, but also absurd. After all, there were other members of the Lancastrian house still living: the incarcerated Henry the Sixth himself to begin with, and his own son, living in exile with his mother.

It made no difference. Margaret Beaufort considered that Henry the Sixth deserved to be locked up: he was a simpleton. As for his wife, she deserved to be in exile; she wasn't called the Bitch of Anjou for nothing. God alone knew what their son was like but with such parents he was probably either vicious or stupid or quite possibly both.

Her own boy, judging from the reports she obtained secretly with the aid of her steward, had inherited much of her intelligence, and he was also healthy. Death visited the world often and in many guises but Henry Tudor, if wisely safeguarded, stood a fair chance of outliving his rivals. If so, then the Lancastrian cause might one day be embodied in him. She thought he would be a worthy representative.

Hands clasped before the rood, she said: 'Not my will but Thy will be done,' and did not mean a word of it. *My* will, said an insistent voice in her brain. *My* will, *my* will. Oh, let my son one day live proudly and openly in the dignity and position he would grace so well. Let it be so. *Let it be so*.

She bore the name of Margaret, like the King's sister who had gone to Burgundy, and like the Bitch of Anjou whose soldiers had burned and slaughtered their way through the England whose queen she professed to be, and so earned their mistress that unenviable nickname.

Margaret Beaufort resembled neither of her namesakes. As Stillington had observed, she had the appearance, and to a great degree the interests, of a scholarly abbess. She had never led an army and she was not a queen.

But if she ever did lead men to war, she thought, they would win their battles. And if she were ever called queen, her dignity would never be assailed. What position she won, she would keep. And so, she believed, would her son.

If he lived long enough.

If ever chance, or God, or providence, gave him opportunity to show his mettle.

PART TWO
WARWICK VERSUS YORK
1469–1471

Chapter Eleven

Petronel: Joy and Fear

1469-70

Geoffrey came home in November, having gone first to London with Warwick and the King to take part in the sealing of the peace. I had worried for him and lit candles for him all through the year, and had eagerly listened to every snippet of news which reached us. I expected, when he came back, that he would be somehow surrounded by an aura of great events, and perhaps still tanned after riding with armies all through that hot summer.

But the Geoffrey who rode over from Silbeck the day after his return was pale and had lost weight. He had a slight cough too, which he said was the aftermath of a bronchial attack just before he left London. He was no godlike figure, but a tired man with a strained face, and my heart went out to him at once in a surge of tenderness. And when our eyes met, I knew that he had felt that invisible embrace. I looked quickly away.

Lionel had ordered an informal dinner round the hearth in our chamber, which was warmer than the hall. I took pains to see that it was a good meal, and not only for Geoffrey's sake. I was better now at running the house and dealing with Ralph, but Lionel was very sharp and critical with me these days. I knew why but there was nothing I could do, except try to avoid the criticism.

Our hearth was indeed warm, but on windy days, as this was, chimneys have a drawback. They could whine mournfully. 'I hate that moaning sound,' Geoffrey said unexpectedly as we ate. 'It makes me think of restless ghosts. There are some abroad in the land now, I fancy.'

'Ay, Warwick's victims,' Lionel agreed. He sang Warwick's praises much less nowadays. 'We've heard most of the news. I told you, you shouldn't have gone. Warwick's knight you may be, but to take up arms against the King . . .'

'I said to you before I left, Uncle, that we didn't think we were doing that. We knights were summoned, as we understood it, to put down a rebellion, and later we were told we were to purge the King's government. The rebels had become allies by then, which seemed odd, but we trusted Warwick. Only then he had the Queen's kin beheaded . . .'

Geoffrey's voice faded. The tautness in his face intensified. 'It wasn't for anything they'd done, you know,' he said at last. 'It was just for being Woodvilles, and – in Warwick's eyes – presumptuous. And the Earls of Pembroke and Devon were on their way to support the King when they were seized. They're dead too. Did you know?'

'Yes,' said Lionel shortly.

'I was there when Pembroke was executed.' Geoffrey said. He had been cutting meat with a knife and now he laid the knife down quickly. His gaze was fixed not on either of us but apparently on some abominable vision. 'I was on guard in his room when he wrote his last letter to his wife. He was a decent man, if foolish in some ways. It gave me no pleasure to see him turned into a headless carcase. He hadn't harmed Warwick. Warwick wasn't paying off a debt. It was just a . . . a gesture of strength, Warwick showing his power.'

I had been so glad that Geoffrey was safe, and so relieved too that I need not struggle to conceal a depth of grief to which I was not entitled. But danger lurks where one least expects it. 'Headless carcase,' said Geoffrey and instantly a hideous picture leapt into my mind, only it was Geoffrey I saw butchered instead of the unknown Pembroke. This, then, was what love did to one. I could not, apparently, hear of any man being hurt or killed without instantly

seeing him as Geoffrey. Geoffrey disfigured, maimed, ago-
nised or lifeless. I broke bread, giving my suddenly shaky
fingers something to do. I dared not meet his eyes again. I
hoped that my candles and my prayers had been part of
what had protected him throughout the war.

Lionel's voice broke harshly in on me. 'Devon and
Pembroke paid the price of stupidity. They quarrelled with
each other when they ought to have been allies. Ay, we
heard that story too. But it's no excuse for what Warwick
did, I grant you. If this peace doesn't last, what will you do
next time, lad?'

'I don't know,' said Geoffrey wearily.

'Well, take care, lad, that's all I can say. And now tell us,
through from the start, all you saw and did.'

It was not an account I enjoyed hearing. It was not only
that I now learned how grave Geoffrey's danger had been in
the fighting when the forces of Devon and Pembroke had
been decimated. That danger was past now and it was in any
case part of his calling as a knight – I knew that. But it was
the sheer nastiness of it all: the men executed who had done
no wrong, the hatred fermenting within one family to breed
such violence. I wondered where Isabel was. She was married to the King's brother Clarence. She had wanted to
marry him, I knew, but was she happy? And would I see her
again?

Well, Geoffrey was home and safe, and for the time
being the troubles were past. I fixed my mind on these facts
and later, when we had finished eating, I slipped out and
crossed the dark, windy courtyard to the chapel to light yet
another candle, this time of gratitude. When I came out
again, I found Geoffrey waiting for me.

I was not particularly afraid of the dark, not as some
people are (Isabel would never walk a yard alone after
nightfall). But tonight, with the wind moaning, and after
Geoffrey's talk of restless ghosts, there were images of fear
in my brain. The shadows in the chapel, the streaming
candle-flames and billowing door curtains had made me

unusually nervous. When Geoffrey's voice close to me said: 'Petronel!' I jumped and almost dropped my lantern.

'I'm sorry.' He emerged from the surrounding darkness. 'I didn't mean to startle you, but I saw you go out to the chapel and I wanted to speak to you alone. I've thought of you so much while I was away.'

'Oh . . . yes?' I said. I stood still, facing him, just before the chapel porch. As always, his closeness did things to my breathing and my heartbeat.

'I thought of you sometimes at the worst moments,' Geoffrey said. 'Listening to Pembroke dictate that farewell letter to his wife . . . and when I had to be part of the guard that fetched him to the block. Petronel knows nothing of all this, I said to myself. She's kind and innocent. She doesn't know what men can be like, how hungry for power and land, how ruthless.'

'Women can be like that too,' I said. 'Margaret of Anjou was. Is still, I suppose.'

'But most women aren't. And you're not. You're sweet. I let you go too easily before,' said Geoffrey.

I said nothing. I wanted to look at his face but the darkness hid it and I hadn't the courage to lift the lantern in order to see.

'That glove you gave me at Smithfield as a favour,' said Geoffrey. 'I've kept it to remind me of you, your gentleness and your virtue. You come often to the chapel, even so late?'

I clutched the lantern handle tighter, knowing that the feelings with which Geoffrey inspired me were not gentle and certainly not virtuous, but they were contained within walls of fear. I dared not tell him I had been saying a prayer of gratitude for his safe return. That would be to take a step towards him and into danger. 'I come now and then,' I said and then added what after all was true. 'I pray that I may give Lionel a son. He wants one so badly and so do I.'

'It's like that, is it?' His hands came out and closed on mine; their grip was warm and strong, too strong. The

lantern handle ground into my palm. 'Yes, I know what my
uncle can be like. Then try me, Petronel! Petra, my darling,
I came out here to ask you again what I asked you in Sir
Anthony Woodville's hall. I made up my mind I would, the
day Pembroke wrote that last letter. I need you, Petra. I
need your sweet love to cure my poisoned memories. But
now I have a new reason to ask. I can give you that son.
Then Lionel will be pleased with you, he'll be happy! Petra,
say yes!'

'I can't! How can I?' The right words came out once
again, all by themselves, even while the grasp of his hands
turned me dizzy. 'Let me go. You're holding me too tight.
The lantern handle . . .!' I gasped. He released me slowly
and I wished he had not. He had kept my glove all this time.
It made me want to sing and dance. 'You ought to marry,' I
said breathlessly. 'Surely your mother would like you to
marry?'

Alison had not in fact said so to me but apparently I had
guessed right. 'Oh yes,' said Geoffrey with wry amusement.
'She does. She even has a candidate. A nice girl, with a good
portion and no conversation. All she ever says is yes and
no.' It was the first I had heard of this girl's existence and I
felt my face turn sickly with jealousy. I was thankful that
the darkness hid me. But as though he had seen all the same,
Geoffrey said reassuringly: 'I don't want her. I want you.
You are not afraid of me, are you?'

'No,' I said shakily. I should have walked away but I
couldn't. 'Not of you.'

'Of my uncle?'

'Yes.'

'Oh, Petra. My darling,' said Geoffrey and there was a
note in his voice which was new, quite different from his
lighthearted courtship of me so far, which I now saw had
had something stylised in it, as though we were characters in
some Arthurian romance. This tone had in it something of
depth, of being shaken, and of understanding. 'Petra, my
dear love. He'd never know. I'd see he didn't. And if by

some terrible mischance he found out, do you think I wouldn't protect you?'

'You couldn't.' I knew Lionel. I was only seventeen and he was in his fifties with whole tracts of experience of which I knew nothing, but I was his wife and there were things about him which I understood very well. I knew that he would never forgive anyone who betrayed him and that he would exact payment in full. Indeed, there was something of that even in Geoffrey. He had said of Pembroke: 'Warwick wasn't paying off a debt,' as though a debt would have somehow justified a man's execution. Must I also be afraid of angering Geoffrey? 'Don't be angry,' I whispered, 'but I must go.'

But even then I hesitated, lingering, and if he had put his arms round me then, I don't know what would have happened. But he stepped back. 'Petra, my heart, I don't want you to be frightened. But my offer stands. Come to me if ever you are in trouble. Promise me you'll do that.'

'Very well. I promise. Yes,' I said, taking pleasure in saying yes to him for something, even for this feeble substitute for the thing I dared not grant. And then at last I fled, running away across the courtyard, indoors and up the stairs, in a turmoil of alarm and joy. Geoffrey wanted me still and I thought he loved me and I was full of delight. But it was only a dream and if I tried to make it real, it would soon become a nightmare. On the stairs I tried to compose myself, straightening my head-dress, slowing my steps. I walked into our chamber, outwardly calm. 'Where have you been?' demanded Lionel.

The room was ready for the night with bedcurtains looped back and candles lit. Lionel was already in his bedgown. He had been waiting by the fire. His ears were red.

'I went to the chapel,' I said warily.

'At this hour? You spend too much time in that place. Piety is all very well but you're a wife now. The nunnery's behind you. Time you realised that.'

'But I do!' I said quickly. I had never spoken much to Lionel about Withysham. Following my mother's instructions, I had either avoided the subject or else tried to give the impression that I hadn't cared for the place. 'I wouldn't want to go back to Withysham,' I said. 'I know I belong to Eynesby now.'

'But you can't stay out of that chapel, can you? What did you go there for this time?'

There was suspicion in his voice. Had he seen Geoffrey follow me out? 'I went to pray and to see that my candle, that I lit earlier, was still burning.'

'Oh yes, Father Chaplain tells me you light candles in there any time you're here and not at Middleham. I give you money so you can buy the gewgaws and trimmings women like and you throw it away on candles. What are all these candles for, hey?'

For the second time that evening, I took refuge in the truth. 'They're votive candles. I pray . . . I pray for us to have a child.'

'A child!' Lionel laughed, not at all pleasantly. 'And you think that's the way to get one, do you? On your knees in a chapel?'

'No, I mean . . . I thought it might help.'

Lionel stood up. 'You mean, I take it, that you light candles to induce God or His mother to make a better husband of me? I'm not as attentive as I ought to be. D'you think I don't know it?' I didn't know what to say and stood there looking nervously into his face. 'I suppose,' he said, 'that it never struck you that there are other ways to encourage a man that's getting older, to do his part? No, you wouldn't. You were bred for the nunnery. That's not the kind of talk the nuns encourage, is it? Well, say something!'

'I don't know what you want me to say. I don't . . . I don't understand why you're angry.'

'I'm angry because although Geoffrey's like my son to me, he's *not* my son. When I first heard he was safe and would be coming back to us, I thought, it's as though my own boy was on his way home. And then I thought, no, I just wish he were my own, because a nephew's not a son. It's not the same thing and I want a lad of my own. D'you hear me?'

'I'm . . . I'm sorry. But what can I do? I want a child too. So I light the candles and pray.'

'Try coming to bed,' said Lionel grimly. 'And let me show you what you can do.'

After three years of marriage, I had thought myself an initiate. Apparently, I was not. That night I learned for the first time of the hinterland beyond the simple sexual act, the manifold other ways by which the male half of it could be stirred.

Some of them could, with a truly desirable man (such as Geoffrey, oh Geoffrey! said my wayward imagination many times over that night), have been a joyful game.

Others could not have been anything but ugly. All in all, Lionel succeeded in climaxing twice in the course of that horrible night. Eventually, sometime in the dead hours, he grew weary, snuffed the candles and slept. I slept too, eventually. I had been physically hurt, but I was exhausted.

There was no child.

Lionel pursued this savage instruction course in the techniques of arousal intermittently over the next few months. I don't like to remember them.

Gradually, these outbursts became fewer and meanwhile I, in self-defence, learned how to forestall him, to initiate things which might arouse him without hurting or degrading me, and thus to save myself. It all died away at last. Lionel appeared to accept, though sullenly, my barren state. I gave up lighting the candles, though. That was a practice which annoyed him.

We saw little of Geoffrey and I didn't know if I were relieved or sorry. He remained chiefly at Silbeck, visiting us only at Christmas and preserving, once more, a formal standard of behaviour towards me. We heard that Warwick was making a great show of being the King's trusted cousin and brother-in-law and right-hand man, but Geoffrey chose not to join the crowd of retainers which the earl kept round him to demonstrate his importance.

Lionel worked for Middleham as usual but dealt only with such people as bailiffs, shepherds and merchants. Warwick and his family stayed away. Isabel sent for me once to join her in the south but Lionel sent word that I was unwell.

'Best stay right away from them,' he said to me, 'like my nephew's doing. We've not seen the end of this feud between Warwick and the King yet, mark my words.'

He was right. In the spring of the next year the fragile peace was broken, and this time it was Warwick who was in flight.

Chapter Twelve

The Plantagenets: A Pawn is Hazarded

1470

Warwick's ship was halfway up the English Channel, bound once more for Calais but this time with fugitives on board, when the westerly breeze turned into a gale. Warwick, denouncing the steersman as a hamfisted wantwit, wrenched the helm from him and altered course to ease the vessel's pitching, which was important.

He brought her into harbour himself. His son-in-law Clarence stood uneasily by, shrouded in a blanket against the spray. From the Tower of Rybank overlooking the harbour came a puff of smoke followed by a rush of displaced air as a stone cannonball crossed their bows and splashed into the water.

'Has the Captain of Calais gone mad?' Clarence shouted. 'You're supposed to be his Governor!'

'I think he regards Ned as the higher authority,' said Warwick grimly. They put about and withdrew beyond cannon range. The small fleet which had accompanied them caught up and he signalled them to stand off. Sea anchors were dropped and a man was ordered into a small boat to parley with the Calais garrison.

'They'll let us ashore when they understand,' said Clarence.

From the cramped cabin whose companionway was close by came sounds at which they both shuddered.

'I hope so,' said Warwick.

'We can't land but they've sent us some wine? How good of

them!' said the Countess of Warwick sarcastically. She took the small cask from the embarrassed Clarence but barred his way down to the cabin. 'This is no place for men. It's hardly a place for women either . . .' She caught at the rail as the ship heeled over in a gust. By leaving the harbour, they had exposed themselves once more to the weather. 'But we were left no choice. We should never have come. Why didn't you listen?'

'We could hardly have abandoned you in Warwick,' said her husband over Clarence's shoulder. 'You'd have been made hostages!'

'I'd rather be a hostage than see my daughter – *your* daughter! – in this state. Nothing would have happened to us. Edward is civilised. But no, you drag her half the length of England on horseback and then up the Channel in a storm when she's eight and a half months gone and . . .'

'Mother!' wailed Isabel from below. The cry ended in a miserable retch. The countess regarded her menfolk with anger: her husband wan with worry for which he was himself responsible, her son-in-law green-tinged with seasickness, offering a cask of wine extracted with difficulty from the Calais garrison as though it were adequate compensation for the mess the pair of them had created.

A couple of handsome, useless visionaries, she thought with fury. She had rebuked her daughter Anne once for criticising Warwick, but the child had clear eyes. Clearer than her father's! Warwick and Clarence had emerged from a poppy-dream of being respectively a king's sponsor and a king, to find themselves hove-to in a gale, denied admittance to Warwick's own harbour of Calais, with Isabel in labour below, crying herself into hysterics with pain and fear. 'I'm coming!' cried the countess as Isabel wailed again, and whisked down to the cabin, taking the cask. Warwick swore.

His wife's contempt angered him. He had done his best, bringing his family out of England into what he thought would be safety, now that his renewed attempt to unhorse the ingrate Edward had failed. The very thought of Edward sent rage coursing through his veins like hot mercury. He had made Ned. All he had ever asked in return was common gratitude, a little respect and a little sense of political responsibility. And what had Ned done instead? Married that woman, swamped the government with Woodvilles . . .

The ship lurched again. From below came another frantic cry.

In the cabin, Isabel crouched on all fours on the pallet which her mother had put on the floor because it was safer than the narrow bunk. Overhead the wind tore across the decks and through the rigging. The floor constantly tilted; jugs, basins and even the pallet itself slid to and fro. Isabel was not only in labour but extremely seasick. Her sister Anne squatted beside her, wiping her face with a damp cloth, offering her sips of wine or a basin as required. Across the cabin, Ankaret Twynyhoe sat on a stool, her face anxious, shearing sheets into squares of cloth and saying over and over like a litany: 'We have no hot water. It is shocking, a girl such as Isabel, so gently reared, and no hot water.' On the floor, beside Anne, crouched the countess.

She was an experienced midwife. She had helped her friends and the women about the estates of Warwick and Middleham. But for all her knowledge she had never seen such a childbed as this. In the most squalid labourer's cottage, the floor at least kept still and candles could be lit. Here the only light was from a porthole which darkened every now and then as another green wave went past, and a lantern swinging crazily from a beam. With as much assurance as possible, she said: 'Take deep breaths, Isabel. In, while I count three . . .'

The ship's stern rose crookedly and toppled half sideways as though one leg had been chopped from under a four-legged table. Ankaret went sprawling from her stool, her linen squares scattering all round her. 'Mother!'

Isabel's voice was full of panic. 'I'm going to die, I know I'm going to die!'

'You're not. Grip my hand.' Over Isabel's tangled head, the countess met the eyes of her younger girl. There was a question in Anne's gaze. *Could she die, Mother? Is that true?*

Ankaret collected herself and her linen and once more set about her task, biting her lips. She knew the answer to that silent question too.

Yes, said the Countess of Warwick's brown eyes to Anne, with truth, and fury.

The Countess of Warwick loved her husband and even now she would be loyal to him no matter how far in the wrong he put himself. But she was under no illusion. In the wrong he unquestionably was. She had watched his obsession grow, all through the winter of 1469, as Edward once more took his power to himself and more and more Warwick, who had once been his lodestar, was subjected to gentle mockery, was unobtrusively patronised and put in his place.

Edward, blandly behaving as a guest all through the time he was Warwick's captive, had made a fool of his former guardian and enjoyed it, and he didn't mean Warwick to forget it. As for the Queen, Warwick had killed her father and her brother and if no one knew what she said to Edward about Warwick at night, behind the closed doors of their bedchamber, one thing was certain: it was nothing good.

The countess had watched her husband, all winter, walking arm in arm with Edward, smiling, outdoing everyone but the King himself in the finery he wore, and seething beneath his fur-trimmed cloth-of-gold with resentment and suspicion. She had heard him afterwards, in private, raging over the subtle reminders of defeat, the offices taken from him and given, most of them, to Dickon of Gloucester instead, the amused expressions he thought he had seen on the faces of others.

And Clarence had heard him too. He had done much of

his raging directly to Clarence and their royal son-in-law had been, in the countess's opinion, much too sympathetic. Probably, she thought, because he considered that some of the offices which had gone to Dickon should have come to him instead.

There had been drinking bouts and one in particular during which, after several flagons had been emptied, they had discussed ways and means of bringing down 'our high and mighty Ned's good opinion of himself' and had somehow or other reached the unlikely conclusion that Clarence would make a better king. 'With me at your elbow and all the Woodvilles gone to the block, it would benefit the country greatly,' said Warwick virtuously.

And then, as though providence were determined to bring matters to a climax, there had come a minor outbreak of Lancastrian violence in Lincolnshire, making it possible for both Clarence and Warwick to call up their men without attracting adverse comment.

And she had not protested. Had she been wrong? She quelled panic as Isabel cried and strained. There was a bang on the cabin door. Ankaret went to it. Clarence peered in. 'How is she?' He caught a glimpse of his wife crouched like an animal on the floor, and recoiled.

'We're doing all we can,' said Ankaret, in a voice laden with dislike.

'Say . . . say to her that we're praying for her,' said Clarence and fled, gulping, whether through genuine *mal de mer* or from horror at the facts of life as presently illustrated by Isabel, was not clear.

'A pretty king he'd make!' said the countess derisively.

But the wind was easing and the wine had at least dulled the edge of Isabel's suffering. Her over-taut muscles were relaxing. Between her thighs, the baby's head appeared. 'We'll do it yet!' said Isabel's mother.

She had been wrong to keep silent. ('Push when I tell you, Isabel. Ankaret, bring those cloths here, quickly, and a towel and scissors.') Nothing had gone as Warwick intended. Edward was too strong. They had had to run and for the first time in his life Warwick, who had ordered the executions of others without hesitation, had recognised the block as a conceivable end for himself. He had wakened her in the night more than once struggling and shouting in nightmare and told her he had dreamed of his own beheading.

He was valiant in battle, she knew, but the block was the other face of violence, the cold and legal face in which death must be faced in cold blood, captive and helpless. She held him firmly until he fell asleep again. But she had known then that she had been mistaken in her silence, that she should have tried to stop him.

Except that it would have been no use. Men pleased themselves. Why waste one's breath? 'Push, Isabel. Now!' Isabel screamed. The child was expelled. 'The cloths, Ankaret!' There was too much blood. She worked furiously, directing Anne and Ankaret to see to the baby while she tended the mother. 'It's no use,' said Anne hopelessly.

'I'm afraid, madam,' said Ankaret, 'that the child is dead.'

No, it would have been no use. Lost in their obsession, neither Warwick nor Clarence would have listened. 'This is men's business,' they would have said loftily.

The Countess of Warwick took her anger and used it. Like a steel mesh criss-crossing the noisome cabin, she set it between her daughter and eternity. Here in this place, *her* will should be heard. The child was dead and beyond help but Isabel should live.

'They're in France,' said Edward, tapping the latest despatch from one of his most reliable agents, the so-called pedlar of so-called Papal pardons. 'Louis is sheltering them. They were stopped from landing at Calais but they came ashore elsewhere.'

The lines on Dickon's face were those of a man twenty years his senior. He no longer looked in the least like a

Dickon and people, tacitly, had begun to call him Richard instead. He said: 'I know you did it to quieten the north and that you gave him other honours in lieu, but I wish you had left John Neville as Earl of Northumberland and not reinstated the Percys. Neville was faithful to us all through that first rebellion. If he turns on us now, will it be surprising? He's Warwick's brother, after all.'

'I know. But the troubles in the north were working to Warwick's advantage. He could make use of them and he did. As it turned out, of course, he merely made use of the ones in Lincolnshire instead! I should have known, I suppose, that there will always be trouble somewhere! I've lost sleep over it, Richard, but it's too late now.'

'I wonder,' said Richard worriedly, 'what Warwick is doing now?'

In a spacious reception chamber in a palace at Angers, in her homeland of Anjou, a woman semi-reclined in a chair with a high, carved back. Gold braiding and gold tassels decorated the cushions on which she leaned her elbows. She was sweepingly dressed in dark red velvet with wide, hanging sleeves which revealed the tight undersleeves of another dress in blue, with gold embroidery. An acute observer might have noticed that the velvet was scuffed here and there and that the embroidery had many pulled threads, and might have deduced that although her suzerain King Louis had lent one of his own palaces to help Margaret of Anjou, he hadn't opened his purse more than absolutely necessary.

But few observers would have been sufficiently sharp-eyed. Margaret of Anjou herself would have held all their attention.

She was still not old and the plait of hair which was drawn through her stiffened head-dress was glossily black. She had a strong face, even with the vigorous eyebrows plucked out of existence. The wide nostrils and broad lips, the flawless teeth, testified to her vitality. Under the obliterated

191

brows, her eyes were amber coloured, a tigress's eyes, and her jaw had that suggestion of underhanging which imparts to a face a trace of animality and much more than a trace of sexuality.

She was enjoying herself. For the last fifteen minutes, in the presence of Louis' representatives and her own household, she had had Richard Neville, Earl of Warwick, her most implacable enemy and England's proudest lord, on his knees before her, pleading for her aid.

Chapter Thirteen

Petronel: Taking Sides

1470

The midsummer shearing in 1470 took place in a drought. After many weeks with no rain, the hillsides turned brown and the streams began to dry up. The wells held out at first and we had on our land a good spring which continued to flow, but the river was reduced to a dismal trickle among parched boulders while our ford (Lionel had never replaced Nicholas Hawes's bridge) became a stretch of cracked, baked mud with a ribbon of water across the middle. The sheep were no doubt glad to be relieved of their fleeces.

The shearing was done by co-operative effort. There were a good many men on the land of Eynesby. I had little to do with them but they mostly lived in the village and split their time between their own rented smallholdings and the Eynesby home farm. As well as our sheep pastures, we also had some fields where we grew oats and barley. Our men and those of Silbeck and Bouldershawe, and some other places in the locality, formed a band to do the shearing for each sheep-owner in turn. But shearing is hot, thirsty work and ale costs money. Lionel encouraged the men to drink the well water and I think it was because of this unusual demand that our well finally failed.

The river water was out of the question. It was trodden in by sheep and cattle and tasted abominable. We still had the spring but it was even further than the river. We tried bringing water in barrels, on a cart, but it was a great nuisance. Lionel became impatient. 'We should pipe the spring water to the house. That's the modern way.' In order to be modern and one up on his neighbours, he was prepared to spend good money. He sent word to York and three days later Robert Welton, Master Founder, put in an appearance.

He came with a team of three men who were instantly set to making a survey. Welton himself, a dour-faced individual with a completely expressionless voice, repaired to the hall with us for food and drink. Geoffrey, who had heard of the proposed installation, had come over to be present. He had not renewed his siege of me but I had sometimes thought he was on the verge of doing so, and from the way he kept glancing at me, I suspected that he might have it in mind now. I half wanted it to happen and half feared it and did not know whether to be thankful or resentful because no opportunity presented itself. We were all nailed in our places as Robert Welton's audience. Welton apparently liked to hear the sound of his own monotonous voice. We listened for an hour while he talked of droughts past and present and the science of plumbing, and consumed ham patties and the best ale, which Lionel had told me to bring out for him. After enough of the ale, he became gossipy.

'Drought's bad for business some ways but does it good in others. There's folk like you, need to better their water supply. Then there's others complaining their pipework's gone wrong. It's the water that's dried up, but it's easier to blame the man who put the pipes in than it is to blame God. Worst bit of trouble I've had lately's had nowt to do wi't'weather, though. I had a big contract on one of Sir John Neville's Yorkshire estates cancelled. Now that were a bad loss, though maybe I should have expected it, seeing how things are.'

'And how are they?' Geoffrey enquired.

Robert Welton looked at the questioning expressions on all our faces with evident surprise. 'You've not heard?'

'Heard what?' said Lionel.

'Why, John Neville's lost t'earldom of Northumberland, that's what's happened! Oh, he's got some other fine-sounding title but it don't carry the income t'old one did. He's not half so wealthy now as he was and I'm not the only one to lose business through it.'

'But why did he lose the earldom?' asked Lionel. 'Did he offend the King? He took King Edward's part last year, even against his own brother.'

'Aye, he did that,' Welton said. 'He gave no offence, no. It was to keep t'north quiet, they say. Harry Percy has Northumberland now, which is what the folk of Northumberland are supposed to want. The King most likely thought to get some peace up there that way. A mistake, that's what a lot of folk think.'

'A mistake? An outrage!' Geoffrey had gone scarlet. He banged a hand flat on the table in front of him. 'If Neville backs his brother now against the King, who'll blame him? He's had a near princedom grabbed from him and for no fault! If he wants payment for it, who'll be surprised?'

We were interrupted then by Welton's men coming back with a problem for their master to solve. But the next day, Geoffrey rode over from Silbeck again. Standing in the middle of our hall, his face shiny from the heat of the ride across the sweltering valley, he told us: 'Warwick's in exile now, but if he makes some move or other – and somehow I think he will – then his men will be called to arms. I've been wondering what I'd do if so. Now I've decided.'

'There's nowt to decide,' said Lionel sharply. 'In the spring you had sense enough to have a bad cough when the summons came. You stayed away and you were right. It was the same trick that Warwick played before: calling men to arms to put down a rebellion and then, when they answered, using them to create one. This time, most of them were glad enough to creep away home when Warwick ran for it, because most of them were none so keen on being caught up in treason. If he calls for them again, to join him in France, that will be treason just the same.'

'I wasn't thinking of going to France.'

'Ah, now you're talking sense.' Lionel was relieved.

'You'll be volunteering to fight for Edward.'

'No,' said Geoffrey, 'John Neville.'

We all stared at him. 'If Warwick calls for his men,' said Geoffrey, 'he'll call on his brother John Neville too. It will be for Sir John to decide whether he supports Warwick or the King. He's had provocation enough to make him back his brother this time. I propose to let him decide for me as well. If Sir John calls for his men, I shall offer my sword to him. I'm a Neville man – I'll have changed Nevilles, that's all. And where this one goes, I'll follow.'

Lionel looked at him disparagingly. 'Why don't you just toss the dice and be done with it?'

'I considered it,' said Geoffrey wryly. 'The thing is,' he explained, 'that staying out of it's no good to me. I'm a knight, it's my business to be in the fight, but how to take sides in this is beyond me. It's not as clear-cut as it was, not since John Neville was robbed of his earldom. If he's faithful to the King, even after Northumberland, I'll respect that. If he deserts him for Warwick, I'll respect that too.'

'You'd do better to keep right out of it,' said Lionel shortly. 'But since you clearly won't, all I can say is, God go with you, and let's hope it never happens.'

It did, of course, but other things happened first. One of them was that the shearing ended and the wool was packed on to the sweating backs of packhorses and we went south with the wool train. This time, Lionel took me with him. It was the dying phase of his violent determination to get a son by any means. He would not let me be apart from him for a single night. In the July of that year, I found myself once again in London.

One of our first engagements in London was to dine with the merchant family we had visited when Lionel first took me to the city after our marriage. We had seen them when we came south for the Smithfield tournament too. Lionel considered it important to keep up his acquaintanceship with the Halford household, for they were the centre of a powerful social web. They had an immense number of friends among merchants, courtiers, knights, landowners and the like, and if you knew the Halfords, you stood a chance of making useful acquaintances of your own.

In fact, Master Halford did not at all mind acting as an introduction broker. I knew that Lionel had on occasion asked if such and such a man, whom he wished to meet 'accidentally', could be invited at the same time as himself, and it was done. A good deal of business was transacted in Master Halford's hall, and political plots had been known to be hatched across his dinner table.

This time, Lionel sent Master Hardynge, our secretary, to the house with a polite notification that we had arrived and, with their permission, would wait upon the Halfords shortly. Hardynge reappeared an hour later with the news that the Halfords had expected to learn that Lionel was in London, were delighted to hear that Mistress Eynesby was with him, and wished to invite us both to a river party to be held the following week, weather permitting. If it did not, then the party would be at the house.

The drought had broken while we were on our way south, but the sunshine had resumed by the time we reached London, and was all the more pleasant because the air and the city streets had been washed by rain. It stayed clear, and on the appointed evening we were welcomed aboard a moored barge close to the Halfords' private landing stage.

It was a calm, lovely evening. Upstream, to the west of us, the river was like liquid gold in the declining sun. In the other direction, the City with its spires and gables looked very beautiful, fretting the sky-line. I remarked on it. 'Yes, I love my city viewed in this fashion,' said Master Halford, handing me to a seat amid a pile of embroidered cushions. 'From here you can't hear it and you can't smell it. Do you have something to put round your shoulders? We shall have a little breeze on the river towards nightfall. May I say what a delightful gown you're wearing.'

I was a disappointment to Lionel in many ways, but I had

learned to do him credit in public and on his side, he saw to it that my clothes were suitable. The gown was brocade, pink with silvery green leaves woven into it. Kat and I had made it up during the last few days, having brought the material with us from the north but waited to observe the London fashions before using it. It was an elaborate design and had meant a good deal of work, but that was intentional on my part. Kat was pining over one of the Bouldershawe men who had come to help with the shearing. He had led her on to believe that he was single and I had had a most exhausting session with her when she learned that he was married. She had cried bitterly for two days and been unable to do any work at all. I was glad that we were coming to London with Lionel since it would be a distraction for her, and I had made a special point of keeping her busy.

Now I gave Kat a smile as she handed me the wrap she was carrying for me, and said: 'The gown is mostly my maid's work; she is a very gifted needlewoman, Master Halford,' and arranged my skirts gracefully. Kat withdrew to sit among the attendants of the other guests, though she remained within call. She looked pleased with my compliment and I hoped she would soon get over her unhappy romance.

Lionel had been seated at a distance from me too. Other guests were now coming aboard and I found that my immediate neighbour was to be a large, amiable, fresh-faced cleric called Dr Alcock. 'Dr John Alcock, to be precise,' said Master Halford, introducing us. 'Dean of St Paul's and Privy Councillor . . .'

'But quite human and easy to talk to, I assure you,' said Dr Alcock, lowering himself heavily on to his cushions. 'Why do you like these al fresco affairs so much, Halford? I'd prefer a settle. It will take two men to pull me up when it's time to go, I warn you.'

'You can have half a dozen if you like,' said Master Halford, laughing, and moved away to introduce Lionel to the man who was about to take a seat beside him.

'Who is that with my husband?' I asked Dr Alcock. 'Over there. He doesn't look English.'

He certainly didn't. I was glad I had Dr Alcock next to me and not Lionel's neighbour for the latter looked like nothing so much as a foreign cut-throat, and the fact that he was most fashionably dressed only made his face worse by contrast. Dr Alcock said: 'He isn't English. I mean he wasn't born here, he was born in Portugal, but he's legally English and he's taken the name of Edward Brampton. I know, it seems a most unlikely name for a face like that, but he is really most respectable, a successful merchant and a loyal personal friend of the King. If you get to know him, you'll probably like him.'

Lionel appeared to be liking him already. Master Halford had left them together and they were deep in talk. I wondered what it was about. Brampton did not seem the kind of man to be enthralled by sheep. It would be politics or money, I supposed. Refreshments were brought and the minstrel who was a permanent member of the Halford household strolled about with his lute and began a song.

'That's a popular air round the court just now,' Dr Alcock told me. 'It's about the adventures of Sir Gawaine, one of King Arthur's knights. Do you ever wish you were a man, Mistress Eynesby, and free to go on adventures? Would you enjoy them, I wonder, or would you be afraid?'

I looked at him in astonishment because he sounded as though he really wanted to know. 'I've never thought about it,' I said at last. The only adventure I had ever been offered, I had refused out of fear. But that was fear of Lionel. Green knights and dragons seemed harmless by comparison. One would not have to live with them for ever, after all.

And of course, behind Lionel had been the demons of hell, which Aunt Eleanor believed to be a real peril awaiting sinners. I had thought less along those lines of recent years; Withysham was slipping into the past and doing so all the faster because I never talked about it. Father Edmond at

Eynesby did not preach much on the subject of hellfire either. But something of Aunt Eleanor still remained.

Dr Alcock was still looking quizzically at me, as though he expected me to say something further. 'I think,' I said slowly, 'that it would depend on whether it was a good adventure or a bad one.'

'And by that, what do you mean, exactly?' he prompted.

'I think I mean I'd be more willing to take a risk for a good cause than for something I knew was wrong. One's soul wouldn't be in peril then, whatever other perils there were.' I sounded prim and knew it, and there was an uncomfortable amusement in Dr Alcock's eyes. They were blue and at first glance had a boyish, limpid expression but when you studied them more carefully, you saw how keen they were.

'Edward Brampton,' he said, 'is a convert. He was not born into the Christian faith. He was originally a Portuguese Jew. He found when he came to trade in London that more favourable terms were available for those who were baptised. Are you shocked?'

I was. Aunt Eleanor would have said that such a man was not worth trusting, that to sell one's faith for gain was the shabbiest form of dishonesty, but Dr Alcock evidently liked Edward Brampton. I did not answer.

Dr Alcock obligingly did so for me. 'You are thinking that such a man might do anything for profit, that he would engage in any adventure, however dubious, if he thought there might be money in it.'

'I . . . I shouldn't say such a thing.' I wondered how this topic had come up. On the face of it, it seemed to be an unexpected change of subject, yet I knew that it was not.

'You wouldn't say it, but you're thinking it. And you are surprised that I, a man of the Church, don't hold the same opinion. The answer is that I am older than you and have a wide experience of human nature. I understand Brampton. He is a man who is not able to give his allegiance to a spirit he cannot see, but that doesn't mean that he has no allegiance to give to anyone. He is the King's man to the death. He owes all his present prosperity to King Edward's sponsorship at the time of his conversion and patronage since. He would enter into no adventure to King Edward's hurt, and into any at all that would assist him, whatever the danger.' He smiled at me, kindly, but with an expression in his eyes as though they were trying to bore into me. 'I wonder,' he said gently, 'if even in a good cause, you would be willing to risk yourself as Edward Brampton would. Is your allegiance the match of his, I wonder? Or is the despised convert perhaps, in this, the better of the two?'

I was embarrassed and also indignant. I had been made to feel young, silly and boastful, but I had been asked questions I could not answer. 'How can I tell?' I asked and heard the anger in my voice. 'No one would ask me to ride into battle. I'm Mistress Eynesby, not Edward Brampton. I hope I would try to serve the King, if I were asked, in any way that was right and proper. I hope I wouldn't be too timid to face any dangers that were involved. But I don't know. I can't know. Forgive me, Dr Alcock, but you are not being fair.'

One's instinctive knowledge of other people is a curious thing. I would never have said that to Lionel. It would have been no use. He would never admit that he was unfair, however true it might be, and the accusation would only make him angry. But Dr Alcock laughed and said: 'You are wise after all. That was a very good answer,' and I realised that I had known beforehand that it was a safe answer to make to him.

The minstrel had begun another song. 'We are belittling this excellent singer,' said Dr Alcock, 'by not attending to him. Let us do so. I think he's about to serenade you.'

The King's messenger, who arrived early the next morning, did not look like a royal servant. He was a plainly dressed man who could have been anyone and he travelled in an ordinary hired boat. Lionel had as usual taken lodgings by the river, which was the City's great thoroughfare, and they had a landing stage entrance.

I was in our chamber on the upper floor, taking Kat to task for her still distracted frame of mind and an item of poor work, although not too unkindly for she had done well with the new gown and I had an uncomfortable feeling that I had been remiss. Before we left Faldene, my mother had told me that it was my responsibility to look after Kat and in due course find her a husband. I had not done so and this unhappy romance of hers was the result.

'When we get home to Eynesby,' I told her, 'I shall see about getting you settled in life. Now, Kat, don't cry. You must marry someone, and you will find that once you have a future to think about, the past will matter less. I have your happiness at heart, but in the meantime, I really must insist that you try to attend to your work . . .'

I broke off as Lionel came up the stairs two at a time. 'Petra, where are you? Ah, you're here. Get thy best dress on.' When he was excited, his Yorkshire accent always became stronger. 'The brocade you wore yesterday will do. Kat, fetch it to your mistress and the jewels to go wi' it. We're bidden to Westminster, an audience with the King, no less.'

'What, now?' I said, astonished. 'But it isn't yet eight in the morning!'

'Aye, now and we've our escort waiting. Thee'll want a clean head-dress, summat smart, and a cloak, you're to wear a cloak . . .'

'But it's already hot!'

'You've not to look conspicuous. Hurry, hurry! It's the King, girl! You want to keep him waiting?'

'But what's it all about?'

'You'll see! Are your hands clean? Your shoes? But hurry!'

In a flurry of contradictory instructions, I dressed in the brocade, buried it under a cloak, made myself clean and tidy so rapidly that I left a basin of water standing and a damp towel on the floor, and clattered down the stairs after Lionel to join the unobtrusive messenger and board the boat, which had waited. Kat did not come with us. We were set down at Westminster's tradesmen's landing stage and taken in at a side door. We climbed a spiral stair and were shown into a room, not very large and in no way remarkable, except for the beauty of the two carved settles and the table which furnished it, and the glowing softness of the rose and azure oriental carpet which hung upon one wall.

There were two men in the room already. One was Edward Brampton, who came forward to take my cloak. The other was King Edward himself.

I had seen him from a distance at the Smithfield tournament and at Sir Anthony's Woodville's banquet afterwards, but never face to face like this before. He was not at all intimidating. He stood up as I entered with Lionel, and shook his head with a smile as I started to sink into the usual curtsy.

'Master and Mistress Eynesby? Be seated, both of you.'

His voice was a little like Geoffrey's and I remembered with astonishment that they were actually half-brothers. I always did feel astonished when I thought about this; it seemed so improbable that anyone one actually knew should be related to the King. Apart from the voices, their hazel eyes were their only real similarity. Both had height and fairness, it was true, but they took these things from their respective mothers not from the father they shared who, according to Alison, had been short and dark. King Edward's hair was quite different in shade and texture from Geoffrey's and his flat, high cheekbones gave his face a handsomeness all its own. Geoffrey's looks were based on the moulding of flesh, not bone.

Perhaps one could say that they shared a love for fine clothes, though. Even at this hour in the morning, Edward was sartorially splendid, and that was also a characteristic of Geoffrey.

We sat down, as bidden, side by side on one of the carved

203

settles. Edward clapped his hands and a page came in with a tray of refreshments. When the page had gone out again, Edward came straight to the point, and he addressed his words not to Lionel but to me.

'Mistress Eynesby, I believe you were once an attendant on the Lady Isabel, now the wife of my brother of Clarence. And I also believe that not long ago she asked you to come to her again. You could not do so because you were unwell. Are you quite recovered now?'

I dared not glance at Lionel for instructions on how I should answer. Edward had spoken directly to me and therefore expected his answer to come from me. 'Yes, my lord, I am quite well now.'

'I'm glad of that.' He sounded as though he were really glad, for reasons of kindness and not only on account of the ulterior motive which he quite obviously had, although what it could be I could not imagine. 'The source of my information,' he said, 'was Dr John Alcock, whom you met yesterday. Dr Alcock makes it his business to know many things and to discover things too, at my request. He suggested your name to me and Master Brampton here, who knows Master Halford, arranged for you all to come together at the river party last night.'

I was bewildered. I did at this point glance towards Lionel and was interested to see that he was not at all surprised. So he knew what this was about.

'At the party,' said Edward, 'you expressed the opinion that you might be willing to engage in an adventure in a good cause. You did not then know that such an adventure might be offered to you. But if it were and you accepted it, I would be grateful, and there would be a reward. And I believe that you, Master Eynesby, indicated to Brampton that you would consent, if I asked your wife to act as my emissary.'

'But emissary to whom, my lord?' I found my tongue. 'To Lady Isabel?'

'No, to my brother Clarence,' said the King.

I waited.

'He and Isabel are now in Calais,' said Edward. 'They are based there while Warwick matures his plans. As far as I can ascertain, those plans don't please Clarence overmuch. Originally, you see, Warwick's scheme was to dethrone me and put Clarence in my place. However, he can't hope to do that now without backing from somewhere and the backing he's after is that of Margaret of Anjou. And in that case, the bait will be the reinstatement of her husband on the throne, which will cut out Clarence.'

'The reinstatement of Henry the Sixth?' I exclaimed. I was startled. Like everyone else I knew, I was used to regarding the former King as a cipher. In fact, I had had a vague idea that he was dead.

'Yes, the halfwit,' said Edward dispassionately. 'Their son is in exile with his mother and would become the heir.' Suddenly he grinned. 'There'd be no room at all for Clarence; he'd have to be content with being a loyal duke. I gather he's annoyed. He's ripe for persuasion back into the family fold. Isabel is of the same mind, and she's more afraid of me than of her father, I gather. She'll help. But I need to be in touch with them. I want you to do that for me. I want you to go to Calais and offer my terms to Clarence.'

'*Me?* But I've no experience, I . . . wouldn't a man . . .?'

Edward shook his head. 'No. First of all, I need someone who looks harmless and innocent and won't easily be suspected of political motives. You are a lady-in-waiting seeking to rejoin the mistress you're fond of. You weren't well enough to go when she first sent for you. Now you can travel, and so you're answering her summons. It will seem perfectly natural. Secondly, I want someone who can talk to Clarence with the voice of the family, of home and domesticity, someone who can speak convincingly of brotherly love. Women do that far better than men. Well, Mistress Eynesby? Will you do it?'

It was plain enough that he had spies in the Clarence household already, I thought, but perhaps they were employed there as servants who would have no opportunity to talk persuasively to their employers. I thought about it while Edward sipped wine, refilled my goblet and Lionel's in the most casual and un-royal manner – the perfect host. Once Lionel made as if to speak but Edward silenced him with a gesture. Brampton ate a sweet cake and said nothing either, but I felt his dark, un-English gaze on me.

'Must I go alone? Without my husband?'

'You'd have a proper escort and could take a maidservant, but not Master Eynesby, no. It will look more innocent without him.'

Regrettably, my first thought then was: I shall get away from Lionel.

Lionel said: 'I've given my consent, Petra.'

'It's your consent we need now,' said the King.

Brampton, who was seated at the far end of the King's settle, stirred. 'You need feel no diffidence, Mistress Eynesby. It's not political negotiation that we need.' His English was accented but clear. 'This is a domestic appeal from one brother to another. You would speak to Clarence as any woman might who was trying to mend a quarrel within her own family.'

'It's a great honour, Petronel, to be asked to help the King,' said Lionel.

I saw that whatever my own feelings, I must consent or he would never let me forget it. And for the duration of my mission, *I would get away from Lionel.* Edward did not know it but he couldn't have offered me any greater inducement. I swallowed once, and then nodded.

There were instructions: what to say, what to do. I had to commit a message to memory. 'Nothing must be put in writing,' Edward said, 'and you must be careful to make sure that no news of your activities reaches Warwick. He would put a stop to them if they did. In particular, conceal them from the governor of Calais, Wenlock. He wouldn't let Warwick land when he first fled the country but he's harbouring the Clarences now and that means he's not trustworthy. Beware of Wenlock. There are others you can trust.' He gave me some names. Then he nodded to Brampton, who went out and came back presently accompanied by Dr Alcock and a shabbily dressed man who appeared to be Alcock's protégé but was a most unlikely person to encounter in the presence of a king. He was introduced to me by Alcock as 'Peter the Pardoner.'

I had been told by Aunt Eleanor how to regard itinerant sellers of pardons. 'They are a plague in society. They pretend to sell the absolution of the church. Buy one of my prettily lettered pardons, they say, and free yourself from your sins. No one can forgive sin but God, my child, through the intermediary of one of His ordained priests. You can't buy absolution with money, only with repentance.'

This example of the breed had gap-teeth and the kind of superficial boldness which dissolves into cringing at a moment's notice. But he did not cringe at the sight of the King. Apparently, they knew one another.

'Mistress Eynesby,' said Edward, 'I want you to look well at Peter here. I want you to be able to recognise him again. You won't see him again on this side of the Channel but when you have been in Calais for a while, he'll find his way to you. Leave that to him. He will carry Clarence's answer back to me. You will remain with Isabel for some months – best of all, until she returns home with her husband to be received by me.' He turned to the pardoner. 'Peter, this is Mistress Eynesby. You in turn will need to know her again.'

'I'll do that, my lord.' He was studying my face as I was studying his. 'I wish you luck, mistress,' he said seriously. 'And I'll be in touch in Calais.' He gave me a grin like a broken fence. 'And if you sin in carrying out your task, I'll give you a pardon for nothing.'

Brampton laughed and Alcock said: 'He's incorrigible, I'm afraid,' in a voice of mock despair. He took the pardoner out again.

207

As we ourselves were leaving, after a few more instructions, Brampton drew Lionel aside and the King came close to me. 'Are you sure you are willing to do this, Mistress Eynesby? You're very young. I didn't realise how young, till I saw you.'

'I'm willing to try, my lord.' I was indeed young. I was even now thinking in terms of a journey to Calais and a few blessed months without Lionel. 'I may not succeed,' I said anxiously, 'but of course I will try.'

'If you even make him wobble towards me, it would help. But be careful. I saw you admiring my wall carpet when you first came in.' I blinked at the *non sequitur*. 'It's made of silk,' he said, 'a myriad myriad tiny knots. Children make them; only children's fingers are delicate enough. Hour after hour, day upon day, herded into sheds, they knot silken carpets for the walls of the wealthy. They never play. They tie knots until their childhood is gone and their eyesight with it. We live in a savage world. Your youth, your sex, may not protect you. I want you to be discreet not only for my sake but for your own safety. That is why I am not giving you a written letter to carry and why I urge you to send nothing in writing back. Word of mouth only is safe.' His eyes and his voice were worried, kind. 'I need you,' he said, 'but by God, I wonder if I should send you.'

'But my lord, surely Warwick would not . . .'

'Harm you? A young woman he has met, who has eaten his salt and served his daughter and perhaps exchanged good-day with him now and then? No, perhaps not, but he is suing for a partnership between himself and the Bitch of Anjou, and that woman,' said Edward grimly, 'stops at nothing. Petronel – if I may call you that – take care.'

I didn't understand. I had only, I thought, to join my mistress Isabel and achieve two conversations without being overheard, one with Clarence and one with the pardoner. It sounded neither difficult nor dangerous and – again the thought came joyfully to me – I would escape from my husband. Nothing but a direct order from the King would ever, I knew, have induced him to let me go out of sight, induced him to surrender for the time being the chance of getting a son. It was good fortune undreamed of.

And if it were not, even if I had not wished to go, I still would not have dared refuse. Lionel would never forgive me if I put him in bad odour with the King.

'I will take care,' I said, 'but I am willing to go, my lord.'

'Lionel Eynesby,' said Edward as my husband and Brampton came up, 'you are the husband of a most valiant lady. I hope you realise it.'

Chapter Fourteen

The Plantagenets: A Pawn is Advanced

1470

The waters of the Loire were smooth, like warm silk under the summer sky. The wake of the official barge, on loan from King Louis, stretched out in a long, v-shaped wrinkle.

'If you look ahead,' said the Countess of Warwick to Anne, 'you can see Amboise Castle. It is supposed to be very beautiful.'

Her voice was more than slightly brittle. Anne studied her mother's face thoughtfully before transferring her gaze to the slim, airy turrets of the castle ahead. 'And King Louis has lent it to Margaret of Anjou just as he's lent this boat to us. She's his pensioner really, isn't she?'

'That's an unsuitable attitude, Anne. Please moderate it.' The countess's face was shadowed by the orange awning which kept off the late July sun, but Anne thought that her mother had flushed angrily. 'Your father hopes that Margaret of Anjou will shortly be reinstated in England as its queen, at King Henry's side. In that case you, as her daughter-in-law, will be a future queen yourself. Disparaging remarks about the people who will bring you these honours are not becoming.'

'I'm sorry, Mother,' said Anne. It was a lie. She wasn't sorry at all.

She watched the turrets of Amboise come nearer and thought of her recent parting from her father, and wished he had not on that day been so exactly the same as he had always been. She would feel less anguished now if only the sun-god she had once worshipped were not still so outwardly godlike.

He had gone away on a dangerous enterprise. Knowing that, she had wept a little in their parting embrace. But in the interests of that enterprise, he was handing her into the power of Margaret of Anjou and into the power also of an unknown youth she had never heard of until now: Edouard, the son of Margaret and her dethroned husband, the ex-king Henry. Anne was afraid of them both.

And her father must know it. He knew Margaret's reputation, but he had placed his daughter at her mercy without hesitation. She remembered how, as they rode out of Warwick Castle to Isabel's wedding, she had taunted Isabel by telling her that she was only a pawn. Only now did she understand what that really meant.

Isabel was not here with her. She and Clarence were in Calais and when, in due course, Clarence sailed to join Warwick in the invasion of England, Isabel would remain there. Anne had started this journey missing her sister. Now she was glad that Isabel was not here to observe her fear and to pity her.

The boat pulled in towards a landing stage. At close quarters the castle was undoubtedly lovely, a place of slender pillars and tall tapering arches, wide, gracious staircases, turret casements. It was a fit habitation for a fairy princess. How very unfortunate that it was more likely to contain an ogress.

The countess reached a hand to her daughter. 'We have arrived. Come.'

Anne shivered. How she had sensed it, she could not have told, but she knew her mother was frightened too.

Her own dread was mixed with anger. She remembered how her father had come back to Rouen, where he had left his wife and younger daughter under Louis' protection, and told them that he had laid to rest all his old differences with Margaret of Anjou. He who had laboured to throw her husband off his throne and install Edward the Fourth on it instead would now, with King Louis' help, undo his mistake. Edward should be cast down and Henry returned to

212

his rightful place. Then Henry ('He's just a gentle madman and fonder of his chapel than his council chamber,' her cousin Dickon had once told her) would reign once more in England with Queen Margaret beside him. Their son, aged sixteen and known in the French fashion as Edouard, would be their heir. And Anne – 'my dearest daughter' – said Warwick lyrically, should marry Edouard and one day be his queen. A betrothal ceremony had already been held at Angers Cathedral, he said, at which he had made the commitment on her behalf. Was she not overjoyed?

They were being taken into the castle. There were people bowing and staring. They followed a liveried guide up some steps and into a lofty chamber. Warm water would be brought and their baggage carried in, he said. Presently they would be conducted to Her Grace, Queen Margaret . . .

'We shall be honoured,' said the Countess of Warwick with most unwonted meekness.

Her mother's congratulations, that day in Rouen, had been so extremely conventional that her misgivings had been obvious to Anne at once. Clearly, nothing had happened since to relieve them. And now they were here, in Margaret's very clutches. In Anne's vitals, what had been a dull ache of dread became a twist of sheer white terror.

Her father had had no misgivings. He had actually seemed to expect her gratitude. At some point during that Angers meeting, Richard Neville, the devoted father, and Richard of Warwick, the slighted earl, had succeeded in locking themselves into the united belief that Anne's welfare and her father's were one and the same thing.

But what it came to in the end was that she was part of a deal, the daughter-to-be-queen, replacing Isabel now that it seemed that Clarence had neither the stature nor the luck to make a ruler. Warwick had offered Margaret of Anjou his support in return for her support, but Anne's advancement was part of the price Margaret must pay for her throne – and also, as Anne had very soon realised, for having made Warwick plead on his knees before she would make terms with him.

Now, as they made ready to meet their hostess, soft summer airs blew in through the window and there were swifts in the bright sky outside. It was hard to believe that out there, in the shining world, what had begun as an internal squabble in England between the Woodvilles and Nevilles had now become Warwick against his King, and that her father was about to set sail for England with an invasion force of Anjou mercenaries and his own followers combined. What if her father were killed or taken and . . . and . . .?

She dared not think of that. She must remember that her father's success – his survival – went hand in hand with this marriage. She was angry with him but not for anything in the world would she see him harmed. She must accept this marriage. She must force herself to it.

Their ladies had followed them up from the barge. 'Mother,' she said as one of them knelt to adjust her skirt hem and another knotted an ornate girdle round her hips, 'do you know very much about Edouard? My father said he hadn't met him. But you must have enquired . . .' Her voice trailed off.

'I understand he's healthy and well-educated. Very much like any other young man of good family,' said the countess austerely. 'You'll see for yourself today. You're fortunate. Many girls have no chance to get to know their husbands until after they're married to them. Are you ready? Someone is tapping at the door.'

A very dignified usher led them down to the great hall. An avenue of attendants in livery – it was King Louis' livery, not Anjou's – lined a path to the dais and, there, seated in a vast chair, was a magnificently dressed woman. A saturnine cleric in a dark gown stood beside her, and on a smaller chair on her other side sat a youth. Anne went down into a curtsy at the woman's feet. Above her head, she

214

heard the usher presenting them. Her mother said: 'You may rise, Anne.' She did so.

'So this is Anne,' said the woman on the dais.

Anne tilted back her head and looked into the face of the Bitch of Anjou, whose men had fought her father's men the length and breadth of England for the right to rule the country when King Henry could rule no longer, the woman who had ordered her men to burn and pillage, and had dishonoured an enemy's body.

Till now, in the back of her mind had been a tiny hope that perhaps the tales about Margaret of Anjou were exaggerated. Now she knew that the hope was vain. There was not a soft line in the face of the woman before her, not a sign of a smile in the amber eyes; nothing but dislike and contempt, and behind them, the dreadful backing of superior power.

She knew why the dislike and contempt were there. To Margaret, Warwick was a foe who had once injured her beyond bearing, by masterminding her defeat. That she must now owe her hopes of rehabilitation to him made him more, not less, detestable. The daughter he had forced on her as part of the transaction was damned automatically for being his daughter at all.

She looked away from Margaret, glanced at the cleric and then stared at the youth, only to be confronted at once by another pair of amber-tawny eyes and another hard, if younger, face in which all the lines were straight; brow, mouth, and precisely centred nose. She did not need to ask if this were Margaret's son. He stared back, but he did not smile, any more than his mother had.

Her own mother was being beckoned on to the dais, given a seat, introduced to the cleric, whose name was apparently Dr Morton. Now Margaret was turning to the youth. 'Edouard, I present to you the Lady Anne Neville, your betrothed, daughter of the Earl of Warwick. No doubt you will wish to talk with her. Take her to see your Battle Room.'

215

'Battle Room?' Anne ventured, as Edouard left the dais and jerked his head for her to follow him. A page and two women attendants accompanied them, the page darting ahead to open doors.

Edouard did not deign to reply until they were out of the hall and crossing an outer chamber. Then he said: 'In here,' as the page threw back a door on the far side. 'It's a way to study strategy,' Edouard explained stiffly.

The room into which he led her was limewashed stone, empty but for an enormous table in the middle. On it, a model landscape had been made. Hills had been fashioned of moulded tin, painted green. There were tiny wooden trees and gates, carved sheep and cattle. There were also some lengths of metal which puzzled Anne until she saw that they represented rivers. And there were whole regiments of painted metal men and horses.

'That's the Battle of Towton,' said Edouard, his voice a clipped tenor, 'where my father lost his crown. I go through it often. Other battles too, of course, but this one most frequently. I try to see what we should have done to win. When I go back to England as its heir, if I have to fight any battles, I intend to win them.' His expression dared her to exchange 'when' for 'if'. 'And when I've won,' he said, 'those enemy leaders who aren't killed fighting, I shall have beheaded in front of me. Have you ever seen a beheading? I have. It was exciting. If you displease me when we're married, I shall have you beheaded too. Why do you keep looking at me like that?'

'Like . . . like what?'

'As if I were an animal in a menagerie. It's rude.'

'I'm sorry,' said Anne, taken aback. Once, when in London with her parents, she had seen the Tower menagerie. The panthers and lions had stared at her with inhuman tawny eyes as if wondering how she would taste. Edouard and his mother reminded her of them and her face had apparently mirrored her thoughts with remarkable fidelity. Her apology stumbled. 'I . . . I didn't mean . . .'

'You did mean! You're still doing it!' His voice rose. 'You're being rude deliberately. How dare you? I shall make you a queen one day, if you behave. You're supposed to respect me. How dare you look at me like that?'

Anne gaped at him and then the latent anger in her flared. 'All right then, I'm not sorry! You're going to make me a queen? My father will have to put your parents on the throne first and without his backing they won't get there. Your mother's a long way yet from being a queen. Real queens don't wear dresses all frayed at the hem. I saw when I curtsied to her. So perhaps you'd better respect me a little bit, too!'

His big-knuckled boy's hand shot out and gripped her forearm. His other hand came up with a two-inch-high silver-painted knight in it. The knight carried a lance like a sharp needle. The needle advanced slowly, glittering, towards Anne's eyes. She screamed and kicked his shins. None of the attendants waiting by the door moved to help her. She struck out with her free hand and the needle scored a line of blood along the back of it.

'What is all this noise?' demanded Margaret of Anjou, appearing suddenly on the threshold.

Her scream had been heard. Anne let out a sob of relief. Edouard released her and she turned to thank Margaret, who had so improbably become her rescuer. But Edouard got in first. 'She was being impertinent to me. I was showing her that she can't insult me.' He put the knight back on the table.

'Were you impertinent?' Margaret of Anjou asked Anne.

The countess was there behind her but although her face was distressed, the little disapproving shake of her head was enough to tell Anne that her mother would not support her. The countess would do nothing to disturb her husband's plans. She would sacrifice her daughter for Warwick if necessary.

217

Anne didn't care. Even her father's interests had faded into the distance. She would rather be thrown to the lions in the Tower menagerie and her parents with her, than be pushed into bed with this abominable boy. 'No, I was not! He was talking about beheadings as if they were amusing and I didn't look amused enough so he . . .'

'Don't lie!' screeched Edouard. 'You stared at me as if I had two heads and then you told me your father was more important than my mother!'

Margaret of Anjou's hand came up, as her son's had done a few moments earlier. This hand was loaded with rings. None was very valuable but the monetary value of a gemstone, as Anne now discovered, had no connection with its virtue as a knuckleduster. Topaz and rose-quartz were as effective as diamonds for that. Indeed these, ostentatiously large, were better.

Anne went backwards, knocked off her feet by a back-handed blow which skinned the side of her face. She bumped into the table. Margaret hit her again and she went down sideways to land sobbing on the floor. Edouard laughed. From his attendants came a sycophantic echo.

'In future,' said the Anjou woman, 'you will treat my son only with the greatest respect. You are both now required in the hall.' Coldly, she watched her future daughter-in-law scramble to her feet. 'In future,' Anne thought. There was to be no escape from that future, then.

'The servants tell me,' said Margaret, 'that an itinerant pardoner is selling his wares in the courtyard. You had better buy some, my girl, to absolve you from your shameless manners today.'

'Ah, the pardoner.' Dr Morton, who had not come with those who first responded to Anne's scream, now appeared. 'I have sent him about his business, ma'am. A questionable character in my opinion. If spiritual guidance is needed, I will gladly offer it.'

He had not seen what happened. He did not look dishonest. If she confided in him, he might be able to help her, to

218

tell Edouard to behave, perhaps. But she would never tell him; she would never dare to ask anyone connected with Margaret of Anjou for help, for fear of misplacing her trust and having her words simply reported to Margaret.

She had never felt so alone.

Chapter Fifteen

Petronel: Escape to Danger

1470

It was on the voyage to Calais that I realised, for the first time, that I was not only unhappy with Lionel, but hated him.

The relief of being away from him was enormous. For months to come I would be free of the pressure of his personality. I understood now what a heavy weight he was, with his constant watching of everything I did, his readiness to criticise and his continual, resentful demand, no less audible for being so often unspoken, that I should conceive. Not to mention the odious act through which he hoped I should accomplish this.

The sun shone, the sea sparkled. I was free as I had never been in my life before. Even when Lionel went to London and left me in Eynesby, I always knew that when he returned I would have to give an accounting of all I had done while he was gone. But my accounting this time would be to the King, not to Lionel, and I did not find him nearly as frightening. I did not find anyone frightening. If Margaret of Anjou in person had sailed up over the horizon, leaning over the bows of her vessel and brandishing an axe at me, I wouldn't have cared, so great was my joy in my liberty.

The only thing that dampened my spirits was the fact that although the sea was calm as the face of an angel, Kat, who was accompanying me as my maid, was horribly seasick the whole way across and by the end of the journey had confessed what I had already begun to suspect, that she was not only pining for her lover, she was pregnant by him.

'You should have married Lionel instead of me,' I said crossly and candidly, sitting in the cabin to listen to her red-eyed admission of guilt. 'Well, calm yourself. I will look after you. I'll see you right somehow.'

'I'll see you right' was a north country idiom. I was becoming a real Yorkshirewoman, I thought. 'Wash your face,' I told her, 'and look out a suitable dress for me. Fashionable but not too showy. I have to ask the Governor of Calais, this man Wenlock, for permission to join Lady Isabel. I must make the right impression.'

Discretion had meant keeping my purpose secret even from Kat, who thought I was merely travelling in answer to Isabel's request, made before the Clarences left England. Since she knew quite well how things stood between me and Lionel, and the reason why he had been so determined to keep me with him that he had for once wanted me to accompany him to London, she probably thought it odd. But she was well-trained now, and asked no questions.

Getting past Wenlock proved unexpectedly simple. Since he was the kind of man who keeps himself informed, he knew who the Eynesbys were. He knew who Sir Geoffrey was, too, and that Geoffrey had joined John Neville. I have thought since that he probably knew already what Sir John Neville's intentions were in this conflict. He offered me wine and fruit patties; I spoke of my smooth journey and my pleasant former service with Lady Isabel, and said how touched I was that she wished me to come to her. Half an hour later, a smart young squire from the Wenlock household was escorting myself and Kat through Calais to the house which the Clarences had taken. And then, in a sunlit solar, with the ladies of her household clustered round us, I was in Isabel's arms.

I had already discovered, making the first journey of my life virtually alone, that I had a talent for what is known as 'managing.' No doubt I had learned something from coping with Eynesby and Ralph the cook. Now I managed with equal success to whisper: 'I must see you alone. Message from the King,' to Isabel without being overheard. 'Leave it to me,' she whispered back at once.

Then, with a laughing but dismissive wave at her ladies, which caused her wide sleeve to sweep a book from a table on to the floor, and an effusive cry of: 'Petra, it's so long since I've seen you! Why didn't you come before? You must hear all my news and I must hear yours!' she drew me away from the rest and sat me down beside her on a window seat where, holding my eyes with her own, she began to chatter in the most natural way of her life as Duchess of Clarence, allowing her voice now and then to carry. I waited, following her lead.

Ankaret Twynyhoe had stepped resignedly forward to pick up the book. That little accident had been typically Isabel-of-Middleham, but the merry, slightly self-centred chatter about her married life, although it was meant so to appear, was not. It was a wary and calculated performance. Isabel had changed. Isabel-of-Middleham would not have made that swift response to my whisper.

As I listened, and heard for the first time of that nightmare childbed on board ship in Calais harbour, I began to understand what had changed her. While she talked, I studied her face. It had matured, but not softened into the plumpness it had once promised. Isabel looked adult now, but not happy, no. She was the kind that needed cherishing and she had not been cherished. She had been exposed instead to physical danger and used in cold intrigue and she was unsuited to either. Hurt and bewilderment and the desire to escape looked at me out of her eyes.

She chattered away for a full ten minutes and if the others had had any interest in what she said, it soon faded. They busied themselves with work and gossip at the far end of the room and Isabel, at last, paused and then, in a voice which would not reach them, said: 'And now what about you, Petra? A message?'

'Not only for you. For your husband. Can you arrange that?'

'Yes. Ankaret will fetch you to us later, when Clarence is alone with me. We can trust Ankaret.'

'Thank you. And now,' I said, playing her game, 'you'll want to hear my news. There's not much to tell . . .'

We were interrupted before I had finished, however. A flustered girl appeared and spoke to Ankaret, who came hurrying over to us. 'Forgive me for intruding, but if I might speak to Mistress Eynesby . . . Mistress Eynesby, your maid has been taken ill. She was unpacking your baggage when she fainted. This girl was helping her, and came running to find you. Will you come?'

I made haste. Kat had come round by the time I reached her and was lying on her pallet looking sickly. 'It was just tiredness,' she said in answer to my questions. 'I was that tired from all that travelling. No, I'm not bleeding or anything of that.'

I settled her comfortably and told her to rest until morning. 'What's wrong with her?' Isabel asked when I returned to the solar. 'Is it infectious?'

'No,' I said with a sigh, and then, because the maids would certainly grasp the situation before long and gossip to their mistresses, I said frankly: 'She's in trouble. I've promised to look after her. I must find her a husband, perhaps when we get back to Eynesby.'

'We may be able to find someone here,' Isabel said. 'A good dowry can outweigh a child and at least I have access to some money. I can see to that. Perhaps Clarence can suggest a suitable man. I'll ask him.' Her blue eyes gazed straight and intently at me and over her left eye the eyelid drooped, just a little.

Ankaret, as senior lady, had a small room of her own adjoining the Clarences' chamber. She was widowed now, I knew, and perhaps had special consideration because of that. Just as we were all retiring that night, she came to the room the rest of us shared, and summoned me. 'The duke and duchess want to see you, Mistress Eynesby. I think it's about her,' she added, casting a stern glance towards Kat, who was asleep on her pallet and didn't hear.

She hurried me out, leaving a pleasurable hum of specula-tion behind us. 'They're wondering if you're to be censured for having brought such a shocking example of immorality into our midst, or if Kat's to be turned out without a charac-ter in the morning or even tonight,' said Ankaret drily as we crossed the twilit ante-chamber between our quarters and the Clarences'. 'Don't worry. I know why you're here. It's to do with that.'

'Lady Isabel said we could trust you. King Edward said so, too.'

'I hope so,' said Ankaret grimly. She settled her starched head-dress and shook her capacious skirts into order before knocking on the Clarences' door. 'Kat's the excuse,' she said, 'but it may be that the duke may really be able to help. Just for once in his lifetime.'

I stared at her amazed, trying to read her face in the gloom.

'He has made my lady miserable,' said Ankaret, softly but fiercely. 'Him and her father. She nearly died on board that ship and the baby did die. I'm not likely to forgive either of them. You know her, Petronel. She's careless with things but she's kind to people. I love her and they've *used* her.' Her knock on the ducal door was positively peremptory.

Clarence and Isabel were in bed, propped up on pillows. I had once danced with George of Clarence and remembered him as a handsome man; I had always understood why Isabel should fall in love with him. But now, as I studied his face carefully, I saw what I had not observed in Sir Anthony Woodville's hall – the broken veins in Clarence's nose and the petulant lines round his mouth. He said eagerly: 'You have a message from my brother, King Edward?'

'You may sit, Petra,' said Isabel kindly, pointing to a stool beside the bed.

I sat. 'Yes, your grace. I will try to give it word for word as he gave it to me.'

'I'm listening,' said Clarence.

The message I had memorised had been put in plain terms:

225

'Tell him, quite simply, that I wish to make peace with him and not only because I want him to fight on my side and not Warwick's. I also want it because I'm his brother and I would rather we were friends than foes. If we end up facing each other across a battlefield, it will break our mother's heart and that of our sister Margaret in Burgundy. What if one, or even both of us were to be killed? How will those dear women ever get over it?' He said 'dear women' as though he meant it. Edward Plantagenet liked women – more than that, he esteemed them. 'Ask him,' he said, 'if he thinks he could face me in war. Because believe me, I can't imagine how I would face him. I'd throw my sword away and embrace him, then and there in the middle of the fighting most likely. And in addition, tell him that by making peace with me he will lose nothing. I will see that he has all that a king's brother ought to have. What can Warwick offer him that is worth more? Warwick won't give him the crown; that's already been hocked to the Lancastrians. Though you'd better not put it quite like that. Simply say that we have heard that Warwick plans to reinstate Henry the Sixth and his line.'

I had memorised it and repeated it back to him and I had whispered it over and over to myself in the cabin of the ship. I was nervous now and stumbled several times, and I also feared that I wasn't putting over the emotional force of the appeal as King Edward would have wished. I felt as though I were being impertinent, saying such things to a duke and purporting to speak with King Edward's voice.

'It's what he instructed me to say,' I explained at the end. 'I have repeated it as well as I could.'

'You've done it very well. My thanks,' said Clarence.

'It is such a kind message. So brotherly,' offered Isabel in a timid voice.

'That's all very well.' Clarence sounded pettish. 'But I can't fight against my father-in-law either! What would you say, Isabel, if I killed your father?'

'He's likely to say he can't fight Warwick,' the King had

told me. 'I'd like him to, personally! I need all the help I can get. It's worth trying it on with him, but if he raises the argument that he mustn't take the field against his father-in-law, this is what you must answer . . .'

'Your grace,' I said, 'the King anticipated that you might feel so. He charged me with one more thing to say.'

'Oh, did he? Well, let's hear it, then.'

'He told me to say that if you did not at heart wish to fight against him, would you help him find a way to put things right in a way which would harm no one? He said, if you are summoned to bring men to England to Warwick's aid, do so. But would you, when you get there, receive an emissary from the King with official peace proposals and try to persuade Warwick to accept them? And in the event of failure, simply not fight at all?'

'I'll receive an emissary from him at any time, naturally,' Clarence frowned. There was a flagon of wine on the table by the bed and he poured himself a drink and swallowed it, thinking. 'What I say to the emissary is something I can't decide now. It would depend on circumstances. I have not been well-treated by either my father-in-law or my brother.' He spoke in a grand voice which I recognised, having used it often enough myself to Ralph the cook. The fair-haired man with the wine-veins in his skin was caught between brother and father-in-law and he was frightened – and trying to hide it. He didn't in the least want to meet the King in battle. I was certain of that.

'You'll be sending back an answer, I take it?' said Clarence. 'I won't ask you how you're to manage it. Tell him what I've said. I'll receive his emissary but I'm making no promises. I expect to be bringing men to England, yes.'

'There is still the matter of Petra's maidservant, dear,' said Isabel. Again she used that cautious tone.

'Oh yes, our excuse for summoning you here. She's been a naughty girl, I hear.' Clarence laughed in a shrill way which made me feel uncomfortable.

'Yes, she has been very foolish,' I agreed. 'But I feel responsible for her welfare.'

'But if you wait till you get home, it may be leaving things rather late?' said Clarence. I disliked him, like Ankaret, I decided. There had been something sly and sniggering in his tone. But he had a practical suggestion, nevertheless. 'I've a manservant who wants a wife,' he said. 'He's older than your girl, but decent. He's been saving his pay for years and he wants to go home to England and rent a shop in a street I own in London, and start an eating-house. I'll send him to you tomorrow and you can inspect him. My wife says she'll contribute a dowry and I'm agreeable. We owe you something for your trouble in coming over.'

From his tone, I was dismissed. I went.

Clarence's manservant was actually one of his under-butlers. His name was Jarvis Taberner and he was as described, a decent man wanting a wife. He was about ten years older than Kat but Kat, who had, albeit with much whimpering, agreed that she ought to marry somebody, seemed to find this reassuring. I left them together to talk and the outcome was that two weeks later they were married in a little church by the harbour. Taberner's own view of Kat's predicament was that at least she had proved she was fertile. No doubt the dowry also had something to say in the matter. I hoped he would be kind to her.

It proved quite a merry occasion. Jarvis's friends attended and three of Kat's fellow-maids. I was present, escorted by Ankaret. We came out of the church into sunshine and the cry of gulls, with Kat's hand on her bride-groom's arm. Her condition did not show as yet and in any case, the fashion then was for high waists and bunchy skirts held up in front. Passers-by smiled at the pair as they led the way towards the Clarences' house and the wedding feast which was waiting in the kitchens. The road skirted the harbour and there were boats bobbing at anchor and shouts from men unloading a cargo of wool. I wondered if any of it had come from Eynesby or Bouldershawe.

Then Jarvis changed direction, steering Kat across the

road, away from a knot of people looking down into the water. They seemed to be watching as something, not a bale of wool, was drawn up on a rope.

'Oh no!' said Ankaret in my ear. 'There must have been an accident. It sometimes happens. They are taking some poor soul out of the water. He will have lost his footing, maybe going too fast down the steps to his boat. The steps are always slippery with weed. I nearly fell in myself the day we arrived here. Don't look, Petronel. Let us cross the road like the others.'

But just as we turned to do so, the rope's burden was hoisted over the edge of the wall and laid on the paved ground and I had looked before I could stop myself.

What I thought I saw made me move closer.

The man had not fallen in and drowned. He had been thrown in, and he had been stabbed first. They hadn't been able, or hadn't troubled, to remove the knife and as the body flopped face down on the ground, the bone hilt jutted from its back. It was this that I had seen. I stared, troubled by something in the back of my mind that would not at first come into the light.

Then someone in the crowd said: 'Anyone know him?' and knelt to turn him over. The dagger hilt grated on the paving stones as he – it – was rolled face upwards. The head fell back and the mouth opened. I recognised the gap-teeth.

It was Peter the Pardoner.

'Be careful,' King Edward had said, his hazel eyes worried. Warwick would probably not harm me, but the Bitch of Anjou would stop at nothing.

But I, silly, immature Petronel, had gaily set sail, thinking only that I was getting away from Lionel, thinking that even the sight of Margaret of Anjou flourishing an axe couldn't obliterate my joy. I hadn't known what danger meant, never having encountered it.

Now I knew. The harbour lurched, sea, ships, the curving wall with the weedy green tidemark, the crowd round the

229

body, all swinging up to meet the sky. Ankaret caught me before I hit the ground.

'You shouldn't have gone so near,' she said when I came to myself again. 'That was no sight for you.'

But it was as well I had seen it, or I might have waited a long time for Peter the Pardoner to come. Had the people who killed him known he was here to contact me? Was I now in danger? And how was I to send word to the King without Peter? I had been forbidden to set anything down in writing and I had no inclination to disobey that injunction. I saw now what it could mean. The Pardoner might not, of course, have been murdered by the men of Warwick or Margaret of Anjou. He could have been caught up in some silly tavern quarrel. But I didn't propose to gamble on it.

Two of Jarvis's friends carried me back to the Clarences' house. Apologetically, I excused myself from attending the wedding breakfast and said I wanted to lie down. While the marriage party celebrated downstairs, I lay shivering, burrowing under the rug as though in search of safety and half expecting assassins to burst in at any moment.

Presently, however, my nerves steadied. It wasn't very likely that any connection had been made between the Pardoner and myself. He was probably killed because he had become known as an agent of King Edward. Certainly no one had tried to harm me yet. I was just one of Isabel's waiting ladies, attending on my mistress. And I was only eighteen. In the eyes of most men, and most women too, I was a negligible creature, being both female and young. As the afternoon wore away, I crept out from my rugs and tidied myself, and when dusk fell I went down to join in the noisy and hilarious business of seeing the couple to their chamber. A gently reared young woman might turn faint at the sight of a murdered corpse, but no one must imagine there was more to it than that.

Next day, I managed once again to whisper to Isabel: 'I must see you and the duke alone again, somehow.'

* * *

Isabel used the excuse of wishing to present me with a length of dress material for Kat. Clarence came in apparently by chance.

'There is no one we can send to England,' they said unanimously, when I had explained that my messenger was dead and I needed another. 'Even Jarvis does not intend to go until this conflict is over,' Clarence said, 'and from what you tell me, Mistress Eynesby, no one travelling alone from my household would be safe. Either something would happen to them, or they would be stopped by Wenlock.'

'But there is commerce, surely?' I said. 'I saw wool being unloaded yesterday. Ships are coming and going. If we could find a trustworthy merchant's agent, or sailor . . .'

'There are eyes and ears everywhere and no knowing who can be trusted and who can't,' said Clarence. 'What would you know about it?' he added angrily and gave that shrill laugh again. I was silent, thinking of silly Petronel on the ship coming over. What, indeed, did I know about anything?

'Petra herself could go,' said Isabel.

'Don't be a fool,' said Clarence. 'She'd be suspect as much as any other.'

'Not if she were dismissed from my service.'

'It would have to be a rather public and noticeable business. How do you propose to arrange that?'

'Petra,' said Isabel. 'Would you wait a moment, please?' She drew Clarence aside.

Over the next ten days we played a most ridiculous charade. To give Clarence his due, I have to admit that he played his part excellently well. He appeared to enjoy it, which was more than I did. If all of it was acting, that is. Ankaret said later that she didn't think it was.

At dinner that first day, my seat was moved, at Clarence's request, much closer to his so that he could address jocular remarks and not quite jocular compliments to me and reach out under the table to squeeze my knee, which he did with only cursory concealment.

231

On subsequent days, usually at twilight, he took to pouncing on me in odd corners of the house and embracing me with enthusiasm, urging me in a whisper which nonetheless had carrying power, to let him send for me that night. I found it all most uncomfortable, for his hands would stray in a fashion not quite called for by necessity. But I would quell my distaste and scramble out of his arms with coy cries of: 'Oh, my lord of Clarence, how can you?'

When we judged that my lord of Clarence's desire to get into bed with his wife's lady-in-waiting Petronel Eynesby had been, as it were, painted sufficiently clearly on the walls, we staged the denouement, in which I was sent for apparently to attend Isabel but, when scratching on the door of the main bedchamber, was discovered by an Isabel who denied all knowledge of the message, declared that she had withdrawn to sleep elsewhere because of the duke's outrageous behaviour, and threw an almighty tantrum then and there.

She made such a to-do, shouting and crying, that half the household came tumbling from their beds to see what was happening. Clarence came out, knotting a loose gown round him, to ask what the uproar was and Isabel, with perfectly genuine tears streaming down her face, rated him as cruel and faithless before rounding on me, slapping me, calling me a treacherous ingrate and ordering me out of her sight forever more.

Even though we had planned it all in advance, somehow her accusations wounded me and I too wept in earnest as I stumbled away. Next morning, Ankaret came to 'see that I packed my things and was gone before my lady could catch sight of me.'

'I would never have thought my lady could pretend so brilliantly,' I said to Ankaret, trying to smile.

'Pretend?' said Ankaret. 'She's been longing to say all that and more to him for a long, long time. He's behaved like this before and meant it. And I wouldn't be too sure he didn't halfway mean it this time.'

'Ankaret!'

'I keep a stricter eye than ever on you young ones in this house,' said Ankaret. 'I'm glad to see you away.'

'Does he know how much you dislike him?'

'I daresay he guesses. But who am I? Just a grouchy widow of no importance. Wenlock's been asked to see that you find a ship today. He won't make any difficulties. There were enough witnesses, heaven knows! You'll have a rough voyage, I'm afraid, the weather's turning, but you'll be safe in Dover by tomorrow. Petra, don't worry.' Ankaret glanced at me kindly, as I stood there with an armful of my dresses, about to put them in their box. 'She upset you last night, didn't she? But she knows you're her friend. It's all *his* fault,' said Ankaret, with venom.

I sailed at noon on a ship called the *Bethlehem*, not merely unsuspected by Wenlock but positively speeded, although there was no invitation to take refreshments with him this time.

Ankaret had been right about the weather. The sea was grey and bitter and there was a vicious wind. But I stayed on deck most of the time, watching astern, still afraid that my duplicity had been discovered and that I might yet see a ship, bearing Anjou's agents, giving chase. The sight of Dover's white cliffs was like the face of a beloved friend. Once I had set foot in England, I thought, I would be safe. I felt very lonely without Kat, who had wept at my going and kept looking at me as though she couldn't believe the reason.

Once I had landed, my way was made smooth. I think that although my return was not expected, the contingency had nevertheless been met. I sought shelter in Dover castle, and was not only given it, but was sent on my way to London next day in another ship. Once in London I went straight to the Halfords. 'I must see either Master Brampton or Dr Alcock,' I said.

It was Brampton who came, and that within the hour. I was glad to see him; his cutpurse countenance had suddenly become a symbol of reliability. He listened to my story and said: 'You want to tell the King yourself?'

'Yes, I think I do.' I hadn't known this till he said it but then I realised that he was right. 'It's such an indefinite answer,' I said. 'Clarence only says he will meet the emissary. He won't promise to make terms. But I had this impression . . .' I was not used to finding words for such subtleties but, once more, I managed.

'He's a frightened man, trapped between conflicting loyalties and dangers and searching for a way out? Have I understood you?' Brampton said when I had finished.

'Yes. Yes! That's exactly it.'

'Then use those words to the King. He's travelling north, gathering men. If I give you an escort, can you ride hard, to catch up with him?'

'Yes.'

I enjoyed that ride north, although much of it was through blustering winds and blowing rain. I was glad Lionel had made me learn how to sit a horse. I rode astride for the sake of speed, skirts hitched and knees bound with leather to protect me from the stirrup leathers, and delightedly breathed in an intoxicating mixture of fresh, damp air, and excitement.

When I had seen the King, I must return to Lionel and this I did not want to do. But surely, now, it would be different? Surely, if I came with the goodwill of the King and perhaps a material reward of some kind, he would respect me more, be kinder?

I had, of course, forgotten what Lionel was like.

Chapter Sixteen

The Plantagenets: King in Jeopardy

1470

'My lord . . . my lord!'

'Yes, what is it, what is it?' Edward Plantagenet appeared, tousle-haired, on the gallery that linked the upper rooms of the Doncaster inn. He had flung a cloak round him to keep off the September chill. Beside him, a page wiped sleep from his eyes with one hand and held up a candle with the other. 'You're one of my minstrels,' said Edward, recognising the man who had roused them. 'But I hardly need music at this time of night!'

'My lord, John Neville is coming! With an army! People are running for shelter into Doncaster town . . .'

'Thank God he's on his way. I was afraid he wouldn't come. I sent for him. I'm here to meet him.'

'You don't understand, sire! He's not bringing the army to you but against you! He's gone over to Warwick. The people running into the town are fleeing from him. He's burning the manors of your supporters!'

Along the gallery, doors were opening. Anthony Woodville came out, gown thrown round him, and still grasping the book he had been reading by candlelight. The eternally cheerful William Hastings appeared, and beyond him Richard of Gloucester, halfway into his doublet and yanking at his hose. Both Hastings and Richard had girls peering from behind them. Edward raised an eyebrow in comic regret. 'My apologies to you all. If this tale is true, I'm afraid none of us will spend tonight in bed.'

'It's true enough, my lord!' said the minstrel in anguish.

'The coast!' said Hastings sharply. He had the knack of responding to sudden changes of fortune. Last night they had been a king and his immediate friends, halted in this town of Doncaster to await reinforcements before turning south again to deal with a threatened invasion. Edward's agent, the wandering pardoner, was dead but he had not been working alone. A man whom Edward had once noticed shouting odds at Smithfield tournament, a little man with bright eyes in a web of fine lines, was now part of Alcock's organisation and he had brought them word not only of Peter's murder but of other things. They knew nearly as much about Warwick's plans as Warwick did.

Which meant that they also knew that if John Neville espoused the wrong cause, they were themselves no more than a handful of fugitives, impossibly outnumbered. 'The coast is our only chance,' said Hastings urgently. 'Lynn's nearest.'

'Then Burgundy if we can get there.' Edward was thinking aloud. 'I was relying on John Neville. You may as well say "I told you so" and be done with it, Richard. I hope to God our horses aren't too tired . . .'

'The Queen!' said Anthony Woodville. 'What about the Queen? My sister?'

'She has instructions to take sanctuary if the invasion comes,' said Edward. 'If the child she is carrying turns out to be a son,' he added, 'he'll be a considerable embarrassment to Warwick. I can't see Warwick injuring a newborn child, but the Anjou female might. If mother and child are in sanctuary, however, they should be safe until I can get back to the rescue. It's as well that Mistress Eynesby has come and gone too. She's nearly home by now, with the charter to a fine manor in her pocket.' He turned to the page. 'Come, my boy, we must dress.'

Hastings was already hustling his girl back into their room and by the sound of it, briskly paying her off. But Richard, steering his own companion into their chamber and shutting the door, said anxiously: 'Jennie . . .'

'Dear saints, I hopes you gets safe away.'

'So do I. Now listen, if I don't see you again, I want you to have this money.' He pulled a box from under his bed.

'There's no need,' said Jennie, slightly affronted. She was the daughter of the innkeeper. Like Kate's father in York, the innkeeper had no objection if his child caught the eye of a duke. But Jennie and Kate were neither of them whores.

'There may be need. Suppose there's a child? You must have something to pay for its upbringing. If there's no child, use the money as a dowry. If I come back, I'll enquire after you, but if not I'll know you're safe and any son or daughter of mine that you bear me. Take it, for God's sake. Goodbye, Jennie. And thank you.'

'Goodbye,' said Jennie disconsolately. He was the King's brother and there would have been no future for her with him even if John Neville hadn't changed sides, even if Dickon got safe away now and one day came back to Doncaster. When he married, he'd choose someone of his own sort, like that cousin he had, Anne, who'd been his playmate when they were young. He'd mentioned her once or twice.

He'd also, and in a special tone, spoken of a girl in York. Even if Dickon had been of her own sort, Jennie thought, she would never have had a serious place in his life because of that girl in York. But he had been a kind lover and interesting to talk to; she'd never forget him. 'God keep you,' said Jennie to the door, as he vanished through it.

The house where Bess Woodville had taken refuge was attached to the Abbey of Westminster and partook of its right of sanctuary. She had need of sanctuary. Beyond the windows, the sky was smudged with smoke where Warwick's men, every day, fired more of the Yorkists' houses, and in the distance she could hear the cries and clangour of the street riots. The men of the City, the vintners, jewellers, goldsmiths, clothiers, caterers and wool

237

merchants, had approved of King Edward. He encouraged their trade and had been himself a valued customer. Furthermore, he had borrowed money from some of them. With visions of their financial security disappearing over the horizon along with King Edward, they were Yorkist almost to a man and clashed daily, fist, knife and cudgel, with the supporters of Warwick and Lancaster.

But the price of safety was stark. Dr John Alcock, calling in response to an urgent message from Bess, looked at the bare stone of the untapestried walls and at the brazier which was the only source of heat in this damp November, and his heart was squeezed with pity. Edward had been gone two months. He was an exile, probably by now in Burgundy, and here in these austere conditions his queen, ironically, had borne the long-awaited son who ought to be his heir.

The child was there, well-swaddled, in a cradle beside Bess's chair. She was well wrapped herself in a thick woollen shawl. Her face was very pale, but she gave him her sweet, self-contained smile as Lady Scrope brought him in, and extended her hand for him to kiss.

'It was kind of you to come so quickly, Dr Alcock.'

'How can I serve you? Are you recovering as you should? You have received the food and wine you were promised, I hope?'

'Yes. They let me have Lady Scrope as midwife and she saw to it that all my needs of that kind were met.'

'I had to demand an audience with Warwick,' said Lady Scrope. 'But he granted it and he was reasonable.'

He had had little chance to be anything else. Alcock had not been present, but he had heard about it. Lady Scrope had swept into the earl's presence preceded by a blast of glacial rage like the breath of an iceberg, and asked him if his daughter's hideous accouchement aboard ship hadn't been enough; was he going to make a habit of warring on women in childbed?

Warwick had risen instantly and furiously to his feet but Lady Scrope stood her ground, hands folded before her, and looked him in the eye until he said: 'I find that accusation offensive. I take it that you are here to represent Bess Woodville. What am I alleged to have done to her?'

'She needs red meat and good wine and an allowance with which to buy them.'

'Is that all? See my steward,' Warwick had snapped. 'He will arrange daily supplies. Tell him what's needed.'

'I have enough material things,' Bess said now, 'but I asked you to come . . .' She glanced at Lady Scrope.

'The child will soon need feeding. I must take him to his nurse,' said Lady Scrope. She gathered the infant Edward up from his cradle and tactfully withdrew.

'It's spiritual advice you seek?' asked Alcock as the door closed after them. 'But you have your own confessor. Of course, anything I can do, I will, but . . .'

'I don't want to confess. Not quite that. Sit down, Dr Alcock. Bring that other chair to the brazier. I asked you to come because I wanted to talk to someone I could trust. I have always felt that you were friendly towards me and . . .'

Unexpectedly, she put her face in her hands. Alcock made an instinctive half-movement to go to her but checked himself. He would have put his arms round any child that wept like that, but Bess was a woman, and his Queen. He waited.

'I'm sorry,' Bess whispered at last. 'But . . . my baby, my baby, Dr Alcock. My husband wanted a son, an heir, but to what will our son be heir now? We're safe enough for the time being, here in this house. But for how long? Does even the right of sanctuary last for ever? What if my husband never comes home again? What if my child and I are left to the mercy of Margaret of Anjou when she comes to England?'

'The right of sanctuary lasts,' said Alcock. 'And if it came to it, you would undoubtedly be given safe conduct to rejoin your husband. You must not brood like this. You have nothing to fear. You are suffering from melancholy,

239

missing the King, no doubt. These surroundings are hardly what you're used to.'

'I wonder who is using my rooms in Westminster?' said Bess wryly.

Alcock knew the answer to that. Long-nosed, feeble-witted, would-be monk King Henry was occupying them. Alcock's official court business was administration and administrators were not supposed to have personal opinions about those they served, but he knew quite well that he wasn't the only civil servant who had had to suppress a groan on being confronted with Henry the Sixth, after being used to King Edward.

He did not, however, express this improper thought, but asked instead: 'Is there anything I can do for you?'

'There's something that I want you . . . to know.'

'Yes?'

He saw that she was trembling. 'I keep on thinking,' she said, 'of the Earl of Desmond and his sons.'

'Oh yes, Desmond,' said Alcock, a little bleakly. 'You want to tell me something about them?'

He had not intended it, but a coldness had crept into his voice. Bess heard it and seemed to shrink away into her shawl. After a moment, she said: 'One must defend oneself. I was – am – the Queen and Desmond called me a grey mare. He practically advised Edward to divorce me. He despised me because I was not aristocratic enough to suit him. I had to show him, and others, that I could not be so belittled. If you want me to show remorse for Desmond's death, I can't. But I never ordered the deaths of his sons. Never. You must believe me.'

'I do. I have never supposed that you did. And I have always understood that you struck at Desmond himself out of fear. I think you acted wrongly, but I believe it was out of fear, as I say. Out of weakness, if you like,' said Alcock, 'but not out of evil. I never believed that.'

'I chose Tiptoft to act for me because he was loyal and powerful and willing for a brutal errand. But . . .'

'What made him so willing,' said Alcock, 'was that he really does possess a streak of sheer evil. And you found that out?'

'Yes.' Bess was whispering again. 'He exceeded his orders. But how many people will believe that? Since I've been here, I have had the same bad dream three times.'

'What dream was that?'

'I dream,' said Bess, 'that the Earl of Desmond comes into this room and seizes my baby from his cradle. I clutch at his arm and cry out to him to stop, but he shakes me off and carries my child away. Warwick is here, and my husband, but they only stand by, pointing their fingers at me and jeering!'

'You are suffering from guilt,' said Alcock. 'Have you sought absolution? You should do so. Then you must try to put this behind you. It is done now. I repeat: I understood why you did it although I didn't approve. And I know it was Tiptoft, not you, who had the boys killed. Tiptoft will pay for that soon. Warwick intends to execute him.'

He hoped he was reaching her. He was more sorry for her than ever, although less admiring. His admiration had begun to falter from the day the news of the Desmond tragedy reached him. The timidity, the vulnerable air which had once seemed so charming and so womanly, had begun then to take on a dubious aspect. A woman should not be too childlike, after all. He repressed a sigh. There was a serpent in every garden, it appeared.

He saw that tears were sparkling on Bess's porcelain-smooth face. 'Innocence didn't protect Desmond's sons; why should it protect mine? My baby is a danger to King Henry, to Warwick. He's the perpetuation of an enemy line. My daughters are downstairs, playing in the garden. Like me, they're female and we may be safe because of that. But my son, how safe will my son be, Dr Alcock? Can you tell me? How safe will he be?'

She had called on him for help. He had failed her. He had no answer.

* * *

In the Palace of Westminster, one of the guests at King Henry's hurriedly reconstituted court sat watching while her serious, ginger-haired, thirteen-year-old son played chess, skilfully for his age, with her steward. The Lady Margaret Beaufort's prayers had been answered. Well, some of them. The Lancastrian cause was alive again and she was once more in the company of her boy. And they were here at Westminster, held in honour, sitting in a room from which tapestries bearing the white rose of York had been removed, to be replaced by hangings patterned instead by red Lancastrian roses. She had taken back the title of Countess of Richmond, which was hers by right of her Tudor marriage but which she had preferred to forget while Edward ruled, not wanting people to say: 'Countess of Richmond? Oh yes, through Edmund Tudor. Wasn't there a son?'

Like King Henry the Sixth (newly released from a cob-webby Tower apartment and eyeing the luxuries of Westminster Palace with pious suspicion), like ex-king Edward (regrettably reported safe with his sister in Burgundy), like her nephew by marriage the spoilt young Duke of Buckingham (still sulkily refusing to consummate his marriage to a mere Woodville), Margaret Beaufort was descended from Edward the Third through his son John of Gaunt. Unfortunately, the wife by whom John had bred Margaret's line, had produced her children before going through the marriage ceremony, a reversal of the standard procedures which Parliament, when passing the Act which legitimised them, had been unable quite to ignore. Legitimate they might be, but they were not entitled to stand in line for the throne.

But Acts of Parliament were the laws of men, not of God. They could be, might be, changed. It was the blood that counted.

The steward, Master Bray, waiting for Henry Tudor to move a pawn, glanced at his mistress and gave her a frater-nal smile. Despite gossip to the contrary, she was his mistress only in the sense that she employed him. They were not and never had been lovers. And because of this very thing, it was to the quiet, competent Reginald Bray that Margaret Beaufort told many of her inmost thoughts. Lovers feared to risk shattering each other's illusions with too much candour. Mistress and servant had none to shatter.

Reginald Bray knew how Margaret Beaufort loved her only son (in that, perhaps, she did have something in common with her namesake of Anjou). He knew that compared to Henry Tudor, Margaret's second husband was only a shadow in her life. He knew that she had named her son after the Lancastrian kings on purpose. And he knew that, in the face of all reality and likelihood, she secretly dreamed that her son might one day become a Lancastrian leader. Might even come to power.

Chapter Seventeen

The Plantagenets: Knight's Move

1471

'But they're bypassing us to the east!' Sir Geoffrey Silbeck's voice was ragged with the effort of arguing with his leader without actually shouting at him. He longed to pound a fist on the table under John Neville's nose. 'They're getting away!'

'And the scouts,' said a captain of archers longingly, 'say their force is small.'

'It is.' John Neville's face was drawn. His smallpox scars stood out. 'I think they expected Harry Percy to send men from Northumberland. He didn't. Sitting on the fence to see which side will win, I fancy.' His voice held no liking for his successor to the earldom of Northumberland. 'And I doubt if they picked up many men in York. But . . .'

His voice trailed away. 'The sauce of it!' said the captain with energy. 'Entering York at all! Entering the country!'

The captain was a no-nonsense midlander who detested what he called 'sauce', and there was no doubt that Edward of York, king or ex-king according to one's point of view, and his brother Gloucester had displayed it in considerable quantities. They had reappeared in England, landing in the north with only a few men, persuaded the city of York to receive them by claiming that Edward had returned only as the Duke of York and did not mean to involve the citizens in any more civil war, and then, having acquired supplies, information and at least a few recruits, they had marched boldly south, with the plain intention of starting the said civil war as soon as possible.

And John Neville, in his castle of Pontefract, was apparently prepared to sit still and let them go past, untouched.

'The scouts estimate,' said Geoffrey persistently, 'that they have no more than fifteen hundred men . . .'

'And the effrontery of Old Nick,' said the captain.

'. . . and they'd be ours for the taking if we rode now. They're making for Doncaster by the look of it. We could intercept them before –'

'I told you, no,' said John Neville.

The captain of archers stared at him in despair and then turned to gaze about the hall of Pontefract Castle, strewn like a supply depot with the bedrolls, packs and paraphernalia of only a small portion of John Neville's considerable army. The castle and the town outside were stuffed to bursting point with the rest of it. Neville had three thousand armed and pugnacious soldiers at his command. And there he sat, unshaven, elbows on a table littered with rolled-up maps and a muddle of pewter and pottery in which an uneaten meal was congealing, and said no.

'My lord!' protested Geoffrey.

'You think we should ride because we outnumber them two to one.' John Neville shook his head emphatically. 'For that very reason, Sir Geoffrey, we shall not ride. It's not a fair fight. Let them go.' He pushed back his chair, got up, and walked away.

Geoffrey went after him. 'Sir!'

Neville paused at the foot of the steps to his tower chamber. 'I want some rest, Sir Geoffrey. I didn't sleep last night or the night before. My cousins of York and Gloucester, let me remind you, were once my friends. One cannot extinguish old affections as though one were blowing out candles. How much simpler life would be if one could. Goodnight, Sir Geoffrey.'

'If you will wait here, sir, my lord of Clarence will be informed.'

Richard of Gloucester nodded and the guard went out.

Left alone, Richard wandered inquisitively round his brother's tent. He fingered the sable furs on the bed and peered at his own reflection in a silver basin. He was extremely dirty. He was trying to get the caked mud off his boots when Clarence's voice behind him said: 'I admire your courage, Dickon, riding alone into a camp full of enemies. Food and hot water are coming. If you can bear to eat my salt, that is.'

'I credit you with enough sense not to murder a lone ambassador, least of all your own brother,' said Richard with asperity. 'As for eating your salt; I'd eat anyone's. I've ridden twenty miles through what seemed like unadulterated bog all the way from Warwick to talk to you. It rained the whole way. You sent word by Mistress Eynesby that you were prepared to meet King Edward's emissary. Here he stands. I'm him. When I talk, will you listen?'

The hot water arrived. 'Naturally I'll listen,' said Clarence when the servant who brought it had gone. His manner was slightly mocking but also slightly conciliatory.

'Why did you do it, George?' Richard asked, beginning to wash. 'Take up arms against us, I mean?'

Clarence flung himself down on the sables and contemplated the tent roof, hands behind his head. Rain drummed. 'I'm a married man, little Dickon. A man owes something to his wife's family. Ned knows that.'

'Was that an answer or a retort?' enquired Richard before he could stop himself. He remembered his brother's words of warning: 'Take care,' Ned had told him. 'George can be the most provoking man on earth but don't undo all Mistress Eynesby's efforts with a burst of temper. I can't afford it, Dickon.'

That was true. Edward had an army, certainly. He had the fifteen hundred men who had come with him and Dickon from Burgundy, together with a few – though very few – from York. He also now had another three thousand brought in by Hastings, who had remained blessedly loyal. And as they went south he had gathered further volunteers, snowball fashion.

But Warwick had more than one army. He had five.

'French allies in the Channel,' Edward had said grimly, counting on his fingers. 'Margaret of Anjou poised to cross with her own men. Warwick's private army here in England – boxed up in Coventry at the moment. John Neville's troops coming south behind us. I think he let us slip past at Pontefract but he hasn't changed sides yet, all the same. And fifth, George has made a separate landing in the south west, following Warwick in. Unless we bring at least one of those armies over to us, we're dead men. Well, you've already talked Thomas Stanley out of backing Warwick, so I knew you have good powers of persuasion. Use them well. George is nibbling the bait. Don't lose him!'

Fortunately, Clarence did not now take offence. 'A retort, I suppose,' he said, quite ruefully, and Richard was encouraged to say, 'We understood that your wife Isabel would welcome it if you made terms with us. And certainly our mother and sister are praying every day for you to do so.'

'Is Ned praying as well? I can understand it if he is,' Clarence drawled to the roof. 'He's in a very nasty position.'

'Look,' Richard sponged mud off himself and weighed his words, 'just what is your father-in-law offering you that Ned isn't? Not the crown, that's certain.'

'Dickon, I swear I never seriously thought, or planned . . .'

'Didn't you? Well, all right, we won't discuss that. But as one brother to another,' Richard turned to face him, 'what's hindering you from making terms with Ned? They're good ones. I'm empowered to say that the honour and friendship which a king would naturally offer to his own brother will be yours if you consent to mend the breach. Why not mend it? Why not, George?'

'Because,' said Clarence, addressing the tent roof, 'even I, Dickon, have some standards of behaviour. I have backed Warwick. To change back to Edward's side now and fight on his behalf instead would be rather too much bed-hopping even for me. I backed Warwick first of all to help him put down the Woodvilles – *not* in hopes of grabbing the throne, Dickon! You don't like the Woodvilles either so you ought to understand. After that, well, Warwick made a friend and confidant of me. What was I to do – come running to Ned with tales?'

You needn't have encouraged Warwick. You needn't have been willing to be his puppet king. And you were willing for that, George, deny it how you will.

Richard weighed his words once more, holding down his anger. 'George, Ned is not asking you to fight under his banner. Did Mistress Eynesby not say as much? We realise your dilemma. What we want you to do is offer to mediate between Ned and Warwick.'

'I know. Mistress Eynesby did her part. But I returned a cautious answer and I'm still cautious, because the first thought that occurred to me was, what if mediation fails? I think it must. Ned will offer Warwick his life at most. For Warwick, battle is a more rewarding prospect. Ah, here comes the food. You'd better have something, after that long wet ride.'

'We know that mediation is shooting at a distant target,' said Richard patiently, accepting a meat pasty, 'but anything's worth trying. And if it failed, you could still simply keep out of the fight and give Ned a better chance that way. Mistress Eynesby said that too, did she not?'

Mistress Eynesby had also reported that Clarence was looking for a way out, was ready to be won over. But it seemed that there was some magic password, some key, which Richard needed to know to bring this about. He took a bite of pasty, giving himself time to think. He immediately put the pasty down, repelled. 'What on earth is in these pies?'

'Donkey, as likely as not,' said Clarence. 'I'm having trouble feeding my men. We keep running out of things, such as money.'

'Really?' Richard eyed the sables and the silver basin expressively.

'We manage,' said Clarence. 'Old donkeys come cheaper than fat sheep, though. We pay for what we take,' he added virtuously.

'Are you telling me that you've been reduced to feeding your troops on superannuated horsemeat in the cause of fighting your *own brother*?'

'No,' said Clarence. He swung his feet to the ground and faced Richard, eyes as limpidly blue and hair as pale as when he was five years old. 'I'm telling you that I've been feeding them on elderly asses and *not* selling my expensive furnishings – I saw you look – in the desperate hope that they'll desert so that I can't fight my own brother. Do you think I want to? Mistress Eynesby said that Ned, if we met on the field, would throw his sword away and embrace me. How can I go to war against him after that? But how can I abandon my father-in-law either? He thinks I'm going to, by the way. That's why he's barricaded into Coventry now. John Neville let him down when he allowed you to bypass him at Pontefract and he's afraid I'll do the same.'

'Yes. He knows you have reason.' To mention the matter was risky, for it was an accusation and might rouse Clarence's ire, but it seemed necessary. 'He originally offered to make you king and he's changed his plans. He hasn't much to complain about, George. He's given you cause to desert him. And you would only be leaving him for the greater loyalty – your brother and your King. Oh, George . . .'

And then something in Clarence's eyes told him what to do. Pushing aside the table with the ghastly meat pie on it, he went straight to George of Clarence, opened his arms and stood there while Clarence came into them. In that fraternal embrace, the ties of blood were made strong again. They had come from the same womb. As children they had shared a bed and kept each other warm in winter, snuggling together like pups in a litter. And big brother

Edward had always been ready to look after them, coming to see them every day when they were within reach, taking on the responsibilities of a father when their own father was gone.

'Peace?' said Richard.

'Peace. I will try the mediation. It won't work, but I'll try.'

'Ned will be grateful. He's in a generous mood, George. He's the father of a son at last. The news reached us before we left Burgundy.'

'A son? Oh yes, of course. So he is. A legitimate heir at last,' said Clarence, and laughed on a note that was curiously shrill.

Geoffrey of Silbeck went into battle just after sunrise on Easter Sunday morning, 14th April 1471. By accident.

The Battle of Barnet had descended like a landslide, despite all Edward Plantagenet's efforts to evade it. Warwick, spurning the offer of last-moment peace ('I put Edward where he is. I'm his benefactor and he'll recognise me as such or else!' he had snapped to Clarence), had concluded that he must leave Coventry and make a bid for London, and set out to race Edward for it. Edward had won by a whisker.

Now Warwick, his brother John Neville and their men waited north of the city, at Barnet, to challenge Edward for it face to face. The odds had evened. A number of wealthy lords, like Clarence and Stanley, were keeping out of the conflict, and Margaret of Anjou had not yet arrived. Edward marched out to meet his foe on something like equal terms.

He had marched at nightfall and taken up his position ready for the morning. Warwick's cannon, gape-mouthed monsters perched on high ground and staring out over the encampment below, had fired intermittently all night, aiming into the darkness in the hope of finding a mark. Their dull booming had kept Sir Geoffrey from sleep and he

251

was gritty-eyed when he rolled out of his rugs at cockcrow, into a throat-catching mist.

He had been told he was to be in the mounted reserve. Once mounted, waiting with his companions at the rear of the centre squadron, he watched while the light grew greyly round them and revealed a world not shrouded merely in early mist, but in a heavy, muffling fog. It was going to be a queer sort of battle in this.

The task of the reserve was to pursue fleeing foes or back up hard-pressed foot troops. Thus positioned, and encased in armour, he was considerably safer than at most tournaments, but he had had himself shriven just in case, though he had not mentioned the glove he carried inside his shirt. It was not a sin to carry a lady's favour. He had never sinned with Petronel and at this moment was regretting it, bitterly and intensely. She would not let him become her lover, and she was right, and it only made her more desirable. He could remember the precise moment when to his own amazement, he fell in love with her and he had thought then that his feelings could go no deeper, but they had. The more he thought of her, the longer she went on giving him glances full of wistfulness and yet still held aloof, the more powerful the enchantment became.

It would be a terrible thing if he died without knowing her. And although his danger was not great, he was uneasy. The wait seemed endless. Globules of moisture formed on his metal-sheathed thighs and he ached with cold. His helmet was not the massive affair one wore at tournaments but it still interfered with his hearing, adding yet another dimension to the swaddled silence which the mist had imposed on this unhallowed Easter morning.

Hidden in that mist, across the fields to left and right were other squadrons, commanded by lords loyal to Warwick and including several of his ubiquitous relatives by marriage. Somewhere to the left, too, was a marsh which should protect them from attack from the east. Near at hand he glimpsed Warwick, on foot, conferring with John

Neville, who was mounted. They were ghostly shapes, barely recognisable. At the sight of Sir John, Geoffrey's uneasiness increased.

John Neville had led them south to meet Warwick, but although they had ridden on Edward's heels, they had not tried to catch him. And night after night, John Neville had stayed awake, pacing back and forth in his chamber or round his camp. Geoffrey had seen and heard him. Now he knew that inside his ornate armour Neville was shrivelled with the sleeplessness of many nights, not only the one which the cannon had just given them all. John Neville did not want to be here, did not want to fight his cousins of York and neither, by osmosis, did his followers.

The conference ended. Warwick and Neville parted, fading into the vapours. A breeze sprang up, and to the east a dull orange circle showed the position of the sun. The mist began to rise in wreathing spirals and for the first time the two armies saw each other. They were closer together than they had thought. War-cries broke out on both sides. Trumpets sounded.

Both sides had seized the moment and were starting to advance. Warwick's archers loosed and a volley of shafts flew through the opened doors of the free-standing pavise shields. The pavise doors slammed shut just in time as an answering volley rattled against them. The cannon crashed anew and there was disruption and an ugly clamour in the oncoming Yorkist ranks.

The horses in the reserve half-reared, gathering their hocks beneath them. Their riders held them back. Then the armies met with a roar of voices and weapons which rolled back to the reserve in a breaker of sound, and in the same moment, the wind once more fell away. The sun vanished, the mist descended more blindingly than ever, and with it descended chaos.

The sound of the conflict changed at once. The war-cries and eldritch counterpoint of colliding blades suddenly mingled with repeated hoarse shouts on a note of alarmed enquiry. Trumpets spoke again and again, trying to collect men scattered in the fog. Then indistinct figures tumbled fighting out of the mist at the very feet of Geoffrey's horse and, without any choice in the matter, the reserve was in the fray.

A shape leapt at the bridle of Geoffrey's destrier. He struck at it and it fell. Warhorses were trained out of the natural equine instinct not to trample living things. Geoffrey glimpsed the last grim moment before the huge hoof descended on the frenzied face, saw the redness spatter over his horse's shoulder. Then he lost sight of it, lost sight too of the men who had been beside him in the reserve line. Had lost himself.

It was all blurred, incomprehensible, interminable. Afterwards, he never knew how long he spent plunging here and there in the fog. The battle had become a collection of little battles, fought between small groups of men, who were cut off from all the rest by the mist and had no idea where they were in relation to them. Men were knocked off their feet and as often as not crawled straight on to the enemy spears. Geoffrey blundered across turf churned and crimsoned and littered with a hideous debris, where broken hedges, broken weapons, broken flesh alike were being trodden down. He almost rode into the marsh at one point. Briefly, and astonishingly, a banner with a white boar on it swam across his line of vision; somehow, Richard of Gloucester had managed to lead an attack across the bogland. Trying to avoid the mud he also lost touch with the struggle against Gloucester but rode by accident into a cluster of his own colleagues, tackling a Yorkist band which had set upon John Neville. He joined them.

And, within moments, what had begun before the battle as unease had deepened into horror and despair. No one was wasting breath on comment but in times of mutual danger, minds were welded at a deeper level than words. Without words they all knew that John Neville was not rallying them as he should. They were being left to fight, each man according to his own judgement, and it was demoralising. Geoffrey's sword-arm weighed heavier and his belief in his own prowess waned. He caught himself thinking: *in a moment I shall be killed*.

A split second later he might well have been, except that the assailant who sprang from nowhere, wielding an axe, had lost his helmet and Geoffrey recognised him. 'My God,' said Geoffrey, sidling his horse to avoid the blow, his fighting skill suddenly restored by anger and a long-frustrated desire for revenge, 'I know you! You're William Hawick! Lost your knight's spurs at Smithfield, didn't you, when you cheated? I've been hoping to meet you again. Here's your pay, Hawick!'

He swung the horse again so that the descending axe which was meant to sweep him from the saddle and put him at the mercy of a poniard, flashed harmlessly past. Then he used his sword. Hawick had sprung from the left and Geoffrey had manoeuvred to keep him there. His sword was in the hand nearest to Hawick. It was easy. Hawick went down. Gasping, sweat-drenched inside his armour, Geoffrey veered away and discovered that a mail-clad angel had arrived, pounding on foot at the head of reinforcements. Warwick, in person.

Geoffrey still did not know where he was or even which way he was facing but Warwick apparently did. He was re-organising them, signalling the reserve back to form up again in a line behind what now emerged as a rank of archers, still stoutly in place. The mists, swirling, widened their field of vision, rolling back. There seemed to be hope again.

The surge of noise came suddenly, sweeping towards them, turning first into a shadow and then a line of men charging from what was now a quite distant wall of vapour. Above them, wildly waving, was a banner which Geoffrey for a frightful moment took for the King's Sun in Splendour. Then he saw that it was not, that the device was the Rayed Star of Oxford, who was one of Warwick's lords.

But it was still charging them. From the ranks of the archers, someone screamed: 'Treason!' Warwick's standard-bearer was shouting and leaping like a madman, brandishing the Bear and Ragged Staff banner of Warwick in the faces of the oncoming Oxford troops. Their leaders had seen it; trumpets were sounding, trying to halt what had clearly been a mistake, if anything in this cloud-bedevilled world could be called clear. But the archers had already loosed. Their shafts sped through the pavise doors with an evil swish and as the pavises shut with a composite bang, Oxford's line dissolved, struggling, flailing, shouting 'treason' in their turn.

And with that the genuine Sun in Splendour, rippling grandly above a tidal wave of Yorkist forces, was upon them. The world exploded around Geoffrey. He struck, wheeled, struck again, surprised to be still alive when all round him lives were going out like doused fires, amazed to be still whole when air and earth seemed full of the stricken faces of men who could not believe they had lost a hand, a leg, an eye, that those were their own guts, slithering out of them on to the cold ground.

He found himself beside John Neville. Neville was still horsed, as he had been throughout. He was fighting a man on foot but wearily, as if too tired to defend himself. Geoffrey's sword-edge was growing dull. He sheathed the sword, snatched out his axe and used that. Neville's opponent fell. Geoffrey was then almost thrown from his saddle as Neville's mount barged into him. Sir John's visor was up. His eyes were furious and pox-scars flamed on his skin. 'You stupid sod, get out my way!'

'What?' Geoffrey shouted.

'You heard them shout "treason", didn't you? Quite right, but I'm the traitor. Let me die, God damn you!' Neville's spurs drove into his horse. He plunged past and vanished across the grass into the fog. A dreadful clamour broke out, Yorkist war-cries and the sound of blades on armour. Geoffrey spurred desperately after Sir John. His horse stumbled on something – a body, an overturned pavise shield, he couldn't see what – and came down. He fell with it and was flattened by its weight. Men streamed past him, some fleeing, some giving chase. The battle was apparently over; it had become a rout. The horse struggled up, eyes rolling. Geoffrey dragged himself up as well and tried to mount but the horse, upset, sidled away. He leant against its shoulder; they were both exhausted. The fog was steadily clearing now. He could see blue sky.

The shouts and clamour were distant now, and receding. He did not try again to mount, but turned in the direction in which John Neville had gone, dragging his horse. It was something to do, an objective. The horse trailed obediently after him. It was alive because no one killed warhorses needlessly. If you slew a mounted foe, his steed was yours. Destriers were valuable.

Other things of value besides horses might be seized on the field. Eynesby itself had once been bought by such proceeds. When he found John Neville's corpse, he was not surprised to see predatory figures crouched over it.

But it was not a sight he could endure. He thrust his exhaustion away. He left his weary horse to stand, gripped his axe and ran at the robbers. He split one crouching back down the spine, shearing through the padded jacket as though it were tissue paper. He whirled the reddened blade and the others fled, taking with them whatever booty they had in their hands. He stood still, panting, weighed down by his mail, and then turned as the tail of his eye caught a movement. A Yorkist soldier, who had crept up behind him, levelled a pike and attacked.

His power to react was almost finished. His axe as he raised it seemed to weigh a hundredweight. But it was in his left hand and although his adversary must have seen it, he had been trained to fight right-handed men and the reflexes of the years now betrayed him. He moved the wrong way and the axe crashed home. Geoffrey saw the man's thorax open and the ends of the splintered ribs show white through the scarlet and heard the last whistling breath go out of him. Then his foe was dead at his feet and Geoffrey was once more alone.

He was sitting by Sir John's body, his head in his hands, when Richard of Gloucester rode up at the head of half a dozen men.

Richard was riding one-handed. The armour was gone from his left forearm and a bulgy, hastily-applied bandage was there instead. 'We heard Sir John Neville had fallen hereabouts,' he said pulling up. 'We seem to have found him. Who might you be, my friend? Stand up and take that helmet off.'

Slowly, Geoffrey obeyed. 'Sir Geoffrey Silbeck at your service, sir.'

'Ah yes,' said Richard. 'Of Warwick's household at one time. We have met.'

They were also half-brothers. Neither commented on this but Richard waved back the escort which had moved as though to surround Geoffrey. 'In this fight,' said Richard, 'I believe you followed Sir John?'

'I did.' Tiredly, Geoffrey brought out the arguments he had once put before his uncle. 'I used to be Warwick's man, but in this war he did not seem to me to have just cause. I can live without his retainer but . . . There is still the matter of loyalty to one's lord. It was a difficult situation, my lord of Gloucester. When I heard that Sir John was going to the war, I decided to go with him instead of with Warwick. He was a Neville, Warwick's brother. If he fought for the King, so would I. If he chose Warwick's side . . .' Geoffrey gazed steadily at Richard. 'Well, he had a quarrel with the King and it seemed to me that his at least was a dispute in which he had a case.'

'Northumberland?'

'Yes, Northumberland. In his following, I could fight for a Neville without dishonour. I did my best,' said Geoffrey, in a tone not far removed from the pettish. He wondered if he would now be arrested but was too tired to care. He ought to have died with Sir John, he thought. He probably would have died if he hadn't been left-handed. His uncle Lionel's unconventional attitude to this eccentricity had saved his life.

'Warwick is dead,' said Richard.

'On the field?'

'Pulled down when he was trying to escape from it, like a deer by a pack of wolves. But it may be best that way.'

Geoffrey nodded. Better for Warwick to die that way than by the cold dismissal of the block. Gloucester would not like to think of his cousin and former guardian being formally executed. He might well not like to think of such a thing happening to his half-brother either, even though Geoffrey belonged through the traditions of his mother's family to the Neville faction, even though they had never been publicly brothers. Richard was speaking again.

'Ships bearing the devices of Anjou have been sighted off Dorset. The courier who brought the news is with my brother King Edward now. Your own Neville lords are dead. Tell me, Sir Geoffrey, are you Anjou's man or ours?'

'Yours?' said Geoffrey. He was stupid with exhaustion.

'Yes, ours. I'm offering you a new allegiance. Sir John wouldn't object,' said Richard. 'Look.' With his good hand, he looped his reins round his saddle pommel, drew his sword and leant down, using the tip of the blade to move aside the loose plates of armour that half-hid John Neville's chest. The robber had had the mail half-off when Geoffrey burst upon them. Under it, the body was clothed in linen and a tabard of red silk. Richard had already seen that on the breast, untouched as it chanced by any wound, embroidered in bright gold thread, was Edward's Sun in Splendour.

Battles might be fought, kings might come and go, but the festivals of Holy Church ought not to be interrupted, and no one expected the Dean of St Paul's to take up arms.

During the days when the conflict was taking shape

around him, Dr Alcock prayed and meditated, prepared sermons and delivered them, just as usual. He conducted several funeral services and memorial masses and although some of them were for victims of the fighting, his homilies made no political references. He presided over meetings of the cathedral chapter and deliberately saw to it that the topics discussed concerned only St Paul's. New appointments to the cathedral clergy and methods of improving the standard of singing among the choristers were the items which received the most attention.

He also welcomed an unexpected visitor who announced himself as 'an old servant of your father, in Hull,' and counselled several young couples who were to be married as soon as Lent was over.

The old servant had never set foot in Hull or met Alcock's father in his life, and a bridegroom who came by himself to see the Dean had been a contentedly married man for six years. After their visits, Alcock each time engineered a seemingly chance encounter with King Edward. When the King went out to meet the foe at Barnet he did it with a knowledge of the number and nature of Warwick's forces which Alcock's innocent-looking visitors had supplied. If, in spite of that, the King were defeated, Alcock's apparent neutrality might protect both himself and his informants.

On Easter morning he celebrated Mass. He had a crowded congregation.

The citizens of London were very well aware that out there beyond the city's northern boundaries, their future was being decided. They had made it plain that they preferred Edward. They had harboured and succoured him and repelled one direct attack by Warwick already. If their royal defender now failed them and it was Warwick who marched victoriously back into the city, there would be carnage in the streets.

The Lord Mayor, panic-stricken 'because he doesn't know which cock to gamble on,' as some cynical wag had remarked, had taken to his bed some time ago with what his wife insisted was plague but a talkative servant of his maintained was a rash manufactured from beetroot juice. Alcock, facing the altar and leading his flock towards God, had the sensation that the congregation was not merely standing behind him but pressing forward on his heels in search of sanctuary. He more than sympathised.

But his carefully neutral behaviour in these past days had not been for defensive purposes only. He was a priest. His business lay with eternal verities which the struggle now in progress at Barnet could not alter. He had tried to concentrate on them lately as a matter of principle too. He tried to do so now. This was Easter. His own mind, and the minds of his congregation, should be engaged with the vista of eternal life and the conquest of death which was the Resurrection's meaning.

But if he was Dean of St Paul's as well as an intelligence gatherer, he was also a Privy Councillor. To which king's council would he belong by the end of today? His own safety apart, might he before the sunset of this Easter Day have been forced to witness the sack of the city?

He did not know and, despite himself, his voice faltered.

Chapter Eighteen

The Plantagenets: Pawn Taken

1471

Years before, when her cause was succeeding and the old
Duke of York, King Edward's father, had lost his life in
fighting against her, someone had thought of presenting
Margaret of Anjou with her enemy's head, rammed on a
spear. ' He wanted a crown,' she said, contemplating this
grisly trophy without any visible sign of revulsion. 'He shall
have one.'

As a child, while still too young to be aware of what was
fitting for her dignity and what was not, Margaret had
learned from one of her nurses the art of weaving baskets
and dolls and other shapes out of rushes. She exercised this
talent now, from a handful of fresh rushes which had been
intended for strewing on the floor. The woven crown she
contrived even had something resembling fleur-de-lis to
decorate it. She herself bound it round her mutilated
enemy's brow and twisted the last knot which held it in its
place.

It was not a deed with which to buy kindness in later
years. Thomas Stanley, the astringent man whom John
Alcock had once observed among Warwick's brothers-in-
law, had shown signs of backing Warwick during the latter's brief ascendancy, but had been talked out of it by
Richard of Gloucester, without undue difficulty. The reason for such easy capitulation lay in the intense dislike he
felt for Margaret of Anjou. He was glad she had been
defeated and glad too that her son, who by all accounts had
been very much the offspring of his detestable mother, was

dead. Stanley, in fact, had acid enjoyment in his voice and no compunction as he said: 'It is my duty, madam, to inform you that your son Edouard, formerly styled Prince, was killed attempting to flee the field near Tewkesbury. He died,' said Stanley, 'squealing like a rabbit when the weasels get it.'

He stood with his helmet under his arm in the parlour of Little Malvern Abbey, where Margaret had fled for sanctuary. The door at his back stood wide and from the river meadows of the Severn the scent of spring grass blew in on a warm wind. Edward had triumphed over Warwick at Barnet in mist and cold: he had conquered Margaret of Anjou at Tewkesbury, in the west, during the first heatwave of the year. 'Surely,' said Stanley as Margaret whitened, 'someone capable of officiating at a posthumous coronation isn't going to faint at a little detail like that?'

The prior had accompanied this aggressive minion of the King to the guest parlour. 'That will do, my lord. As a matter of decency, I must ask you to withdraw while these ladies compose themselves. They cannot run away.' He was a Welshman, short of stature but not short of dignity, and he was annoyed. Thomas Stanley had almost forced his way into the Abbey.

'Very well, but they must be ready in half an hour to come with me to King Edward's headquarters.' He allowed the prior to escort him out. Neither glanced more than cursorily at Anne Neville, standing stiffly beside her mother-in-law.

As the door closed, Margaret's mouth went square. She put a hand blindly behind her, found a bench and sank on to it.

'Go on,' said Anne viciously, 'weep for him. You were the one who taught him to love killing without understanding what it meant to die.'

Margaret stared at her and her tears were overtaken by rage. 'Hold that savage tongue of yours! I bore with you when you grizzled for your father!'

'I loved my father. He wronged me when he tried to throw me to your son but I still loved what was best in him, and mourned for it. I knew what my father was like. You never knew what your son was like. But I must thank you, madam, because hating my father as you did and me with him, and resenting my marriage to Edouard, you would not let him bed me till his cause was won. Did you never realise that your hatred had no finer weapon against me than Edouard's embraces?'

Margaret came to her feet, hand raised. 'Go on,' said Anne contemptuously. 'Hit me as you did once before. As you would have done a good many times since, except that King Louis made a pet of me and even you could see that it wouldn't do for the guest of honour to arrive at a banquet with red eyes and bruises. Do as you please, madam! You can't force me to sleep with Edouard now and nothing less is likely to frighten me. I'm glad he's dead, do you hear?' Amazed, Margaret let her hand drop. 'You're a great woman,' said Anne. 'A queen. You've led armies, signed treaties with your own name. How would you like to be nothing but a pawn, paired off to a boy you loathe, to suit someone else's ambitions?'

'How would I like to be . . .? You stupid girl,' said Margaret. 'You'd do better to ask how I *did* like it! What else was I when I came to England at fifteen years old – no older! – and found myself married to a pale, meek halfwit who thought women were devices of the devil to tempt men from the paths of purity? I rose above it. I showed my strength. I'd have made a better man than either my husband or my son, who had too much of his father in him. It's been said that Henry didn't father Edouard, but he did. Henry slept with me,' said Margaret bitterly, 'every night for one month because his Council told him it was his duty to the country. He also prayed every night throughout that month, in my presence, that he might be forgiven this lapse from chastity, which was due only to his sense of responsibility and not to anything as sinful as desire. What do you think that was like, my self-pitying, self-righteous little Anne? I overcame it. You could have overcome Edouard's shortcomings in the same way. I know more about them than you think. He was weak, despite all my efforts to toughen him. I am not the blind fool you suppose.'

'I . . .' began Anne and then could not go on. She had never before wondered what Margaret of Anjou had been like at fifteen. She looked at her mother-in-law's strong, sensual features and suddenly visualised her partnered not with the half-monk Henry but with a man as vigorous and carnal as herself. Margaret, queen to a king who knew how to rule, wife to a husband who was not afraid to be a man, would have been Margaret fulfilled, a free-flowing river, not dammed-up and dangerous . . .

In a million years, thought Anne, she would never have expected this. In a million years she would never have imagined herself cradling Margaret of Anjou's dark head against her shoulder and speaking words of comfort for Edouard's death, as she was doing now.

The Painted Chamber at Westminster Palace, with its inner window overlooking a chapel, was full of colour. From the midst of a sky-blue mural, Edward the Confessor all in silver leaf gazed out over the Council table. Mailed knights in silver-gilt stucco galloped across the opposite wall. The other two walls had vivid tapestries. A war-fleet made landfall; a woven city was besieged; a knight for some unexplained reason beheaded a lady. John Alcock's eyes kept on being drawn to this. He could think himself fortunate, he told himself, that he was not being asked to approve a course of action quite as objectionable as that.

The one the Council was being obliged to approve instead was odious enough.

Margaret of Anjou could be allowed to go on living, yes. The deadly disease of Lancastrian blood did not run in her veins; no one would launch a rebellion to put a crown on Margaret's head. In accordance with normal chivalric practice, she could be ransomed by her countrymen for a healthy sum (it would be useful; wars were expensive), and sent home to Anjou.

But her husband, who had once been Henry the Sixth, and who was now referred to as Henry of Lancaster, could not be so easily neutralised. He would for the rest of his life be a possible focus for rebellion, by those who truly believed his line to have the right to the throne, and by those who wished to take advantage of his feeble wits in order to rule through him.

It would therefore be advisable to see that the rest of Henry's life was as short as possible. The land had seen enough of the destruction and the costliness of civil war. Alcock understood this perfectly well, but it did not make the elimination of Henry any pleasanter. This was one of the times when he longed to turn his back on the whole world of court and state and political intrigue, flee to St Paul's and kneel there, hiding his head in prayer.

But a responsible Councillor could not behave like that, so he sat quiet while a man's life was disposed of, and felt as though his own instinctively kindly nature, not to mention his Christian principles, were being subjected to a form of rape. He knew that across the table Cardinal Bourchier, the Archbishop of Canterbury, felt very much the same.

But their silence, however miserable, was still silence. The one man at the Council table who apparently didn't understand the situation sufficiently to hold his tongue was Richard of Gloucester, whose protests were vociferous. Edward had listened to him patiently, if unyieldingly. It was Thomas Stanley who was now trying to argue with him. Stanley's veering allegiances, to Warwick and back again, had done his reputation no good. Alcock had actually heard a group of Council members raising their voices and dragging the topic of *weathercocks* into their conversation when Stanley entered the room. Thomas Stanley's expression these days was more than ever that of a man who has been eating sour fruit. He was trying to redeem himself by a devoted support of whatever policies Edward chose.

But Richard, unimpressed, was shouting him down. 'It's shameful. And what do we put it out as? Natural death? Do we tell the populace that he died of sheer displeasure and melancholy? Will anyone believe us?'

'He's in poor health,' said William Hastings gloomily. He doesn't like this either, Alcock thought.

'And as for the notion of pretending to him that he's being escorted to a ceremony and then striking him down from behind . . .'

'God's teeth, Richard, do you *want* him to know it's coming?' Edward lost patience. 'Do you think any of us will enjoy disposing of a poor old man who'd have been happier as a monk?'

There was a silence, during which the image of Henry, the long, gentle face and the tendency to round shoulders, the look, at once touching and exasperating, of complete defencelessness, hovered before the mental vision of all present. Then Thomas Stanley said: 'He was born to the throne. He should have faced up to his responsibilities. He failed them and so all the rest of us have been forced to take sides when we would prefer simply to serve a king.'

And with that, with the responsibility for Henry's misfortunes deposited firmly on Henry's bent shoulders, all but Richard shook themselves like dogs shaking water out of their coats and Edward said: 'The decision is taken, openly, in Council, as it should be. We are not committing a hole-in-the corner murder but defending the peace of the realm. And that is that, my lord of Gloucester.'

'I have business in Kent soon,' said Richard. 'I shall leave as soon as this session closes. I would prefer to be out of London before the deed is done.'

'As you wish,' said Edward coldly. 'We will go on to the next item.' The officiating clerk cleared his throat but Edward, who always knew his agendas by heart, forestalled him. 'It concerns a new appointment to the Council. My lord Archbishop?'

Bourchier was well-connected enough to be a major political force in his own right but he wasn't interested. He was another who disliked taking sides. To Bourchier, the York versus Lancaster rivalry was a tedious waste of time and talent. They all knew his views. Even so, what he had to say about the proposed new appointment came as a shock to most of them. '*John Morton?*' said half a dozen scandalised voices.

'Dr Morton has been one of Margaret of Anjou's most staunch supporters,' said Stanley seriously. 'Surely he himself can't want . . .'

'He does want,' said Edward. 'And why not? He is an extremely able and ambitious man who has had to spend years in the shadows. It's to his credit that he never tried to change sides before. He remained true to Lancaster until there was no longer a house of Lancaster to be true to, and I can appreciate that.' He wasn't looking at Stanley and probably wasn't even thinking about him, but Stanley's sallow skin flushed faintly. 'Morton,' Edward said, 'was a very able Privy Councillor when Henry was king. As he has just told you, Cardinal Bourchier here knew him personally and in fact brought him to the notice of the King. After Towton, he was arrested for supporting the Lancastrian cause. But although Henry of Lancaster was by then quite unfit to rule, nevertheless, the school of thought which backed him simply because he had once been an anointed king cannot be called criminal or treacherous. Misguided, perhaps. I do not consider Morton to be a treacherous man. I didn't even then. The arrest was one of those heat of the moment mistakes. I saw to it, personally, that he escaped from custody. He knew who had arranged it and he hasn't forgotten. He's very willing indeed to serve me now and on my side I'd welcome the services of such a capable administrator with so much financial acumen. It was I, my lords, who sent Bourchier to him to negotiate.'

'He has made just one stipulation,' said Bourchier. 'The whole Council must invite him.'

269

'Naturally,' said Edward, 'I expect that my Council members will allow me to guide them on this point.' There was a grim silence.

'I've met him and I don't like him. I don't approve,' said Richard flatly.

'That's not a sound reason,' said Edward.

'There, I agree.' Alcock sighed as he spoke. He too had met Dr Morton and he hadn't liked him, either. It was probably mutual. Despite their similar professional qualifications, they were opposites. Alcock was large, fresh-complexioned and friendly; Morton was lean, dark, cadaverous and self-contained. Alcock was a north-countryman and Morton came from Dorset; Alcock was a Cambridge man and Morton was Oxford educated. Ancient rivalries, between the universities of Oxford and Cambridge, and between the north and the south, had stirred at that encounter. But none of it amounted to a reason for not appointing the man. 'I didn't take to him either,' said Alcock, 'but I don't question his integrity or his ability. I would say that he has both in full measure.'

'As a matter of sheer good taste,' said Stanley, 'not to mention caution, we should exclude him from our plans for Henry of Lancaster. He had best have the same story as everyone else. Natural death, from heartbreak.' His voice held a shrivelling cynicism. Alcock found himself in sympathy with it.

'We are discussing Morton,' said Edward coolly. 'I take it, my lords, that Cardinal Bourchier may inform him that the Council, as a body, have invited him to join them?'

'I say no,' said Richard.

'Richard.' Edward's voice was gentle and inexorable, both at once. 'It's an order.'

Richard, having demanded private speech with his brother, stood facing Edward in the latter's private rooms. Edward was in the long loose gown which he wore when preparing for bed. Beyond an inner door, Bess Woodville awaited him. There was a touch of her exotic sandalwood perfume in the air. 'I hope that whatever this is, it's important,' Edward said.

'It's this!' Richard flourished a parchment scroll with the royal seal attached. 'It instructs me to go to the Tower before I leave for Kent, and require the Constable to be ready to surrender Henry of Lancaster's person to Sir James Tyrell and his men. Who on earth is this Sir James Tyrell, by the way?'

'A most able and well-spoken young man from Suffolk. I knighted him on the field at Tewkesbury as a reward for exceptional valour. Go on. I take it that you don't wish to carry out your orders and want to know why the devil I signed them?'

'Yes, I do. I am being publicly associated with this . . . this killing. Why can Tyrell not present these instructions at the Tower without me, if presented they must be?'

'They must, Richard. There are really very few places for a former king to go except into his tomb. I've tried to keep Henry out of his, but I dare not try any longer. As for why you must be involved, I will say this. In private, argue with me all you like, but in public I must have your loyalty and your obedience. After your attitude at the Council, I am obliged to demonstrate to its other members that I still command those things from you. The insignia of my house may be a white rose, but if you imagine that the crown of England is made of roses, you're mistaken! I have had to fight to get it and to keep it, and I need your support. If you, my brother, can't be trusted to support me, how can any other members of my Council? One brother has already behaved in such a way that I cannot have him on it. Be good enough yourself to be an asset to it and not a leader of dissension. Will you carry my commands to the Tower and prove that in the last resort you stand with me whatever your personal views? Or do I put you under arrest until you come to your senses? Make no mistake, Richard. I mean to be rid of the Lancastrian menace and I also mean to have the men I want on the Council. Even John Alcock supports me and no one is more peace-loving or respectful of human life than he is. But he accepts reality. I hope to make him a bishop within another year. He's a worthy man and gives me incomparable service.'

'You threatened to arrest me once before,' said Richard, 'long ago when I was a lad and Warwick was wooing me and you thought –wrongly – that I was being won over.'

'Yes. You kept faith with me then. And now?'

Richard looked with hatred at the parchment cylinder in his hand. 'That you should charge me with faithlessness because I don't want to see either a defenceless man slaughtered for being born a Lancastrian *or* a proven Lancastrian adherent on your Council, makes me feel very bitter, Ned. I have never been anything but loyal to you and I think you know that. I take the views I do because of that loyalty. I will carry out this order if you insist, not from fear of arrest but out of fidelity. If you still insist, that is.'

'Oh, I do,' Edward assured him. 'I do!'

'Edward is setting out to wipe out the house of Lancaster. Sooner or later, he'll remember your existence. Get away to the Continent and stay there.'

'But I don't count. I mean, I'm debarred from the succession. My line is only half legitimate.'

'Act of Parliament!' said Margaret Beaufort impatiently. 'Words on paper! Words on paper can be scratched out and other words written in. Do you understand? You must go, and at once.'

'Very well,' said Henry Tudor unenthusiastically. His mother knew best, he supposed. Sometimes he longed for stability, to live in one place, belong to one place and know precisely who he was.

'I shall miss you,' said Margaret Beaufort. 'God knows, I shall miss you. I shall attend an extra Mass for you, every day. But one day . . . God go with you, my son. And remember, you are all that is now left of Lancaster.'

PART THREE
KITH VERSUS KIN
1471–1478

Chapter Nineteen

The Plantagenets: Knight and Lady

1471

There were worse fates, Nicholas Hawes had discovered, than being obliged to leave one's native city or one's calling. But for his ejection from York, but for his gambling disaster at Smithfield, he would have passed his life as a struggling nonentity in the building trade which he had hated since he was first forcibly apprenticed to it by a father who said it was 'a good living'. Now, because for want of any other goal he had adopted Geoffrey Silbeck's half-insulting suggestion that he should go on pilgrimage, he was a travelled man who had been to Jerusalem and back.

He had done more. He had seen great ships and strange cities on the way. He had eaten extraordinary dishes, haggled in unfamiliar currencies with Venetian galley captains even more rapacious than himself (before finding out that the official return fare for the sea trip between Venice and Jerusalem was a straight fifty ducats with visitors' fees at designated shrines thrown in) and he had seen the Alps.

He had also looked on the Mediterranean and carved his name illegally on the walls of the Holy City. He had had his purse stolen on the site of St George's martyrdom and recouped his loss by staging a fit of religious ecstasy in a Jerusalem street, a performance guaranteed to attract alms from devout passers-by. He had learned the ropes.

Now, back in London, he was selling his knowledge. Master Hawes, experienced traveller, will undertake to guide pilgrims to Jerusalem and back by the Dover-Calais-St Bernard's Pass and Venice route. Journeys are fully organised: food, transport, accommodation all attended to. Intending travellers may find Master Hawes at the Sign of the Palm Branch in Candlewick Street.

In an average season he would leave London at the end of April with his party, bring them back in September and at once begin the search for the next season's clients. He would wait on better-off prospects in their homes, travelling some way if necessary. It was because he had been calling on a likely customer with 'Sir' in front of his name and a position in the Queen's household that he chanced to be actually in the great hall of her house in Sheen, near Richmond, some miles west of the City, on a crisp autumn morning in 1471.

He had made his way to Sheen the night before and seen his client early. It was still early when, having successfully concluded his business, he prepared to leave. But he stopped and moved back like everyone else in the hall as trumpeters sprang to attention in the doorway to sound a fanfare, and five magnificently clad persons entered. As everyone round him bowed, curtsied or saluted, he realised that one of the five must be the King. He whispered a question to a neighbour.

'The King's grace is with the Queen. The others are the King's brothers and my lady of Clarence,' the neighbour whispered back. 'They've been to Confession.'

Nicholas, straightening up from his bow as the quintet swept past, thought that if so, they had lost no time in re-infecting their freshly cleansed souls. With complete disregard for the interested household population, they were indulging in a quarrel of the most unholy proportions.

They were so engrossed that they let themselves slow to a halt halfway down the hall as the King swung round to face the others. Edward's strong voice boomed out. 'You're not being reasonable, George. Are you going to keep hold of the girl for ever? Why you should want to stand in Richard's way . . .'

'I don't want to stand in his way!' retorted Clarence. 'He can marry Anne with my right good will and I'll give her away at the wedding. But I won't give her estates away. They're mine, I'm Warwick's heir. For the love of all the saints, hasn't Richard got wealth enough already? If he's in love with the girl . . .'

'I'm not in love with her!' shouted Richard, as though refuting a particularly scandalous slander. 'She's the obvious choice for me, that's all. It's high time I married. Anne and I may have been playmates at Middleham as children but that isn't the point. What is the point is that Anne Neville is suitable for me and . . .'

At the word 'suitable', the superbly gowned lady, whom Nicholas had by now identified as the Queen, shot Richard a sharp, uneasy glance and seemed to become aware of their public circumstances. 'Surely,' she said, 'this is not the time or the place . . .'

Her voice was gentle, cool, a little flurried. Richard ignored it. 'I naturally assume that my wife's inheritance comes to me with her as a matter of right – her rights as well as mine. A pretty service I should be rendering her if I let you rob her of her patrimony, George. You have the use of your own wife's portion. Be content with that. You're damned lucky to have it. Your father-in-law died attainted of treason and only Ned's generosity leaves his daughters the right to inherit anything at all!' He turned sharply to the other lady, who stood biting her lips at Clarence's side. 'Isabel, you're Anne's sister. Have you nothing to say on her behalf?'

'Naturally Anne is my sister,' said Isabel, 'but with George to look after her interests, she's in the best of hands.' Clarence patted her arm and she smiled nervously. Isabel had learned a method of managing her wayward husband now. Clarence responded to flattery and therefore she assiduously flattered him.

Richard was not impressed. 'Oh is she in good hands? George wants all the estates you've got between you. Is he going to marry the two of you, then, like a bloody paynim?'

Isabel flushed and turned away. A draught blew through the hall from an imperfectly shut door and she crossed her arms to chafe her elbows. A dignified waiting woman quickly stepped forward with a shawl. 'Thank you, Ankaret. I can always rely on you,' said Isabel, with a gratitude which was revealing. Somewhere in her life others had proved less reliable.

Clarence said heatedly: 'That's a disgraceful thing to suggest, Richard. You're the one who's greedy.' Hawes had the impression that Clarence too had become aware of the fascinated audience but that he, unlike the Queen, was enjoying it. 'Look at the honours you hold!' said Clarence resonantly and proceeded to list them. He made the title of Great Chamberlain sound like a crime of which Richard had been convicted and Constable of All England like a species of epithet. 'I'm Ned's brother just as much as you are,' he concluded, 'and I have barely enough money to pay my bills!'

'Jealous?' Richard glared at him. 'Well, I didn't take up arms against the King, did I? Did you expect Ned to reward you for it?'

'I expected to be given what was due to the King's brother. You promised me that on Ned's behalf, didn't you? I rebelled in the first place only because of the treatment I had had. I was forbidden to marry where I chose . . .'

'It didn't stop you,' Edward remarked. 'You bribed the Papal Adviser to get yourself a dispensation to marry a cousin and went ahead regardless.'

'Then Richard can go ahead regardless.'

'Without the dowry?' asked Edward.

'Yes! And until you accept that, Richard, you don't go near Anne. Understand that!'

Gently, as though in an uncertain attempt to make peace or at least divert the conversation a little, the Queen said: 'My lord of Clarence, where is Anne now? I have not seen her in weeks.'

Clarence smiled, a mischievous smile which revealed how

in other circumstances he might charm and beguile. Even the fact that these days he had pouched eyes and drinker's veins round his nose did not quite mask that charm. 'Ah,' he said, 'now, that would be telling.'

Richard was half-way down the hall, pale with anger, flinging away in search of fresh air and less maddening company, when his sleeve was plucked. 'Yes?' he said impatiently to the small red-faced man who had plucked it.

'Sir, I couldn't help but hear. If you want to find the Lady Anne Neville, I may be able to help.'

'May be able to help? Are you sure? Who are you?'

Judging that Richard of Gloucester was in no mood to be tantalised, Hawes put what he had to say in the tersest possible terms. 'My name is Nicholas Hawes, sir. I lodge in Candlewick Street. I organise pilgrimages for a living. When I am at my lodgings, I sometimes eat in a cookshop nearby . . .'

Anthony Woodville was married but the rooms he used at Westminster were bachelor quarters. He found his wife dull and she found his intellectual tastes bewildering. She never came to court and his quarters showed the mark of only Anthony's taste and character. In the principal chamber, the big curtained bed, which should conventionally have been the centrepiece, had been pushed aside to make room for other things, including a shelf of books, among them some valuable illuminated manuscripts and some of the printed works now being imported from Germany. A map of the known world hung on the wall, partly obscuring a lurid mural of St Stephen's martyrdom. This was probably a deliberate arrangement; Anthony was fastidious. A table stood under the window and on this was a stand, of Anthony's own design, in which were placed maps and charts, rolled into tubes and neatly labelled. Also on the table was a curious device, three feet high, of cogwheels set at differing angles. If the chief cogwheel were turned with a handle it set the rest turning with it.

The afternoon had turned wet and dark. Anthony needed both a candelabra and a magnifying glass in order to adjust this strange assembly. Bits of it lay on the table. Dr Alcock, leaning over the table at his side, was steadying a wheel for him. Alcock's easy temper and interest in learning appealed to Anthony, who had invited him along to examine the device. The three other people who were lounging about the room had sauntered in uninvited and both Anthony Woodville and John Alcock wished they would go away. They kept fiddling with the detached pieces of machinery and at any moment might mislay or break something. Two of them were Anthony's nephews, the Greys, Bess Woodville's sons by her first marriage. The third was older, a stocky young man who had been a friend of the Greys for some time but who would not have been brought on a casual visit to their Uncle Anthony before he acquired his knighthood. His name was James Tyrell. He was a little shy of Anthony and his behaviour was therefore slightly less aggravating than that of the Greys, but he was broad-built and kept getting in the way of the little daylight there was.

'I know it's raining but can't you three find something else to do?' Anthony grumbled. 'There isn't space for you all in here.'

The sixteen-year-old Thomas Grey let out a snort of laughter. 'Here comes another one! You're popular today, Uncle.'

'What in the world is that extraordinary object?' said Richard of Gloucester from the doorway.

'It isn't in the world, strictly speaking.' Anthony, elbows on the table and fingers edging a tiny camshaft into position, did not look round. 'It's a model illustrating the movements of the sun and moon and earth and all the planets. I've just had it delivered.' He pushed a hanging sleeve carefully out of the way. 'Mars is out of alignment.'

'When he's got it back into alignment,' said Thomas, perching on the table edge and ignoring Alcock's reproving tut-tut, 'he'll tell all our fortunes.'

'These wheels,' said Anthony sententiously, 'admittedly remind me of the concept of the Wheel of Fortune, which turns as it will for us all, although Dr Alcock here does not agree . . .'

'No,' said Alcock, 'or where is the doctrine of free will? If there is no free will, there is no good or evil either, or at least no choice between them. Predestination must therefore be nonsense. And so is astrology. It follows.'

'I am myself of the opinion,' said Anthony, 'that free will exists but within limitations. Some of the limitations lie in one's own nature or circumstances, which preclude certain options . . .'

'Have I interrupted a metaphysical discussion?' asked Richard.

'No,' said Anthony, squinting into the depths of the machinery. 'That was interrupted some time ago by my two nephews and their friend here. I was going to say, just now, that although I believe to some extent in fate, I too have doubts about astrology.'

'But the device could be adapted for astrological use if one wished, sir?' said Tyrell enquiringly.

'There's no doubt about your fortune,' said Thomas Grey impudently. 'You've been noticed, really noticed. You could reach any heights!'

Tyrell aimed a friendly punch at him. Thomas yelped: 'Peasant!' and leapt on him. They rolled wrestling on the floor, collided with a table leg, shook a chart of the November heavens and a map of the Sussex coastline out of the stand, and misaligned Venus as well as Mars. The younger Grey boy climbed on to the table out of the way, perturbing the conjunctions of the planets still more. Anthony swore and aimed a decidedly unintellectual kick at the nearest of the two tight-hosed rears bumping about below. 'It's the weather. They've nothing better to do. Have you come to take them all away, Richard? I'd be grateful!'

'I've come for information,' said Richard. 'On a . . . a private matter. I didn't want simply to send a man-at-arms or a squire to make enquiries. There are delicacies in these things. Anthony, Dr Alcock, any of you: have you by any chance heard of a cookshop in the City known as Master Taberner's? It would be near Candlewick Street. It may be quite new.'

The combatants on the floor broke apart and sat up. 'A cookshop?' said Thomas Grey incredulously. 'An ordinary cookshop?'

'My dear Richard, is it likely?' Anthony laid down his magnifying glass and stooped to retrieve his charts. 'Would any of us frequent such places?'

'Who *would* know?' Richard persisted.

'What is it you need to know about it?' Alcock turned to examine Gloucester's thin, tight countenance. 'What is the matter, my lord? I can see that you're worried.'

'I want to know exactly where the place is and whether it's respectable, to begin with. And I didn't wish to pursue the matter with the man who first mentioned it to me, any more than with a man-at-arms. He didn't strike me as at all respectable,' said Richard.

'I believe I've seen it.' Tyrell rose and dusted his clothes, bowing rather hastily to Richard. 'If it's the one I'm thinking of – yes, it opened recently. I've never been into it but I think local workmen and apprentices eat there during the day. It's closed in the evening. I'd say it's quite respectable. The proprietor was once employed by the Duke of Clarence, I believe.'

'Indeed? Then it almost certainly is the right shop. Clarence is probably the landlord, come to think of it. Tell me,' said Richard, studying Tyrell hard, 'would you be willing to do me a service?'

'Of course, sir.'

'Would you go there as a customer, dressed in ordinary-looking clothes and find something out for me?'

'Certainly.'

Alcock watched them with interest. Richard had said some hard things about Tyrell after the demise of Henry of

282

Lancaster, but Alcock thought Tyrell was decent enough; a tough young man, but entirely honest, prepared to carry out the orders of the King and Council even if they involved unpleasant tasks, and now prepared to carry out the orders of the King's brother with similar efficiency and lack of question. Richard appeared now to be recognising these things. The two of them had much in common. They were much of an age, neither quite twenty, and both had borne responsibilities beyond his years. They might well be drawn to one another.

'What must I enquire about?' Tyrell asked.

Richard said: 'Find out if Anne Neville's there.'

She had been the daughter of the Earl of Warwick and the daughter-in-law of a king. Now she was rolling pastry in a London cookshop. It was a strange sort of life for someone with her personal history, Anne Neville thought.

She supposed she should resent being sent here, but when she first arrived, after being bundled off by Clarence at an hour's notice, concealingly cloaked, on foot and in the charge of two manservants, she had been too tired and battered of spirit to care. She had been whirled from place to place, from person to person, too often and too fast. She had hardly even had time to mourn for her father. She wanted to stop, to be still, to have time to think and understand. Anywhere would do, and any company. Master Jarvis Taberner's Cookshop was good enough.

The cookshop was in a turning off Candlewick Street, wedged between a saddler's and a linen seller. Inside it had a sawdust-strewn floor sunk below street level, trestles and benches for customers wishing to eat on the premises, and a counter at the back where people bought food to eat elsewhere. It smelt of cookery, steam, grease and inadequately washed humanity.

But soldiers on campaign often put up with worse and Anne had learned something now about campaigning. Fleeing from England with her parents and Clarence and Isabel, ten hours a day in the saddle for two days and five on the third, with Isabel's horrifying childbed on board that tossing ship afterwards, following Margaret of Anjou's army to Tewkesbury over hot summer roads with the dust hanging in the air from the troops who marched ahead, she had discovered the meaning of hardship. By comparison, the cookshop was almost a haven.

Certainly no one was unkind to her. Taberner had once been an under-butler to Clarence, was still a tenant of his, and did what his powerful master told him, which in this case was to hide Anne from her cousin of Gloucester by dressing her as a cookmaid and giving her work in the shop. But he was respectful enough, possibly because Clarence had given him orders about that too. And then, there was Kat.

She had recognised Kat at once. The last time Anne had seen her, Kat had been maid to Mistress Petronel Eynesby, who had attended on herself and Isabel at Middleham. Kat was more than respectful. Anne had actually overheard Master Taberner lecturing his wife quite sternly on the importance of treating Anne as though she were just another employee. Kat could not be trusted not to curtsy or blurt out 'My lady!' when addressing Anne. But her friendly presence and the example she set the girls who were Anne's fellow employees was reassuring.

If there had been disrespect from anyone, it had been from the other girls. Master Taberner had explained her well-bred accent and any other inadvertent signs of nobility to them by saying that she was a byblow of some unidentified lord 'now dead, so the money supply to his mistress has stopped. The girl's been reared above her station but don't hold it against her. She's willing to work and not proud.'

But the girls had not unnaturally stood back for the first week or so, to see if this wench with the unofficial noble blood and the over-exalted education would acquit herself well or ill. Anne herself had been nervous. She was not allowed to serve customers for fear that her face might be recognised or her voice provoke gossip. Her duties therefore consisted of work in the kitchen, and that meant cooking.

It was fortunate, she realised, that her mother had encouraged her and Isabel to learn cookery. It was true that at home, she and Isabel had mostly concentrated on making sugared violets and modelling flowers or houses in marchpane. But somewhere along the way, Anne had also learned how to make several kinds of pastry, and prepare a variety of pie fillings. Now, these skills proved their worth. They had been her first step towards acceptance. She took the second when one of the others asked snidely whether she found their communal mattress to be a 'bit crowded and not what you're used to' and Anne, remembering the lurching ship outside Calais and the stifling tent outside Tewkesbury. replied quite sincerely: 'Why, no, I sleep very well,' which surprised them all into silence. By the end of the fortnight, when she had proved that she could not only make excellent pies but was willing to do extra to cover for a girl who wanted to slip out and meet a sweetheart, she had become simply 'Anne – she talks a bit la-di-da but she's all right.'

The day that Jarvis Taberner's errand boy came back from the spice merchant's, and said in innocent excitement that the Duke of Gloucester and six armed men all on foot had just turned into Candlewick Street, she was in the rear kitchen, kneading dough alongside a girl called Joan and answering questions on 'what the big houses were like where you grew up'. Anne was describing the kitchens of Middleham, circumspectly not mentioning the castle's name and implying that helping cooks was part of the arrangement under which she lived there. She broke off, startled, as Master Taberner hurried in and caught her arm. 'Gloucester, coming down the street,' he said shortly, regardless of Joan's presence. He nodded towards the stair which led up from a corner of the kitchen to the floor above. 'Up there!'

'You mean this duke's coming here after *her*?' Joan was open-mouthed.

'Family feuds. These great people have all sorts of funny goings-on,' said Taberner resourcefully. 'Not a word, if he comes in here, do you understand? Upstairs, Anne!'

There were three rooms upstairs, leading out of one another. The stairs led straight into the big bedchamber where the Taberners slept with their small son in a cot by the bed. The next one housed the female staff. The men-servants slept downstairs, under the counter, and the third first-floor room, which was not much larger than a fairly capacious cupboard, was used as a junk room. Taberner, hurrying after Anne, hustled her through to the junk room, pushed her in and turned the key on her. The place was dusty and cold, with a low sloping ceiling and a miserable view through a slatted window into a backyard full of debris. There was a chest, a pile of stacked truckle beds, a couple of benches, standing up on end and leaning against the wall, and a table with a wobbly leg. Anne sat down on the chest, clasped her hands in the lap of the flour-dusted apron she wore over her brown woollen dress, and waited on events.

Once again, she supposed she should have protested, but it was too much trouble. Master Taberner was only obeying orders he dared not defy and she herself had no wish to see the Duke of Gloucester. She remembered him, of course, from the days when Warwick had frankly encouraged his wards Clarence and Gloucester to make friends with his daughters. The two York boys had danced with her and Isabel, escorted them out hawking, shared their games and lessons. She had liked Richard – or Dickon as everyone called him then.

But all that was long ago. Now he was coming after her with armed men and all she wanted was peace, escape from wars and dangers and male ambition.

After Tewkesbury, if only Clarence had taken the trouble to ask her what she wanted to do, she would have answered: 'Withdraw to a nunnery.' Sitting on the chest in the chilly lumber room, she imagined one. A quiet priory, serene behind protective walls, with fruit growing against the south-facing ones, and days divided evenly and predictably by the singing of the Office. Even the Duke of Gloucester wouldn't be able to get at her there. Neither would Clarence, of course, unless she consented, which was no doubt why the expedient of a nunnery hadn't suited him. He wanted her and her estates to remain under his hand.

Downstairs she heard the tramp of feet. Voices were raised in sharp enquiry. Master Taberner answered on a histrionic note of indignation. She couldn't hear the words but she knew what he was saying. The Lady Anne Neville here? Why in the world should the Duke of Gloucester expect to find a lady of such rank in this humble place?

'Why indeed?' said a voice sufficiently ringing to be intelligible through the floorboards. She had not heard Richard's voice for nearly two years but she recognised it instantly. He gave some sort of command. There were scrapings and bangings as though benches were being pushed aside, some alarmed exclamations probably from customers, another sharp order from Richard, expostulations from Jarvis. Then feet on the stair. The building was timber and the sound vibrated through it. The feet tramped towards her through the other rooms and someone tried the door. She sat quietly, watching it shake.

'Anne? Anne!'

She said nothing.

'Open this door, Master Taberner!'

'I can't, my lord. It's a disused room and the key is lost.'

'Very well. Scrivener and Green, come here!' More rapidly ascending feet. 'Break this door down!'

Jarvis Taberner's voice came again. 'There's no need, my lord. I was doing only what my lord of Clarence bade me. I owe my livelihood to him. He could throw me out of this house if he chose.' Somewhere, Kat Taberner was sobbing – with fright, Anne thought.

'I realise that. If he does, come to me.' Richard spoke calmly. 'The key, please.'

She heard it grate into the lock. Then he was in the room.

He kicked the door shut behind him, leaving everyone else outside. Across the little room, they stared at each other.

'You must have heard me calling your name. You didn't answer. Why?'

She heard the unfriendliness in her own voice as she said: 'Why should I, particularly?' She knew that her chin had risen an inch. 'How did you know I was here?'

'A man who eats at this cookshop had heard gossip that a girl was here who was new, used to noble houses and her background was a bit of a mystery. He had also heard you referred to as Anne. I sent a friend to investigate. He knows you by sight. He managed to look through to the kitchen while he was leaning up against the counter. He told me he thought he had recognised you, not that you looked much like yourself. I came at once.'

'So I see. Now it's my turn to ask why.'

'Why? I'm your cousin, if nothing else. Did you think I would leave you in a place like this?'

'George of Clarence is my cousin. In fact, he's also my brother-in-law, and he sent me here.'

'To keep you out of my reach?'

'So he said.'

'I see.' Slowly, as if to avoid startling a nervous colt, Richard pulled a truckle bed off its pile and sat down on it. He set his elbows on his knees and framed his face between his hands. Despite the slightness of his build, his forearms were powerful and the shoulders above them had thick pads of muscle. The right shoulder was a little heavier than the left. Somewhere on his stormy progress through the shop, he had torn his left sleeve and then impatiently pushed it back; she could see a thick red scar on his forearm. He had been wounded at Barnet, she remembered someone telling her.

'Have you been ill-treated here?' he asked.

'No, your brother said I was to be used with courtesy.

The other girls didn't take to me at first but I've avoided giving offence and, as it happens, I can make pastry. I get along with them very well now. It's easy. I've only to be polite and do a good day's work.' She knew that her smile was sour.

So did Richard. 'In a few more years,' he remarked, 'you could turn into quite a shrew.'

'Thank you,' said Anne icily.

Richard gazed around at the cobwebby rafters and the ill-fitting floorboards. One could almost see the cooking smells which filtered up between them. 'Why are you so angry? You can hardly want to stay here.'

'I don't, but I've been less frightened here than when I thought I'd have to be Edouard's wife. He threatened to blind me once, and his mother hit me. No one hits me here. It isn't paradise but I've known worse places.'

'I take it that you know I have the King's permission to marry you? Am I to understand that you think that might be worse than this? Can you see no difference between me and Edouard? I've heard all about him, by the way. If you can't distinguish between us, I don't regard that as a compliment.'

'What I'm trying to tell you – I think –' said Anne, her voice taut and high, 'is that for all your pretty talk about being my cousin and not willing to leave me in a place like this, I don't believe that you or anyone else cares a farthing what happens to me. You only care for your own convenience, your own gain, all of you. All my father thought about when he handed me to Margaret and Edouard was that the marriage was a good thing for him. Clarence put me here so as to hold on to my inheritance. Now you want to marry me and that will be a good thing for you because you'll get your hands on my inheritance instead. All right, you've found me and you've brought soldiers so I suppose I can't resist. If you'll let me put my few things together – they're in the next room – I'll come with you and do whatever you say. You've got the King's consent to our marriage and I suppose that's much the same as the King's order. I shall do as I'm told as usual, but I need not pretend I like it and you need not pretend that you care whether I like it, either.'

'How dare you?' shouted her cousin, as though they were children at Middleham again and she had snatched an unfair advantage in a game of tag. 'Of all the . . .'

Staring at him, and reminded of those happy days of innocence, Anne felt the tears come into her eyes. He saw them but it made no difference. 'How dare you suggest that all I want is your money? What the devil gave you that idea?'

'Clarence said so.'

'Clarence! One of these days someone will murder Clarence. I'm fighting to get your inheritance, yes, but for you! Don't you want it? Do you want to spend the rest of your life either as Clarence's pensioner or my wife, having to be grateful to someone else for every mouthful you eat and every yard of cloth you wear? I shall protect your self-respect and your worldly goods even if you won't. You're Warwick's daughter, let me remind you. Listen to me. Marry me and you'll be safe. You'll have the position you were born to, a secure home and proper treatment and, God willing, children. When we were children ourselves, we were friends. It's time I was married and you're a suitable wife for me but the real reason I want to marry you *is* because we were once friends and we could be again. I've begun realising that all the while I've been searching for you. Is it such a bad bargain?' Deliberately, humorously, he let his accent become more northern, and in his tone, persuasiveness took over from indignation. 'I'd call it a reet good bargain, lass. What about it?'

Anne sat still, not knowing how to answer. He was different from the Richard she remembered, a man now instead of a boy. And a human being, willing to negotiate, instead of just a duke with six armed men and a king's backing.

The silence went on and on.

At length, he said: 'There's no need to answer me now. For the time being, let me simply take you out of here. Where would you like to go?'

Anne said: 'Into sanctuary.'

Halfway down the stairs, she said: 'I was never really Edouard's wife, you know.' And knew that although for the moment she was bound for the sanctuary of St Martin le Grand nearby, she had just implied capitulation.

Her cousin, descending ahead of her, glanced back and smiled. 'Thank God for that, for your sake. Judging from all I've heard about him, it would have been no pleasure for you. I'm the one with a past, I've two children by a girl in York – she died of an ague last winter and a tenant of mine up there is caring for them. The mother of the third child is married now and the boy is out to nurse. You're entitled to know all this. I hope you don't object.'

'I knew most of it already. You seem to be a conscientious father.'

'You're smiling!' said Richard. And as they arrived in the shop below and walked through it, he tipped the astonished Master Taberner two gold nobles.

Chapter Twenty

The Plantagenets: New Beginning

1472

'It's the season of spring and the springtime of this new marriage,' said Edward lyrically. 'We shall give a feast and a dance for Richard and Anne at Windsor. The great hall must be decorated and the pages garbed appropriately. Hastings, I look to you for ideas.'

Will Hastings loved a revel and was rarely short of ideas in any circumstances – 'All too often concerning other men's wives,' Richard had been known to remark acidly. When Edward told him that Hastings was to organise the feast and gave the latter's gift for ideas as a reason, he commented: 'I'm glad to hear that he's turning his mind towards celebrating the holy estate of matrimony for once.'

'Don't be so righteous,' said his brother amiably. 'What about your little Kate in York? And Jennie? You're hardly a pattern of virtue.'

'Neither of them was married at the time. Now that I'm about to be, I propose to be a faithful husband.'

'Admirable! But I didn't know you disliked Hastings.'

'I don't. One couldn't. He's loyal, to us even if not to his wife; he's brave, resourceful and excellent company. But where women are concerned – that's a side of him I can't admire.'

'Bess agrees with you.'

'Very proper,' said Richard. 'Well, what has Hastings suggested for the theme of the celebration?'

'A green and red colour scheme. Green for the young leaves of springtime and red for hot young blood – that's yours and Anne's. The pages' costumes are being made now. But I'm not quite sure,' said Edward doubtfully, 'how it's all going to look.'

It looked, most of the guests agreed, somewhat peculiar. The red and green bunting which festooned the dais at the end of the hall, where the King sat with his family and friends, did not seem bright enough to be festive. Edward himself, confronted by a bowing page with one crimson leg and one green one, and a velvet tunic quartered shoulder and hip in gules and vert, closed his eyes with a groan, requested a goblet of 'good strong wine, please,' and gave the page time to go away before opening them again. 'You've broken the laws of heraldry, Hastings. Never put colour on colour or metal on metal. Green and gold or red and silver, but never gold on silver, or green on red. I should have realised when you first told me.'

'This is a feast, not a coat of arms,' said Hastings unrepentantly. 'And I enjoy breaking rules sometimes.'

'The point is that one can now see the point of the rules! Never mind. Actually, I think it could grow on one.' Edward decided to soothe his friend's feelings, not that Hastings showed any outward sign of hurt. 'And the banquet was superb. So is the music. Our newlyweds are about to lead the first set and they're delightfully besotted with each other, don't you think? It's always such a relief,' said Edward contentedly, 'to see a young couple merry and inclined to cling together the day after the wedding. First nights aren't always a success.'

'No, but I think this one was,' Hastings said, chuckling. 'Those two look downright smug. Here comes the page with your wine.'

Edward, accepting the goblet, this time kept his eyes open and observed that the boy inside the remarkable parti-coloured clothing was a stranger to him. 'I don't know you, do I? Surely I'd remember if you were one of mine.' The boy had shining light-coloured hair in a bob, and a clean-etched aquiline profile. They added up to an air of distinction. 'Where are you from?'

'This is William Catesby, my lord,' said Hastings. 'He's from my household. Later, he hopes to study law.'

'I wish you well, boy. You've a deal of hard work ahead.'

'I hope to perform it successfully, sir.' The boy smiled, responding easily as people generally did to Edward's geniality.

'God send you good fortune. Fetch wine for everyone on the dais here, will you?'

'My lord, I have a party of guests across the hall there,' said Hastings.

'Waiting for you, are they? Away you go then, William Catesby, attend your master's wishes.' Edward turned to his wife who was sitting beside him, watching as the first set formed up. 'Bess, are you able to dance?'

Bess Woodville was pregnant again and even under a skilfully applied layer of pale powder based on a ground eggshell, her skin was sallow. 'It would be better if I did not. Why not lead our daughter out instead?'

The six-year-old Elizabeth was seated on a stool at her mother's feet. She looked up hopefully. 'With pleasure,' said Edward, and held out his hand.

With a last zestful flourish on the tabors, the music ceased. The dancers saluted their partners and Edward, escorting his small daughter with as much grave dignity as though she were a dowager princess, brought her back to the dais. 'Thank you, sire. I do enjoy dancing so,' said Elizabeth in a grown-up voice. She was a fairy-like child with silver-gilt hair like her mother's. It swirled about her small head, fine as gossamer, escaping from its jewelled snood. Her face had a maturity beyond her age. 'I want to dance with Uncle Richard, too.'

'Later, darling,' said her father, handing her back to the stool. 'He's dancing with your new Aunt Anne now. They're only just married, you know.'

Elizabeth pouted.

'No, you must not make faces,' Bess chided. 'You are

privileged to be here at all. On most days, you would be in bed by this time.'

The March day was indeed fading and the flambeaux were being kindled. The smoky light glittered on silks and gems, buried itself opulently in velvet pile and flashed from satin slashings. The extraordinary decor suddenly took on depth and strength. At the back of the dais, Dr John Alcock, who had been politely acknowledging congratulations from his namesake Dr John Morton on his forthcoming promotion to the bishopric of Rochester, and attempting to make conversation about educational projects in his prospective diocese, interrupted himself to say: 'This is a magnificent function.'

'It is indeed, and very well attended. The young Gloucesters seem popular.' Morton inched his chair closer to Alcock's. 'It occurs to me that this is the first opportunity we have had of an informal talk. We need to know each other better, since we must work together on the Council.'

'Yes. Many of the Council members must be strangers to you, or near-strangers. Even I am having to adapt myself,' Alcock said. 'There have been so many changes.'

There had indeed. Morton himself represented a sudden new element, while one which had vanished and was missed to a surprising degree was that of the Nevilles. Wayward, gifted and good-looking, they had been a sometimes disturbing influence but they had had glamour. No one had been quite indifferent to it. The Council chamber seemed oddly quiet without them. But Warwick and John Neville were dead, and Archbishop Neville was under lock and key, and ailing. Edward had ordered that he should have medical care but it looked as though his sickness would be mortal. Morton was speaking again. Alcock emerged from a reverie on the Nevilles, to find his own character under scrutiny.

'. . . I must say I find you something of an enigma yourself, my dear Alcock. A few moments ago I congratulated you on your forthcoming appointment as a bishop, but you virtually changed the subject in order to talk of the monastic schools in your future diocese and the improvements you hoped to make in them. It was almost as if the schools loomed larger in your mind than Rochester Cathedral. Now that I find surprising.'

They were present as guests, by right of being Council members but although able-bodied, regarded themselves as constrained by their priestly orders not to dance. Alcock now regretted this, as it seemed to have marooned him in Morton's company and try as he would, he could not make himself like John Morton. But another set had begun and all round them, people were leaving the dais for the floor. Alcock resigned himself.

'I care very much about good teaching and good educational opportunities for the young,' he said reprovingly. 'After all, they are our future churchmen, lawyers, administrators. In some of the schools over which I shall shortly have some jurisdiction, I've found that there is too much severity. I disapprove of that. Boys can be made to hate learning, and driven into turning away from what might in other circumstances have been their greatest source of joy. I'm sure that beating does nothing to impress lessons on their minds. The tough ones merely grow tougher and more resistant, while the sensitive ones become terrified and lose such wits as they possess. I hope to found a school one day. You, perhaps, go in less for dividing your energies?'

'I need occasional relaxation.' Morton's saturnine face did not, however, smile. 'I have a mild interest in growing new varieties of vegetables and fruit. Wherever I am, I manage to have a garden of some sort, but I also manage to have at least one gardener to look after it. I merely walk round of an evening and give instructions. For me, my daily duties amount to a time-consuming business which keeps me from side issues. I don't like to miss opportunities.'

'Yes, you must have found it hard, being in exile. It was a credit to your integrity,' said Alcock, firmly doing his companion justice, 'that you did not abandon Margaret of Anjou for gain. I respect you for that.'

'I am sure you would have acted in the same way, Dr Alcock.'

'I hope I would,' said Alcock, a little absently. He had begun to watch the dancers and his attention had been attracted by one or two interesting partnerings. Intelligence gathering was not a matter confined to his subordinates, or to certain days or hours. One did it all the time, automatically. He had, for instance, just noted and mentally filed the fact that William Hastings had apparently acquired a new mistress. Alcock knew who she was; it was part of his business at these functions to know who people were. That merry little lady with the daffodil-coloured hair did not belong to the court, but was a guest from outside, in fact from London. Her name was Mistress Shore and her husband had been a City goldsmith. The marriage had been annulled because of his incapacity. No doubt she found Hastings a welcome change. There was no doubt that they were on intimate terms; one could tell that from the way they moved as they danced.

One could equally sense closeness in the way the Gloucesters danced, as they in turn came past the dais. 'Now many people,' said Alcock, 'find Richard of Gloucester enigmatic. Have you found an opportunity to get to know him?'

'Not very much of one. Of course, people talk about him. An astute individual, by all accounts. He appears to have bargained like a horse-dealer with his brother Clarence over his bride's inheritance. The Gloucesters are to have Middleham Castle, which apparently they both have a sentimental attachment to –' Morton's voice was indulgent, as though affection for a childhood home were a form of weakness, albeit forgivable ' – while Gloucester has resigned several valuable appointments to his brother. But I fancy he will wield considerable power in the north as the King's representative there. He has no doubt made a very sound bargain. Have I passed my examination?' enquired Morton, drily and unexpectedly.

He had a sense of humour then, of a sort. But you don't strike me as a man who enjoys life, Alcock thought. There's something calculating in you. I doubt if you even really enjoy growing better strawberries and radishes. You take your hobby as though it were medicine. There's no mischief in you. I can't deny your integrity. You may have more than I. I ought to like you, but I can't.

Aloud, he said: 'I would give you – shall we say seventy marks out of a hundred, Dr Morton. The key to Richard of Gloucester in my view is that he sees himself, first and foremost, as King Edward's brother, representative and steward. I think he may value his prospects in the north mainly because of the service he can render the King in being there.'

'Ah,' said Morton, showing no trace of discomposure, 'you would no doubt know better than I. You like him, evidently.' He succeeded in implying by his tone that Alcock was prone to irrational likings and to making excuses for people on the basis of them. Alcock held down his annoyance and avoided an immediate reply by once more taking an interest in the dancers. They were now leaving the floor as the music ceased. The interest at once became genuine. If Hastings had a new mistress then so, apparently, had Harry Buckingham.

'There goes someone I don't like,' he observed lightly. 'Harry Buckingham has not been dancing with his own wife and in fact has never been known to do so. She is over there, in that group of young women. He has ignored her all evening and will go on ignoring her.'

'Ah yes. I see,' said Morton.

The Queen's sister, Catherine Buckingham, aged eighteen, was chattering with noisy animation to a group of half a dozen ladies of her own age. She was pretty, not as silvery-fair as Bess, but graceful and with a charming laugh which was now working hard. Catherine was telling the others an amusing story, leaning close to them, giggling. *Why should I mind if my husband dances with other women but never with me? I'm too preoccupied with my own friends to notice.* Alcock and Morton, both men of the world in spite of having officially renounced it, knew the forced merriment for the face-saving lie it was and paid it the tribute of a brief sympathetic silence. Although each had by this time recognised the other as a rival, they were, just for a moment, in accord.

'She needs advice,' said Alcock. 'Or a child. Or at least a way to fill her days. Have you ever met the Lady Margaret Beaufort? A woman of highly cultivated intellect. More attention should be paid to the education of girls in general. Intellectual interests can be an immense comfort when other things go wrong in one's life.'

'Except that that young lady is not of an intellectual sort,' said Morton. 'I have indeed met Margaret Beaufort. She has nothing in common with any of the Woodville women.'

Edward had not returned to the dais after the set. He could be seen in the distance, however, making his way towards Will Hastings's party. The minstrels were resting and a group of tumblers were out on the floor, starting their performance. The Gloucesters came back and reclaimed their own places on the dais. Alcock saw Richard's eyes follow Bess's gaze across the hall to where King Edward was just being offered a place on a settle among Will Hastings's guests.

'Madam, can you not dissuade my brother from spending so much time in Hastings's company?' Richard pitched his voice low but it reached Alcock nonetheless. 'Hastings is a pleasant fellow but he is given to roistering.'

Across the hall, Mistress Shore was pouring wine for the King, watched intently by Bess, who was plainly oblivious of the tumblers. These had now climbed on each others' shoulders to form a human tower and amid gasps from the audience were pretending to overbalance.

'I know. I too worry.' Bess spoke gently. 'The King works so hard that I often think he needs rest more than noisy company and so much wine. But it is for him to say. What pleases him must content me. I would never try to influence him against his will. Could you not try to persuade him yourself? Your powers might in any case be greater than mine.'

Bess was good at keeping her own counsel, Alcock thought. A subtle smile, a cool expressionless phrase, could hide fear or hurt or self-doubt as effectively as a damask cloth could hide the scars on a hardworked table, and Bess employed them accordingly. But at this moment, she was doing something more. He recognised it for he had heard her speak to Richard in this manner many times before. Too many times and always in vain. Behind her tranquil words was self-deprecation and it meant that she was trying to placate him. She was saying: 'Please put aside your hostility, please forgive me for marrying your brother and making dreadful mistakes. Please look at me and see that I am a real person and that I too can be hurt by the Mistress Shores.'

And Richard, this time as ever, had failed to grasp the point. He clapped the tumblers as the human tower tottered, sprang apart and formed anew in an even more dramatic feat of balancing, and he remarked: 'Unfortunately, I shall soon be in the north and far away from my brother, and in any case my attempts to talk to him about Hastings have so far met with scant success. I shall have to leave him in your hands. I'm sure you are too modest about the power you possess.' He withdrew his gaze from the tumblers to look directly at Bess. 'I believe your power is very great, madam. Power of life and death, one could almost say.'

It was done so smoothly that for a moment Alcock almost took it for the compliment it appeared to be. Then, as he caught up grimly with the fact that Richard had left his blunt youth behind and learned considerable subtlety, he

301

saw Anne give her new husband a quick glance. Richard turned to her with a smile, and she relaxed. Alcock, himself taut as a lute-string, allowed his head to swivel slowly, and met Morton's eyes. Their expression was a mixture of comprehension and enquiry. Morton had recognised appeal and refusal and he had sensed something amiss with that piece of seeming flattery, but he had probably never heard of Desmond and he could not interpret this.

He would never hear the story from Alcock. All Alcock's old instinct to protect Bess Woodville had come alive again. He kept his own face blank.

But he knew that like himself, Morton had understood Bess's stiffly upright back and her ivory pallor as signs of anguish, and that Morton too was relieved that she had this gift of dignity under attack. Whatever her other shortcomings as a queen, in this respect she was admirable.

On the far side of the hall, Edward said to Hastings: 'The dancing will begin again soon. Permit me to borrow your partner. And would you do me a kindness? Lead out Catherine Buckingham. Show her some attention and make that laggardly husband of hers jealous. I made that marriage and I want it to succeed, but there are places where the King's writ doesn't run and other men's bedrooms are among them. I can't order him to consummate the marriage. The only way is to provoke him.'

'I have heard a rumour,' said Morton civilly as the new set commenced, 'that in due course, when the young Prince Edward is given a separate household, you may be put in charge of his education. If so, your extramural interest, as it were, will have brought you an excellent further appointment.'

'The idea has been mooted,' Alcock said, 'but it hasn't been confirmed. The time hasn't come yet and the King might change his mind. It will be hard on the child's mother,' added Alcock, lowering his voice, 'to have him taken from her so young. But she tells me she has confidence in me. I hope I do receive the appointment, but not only for my own sake.'

'It may be to the child's advantage to be reared away from the court,' said Morton quietly. 'Look at that. That's no example for a young prince, I fear.'

The dancing had begun again and now that the evening was wearing on and a good deal of wine had been consumed, it was less decorous than it had been. Some couples were forgetting their obligatory bow as they passed the royal dais. In the midst of the floor, Hastings had crossed hands with Catherine Buckingham and was spinning her so that her embroidered skirts flew out. And King Edward, in the company of Mistress Shore, was also spinning his partner, but side by side with her, his arm about her waist and their shoulders packed together. Both were red with wine and exertion and as they danced, they turned to one another and set mouth on mouth and kissed.

Chapter Twenty-One

Petronel: Over the Edge

1470–1473

I must have returned to England a short head in front of Warwick's invasion fleet. I learned later that he landed almost on my heels and that King Edward was obliged to flee for his life the day after I left him.

But I saw little of the conflict. I rode home to Eynesby with the escort Brampton had provided (Brampton, as a merchant, managed to stay in London throughout all the troubles, keeping his head down and his eyes open and no doubt sending useful intelligence to Edward in Burgundy when possible). When I reached home, Lionel greeted me formally. We stood in the hall, looking at each other. And I had the dreadful sensation that, after all, nothing had changed.

I had thought it might. I was different now. I had played the game of deceit for high stakes, the future of a realm and my own life among them. I had not been found wanting. Surely, therefore, I had outgrown my fear of Lionel. I had walked proudly as I entered the hall, but the colourless eyes on either side of the long nose were still the eyes of one who had power over me and considered me to be in certain vital respects a failure.

Now, standing before Lionel, I felt my self-assurance draining out of me as I said: 'I carried out the King's mission well enough to please him and he has rewarded me. He has granted me a manor. It marches with Bouldershawe. Thornwood, it's called. But of course,' I heard myself say, 'it's as much yours as mine.'

305

Oh yes. I was still afraid of him. The sound of that sooth-ing, dog-bringing-a-bone note in my own voice, made me want to be sick.

I handed the charter over to Lionel. 'Aye,' he said when he had read it. 'You made an impression on the King, right enough. That's plain from the terms.' It certainly was. The thing was larded with phrases like 'our right well beloved Petronel Eynesby' and 'for services most loyally rendered to us.'

Lionel's ears had gone red. I was not surprised by his next words. 'But now you've pleased the King and got us all into his favour, provided he stays King, which is doubtful, it's time you started rendering a service or two most loyally to me. You've been gone a good while and I'm not getting younger. I want a son before I'm done, Petronel.' He could still say that, I thought wearily, even after all this time. Had he not accepted, even yet, that it wasn't likely to happen?

Apparently not. My absence had merely given him time to brood and regain what I had thought was his flagging enthusiasm. My homecoming night was not pleasant. I sus-pected that an element of revenge was involved; I had pleased the King but failed my husband. I had become a landowner in my own right and I had grown. For he had seen how I carried myself as I walked into the hall, and he didn't like it. That he had almost ordered me to agree to perform the King's mission, I think made him more, not less, bitter. I did not expect to see much of the proceeds from Thornwood, or be allowed any personal control over it. And I was right.

We entered now on that alarming era when King Edward was first in Burgundy and then came home to face the fields of Barnet and Tewkesbury. Geoffrey had gone away with Sir John Neville and we did not know what had happened to him. Meanwhile, Lionel considered that we should behave circumspectly. So in all that time, we never left Eynesby. John Steward went to York at times for household supplies and brought back news, but it was often garbled. It was a sign of the nerve-racking times that our Eynesby villagers, who usually had little time to spare from their hard-working lives, would desert plough or workshop at a moment's notice to pounce on any stray traveller for news, and the unexpected ringing of a church bell (as happened one day when someone's adventurous goat got into the church, climbed the belfry stairs and tried to eat a bellrope) brought them running from their fields and homes to speculate on invasions and victories and sudden deaths of the great.

But no violence came near us and life went on, by night as well as by day, though Lionel was no longer young enough, I think, to keep up the energetic nastinesses with which he had welcomed me home. Between us, things seemed to settle back into the old pattern. I was not happy and I was always wary, but it was no worse than that.

In other places, life continued, too. From Faldene came the news that my half-brother Tom had made an advantageous match. I hoped he would be happy but my mother's letter said little about the bride. It only enlarged on the financial gains. I despatched John Steward to York to buy a set of goblets and some fine linen to send as a gift. He came back accompanied by a courier, who brought us news from Geoffrey, at last.

At long last we had reliable information about Barnet and Tewkesbury. Lionel was thankful to learn that Geoffrey was still alive, and approved of him for making peace with Richard of Gloucester. And the next news brought me great, though secret, pleasure. Richard of Gloucester had married Anne Neville; they were coming to live at Middleham and Geoffrey was coming back with them.

We were bidden to Middleham almost at once. Geoffrey had apparently convinced Richard of Gloucester that Lionel's services would be as useful to him as they had been to Warwick.

'I suppose you will attend on the Lady Anne,' Lionel said

to me. 'You'll have to take Chrissy,' he added.

Since Kat had not come back to Eynesby with me, Chrissy had acted as my maid. She came to Middleham very willingly, for she had recently borne and lost yet another child. 'I'm getting past the age for these capers,' she said to me, 'and watching a baby die is summat you can't take easily at any age. Maybe a change'll help me get over it.'

At the castle we found the old familiar bustle and crowd. Lionel went off in search of Geoffrey while Chrissy and I were shown to our quarters. We set to work to empty hampers and put away clothes and were busily occupied with this when Lionel came in, bringing Geoffrey with him.

I stood there, my arms full of furs, and stared. Eighteen long months without sight of Geoffrey, and now, here he was, just like that. I had the illogical feeling that after so long out of my sight he should have reappeared in gradual stages. He looked well and embraced me with warmth. 'My dear Aunt Petronel.'

'I've been telling the lad,' said Lionel, banging down the lid of a chest in order to sit on it, 'all this time away and now here he is within twenty miles of home and hasn't spared a day for his mother. And her fretting her heart out at Silbeck for you, Geoffrey. When do you mean to put things to rights?'

'Very soon, Uncle,' said Geoffrey. 'I haven't had a day to myself since we reached Middleham. There's a great deal to do when a new man takes possession of a place like this.'

'Alison minds.'

'I sent letters,' said Geoffrey, mildly defensive.

'Not often enough nor long enough. Now, sit you down on that window seat and tell us all the rest of it.'

He did as he was told and talked for more than an hour. We heard how John Neville had deliberately let the King go unscathed at Pontefract, and how he had walked the floor in indecision night after night before Barnet. And how he died on the field there, calling himself a traitor and wearing the Sun in Splendour embroidered on his jerkin.

We heard too how Geoffrey had been lost in the mist at Barnet, and how he had slain William Hawick. I had been enthralled by the narrative up to that point, but when he spoke of Hawick something within me checked, brought up short like a horse when you jag its mouth. 'But . . .' I said.

Geoffrey smiled at me. 'There's this in both my uncle and me, Aunt Petronel. We pay our debts and we make our debtors pay us. But he was fighting on the opposite side, you know. I was supposed to be there to kill the enemy, after all!'

I remembered Alison saying: 'Men'll go to war and do things in battle that we can't stand to think of.' Geoffrey's smile was saying something similar. It told me that I wasn't expected to understand, even that my failure to understand was charming, and that I needn't worry, he knew right from wrong and if he had done it, it must be all right.

I supposed it must. And after all, it was true that Hawick had been one of the foe.

'Let t'lad go on,' said Lionel impatiently. 'How did Warwick die?'

Geoffrey went on with his tale. He told us how Warwick had been killed trying to flee the field, and how very nearly he had been killed himself, except that his left-handedness had saved him. He told us about Tewkesbury field and how Prince Edouard had fallen. He described how Margaret of Anjou had been seized at Little Malvern Priory.

'Henry of Lancaster is dead now, too,' he said. 'It's said he died of pure displeasure and melancholy. Though,' he added soberly, 'not many people believe that. Margaret of Anjou is in custody. She'll be ransomed, probably, and sent back to France.'

He went on to detail the rejoicings at the marriage of Richard of Gloucester and Anne Neville, and how Gloucester had rescued her from, of all places, an eating-house. 'Clarence put her there. People are saying he's not quite right in the head.' The Queen was expecting another child, he added, and everyone hoped that this too would be a son. 'This too?' queried Lionel.

'Oh yes. Did the news not reach you? It was when the King was in Burgundy and the Queen in sanctuary in London. She had a son then, little Prince Edward. Why, he's not far short of a year and a half now. He's to have a household of his own very soon.'

'We'd heard various rumours,' Lionel said. 'A son, a daughter, a stillbirth; all sorts of things. No one knew what to believe.'

'Well, it was a healthy boy,' said Geoffrey, laughing. 'Warwick behaved very well. He sent meat and wine to the Queen during her lying-in and offered no affront to her or the baby. Though what would have happened if the Anjou woman had got back into power, no one likes to guess!'

A page tapped on the door. Always, at Middleham, Lionel had been liable to be summoned at five minutes notice to this conference or that. The old regime and the new were evidently identical in this. 'But I shall only be five minutes,' Lionel said, having heard the page's message. He went away and Geoffrey, turning to Chrissy, asked her to fetch us something to drink. As soon as she was out of sight, he put his arms round me. I stood stiffly within them and he shook me gently. 'Oh, Petronel, I've missed you. Is the answer still the same? No and no?'

'It's still the same,' I said and he let me go. But there was a provocative smile on his face. 'Lionel will be away tomorrow night,' he said. 'He's going out to inspect the flocks. I was in the hall earlier listening to Gloucester discuss his programme for the week; that's how I know. Petronel, Petronel, can we let such a chance slip by?'

'We must,' I said. I drew myself away. 'Chrissy sleeps with me when Lionel is absent.'

'Turn pettish, tell her she snores and send her to share the maids' room with her fellows as she usually does. Petronel,' he said, turning serious, 'did I shock you when I spoke of killing Hawick? That was part of the world I live in. It's not pretty – it just is so. It need not concern you.'

'I wasn't shocked,' I said, and indeed the shock had

passed by then. 'But nothing,' I told him, 'has changed. You know why. It has nothing to do with Hawick. No, don't!' He had taken hold of me again and was trying to pull me back into his arms. 'Stop it! Someone's coming!'

And when Lionel reappeared a moment later, Geoffrey was back on the window seat and I was sitting on the chest, while he told me how amazingly regal the Lady Anne could look and how surprised I would be when I saw her.

Life's great transitions can be very sudden. At fourteen, I had been whirled in twenty-four hours from novice nun to prospective bride. At Middleham, I went over another cliff-edge, in the same unheralded fashion, within twenty-four hours of declaring that I never would.

We dined that day in the hall and Richard of Gloucester proposed a toast to his brother the King and to the young heir Prince Edward. That night, Lionel dismissed Chrissy, barred the door after her, stood with his back to it and said: 'So the King has a son. Tonight we drank his health. Do you know how much I've longed to drink my own son's health in my own hall at Eynesby? I took you on, d'ye realise that, to get that son? I could have got Bouldershawe in the end without you, but I agreed to the marriage because women customarily have children. And what have you brought me instead? You're no more of a woman than I am. Did you think I was pleased when the King picked you as his mouth-piece? I'd no choice, my lass. But I know this, he wouldn't have done it if you'd been a proper female. Carrying secret messages into enemy territory, that's work for a man. The King sent you to do it because you might as well be a man. And he's rewarded you as though you were a man. Giving you a manor in your own right, to will to whom you choose . . .'

'You're jealous!' I said.

'. . . and teaching you to think as well of yourself as though you were a man, to walk with your chin up in the air, ready to defy me.'

311

'But I said Thornwood was yours as much as . . .'

'Very generous of you.' I had never seen his ears go as red as that before. 'You're uncommonly gracious to your poor inferior husband who stayed at home while you went adventuring and hobnobbed with kings and dukes. The Queen spent the war in sanctuary, keeping out of men's affairs and bearing her husband a son. That's a woman's business, and it's time you performed it!'

It was as though he had convinced himself that I could have a child, a son, to order and was wilfully withholding it from him. I did not know what to say or do. 'Come to bed,' I said inanely at last.

'I intend to,' said Lionel grimly.

But when he did, the old difficulty reappeared, the one which had bedevilled us since our marriage night, which had driven him to so many ugly, artificial devices to outwit it.

There was nothing new in that. What was new was that this time, openly, he blamed me. I was doing my best to help him according to the lore in which he had now instructed me, but it was no use. 'If you were a proper woman, this wouldn't happen!' he shouted. 'Crossing the Channel on political affairs, galloping up and down England, chasing after the King astride your horse like a courier boy. How am I supposed to make love to that?'

Perhaps I had changed after all. Before I went to Calais, I would never have spoken my thought aloud. As it was, I retorted: 'Is that what you call it?'

We were on the bed, half lying, half sitting. He came upright on the instant, yanking me up with him. 'You don't find me good enough? You've destroyed my manhood! You've no respect! Perhaps this will make you respect me!' I saw his fist, the bony knuckles foremost, a split second before it landed.

The force of it was incredible; it was like a hammer, a thunderbolt. I rocked backwards and crashed off the bed on to the floor. One whole side of my face had become a single enormous, world-filling pain and I knew that blood was running from one nostril. I tried to get up and met the fist a second time.

I fought back, anger and terror joining hands in me to help. I snatched up an earthenware jug and struck at him with it. It broke and as he came at me again, with blood now running down his own temple, I tried to grab a bedrug and throw it over him. But he was agile despite his years and flung it aside. I screamed for help, which didn't come. I remember that scene, still, with crawling nausea. I resisted, defended myself, for a long, long time against that hail of violence, the violence which I had always sensed in him and always feared. But it went on too long. There was a time when he demanded words of apology, obeisance and respect and I shrieked that he was unjust, that I hated him, that he was a fool to think himself entitled to respect because he was stronger than I; did he respect oxen for their muscles? I bit and clawed and screamed at him that our barrenness was his fault and not mine, but he shouted back that I was a slut to say such a thing, that such shortcomings were never those of the man. Shortly after that came a time when, sobbing and defeated and in pain so intense that I did not believe it could be happening, I said all that he wanted me to say.

It was degrading, it was squalid, and it cured his impotence. The repulsive games he had so often made me play had sometimes flirted with violence, but it seemed that Lionel needed the real thing.

In the morning, I stayed in bed and Lionel, although he would not speak directly to me, summoned Chrissy to attend to me. We had a medicine chest with us containing the usual things; salves and bandages and remedies for coughs and toothache. She anointed my weals and bruises, clucking sympathetically, and fetched me some frumenty porridge to eat and milk to drink, since I found it impossible to chew. But when she said: 'Tha shouldna provoke him, my duck,' I turned my face away and would not talk to her.

When she had gone away, I lay and examined the seething

313

fear and fury and contempt within me, but I was too
exhausted and despairing to decide on any course of action.
It did cross my mind that I had it in my power both to save
myself and take a secret revenge. But left to myself, I would
not have had the spirit to use my power. Only, I was not left
to myself.

Lionel had gone about his day's business, which meant
riding out to the sheep pastures. Before he had been gone an
hour, Geoffrey came to me. I had not had the strength to
get up and bar the door after Chrissy when she went, and he
walked straight in. 'Lionel came into the hall to break his
fast this morning with scratches down his face and a black
eye and I got hold of Chrissy just now and she told me . . .
Petronel! Oh, my little Petronel! Oh my darling, what has
happened to you?'

A moment later I was clinging to him and sobbing my
misery out in his arms, thankful to be with someone who
was friendly, who would take my part and not make it out
to be my fault. He tilted back my head and looked at my
face with horror on his own. 'Lionel did this?'

'That and more, much more. Don't!' I moved his hand,
which was pressing on a bruise.

'But why?'

'Geoffrey,' I said, holding him in feverish hands, 'I have
to have a baby!'

He demurred a little because of my injuries, but the bed
was stuffed with down and Geoffrey's body, warm and
strong, his weight carefully disposed for my comfort, was
itself a salve. We played no games of arousal for he did not
need them and I was not seeking pleasure, which I did not
even know existed. When it came, it filled me with astonishment. I felt my own eyes widen and saw Geoffrey laughing
down at me. The wonder grew and grew and exploded and
left me gasping.

'Geoffrey!'

'Petra!'

And it was only then, afterwards, that I really, fully

314

realised that if the result were what I hoped, if Geoffrey had achieved what all those candles to the Virgin had not, then I should not only preserve myself from Lionel's campaign of resentment, but also fool him into acknowledging his nephew's baby as his own.

In fact, it didn't happen so quickly. Perhaps Lionel had frightened me too much and my body shrank from conceiving. A woman carrying a child is vulnerable, after all, for she must protect two lives while physically at a grave disadvantage. It was many months before the marvellous week passed when the scheduled course failed to appear. But it didn't matter. Lionel didn't attack me again. I think he was ashamed of himself and throughout the rest of that year, he approached me only rarely, and as though he were performing a rather dull job of work. As for me, I endured him and thought of Geoffrey.

I had flung myself at Geoffrey while terrified and in pain, crying that I must have a child. I should have added, 'and I must have you'. As far as Geoffrey was concerned, I fell into a madness of love and did not care that I remained apparently barren. It gave me more time, more freedom to rejoice in his kindness and his strength and his beautiful body, which was so gloriously unlike Lionel's. Geoffrey, not procreation, obsessed my thoughts and his feelings appeared to be in accord with mine. We met whenever we could, seeking each other without conscience or restraint.

I remember that year of 1472 as an enchanted interlude. Only with difficulty can I recall Lionel and the counterpoint of our wary, uneasy daily life together. What comes to mind is Geoffrey, and the stratagems we invented and the chances we took. We were like a pair of children circumventing a tutor . . .

'Alison, shall I come over to Silbeck for a day while Lionel is in York next week? You said you wanted to check your stores and I could help you . . .' And when I was at Silbeck:

'Geoffrey! You made me jump! We'll have to be careful. I'm supposed to be counting these salt pork barrels for your mother and it won't take long; it's the end of the season . . . What's that sheet for?'

'So that we won't get dirty on the cellar floor. Come behind the barrels and then even if anyone does come in, they won't see us. It's been a whole week, my little gosling . . .'

'Uncle, I've been trying a new goshawk. Hawking's the great sport at Middleham now; Gloucester's an enthusiast. I know you don't care for it but could my Aunt Petronel come out for an hour? We'll bring you back some larks for a pie . . .'

'In the open, Geoffrey?'

'Why not? What better bed than a dip in the heather and what better ceiling than the sky? No one can see us from the track. We're safe here in our own world. Can you hear the skylarks? We ought to be hawking for them but . . .'

'I'd rather hear them singing, just now.'

'So would I. How drugged and sleepy the grasshoppers sound.'

'Isn't it strange how one can hear them but never see them? Oh Geoffrey, *Geoffrey*, get up quickly!'

'Darling gosling, what's the matter?'

'We're lying on an ants' nest and they're red ants! They're biting! Quick, brush them off me. They're on you too.'

'Damn the ants. Come over here, hurry, hurry, I can't wait for you any longer. Oh Christ, Petra, no one but you can make me feel like this . . .'

'Geoffrey, what on earth . . .?'

'It's all right. My mother's gone to Eynesby to the Michaelmas Fair. You'll have to put in an appearance there tomorrow, but for today we have the house to ourselves except for the minstrel I've hired from York.'

'The what?'

'The minstrel, darling. Don't worry, he's used to being paid to be discreet. I prepared the bath myself.'

'The *bath*?'

'Yes, darling. We shall start the afternoon by sharing a perfumed tub while the minstrel serenades us, and on a board across the tub I've set out my mother's best wine in her best goblets and some cinnamon cakes which I got her to make yesterday.'

'Geoffrey, you're quite mad!'

'I know, but it's a grand kind of madness, eh, lass?'

There was the time I met him by appointment in a ruined cottage at Eynesby for thirty wild minutes when I was supposed to be visiting the chandlers. There was the time when he took me to see the fine white colt bred from his best mare and the premier Jervaulx stallion and we repaired to the Silbeck hayloft instead. It became a way of life. During those days, the whole world seemed more vivid, the sun fresh-kindled, all the green leaves astoundingly brilliant. Even the moors I had once thought forbidding were beautiful to me because on any skyline, Geoffrey might appear.

In the autumn he had to go to London with Richard of Gloucester and I had to accompany Lionel to Middleham. I fretted, and all the more because I must try to hide it. Six weeks crawled by like six centuries. Then we returned to Eynesby and Geoffrey too came home, in time for Christmas.

But I did not see him at once, for he promptly fell ill with one of the bronchial attacks which now and then confined him to bed. I sent conventional-seeming messages which came from my deepest heart and when I heard that he was recovering I shed a few sentimental tears of relief.

He was well enough to come over with Alison just before the twelve days of Christmas ended. We forthwith made occasion to come together. It was a hasty, chilly, brief reunion in one of the attics, which I was supposed to be inspecting to see that it was clean in case any of our guests fell ill. It had a truckle bed and there we fell on one another, clutching, biting, invading, absorbing, wild with weeks of famine. And it was there, in that cold attic, that I at last conceived.

Afterwards, my delight was tempered by a nervous fear that Lionel would keep track of time and work out when it must have happened. He had been unable to play the husband all through December and right to the middle of January. If necessary, I would have to pretend the child was early, I thought, and delayed telling him the news so as to let his memory blur.

But it was soon impossible to conceal the fact that I was being sick every morning. 'So ye've mended your ways at last!' he said ungraciously when I admitted the cause. But he showed no sign of suspicion and gradually warmed towards me, bringing me gifts and asking after my health. I felt no guilt, only thankfulness. His resentment and his violence would have surfaced again in the end, I knew, unless I had become pregnant. The need to do so would soon have dominated me again. I felt infinite gratitude to Geoffrey.

The baby was born in September 1473, just one month after the Queen in London had – after an intervening and shortlived daughter –presented King Edward and the realm with a second male child, a back-up to the infant heir. News was travelling reliably again now and reached us within a week. He was named Richard after his uncle and his grandfather, Duke Richard of York. When my own baby proved to be a son as well, I suggested, and Lionel agreed, that he too should be named Richard, after the baby prince – and also after his grandfather Duke Richard of York, although naturally I did not tell Lionel that. It would be a little joke to share with Geoffrey when we met again, I thought.

But we did not meet for some time, and before we did a change had taken place in me, for by then I had had time to think.

It was illness which gave me the time. It had been a bad birth. When I made my suggestion about my son's name, I had spoken in a feeble whisper. I recall that during the endless day and night it took me to produce my baby, I cried out that I hoped the Queen had had an easier time of it. Alison and Chrissy afterwards admitted that they had thought they would lose me and the child as well. I can dimly remember the succession of hot cloths they placed on my stomach, and Alison holding pepper under my nose in the hope of jerking the baby out with the force of a sneeze. Chrissy later told me that they had resorted at one point to charms, placing opened oyster shells under the bed, and a sharp knife with them. During the night, I saw both Chrissy and Alison kneel beside my bed, palms together and heard them pray aloud to God to bring forth that which He had formed, for they had done their utmost to no avail. They were like figures in a dream, their upturned faces with eyes closed wavering in the uncertain candlelight and beyond a haze of pain.

When at last the baby did deign to emerge Chrissy looked at the tiny wailing scrap and cried in amazement, 'Mother of God, how did *that* cause so much trouble?'

'He may be a little early,' I said weakly, glad of the chance to make the point. I heard them say that he ought to be baptised at once, just in case, and that was when I managed to whisper my wishes concerning his name. Then I slept. I was very sick indeed for the next two weeks.

When I was once again able to attend to my surroundings, I found that my baby, after all, was thriving. Chrissy had found a wet-nurse, the wife of one of our shepherds, and brought her to the house so that she and the child would be under our eyes. I saw for myself that he was picking up strength and alertness. Indeed, he acquired a nickname because of it. Chrissy kept calling him a 'proper little Perky Dick' and Perky Dick he became for ever after.

He was delightful, a relief and a joy both at once and I could not as much as see him without tumbling into a bottomless pit of devotion. It was deeper even than my love for Geoffrey and far more protective. As I gradually ceased to worry about my baby, I began instead to worry about Geoffrey.

Pregnancy had ended my hunger for him, put a stop for months to our frolics. And now, as I believe often happens after childbearing, desire was slow to awaken again. For the first time, I could see Geoffrey and our situation clearly.

I loved him. It was as though he and not Lionel were my husband. And he had saved me from Lionel's disappointed rage which would have broken out again before long. But what now?

For although I had turned to him to save me from Lionel in one way, I had put myself at risk in another. During our year as lovers, Geoffrey and I had taken insane chances. It was a wonder we had not been caught. If we ever were . . .

I knew now what Lionel's fury was like. Geoffrey was a man and could defend himself but Perky Dick and I were Lionel's chattels. I lay in the little attic room where Perky Dick had had his beginnings – and which, by coincidence, had been furnished as my lying-in chamber –and watched the moors beyond the window come into their September purple. I remembered how we had made love in the heather, and had to flee from an ants' nest. The memory made me want to laugh and want to cry at the same time for I could not believe that such a time would ever come again. Whenever I thought of Geoffrey now, I was reined back by a dreadful sense of hopelessness. For us, I could see no way forward.

So when he came to give his congratulations, which was soon after I at last became well enough to go down to the hall, I whispered to him my little joke about Perky Dick's name, but I would not let him snatch a secret kiss. He looked puzzled but did not persist.

I chattered brightly and feverishly about the visit Lionel and I must soon pay to Middleham, and how we proposed to take Perky Dick and the wet-nurse with us. Anne of

Gloucester had had a son that summer, too. We would enjoy showing each other our babies, I said. I went on and on and I think both Geoffrey and Lionel thought I was still unwell.

But I was not ill any longer. Only afraid.

Chapter Twenty-Two

Petronel: The Rocks at the Foot of the Cliff

1473

I still thought of myself as one of Isabel's ladies but although she had invited me twice to join her for a while, Lionel had not permitted it. Obsessed with Geoffrey, I had myself preferred to stay in the north, near Silbeck which was his home, and Middleham where his lord lived.

Meanwhile, it was tacitly understood that I would accompany Lionel when he went to Middleham and that, while there, I would attend Anne of Gloucester.

I had not, previously, known Anne as well as I knew her sister. I had thought of her as being a little bit prim, even censorious. But marriage to Richard of Gloucester had made a difference.

Richard of Gloucester I had only seen before at a distance, in Middleham and London, and even now I didn't see him often. He was much occupied with taking control of Middleham and seemed to be closeted almost continuously with stewards, petitioners, auditors, messengers, advisers such as Lionel and tradesmen courting his custom. He occasionally joined the ladies to dine or listen to music and then he generally spoke a few words to each of us, but I found him hard to fathom. Unlike his brothers he was slight, with a thin face and dark brown hair hanging straight on either side. He wore superb clothes and jewellery but with a preference for deep colours: rich brown, midnight blue, purple, dark green; and for thick, heavy rings. Surprisingly, they all seemed to suit his thin body. I did notice after a while that the slightness was deceptive. Once on a hot day I went to the audience room with a message from his wife and found him sitting in conference with his sleeves rolled up above the elbow. His forearms were massive and hairy; they looked as if they belonged to a man twice his size, and one of them carried a noticeable scar. He had astonishingly well-muscled shoulders, too. The shape of them wasn't, after all, dependent on the padding in his doublets.

He seemed in fact to be a man of contradictions and to this day I still don't know what to make of him. Many things have been said of him and they are contradictory too. But I did see what he had done for his wife Anne.

The prim child had gone. She had taken on dignity, as women will when they become mistress of their own home, but she had also taken on generosity. Despite her diminutive size, she had become a lady of stature, respected by her household but friendly towards them, someone to whom any of us could turn in trouble.

She introduced changes at Middleham, using rooms for different purposes and having meals served at different times. The first time I went into the hall after her arrival, I was surprised by a sweet pervasive smell which had never been there before. Then I saw that dried violets were strewn among the rushes, giving off their perfume as they were crushed underfoot. That was one of her first innovations.

But the most startling thing concerned her relationship with her mother, the Countess of Warwick. She was there, for her daughter and son-in-law had fetched her from the south coast sanctuary where she had sheltered after Warwick's death. Perhaps she had stepped back deliberately to make way for her daughter or perhaps it was widowhood that had changed her, but where once she had carried her rank like a cloth-of-gold mantle, now she was only a sad woman in middle age, gently spoken and devout and although Anne was unfailingly courteous towards her, it was Anne who now commanded and her mother who gave way. There was no doubt whatsoever which of them was chatelaine of Middleham.

When we went to the castle in the autumn of 1473, we took Perky Dick with us as we had planned. As I had known she would, Anne at once summoned me to bring him to the nursery where her own little Ned was, so that we could admire each other's offspring.

I was glad to immerse myself in the world of babies, to talk about childcare with Anne and the nurses, for I knew that I was on the brink of a dreadful decision. I needed time to think. And I needed a quiet place in which a decision could grow.

Geoffrey was at Middleham and not by chance. He had already found an opportunity to corner me and whisper: 'I've managed it! I'm here at the same time as you. When can we meet?'

'It will be difficult,' I whispered back. 'Let me try to arrange something. I'll find a way to tell you.'

Oh God, I thought as I slipped away from him. What am I to do?

I was balanced between two opposing forces. One was my love for Geoffrey and the other was my dread of its consequences. The sight of his face, the mention of his name, pierced me like a sweet knife and as I regained my strength, need had begun to return as well. But although I no longer carried Perky Dick within me, he was still my responsibility. If Lionel ever found out the truth, his vengeance would be beyond my imagining.

There were, it seemed to me, only two alternatives. I must eschew Geoffrey henceforth, or join him. And if I were to go to him, leaving Lionel, what then?

I had never heard of anyone doing such a thing openly. People lived with their lawful spouses, whatever private arrangements they made. It was difficult to imagine what would happen; I had never seen a demonstration. But as I thought it over, day by day, there were some things I could foresee.

To start with, the church would be on Lionel's side.

Every priest for miles, perhaps even the bishop, would descend on us to demand that I return to my husband. I might be refused the sacraments. Our neighbours would be scandalised. Lionel might well try to get me back by force and he might succeed.

And what of Perky Dick? I thought of the pawn he would become, and shuddered. From one point of view, I had every right to take him to Geoffrey, who was his father. But in the eyes of the world, Lionel was his father. Even if I were not snatched away by violence, my baby certainly would be and once Lionel got hold of him, he would make Perky Dick a hostage to compel my return. I knew it. I knew Lionel.

Our only chance would be to leave England, but how could I ask Geoffrey to give up his home, his inheritance, for me? I had already robbed him of Eynesby. Could I cut him off from Silbeck too?

I could not and if I did, he wouldn't agree. I knew that too. Since having Perky Dick, I seemed to have made another step forward in this slow business of maturing. I remembered Alison admitting that when Geoffrey first came to Faldene with his uncle, he had only been putting a good face on his anger. I remembered Geoffrey himself telling us how he had killed William Hawick. My lover wasn't the man to let go of his rights.

And so my thoughts went round and round, and day followed day, and still I did not know what to do.

Fortunately, Geoffrey was being kept busy. 'My husband thinks regular military exercises will keep his men occupied as well as making them ready for any emergency,' Anne told me. As well as the usual practice in horsemanship and weapon-play, the men were going out after dark to play games of war. 'One group goes ahead and camps on the moors and another creeps up on them and tries to surround the camp without the sentries discovering them,' Anne explained.

I wished, fiercely, that Geoffrey were my husband so that

when he came back, we could meet without subterfuge and he could tell me about it. I wished Lionel would die so that we could marry. Since they were uncle and nephew I might need a dispensation but I would sell Bouldershawe and Thornwood gladly, I thought, to buy one. Then the conversation in the nursery veered back to oyster shell charms and the importance of not letting wet nurses drink too much ale. I joined in but now only the surface of my mind was engaged with it. Beneath the surface, I was in a ferment of fury against the circumstances of my life.

We had arrived in beautiful autumn weather, crisp and a little sharp, like an apple straight from the tree. But presently came a day when we woke to wind and cold, slashing rain. The men had been out overnight on an exercise and next day, although some of them appeared in the hall at dinner, Geoffrey was not there. Early next morning his squire came scratching on our door to tell Lionel that his nephew was ill.

The squire was not Giles, who was now a knight himself and had taken service elsewhere. His replacement, Matthew, was the son of a friend Geoffrey had made while riding with John Neville. He was very young and earnest. 'I don't know what's best to do,' he said worriedly to Lionel.

Lionel pulled his robe on. 'Where is he?'

'In the north-west tower, in the sick quarters. We helped him there, another squire and me.'

'Helped him there? Is he as bad as that?'

'Well, he could walk, sir. But we carried his bedroll and things. He isn't . . . he isn't at all well,' said Matthew unhappily. 'It was being out on the moors at night in such bad weather that brought it on, I think.'

The infirmary room was clean but comfortless. Geoffrey was lying on his pallet and I saw at once that he hadn't enough rugs. The brazier was fuelled but not lit and the cupboard where the remedies were kept was locked. Geoffrey himself was flushed, his eyes both bright and heavy, and when Lionel asked him what was wrong, he said: 'One of my colds,' in a voice which was no more than a hoarse thread of sound.

I turned to Matthew. 'Move the brazier under the louvre there and light it. Is that chest in the corner his?'

'Yes, mistress.'

'You have the key, I take it. Open it up. He usually carries some medicines for this sort of thing. He's prone to it. And put some water to boil on the brazier.'

Geoffrey, shivering, croaked: 'Cold.'

'And fetch more rugs,' I added.

'And a basin and a thick towel,' said Lionel.

In matters such as this, Lionel and I could work well together. Between us we showed Matthew how to prepare a balsam inhalation and a dose of horehound in honey. We made Geoffrey as comfortable as possible under an adequate pile of covers, and then Lionel went to find a steward and request the presence of a physician, while I took Matthew to the kitchen to fetch a measure of wine.

There were two or three servants about the castle who looked after the infirmary as part of their duties, but if anyone who fell ill had attendants of their own, these were expected to do the work rather than the servants – not unfairly, for in Middleham the serving men and women had more than enough to do. Lionel, of course, did not regard day to day nursing as part of his business and in any case was busy about Gloucester's. He had come to Geoffrey in the first emergency; thereafter, caring for him fell to me and Matthew.

For the next seven days, we thought of little else.

We nearly lost him. He grew delirious at sunset on that first day and croaked away to himself all night. In the morning he was rational again but still in a high fever and in great pain from his throat and chest and the aching in his limbs. The physician came, approved the medicines we were using and prescribed others, some of them revolting. That night, Geoffrey's breathing became harsh and laboured and he was delirious again for a while, before losing consciousness in the small hours.

Chrissy brought us food. Lionel came each day to see how Geoffrey did, but never stayed long. I surrendered Perky Dick entirely to the nurses and, with Matthew, stayed on duty at Geoffrey's side. Matthew and I slept in snatches, taking turns on a truckle bed which we put in an adjoining room. It was very strange. I was free to be with Geoffrey as much as I wished, to perform personal services for him, without the slightest question and indeed with approval from all sides. I held him up while he inhaled medicated steam, my arm about his hot shoulders. I held cups while he drank. I helped to steady him out of bed to relieve himself. Matthew fretted about this and kept saying: 'I should do that,' but he was a slight boy and it needed both of us.

At first, Geoffrey seemed to improve every time daybreak came, although he would slip back later. But there came a morning when even this intermission failed to appear. He lay with his eyes closed, his face grey except for a dull red stain on the cheekbones. His skin was dry and burning and his breath rasped in an ugly way. The physician sent for Lionel and for the chaplain. When they came, the Gloucesters came with them. A knight in Richard of Gloucester's household did not die ignored by his lord and Geoffrey was Richard's brother, after all. We all knelt together (much as Alison and Chrissy had once done for me), while the last rites were given. Tears ran down my face but no one thought it odd. Lionel was weeping too.

But all that day and through the following night, somehow or other, Geoffrey held on. Every lungful of air he drew crackled and bubbled in his chest, but he went on drawing them. The physician stayed with us and took the watch in the dead hours while Matthew slept collapsed on a second pallet we had brought into the room and I drowsed uneasily next door. Just before dawn I awoke to find Matthew, candle in hand, shaking me.

'Mistress, wake up!'

'What is it? Is he . . .?' I had lain down fully dressed. I rose at once. 'Tell me, quickly!'

Then I saw that although there were tears in Matthew's eyes, glistening in the candlelight, he was smiling. I ran into the other room. The physician was bending over Geoffrey. He glanced round as I came to his side. 'There is a chance,' he said quietly. 'Only a chance, but he may be going to live.'

I placed my hand on Geoffrey's forehead. It was wet. His hair was wet too, as though it had been plunged into water, and his skin was cool and his breathing, though still harsh, was much quieter than it had been. I looked at the physician.

'The fever's broken,' he said, 'and the chest is easing. There's a long way yet to go. Weakness can be as dangerous as the pestilence itself. But there's a chance.'

Mindful of the proprieties, I said: 'Matthew, Master Eynesby should be informed as soon as he wakes. I will remain here and help the doctor if I can. You can rest until it's time to go and tell my husband.'

Then I sat down beside the bed to share the physician's vigil and secretly, in my heart, with all my heart, I prayed.

By the time another day and night had passed we knew that he would live. But he regained his strength only slowly and throughout all that time he seemed changed; grateful for all that had been done for him, but curiously remote and formal in the way he expressed his thanks, even to me, when we were briefly alone.

By early December he was able to keep his saddle and rode back to Silbeck with us when we returned home. We left him there and went to Eynesby. To our surprise, he did not come to us at Christmas although Alison sent word that he would come in the New Year. He was much pulled down but was improving and we were not to worry.

We had our usual Christmas revels, which were very rumbustious that year because everyone was so pleased with the advent of Perky Dick. As was customary, we elevated a humble member of the household – it was one of Ralph's downtrodden undercooks – to be Lord of Misrule for a day. We plied him with plenty of ale and got him to command a game of forfeits. I hoped that he would make our dictatorial chief cook do something really undignified, such as get down on all fours and beg for his dinner like a pet dog, a fate which had once befallen Lionel at a Middleham Christmas. But even in his cups, the undercook was too afraid of Ralph for that and only asked him to drain a flagon of elderberry wine in one swallow, which Ralph could do with ease and enjoyed doing as he was proud of his accomplishment.

Lionel then seized back his prerogative as master of the hall in order to declare a toast to the two young Richards, the new prince and Perky Dick. The Lord of Misrule at once wagged a forefinger, said he was the one who ought to make the speeches, and launched into a complicated address to the effect that a woman who had borne a son automatically became a queen even though she were a beggar. He lost the thread after a few sentences, waved his goblet vaguely in my direction and fell forward with his nose in the custard. It was all very hilarious and I was even glad that Geoffrey was not there.

For I knew now what my decision must be and I dreaded the moment when I must tell him, and set him beyond my reach for ever. He would renew his suit when he was well; of that I was certain.

We were bidden to Middleham again the next day, to share in their revels. Geoffrey was not there either. We came home to Eynesby just as the twelve days of Christmas ended, and just ahead of gathering snowclouds. When I went next day to help Chrissy remove the decorations in the hall, and carried an armful of withered holly out to the rubbish heap, I stepped into a bitter wind and saw an iron-coloured sky settling over the moors. We must see that the sheep were brought in from the high pastures, I thought. I looked towards the pastures and then, because I could see no sheep there, turned and looked across the valley towards Silbeck, and saw a rider coming.

Whoever it was, was coming at the gallop. For a moment I thought: Geoffrey! And whatever distress his renewed attentions might bring, my first response to the prospect of them was a stab of sheer delight. Followed by disappointment, for as the rider came nearer, I realised that it wasn't Geoffrey after all.

It was Alison. She came pell mell, riding astride, yanking her horse to a skidding halt in the courtyard. Someone ran to take the bridle as she scrambled down. She rushed up to me. 'Where's Lionel? I mun see Lionel!'

'In the house. What's the matter?'

'It's Geoffrey, that's what's the matter. He's ill in his head!'

'Geoffrey? Ill?' I ran beside her as she made off towards the house. 'In his head?'

'Aye, running mad. Oh, where's Lionel? Lionel can stop him. He'll listen to his uncle. He won't listen to me. Set on going, he is, set on going . . .'

'Going where? Alison, what are you talking about?'

'He's going to Jerusalem, that's where he's going!' said Alison and as we came into the hall, she burst out bawling, red-faced and noisy like a hurt child. I caught her arm, said: 'Hush, now, hush,' and somehow or other steered her up to our room. Lionel arrived almost at once, which was understandable, for the noise Alison was making had rung right through the house. She clutched at him. 'Lionel, tha mun come and talk to Geoffrey. Happen thee can get some sense into his daft head!' It took Lionel some time to establish what Geoffrey's daft symptoms actually were and when he did, he was not sympathetic.

'Stop that din, Alison. All this to-do because Geoffrey wants to make a pilgrimage to the Holy Land! Why shouldn't he? Thousands go each year, women even. It's a great adventure. He'll be gone a year, maybe, and when he comes back he'll likely be ready to settle down and get married . . .'

'Married!' Alison burst into fresh wails. 'I had a girl in

mind for him but her father's gone and fixed her up with summun else. Not that that's what matters, any road. Come home, tha says! How do I know he'll ever come home? Jerusalem's that far, he might be going to t'moon! Jerusalem's a place priest talks about in church. Real people don't go to the Holy City any more than real people see angels!'

I remembered that Alison disliked travel. She had travelled with Cicily Neville in her younger days only because she had to. Once freed of the necessity, she hadn't stirred out of the valley. I tried to make comforting noises while Alison rubbed her eyes with red knobbly knuckles and cried harder. 'What if he gets ill again?' she demanded. 'He well nigh died at Middleham, didn't he? I've tried and tried to talk to him but no, he mun send to Middleham for his lord's consent and to the Bishop for a pilgrim's licence and he's got them both already!' Her voice shot up. 'He's made his wi . . . i . . . ill!'

'Hush!' said Lionel.

'I canna hush! He's bought pots and pans to take. He got a book from the Bishop, all about how to make ready for a pilgrimage. It said, take cooking pans.' Out tumbled the pitiful details. 'Listen to thy mother, lad, I said. But he won't listen!' lamented Alison.

'Get her some mulled wine, Petra,' said Lionel.

I fetched it, glad to be away for a moment from her noisy crying, because while I was in her presence, quite literally, I could not hear my own thoughts. Geoffrey to go to Jerusalem? It was simultaneously as though an anxiety had been removed, and the floor had fallen out of the valley. I longed to be alone, to look inside myself and understand what this would mean to me, and in silence and solitude heal the wound which I knew had been dealt me, although it had not yet begun to throb.

When I returned with the wine, I found her in a new paroxysm of tears because in my absence, Lionel had categorically refused to interfere with Geoffrey's plans. We made her drink the wine and lie down. Lionel then said he had work to do and walked decisively out of the room. I sat down beside her, not liking to leave her alone. Alison put out a thin cold hand and gripped my arm. 'If Lionel won't talk to Geoffrey,' she whispered, 'happen you could. Happen he'd listen, seeing what thee've been to one another.'

I looked down at her and felt myself grow chilled all through. 'What in the world do you mean, Alison?'

She gave me a sly, sideways glance. 'Think I didn't know? I helped thee, even. Made sure thee had the house to thysen, once. I've known for a long time how he felt about thee. "Mother," he said to me one time, "I'm mad for Petra, crazed for her. I canna sleep for thinking of her." "Well, what thee does is up to thee," I told him, "but seeing how things are, with no bairn coming along, thee could be doing t'lass a favour." And it were plain enough after he came back from t'war that something were afoot between thee. I soon had it out of him. But I've not told a living soul, tha need not fear me, girl. But if anyone can help me now, it's thee.'

I felt dizzy with shock. Alison had known, then, all that time. Had it been plain to anyone else that 'summat were afoot'?

Was it fear of gossip that was sending Geoffrey off on pilgrimage now? That he should lay plans to go and never even whisper them to me . . .

And now the pain which at first had not appeared, arrived suddenly and laid hold on me and grew. If Geoffrey went away I would wither without him, die of a deprivation as tormenting as hunger and thirst. And I had saved his life – well, helped Matthew to save it. Did he truly mean to go off and leave me without a word? And leave his son?

I rose to my feet. 'I'll give you my company back to Silbeck. No one will think that strange, considering the state you're in. Then I'll talk to him. Alison –'

'Yes?'

'Does anyone else know, or guess?'

'No, no one. I said, I didna blab. Don't think I blame

thee, lass. You had reason and to spare from all I've seen.'

The pain was like a lump of cold iron in the pit of my stomach. Anger, bewilderment and hurt were all part of it. 'I'll order the horses,' I said. 'You'd best take a fresh one, I think.'

'He does nowt but write letters,' Alison informed me as we rode to Silbeck. 'To friends here and friends there, telling them he's going, settling things with the ones he's going with. He's to meet some others in London and set out with a guide they've hired, come the spring. It's as if there's nowt in this world in his mind but Jerusalem.'

He was writing letters when we arrived, sitting at a table in the hall with his back to us. He was already wearing pilgrim grey; the strong, beloved line of his back was made unfamiliar by it. Alison dragged me into the hall, said brightly: 'Geoffrey! Here's Petra come to see thee,' and then left me to it.

I cleared my throat. Geoffrey very slowly laid down his quill and turned round. He was thinner since his illness and his face had lost all its light bronzing.

'I'm sorry, Petra. My mother shouldn't have brought you here.'

'I don't understand what's happening. Alison says you're going to the Holy Land. But were you going without telling me, or Lionel? You've never been near us since you came home, never sent us any message. Geoffrey – why?'

'Oh, my poor Petra,' said Geoffrey helplessly.

I sat down on a settle. No one else was within earshot of us. I spoke flatly. 'You're ending it, aren't you?

He did not speak in answer, but he nodded.

I had meant to end our liaison myself. I had decided, long since, that ended it must be. I had even rehearsed the words in which I would tell him. Now I wondered if I would ever have brought myself to say them.

But even if I had, I thought that at least Geoffrey would

still be here at Silbeck. I would see him sometimes, I would not be quite alone.

I heard myself say: 'Geoffrey, you can't!' and I sprang impulsively from the settle to kneel down by his side. I reached up to him. He put my hands away, kindly but decisively. 'No, Petra, not that. Never again. Sit down, now, and listen.'

It was as though the pilgrim grey were a rampart behind which he had withdrawn. I drew back, though not as far as the settle because I needed, still, to be within touching distance of him even though he would not let me touch him. There was a stool and I pulled that towards him and sat there instead.

'You should have told me,' I said. 'I'm Petra! There's Perky Dick!'

'There is indeed. Petra, I hoped to slip away because I dreaded the thought of seeing you, of explaining . . . It's because of you and Perky Dick that I must go.' His face was paler than ever. 'Please don't make it so difficult for me.'

'What do you mean it's because of me and Perky Dick? You have got to tell me!'

'When I was ill,' he said, 'at Middleham, do you remember – there was a time when everyone thought I was going to die, and a priest was called? He gave me final absolution. Go forth, Christian soul, out of this world. I heard those words. I was drifting in and out of the world, I think. I came to for a moment just then and my eyes opened. I saw people kneeling by my bed. You were there and so was Uncle Lionel. His eyes were tight shut and his face was so unhappy. And then,' said Geoffrey simply, 'I remembered that I owed my life to him.'

'Your life?'

'On Barnet field. I was in danger many times and twice at least I would have been killed except that I'm left-handed. It was Uncle Lionel who let me train with my left hand. Most men would have made me fight at practice with my left hand tied to my belt, but Uncle Lionel allowed me to use it. He taught me how to use my right hand too but he never forced me to pretend I was right-handed. And I'm alive today because of it. Lying there at Middleham, I thought: if I'd been his son he couldn't have done more for me, and what have I done for him in return? Stolen his wife and passed my son off as his. All I can do now is to take the palm branch in my hand and go to Jerusalem and hope to find God's forgiveness. It's the only way I can begin to put it right.'

'You saved me,' I said. 'Lionel was ill-treating me because we had no child. I was terrified of him. Sooner or later, he would have . . . I don't believe he can get his own children. You've given him his heart's desire, you know. I don't think you need so much forgiving. And you've shown me what there can be between a man and a woman. If you must go to Jerusalem, you must, but don't say that what has been between us was wrong. Dangerous, yes. I've thought that myself. Oh Geoffrey, don't go! Or else take us with you, me and Perky Dick! Take us with you! Let's make another life in another country!' The words came out by themselves. Even before Geoffrey fell ill I had sworn never to suggest this to him. And now here I was, blurting it out, knowing as I spoke that it was useless, a blunder, but unable to help myself. 'I know there'll be hardship but I won't mind if I'm with you. Perky Dick will be with both of us, his proper parents. Don't you want that, don't you want to see him grow up? Geoffrey . . .'

'Stop it, Petra! Stop it, I say. Petra, I wanted to avoid a scene like this partly because I still haven't the strength to . . .'

'Then how can you talk of travelling all the way to Jerusalem? All right, we'll end it if you wish – perhaps that would be wiser, safer, anyway. But don't go away. Stay here at Silbeck, near me. I need to know you're near!'

'You are safe now. Lionel has his son, or so he thinks. And Perky Dick will have Eynesby. I'm pleased about that. It may be wrong of me. In my pilgrimage I am seeking

337

forgiveness for that too. But I can't avoid it. I am glad that my son will have Eynesby.'

'What if something happens to him?' Perky Dick seemed healthy now but the strongest babies were frail craft and the world was full of accidents and pestilences waiting to overwhelm them. If we lost him, I would be more than bereaved. I would be in danger again. 'I'd be left alone with Lionel, a childless Lionel, and he'd expect . . .'

It was another blunder, and a worse one. Geoffrey's face froze. 'Is that all I was to you, Petra? A stallion?'

'No, of course not! Yes, I know it was why I gave way to you in the first place, but you knew that then, and it made no difference. You still loved me. And I love you. Geoffrey, I do! That, and needing you to protect me from Lionel, they're tangled together and I can't separate them but . . .'

'I wonder.' He sat resting his hands on his knees and gazed at me. 'God forgive me, I was in love with you and believed in you. But since I was ill, and had time to think, I have come to wonder. You were very remote and strange just after Perky Dick was born. I think Perky Dick is all you wanted of me, if the truth be known. And that now you have him, you would be content except that you would like to keep me close by in case of an emergency.'

'No! Geoffrey, that's not true!' But I knew that I had hurt him and that the twined-together nature of my feelings for him and my terror of Lionel were too complex for him to understand.

'But I shouldn't condemn you,' he said. 'I'm no better than you. I think there is something I should tell you, Petra. It might be best if I do, because then I think you will cease to want either to come away with me or to keep me here, and really, that would be a relief to me.'

'What do you mean? What is there that I don't know, that you ought to tell me?'

'When my uncle married you,' he said, 'I lost my chance of inheriting Eynesby. I minded that.'

'I know, I understand.'

'I came to Faldene to do the correct thing that my uncle expected.' Geoffrey went on as though I hadn't interrupted. 'I came along to pretend my approval, but at heart I was sick with rage. And then I saw you. You were very sweet and it was hardly your fault. I felt sorry for you, married to a man my uncle's age, when you were so young.'

'Geoffrey, I already know all this.' I remembered that Alison had told me most of it and that he might not like that. 'At least,' I amended, 'I guessed at it. It was all natural and . . .'

'And I thought,' said Geoffrey steadily, 'that it would be quite amusing to take you away from my uncle. I thought you might prefer me, anyway. Later, when you and he produced no child, I saw that I could go one step further and that at least, if I could not inherit Eynesby, a child of my body could. That's why I'm so pleased that Perky Dick will have it. After letting me think for so long that one day it would be mine, my uncle somehow owed me Eynesby. The only difficulty was that you resisted me. But then . . .'

I was silent.

'Last summer wasn't a lie, Petra,' he said. 'I'm not as bad as that. I did indeed come to love you. I can tell you the very day and hour when the love became real. It was after I came back from Warwick's first rebellion and I spoke to you just outside the chapel, after dark, and you told me you were afraid of Lionel. I was sorrier than ever for you then and . . . yes, from then on I loved you. But it was rooted in calculation and but for that would never have begun at all. And if it had begun, I might not have pursued it.'

'Does your mother know all this?'

'Most of it, yes. We're close. I tell her most things sooner or later. She understood. She said I'd be doing you a favour and would only be claiming what was fair from my uncle. There'd be a bit of interest on the deal, she said.' His voice held amusement now and as often happened when he was jesting, his trace of northern accent deepened. 'She wants me to marry, of course. She wants a child to inherit Silbeck. But she said to me that not only Eynesby, but Bouldershawe too would go to my lad, or my lass, as the case might be, if you and I had a child.'

'And Lionel's her brother!'

'Half-brother. I'm her son.'

I studied him, taking in for the very last time the face and form I had loved so much. I saw him at last with perfect clarity, Lionel's nephew, who made good bargains and claimed his debts and expected both to pay and receive interest. I was a debt he had recovered from Lionel and with this pilgrimage he was discharging one he had incurred. Love? Yes, he had loved me in his fashion. But before Geoffrey was a lover, he was a big handsome man of business, and after that, a mother's boy who had told it all to Alison.

Even my feelings for him now seemed foolish. When, after all, had we ever talked of anything that mattered? I had never asked him what he felt about Eynesby, never asked what his hopes and dreams and angers were, never told him mine. We had become drunk on each other's bodies, and that was all.

'I owe you my thanks,' I said, 'for a beautiful dream, although it was nothing more.' I stood up. My legs were trembling but I forced them to behave. The capable Petronel helped me – the girl who had come into being during that mission to Calais when realms and heads were at stake and my own life might depend on my ability to keep my nerve.

'Thank you,' I said, 'for defending me from Lionel and for giving me Perky Dick, my child as well as my shield. Go to the Holy Land, Geoffrey. I wouldn't detain you for the world. When you get there, I suggest you stay.'

Then I turned my back and went out of the room to tell Alison that I had failed, to give her what comfort I could (be careful with Alison, said a warning voice in my head, for she knows too much) and then to go home. There, in what privacy I could contrive, I would mourn my lost dream and after that become wholly and for ever the mother of Perky Dick and, holding my fear and dislike at bay as best I could, Lionel's wife.

Chapter Twenty-Three

Petronel: Warning

1476

When I was a girl at Withysham, there was a mad nun. She was kept incarcerated in a separate building – a converted barn, I think it was. We young ones were not supposed to go near her but an inquisitive novice and I did venture once to take a closer look. We ran away quickly, however, frightened by the fierce pale face, grey hair straggling from under a wimple all askew, which peered at us from behind a barred window and spat obscenities from a twisted mouth.

Shortly after that another nun, the gentle Sister Honoria, also became afflicted in the mind. But she was not shut away. She was given a room to herself, and on her bad days, when she literally did not know who or where she was, she was kept in it with an attendant. On other days, as long as someone were with her, she was free to go about the abbey and attend the services. At these times she was almost normal except that she was always excessively worried about other people's safety. If she saw anyone going near a candle, she would call out to them to be careful of their veil; in cold weather, she begged everyone she met to wrap themselves well for fear of falling ill. She actually fainted one day when she saw one of the nuns slip on the steps of the chapter house and sprain an ankle.

We were allowed to visit Sister Honoria even on her bad days, and we used to take her little gifts – flowers from the garden and the like. Once I asked Aunt Eleanor why we kept away from the other one.

'What you must understand,' said my aunt, 'is that

madness varies with the person. It's my opinion that people who are mad don't so much take leave of their minds as expose them. Sister Honoria has been always thoughtful for others and now that God has seen fit to take away her power to control what she says and does, the thoughtfulness remains and dominates. But Sister Agnes, we keep you away from her – or try to –' said my aunt meaningly, 'because her madness is evil. She spits hate and profanity. And she was eaten up with hatred and unspoken ravings long before she lost the power to hide them. I knew her well; I sensed it. So be warned, Petronel. Never let such sins command your soul even in secret. One day, you may not be able to keep that secret hidden.'

Over the next few years, I remembered often what my aunt had said, for I had to hide so many secret feelings, and such violent ones. I carried locked within me the secret of Perky Dick's parentage, and a longing for the sight of Geoffrey's face which persisted and even seemed to grow, even though I had myself told him to stay away, even though I was sure I had ceased to love him. He had taken me at my word and not returned to England. We heard he had reached Jerusalem, and then taken service with a lord he had met there, whose home was in Spain. Alison grieved, though Lionel said that with Geoffrey's tendency to chest illnesses, he might well live longer in Spain than in England.

When I first heard that news, I at once felt a surge of rage and yearning mixed. Geoffrey had after all done the very thing I had asked of him, but without me. He had gone to live abroad. So why could we not have gone with him, Perky Dick and I? To salve his own conscience, he had left me here to spend the rest of my life in Lionel's power and, oh, how I hated Lionel.

That was another secret to be kept. During those years, there were times when the strength of that hatred terrified me. It was so intense that I could not understand why he did not see it, despite my bland face and fair speaking. And then I would remember mad Sister Agnes and wonder, horrified, if one day I would be stripped of the power of concealment, so that all the hate would burst out as profanity.

About three years after Geoffrey had gone, my fear increased, for I saw my aunt's theory proven and illustrated by my friend Isabel Neville's husband, George the Duke of Clarence.

Lionel was pleased with me for a time after Perky Dick was born but of course the euphoria soon wore off. What had I done, after all, but my duty as his wife? However, he did slightly soften in his attitude to Isabel Neville. When next she sent an invitation for me to join her, he allowed it. He was grudging about it, and was so disagreeable when I returned, carping at everything I did, that I privately decided not to go again. However, when Isabel was expecting her fourth child and was very unwell, she sent for me once more and I changed my mind. It was clear that she wanted me very badly. Again, Lionel gave a reluctant consent, and so I left Perky Dick with Chrissy – leaving him grieved me but I could trust Chrissy – and set out. In mid-September 1476 I found myself dismounting in the courtyard of the guesthouse at Tewkesbury Abbey.

The abbey stood close to the battlefield where Margaret of Anjou had been finally defeated. The climate was milder here than in the north; the meadows all round were green and lush and the Gloucestershire air was soft. It was a good place for an infirmary and the abbey was known all over the land for its ample space and staff of excellent resident physicians. Since the Clarences had property in Tewkesbury, it was a natural choice for Isabel's lying-in. No fault could be found with these arrangements. Nevertheless, Ankaret Twynyhoe came hurrying into the courtyard to meet me, and whisked me straight indoors for the purpose, it transpired, of relieving her feelings by telling me her opinion of the duke.

'My lady always has a terrible time in childbirth. Ever

since that first shocking business on board ship. She's had two since then, as you know, but she well-nigh died each time and the boy's simple. He was too long coming into this world, that's what caused it. That and his parents being cousins, maybe. If the duke had any decency, he'd leave her alone. He finds consolation elsewhere as it is!' Ankaret looked older, smaller, more lined than I remembered from my last visit, but her personality, with its combination of passion and dignity, had not changed.

'That might upset Isabel even more,' I said.

'It probably would,' said Ankaret with a snort. 'She still has a softness for him. But it wouldn't *kill* her.'

'Ankaret! You're not saying . . . Oh no!'

'Oh yes. It happens every day to some poor woman somewhere. I was lucky. Mine popped out as easily as could be. But Isabel takes her life in her hands whenever she conceives. And all her husband does is congratulate himself on his prowess. That man,' said Ankaret, 'is the vainest creature I have ever met and this time round – well if Isabel comes through, it will be a miracle, and if she doesn't, she'll have been destroyed by his vanity!'

I had not seen the duke since I left Calais. My other visit to Isabel had taken place when he was away from home. Isabel herself arranged matters thus. In view of the stratagem by which I had escaped Calais, I thought this prudent. But now, ill and wanting her friends round her, she had let that go. When Ankaret took me to Isabel's chamber, Clarence was there.

I must not be unjust to him; he did have some feeling for her, although there were times when it was hard to believe it. When I arrived at Tewkesbury, he caused me no embarrassment. He did not remind me of his semi-real pursuit at Calais and certainly he did not renew it. He was taken up with anxiety about Isabel and hardly registered my existence.

She was ailing badly. She could not eat. 'I feel so sick,' she would protest tearfully when we begged her to swallow a little chicken broth, a few spoonfuls of frumenty, a mouthful or two of bread soaked in wine or milk. The physicians said we should try to obtain anything, no matter how exotic, that she said she fancied. I think Ankaret took great pleasure in making the Duke of Clarence purchase oranges at great expense and personally fetch preserved strawberries to his wife's bedside.

On the 4th of October, her pains began and on the 6th, a baby girl, a little scrap of a thing almost too weak to breathe, was born. Isabel slept for some hours and we hoped she would wake refreshed, but by the next day she was in a high fever.

We fought for her, Ankaret and I, just as Matthew and I had once fought for Geoffrey. Isabel seemed to fret when others tended her; she apparently had a special affection for Ankaret and myself. Perhaps it was because we were the two among her ladies who loved her best.

We fought for thirty-six days, giving her cooling medicines, keeping her clean, coaxing her to take nourishment. A wet-nurse was found for the baby. The child ailed and cried and did not gather strength, but at first Isabel did gradually improve. At the end of thirty-six days, although she was still weak and intermittently feverish, I think we might have won through with her, had it not been for the stupidity of Clarence.

He took it into his head to decide that her recovery was too slow, that we were not taking sufficient care of her – I thought Ankaret would have an apoplexy when he said that – and that she should be moved to Warwick Castle and the care of his personal physician there.

'The castle is her proper home,' he said when we protested. 'Our son is Earl of Warwick now. And she lived there as a child, she will make better progress in familiar surroundings. You may stay with her if she wishes,' he added to Ankaret and me, 'but my physician will supervise you.'

We pleaded that it was unwise to move her. The abbey

doctors added their voices and Isabel herself begged to stay where she was. But despite the weather, which had turned very raw and damp, and despite the fact that Isabel was still so frail from the fever and so tender from the hard birth that any kind of jolting made her cry, she was put into a litter and carried, a whole day's journey swinging between two horses, all the way to Warwick. She was shuddering with cold and pain and exhaustion when she was carried into the castle and although she lingered on for another month after that, from the day of that journey, the battle was lost.

She was in such pain at the end that she whispered that death would be a relief. I was holding her in my arms and trying to comfort her as best I could. The physician stood beside me, shaking his head sadly. The priest was there, but Clarence had been called to his audience chamber earlier that day and although the physician sent for him when we saw that the last crisis had come, she went before he reached her.

Clarence came in, in fact, just as I had laid her down. The priest was kneeling, murmuring a prayer. Ankaret was closing Isabel's eyes. Clarence knocked her hand away. 'What are you doing? Isabel, wake up! It's your husband!'

'My lord!' The physician began to speak but Ankaret cut him short. She loathed Clarence and had never taken much trouble to hide it. Now she took none. 'She is dead, my lord!' said Ankaret with fury. 'And the fault is yours!'

Clarence turned from looking at Isabel's quiet face and stared instead at Ankaret. 'I don't advise you,' he said softly, 'to tell me that my wife's death is my fault.'

He swung round and left the room. 'You see?' said Ankaret furiously. She kept her voice low, out of respect for the dead, but her anger filled the room. 'He thinks the world begins and ends with himself. I think he thought Isabel was insulting him by not waking up when he called her – when she's dead!'

'Hush!' I said. The doctor and the priest were looking at her in alarm.

'My dear lady,' the priest said kindly. 'You are overcome

with grief but you must be careful what you say.'

He was right, as it turned out, very very right. But Ankaret was right as well. Clarence was vain, and in the course of the next year when he apparently went mad as well, the vanity was, I think, at the bottom of it. It made him long for power and position beyond his abilities and when others – sensibly – denied him these things, it consumed his reason.

Chapter Twenty-Four

The Plantagenets: Madness

1477–1478

By decree of King Edward, Ludlow Castle was to be home for his eldest son. 'He's going to be Prince of Wales. He should have a base near the Welsh border.' The castle was not richly appointed and its architectural charm was variable. Over the centuries since the Normans first began it, it had grown in an unplanned sort of way, the rounded walls of the Norman chapel of St Mary Magdalen in the inner bailey, and the cavemouth Norman arches of the keep, making to most eyes a curious contrast with the elegant mullioned windows of the new palace, with its lofty hall and gracefully proportioned private quarters adjoining. King Edward, however, liked it.

'The new palace sits within the curve of the old Norman wall like a bride in the arm of a big tough bridegroom,' he had once said, in that occasionally lyrical way of his. And there was no denying that the outlook over the River Teme in its green valley was beautiful. As far as the young prince's guardians, his uncle Anthony Woodville and his half-brother Richard Grey could see, the boy was happy there. His tutor, John Alcock, agreed with them.

'I'd have preferred the Gloucesters to have him,' Edward had said frankly to Alcock. 'Gloucester will have to be his guardian if anything happens to me – that's confidential, by the way. I'd need a blood relation of my own in those circumstances. But although I could have ordered the Gloucesters to Ludlow, they wouldn't want to go and besides . . .'

And besides, there was Bess.

Edward, initially, had toyed with the notion of putting his son in Richard's care and sending the Gloucesters to Ludlow regardless. But his very first, casual mention of this to Bess produced results which staggered him. They were alone together, about to retire. Bess turned white and sat down suddenly on the edge of the bed. 'No,' she said. Her voice was low, as always, but shook with strong feeling. 'Not the Gloucesters. Not the Gloucesters!'

Edward, who had been standing by the hearth to drain a nightcap goblet, gazed at her in astonishment. He had not heard her sound so vehement since the day when, through flowing tears, she told him why she had sent John Tiptoft to kill the Earl of Desmond. Even on occasions when he had been with a mistress and knew she must be aware of it, she had remained calm and complaisant, apparently oblivious. 'Bess?' he said questioningly. He put the goblet down on a table and came towards her.

'Not the Gloucesters!' Bess shook her head from side to side. 'No, please!'

'But why not?'

Bess bit her lip. She stopped shaking her head but her hands clutched at the furs and embroideries of the bedcovers.

'Why not?' Edward persisted.

'Richard of Gloucester despises me.' The words came out in a hurry. 'He'll teach my son to despise me too. He hates my family. He'll teach our son that as well. He . . .'

'Richard was loyal to me when Warwick rebelled and attacked your family,' Edward pointed out. 'And he certainly doesn't hate your brother Anthony. They get on well.'

'Yes, but he hates all the others. You know he does. One day . . .'

Bess stopped. Her eyes filled and overflowed. She let the tears fall, taking care despite her distress not to distort her features with grimaces, or redden her eyelids with rubbing. She always cried in this fashion. It was a performance which never failed to stir her husband's admiration. When

Bess wept, her face was like alabaster adorned with pearls and he had never met another woman capable of such a phenomenon.

But the anguish responsible for it was real. He sat down beside her. 'Come, Bess. Come, I hate you to be unhappy. What were you going to say? One day . . .?'

'I can't bear to think of it.'

'Of what?'

'Anything happening to you! But if it did, if it did . . .!'

'Our son would be king? Is that what you are trying to say? Well, so he will, one day.'

'And when that day comes,' said Bess, 'I would like to think that he would be good to his half-brothers, to his cousins and uncles on his mother's side. I don't want him taught to be their enemy. A king is a dangerous enemy! Richard of Gloucester would make him hate them.'

'I'm sure Richard would never –'

'He would, he would!' The tears still streamed. 'He despises me, I told you. He's polite when we meet – but even then he says things sometimes, things with second meanings. I'm glad we don't meet often. And even when he isn't saying things, I can see in his eyes what he thinks of me. Oh Edward, couldn't someone from my side look after him? Anthony's educated and a splendid knight and he's kind. Could he not be the one?'

He wanted to please her and stop the tears, and in any case, some of her arguments had force. He did not think Richard could hate Bess as much as she supposed. She was too tender-skinned on some subjects. This might be as well, since he didn't want a repetition of the Desmond scandal, but it might incline her to imagine that remarks were double-edged when they were not. Nevertheless, it was true that in some ways Anthony Woodville would make a better guardian. He was as knowledgeable as Richard in knightly matters and would be as good an instructor in manners, arms and heraldry, and he was, frankly, better educated. Anthony was trilingual, as fluent in Latin and French as in

English. One of Bess's older sons, the Greys, could help him look after the prince. It would make a family unit: Anthony and two nephews.

'Anthony Woodville – well, Lord Rivers as he is now, of course – should be reliable,' he said to Alcock. 'But if anything does befall me, young Edward will become a boy king overnight and he'll have to go through a complete change of mentors. I would want you to stay with him whatever happened, to give him continuity, stability. That means that you'll be taking on an appointment which will last a long time. I sounded you out on the question of being Edward's tutor some time ago but this may make a difference. It's an extra responsibility. What do you feel about it?'

'I welcome the opportunity,' said Alcock.

An appointment to teach, and teach the heir to the throne at that, with every prospect of seeing it right through to the boy's adulthood, was so much to his taste that it outweighed even the bishopric of Rochester where he had lately been installed. In addition, the boy was Bess Woodville's son as well as the King's and once – he could admit it now that it was over – he had been almost in love with Bess. She had proved too flawed for a bishop's daydreams, but he was glad to have had them, and he would do well by Bess's child by way of gratitude.

He had to begin his task from a distance, since his diocese and his intelligence network and the King's Council chamber often summoned him. But with the help of Anthony Woodville and Richard Grey, he appointed under-tutors to teach the child his letters and gave Anthony careful advice as to the course the prince's training should follow after that.

After a time, Edward Brampton proved able to act in his stead in much of the intelligence gathering, and an appointment to the Bishopric of Worcester, which embraced Ludlow, enabled him to spend more time with his pupil. The Council still called him away on occasion but at least his base was now in Shropshire. As he at last drew close to

352

the prince, what he found was beyond his most optimistic expectations.

He had intended that the boy should be literate by now and grounded in languages. Anthony was currently making a French to English translation of a book called *The Sayings of the Philosophers* and meant to have it printed in London where a man called Caxton had set up a press on the German pattern, and he had been entrusted with seeing to the languages.

But not until he was himself on day to day terms with the prince, did Alcock realise how very responsive and advanced in his studies the boy was. He was not only, it seemed, in charge of a pupil who would one day use his education to rule a kingdom. The prince was also highly intelligent in his own right. He was to be valued not just because he was King Edward's son, or Bess's son, but for himself, for his own bright mind and promising intellect.

In his prayers now, Alcock regularly included a petition that this splendid boy should not be forced into kingship too soon, that his father would live long and let the son grow well into manhood first. A minor on the throne was a wretched position; Alcock had seen it all with Henry the Sixth when he himself was young. Boy kings were fought over like tasty titbits by factions eager to rule through them and at the moment there were too many factions in the country anyway. Richard of Gloucester disliked the Queen and all her relatives, except perhaps Anthony Woodville; the Woodvilles understandably distrusted Gloucester; and there were latent Lancastrians still in existence, although at the moment they had no focus. There had even been growling noises from the north where Harry Percy of Northumberland had been heard to complain that Richard of Gloucester's influence there was too great. Northumberland considered himself to be the viceroy in that district and Gloucester was proving too big a rival.

In such a country, the king needed to be adult, experienced and wily. As a future king, Prince Edward could not be protected from knowledge of these things, but he could and should be kept throughout his boyhood in the position of onlooker. He should be encouraged too, Alcock thought, to love learning for its own sake, and to that end Alcock tried to make his studies interesting. The boy, like most children, enjoyed tales, and of wholesome stories, full of noble deeds and wise judgements, Alcock saw that he had plenty. In the process he discovered a childlike vein within himself. The tutor enjoyed the stories nearly as much as the pupil. When Edward said: 'Tell me the story of Sir Gawaine and the Green Knight again, my lord bishop,' Alcock was always happy to comply.

He was in the middle of Sir Gawaine's story, sitting with Edward in a quiet top floor chamber next to the hall, with windows facing out across the Teme and away from the courtyard bustle, when Anthony Woodville strode in and said without preamble, and as though his small nephew were not there: 'Clarence has gone mad. He's murdered Ankaret Twynyhoe!'

With deliberate slowness, Alcock laid down the book from which he had been reading. He knew that on the window seat beside him, Edward had stiffened. Superficially the prince was his mother's son, with the silver-gilt Woodville hair and a skin somewhat fair for a boy. But his almond-shaped hazel eyes were those of his father and the skill of remembering names and faces, which all royalty must learn, apparently came to him naturally.

'Mistress Twynyhoe?' he said, looking questioningly from one adult face to the other. 'She came with Aunt Isabel when my lord and lady Clarence were here to see me. I remember, I think.' It had been a year ago, a long time for a child. 'She was an older lady,' he said. 'She told me a story about a dragonslayer.'

'And gave you sweetmeats, yes. What is all this about, Anthony?' Alcock regarded Lord Rivers disapprovingly. 'Is this quite the time or the place?' he said.

Anthony dropped into a settle. 'My apologies, but the

354

courier has only just arrived and when I heard the news I was so shaken ... It even *sounds* insane,' he said exasperatedly. 'The woman has – had – such an extraordinary name. She sounds too comical to be in the middle of a murderous plot but . . .'

Edward turned to Alcock. 'You told me Aunt Isabel had died, and so she couldn't come here again. Has Mistress Twynyhoe died too?'

'Yes. Not from the same cause,' said Anthony, 'but yes. I'm sorry, my lord prince, but these are things you have to know.'

'How did she die, then? You said Aunt Isabel went to heaven when she was trying to have a baby. But Mistress Twynyhoe was . . . was . . . mur . . .?'

'Murdered. Her death was caused because someone else wickedly willed it so,' said Anthony.

'She and your Aunt Isabel are both in heaven now,' said Alcock firmly. 'Would you like a Mass to be said for their souls?' The child nodded and Alcock, closing the book, rose. 'Then we'll go and find the chaplain and you shall tell him that you want him to arrange one.'

Ten minutes later, walking on the walls with Anthony after leaving Edward with the chaplain, he said: 'It was unwise to burst in like that with the news, my lord. Edward has reached the age when he has just begun to grapple with the idea that people don't live for ever. You should have left it to me to break the news.'

'When you call me "my lord", I know you're annoyed,' said Anthony. 'I'm sorry, but he is to be a king and he must know what the world is like. And preferably, he should learn before it reveals its inherent beastliness to him and takes him by surprise. You over-protect him.'

Alcock rested his forearms on a crenellation and sighed. 'Perhaps. A man who takes priestly orders, forfeits the right to have sons. Perhaps I've begun to think of Edward as a son. I know I try to keep evil influences away from him. What did you mean when you said the Duke of Clarence had gone mad? You had better tell me the whole story.'

'You can read the courier's despatch presently. It's direct from King Edward. But I can tell you in my own words now. When I said Clarence was mad, I meant just that. There have been signs, you know. The way he veered about between Edward and Warwick, and then the way he tried to hold on to Anne of Gloucester's inheritance. That was sheer childish temper because he was jealous of Gloucester. He's never behaved as though he were grown up. Fancy trying to hide the poor girl in a cookshop! How long did he think he could keep her there, one asks oneself! Quite seriously, I think Clarence is sick in his mind. Look at the Burgundy business – come to think of it, that's connected to this affair of Ankaret Twynyhoe – it was showing itself then.'

'You can hardly claim that Clarence's desire to marry Mary of Burgundy was evidence of insanity. You wanted to marry her yourself!'

'Not for the same reason.' Anthony was impatient. 'You know my marriage to Liz was never close. I hardly noticed when she died and that's the truth. Then, coming back from a pilgrimage, I visited Burgundy to see the Duchess Margaret and there was her stepdaughter. The Burgundian court is appallingly stiff. People are so formal their clothes might have been sculpted rather than sewn! And there in the middle of it was this girl like a rose – only she's heir to Burgundy, since the Duchess Margaret has no children, and whoever marries her will virtually rule it and King Edward warned me off being quite so ambitious. He may have been right. I haven't the nature of a ruler, I like my private hobbies too much, my books and my maps and my astrolabe and riding in the lists. I could see that, and I could accept the King's prohibition. Mary of Burgundy is a darling but she isn't for me. But *Clarence* . . . I should begin this tale of Ankaret Twynyhoe at the beginning, shouldn't I?'

'I really think it would be advisable,' said Alcock drily.

'It begins,' said Anthony Woodville, 'with Isabel's death . . .'

'You may not have heard it all,' Anthony said. He leaned on the wall beside Alcock and they both gazed out over the river valley. 'You just heard, perhaps, that she had died in childbed?' Alcock nodded. 'Nothing so simple!' said Anthony. 'She had the baby at Tewkesbury and she took the childbed fever. While she was still ill, Clarence for reasons best known to himself took it into his head that she must be transported to Warwick Castle! He behaved like a complete bully and dragged her all the way there in a litter. Then when she not surprisingly died, he behaved as though she were the light of his life, torn from him by a malignant fate instead of by his own callous stupidity!' Anthony Woodville was a good-humoured man as a rule but the face he turned to Alcock was now angry. 'And then, almost straight away, he made his bid for Mary of Burgundy. You should have been there when he asked for Edward's consent! He talked about his agonising grief for Isabel for five full minutes and then launched into his demand to be allowed to apply for Mary's hand without pausing to take a breath. "As a solace for loneliness or to get your hands on Burgundy?" Edward said to him, and then Clarence began to rant about how he'd always been brushed aside and overlooked and in the same breath, how Isabel had been the one person who loved him and the world was dark without her . . .'

'I see what you mean about madness,' said Alcock thoughtfully. 'But where does Mistress Twynyhoe come in?'

'Bear with me, I shall arrive in due course. Edward said to Clarence: "What a pleasant prospect for Mary," and then told him that the answer was no and that was final because Clarence wasn't fit to rule Burgundy or anywhere else. After that, Clarence went from bad to worse. He started the most disgraceful rumours.'

357

'Yes, those I have indeed heard about. But they were all quite absurd – nonsense about King Edward not being his father's son and some rubbish about a prophecy that the next king's name would begin with a G. I couldn't take them seriously.'

'I don't think many people did. The King was angry, but not alarmed. And that made Clarence more furious than ever. His spleen needed an outlet perhaps. Be that as it may,' said Anthony, 'his next victim was Mistress Twynyhoe. She was one of the ladies with Isabel of Clarence when Isabel died. The baby died shortly after its mother, and Clarence accused Mistress Twynyhoe of poisoning them both. She'd gone back to her home in Devonshire by then. He had her dragged from her house and fetched all the way to Warwickshire. In Stratford-upon-Avon, he had her tried for murder, and surrounded the court with armed men to intimidate the jury. She was hanged the same morning.'

In London Bess Woodville was shaken by the news but it was not from his queen that King Edward heard the most scathing condemnation of his brother. It was his mistress, Jane Shore, who burst into tears of horrified fury. 'The jury were all cowards! I've met Mistress Twynyhoe! Of all the innocent, decent, harmless bodies . . . Oh, it's wicked, wicked!'

'I fancy the jury did it because they knew Clarence would have their heads – or at least their freedom and their livelihoods – if they returned any verdict but guilty,' said Edward candidly. 'He packed the court with his retainers. Some of the jury asked her pardon before she went to the gallows.'

'How could anyone be cruel enough to send her there?'

'You have the kindest heart I've ever come across,' Edward told her. 'Even your lovers' wives like you. It's a rare state of affairs.'

It was true. Jane Shore, the goldsmith's ex-wife whom

Edward had taken casually away from Hastings, had a warmth which found a response in the most unlikely people, even in her rivals. Jane had been christened Elizabeth but would no longer use the name because she said it would be disrespectful to the Queen. And Bess Woodville, who had begun by tolerating Jane in silence because she herself was too realistic to expect complete fidelity from her dazzling husband, and too afraid of offending him in any case to express even justified jealousy, had ended by receiving her in private and telling her: 'Better you than some others. But don't encourage him to drink too much.'

But now Jane said: 'It isn't me we're talking about.' She had a husky voice which Edward said sounded as though her throat were lined with velvet. 'And I don't feel kind-hearted about Clarence. I've no pity for him, whatever happens to him. He is no better than a beast. He's worse!'

Edward attempted to offer a conventional religious consolation. 'It's all over now. Ankaret's safe in heaven.'

'A good woman like Mistress Twynyhoe could have got to heaven quite well without going through hell first.'

'Yes,' Edward admitted, 'I know.'

'And I know that the Duke of Clarence is your brother. But . . .'

Sombrely, Edward nodded. 'I understand. You think I should take steps, and you are quite right, dear heart. The time is coming when I must.'

Catherine Buckingham, the Queen's sister, heard the tale of Ankaret's death from her husband, who strode into her bedchamber in their house near Westminster, ostensibly to tell her. But while he held forth on the demented behaviour of Clarence, he prowled the room suspiciously, slapping the hangings and peering into a clothes closet. Catherine paid little heed to the tale of Ankaret's demise but watched Harry Buckingham's antics with interest. As he finished his story, she dismissed her maid with a glance and said: 'What in the world are you looking for?'

359

Buckingham abandoned his pretence of interest in Ankaret, stood with a scowl disfiguring his handsome face and answered bluntly: 'Hastings.'

'Behind my tapestries? Well, really!' Catherine picked up a pair of tweezers and began to attend to her eyebrows.

'He's hovered round you on and off for years! Lately, it's been more blatant. Is he your lover? Or are you too innocent to know his reputation?'

'If I'm more innocent than a married woman ought to be, whose fault is that? But of course I know his reputation.' Catherine leant forward to study her handiwork in a silver mirror. 'My sister warned me. She hates Hastings because he takes the King on girl-hunting expeditions. She'd rather he just kept to Jane Shore. But I find Hastings amusing.'

'Is he your lover?' Buckingham repeated.

'No,' said Catherine regretfully. 'He hasn't asked me,' she explained.

'And would you say yes if he did?'

Catherine swung round to face him. Her fair hair flew round her face as she did so. Its light strands were like the gold-coloured spun-sugar confection which had appeared on the royal table at last night's banquet. It disturbed him, which made him angrier. He did not want to be disturbed, in that way, by Catherine Woodville or any Woodville and it was as a Woodville that he thought of his wife, never as a Buckingham.

'Does it matter a straw to you?' she demanded of him now.

'You're my wife.'

'Am I? You walk in and out of my bedchamber but I could apply for an annulment if I chose and get it. You realise that? I've been considering it.'

'Have you now? You'd have to be examined by a panel of matrons and stand up before a solemn row of ecclesiastical judges to explain that your husband can't bear the sight of you. Do *you* realise *that*?'

'Oh, you can bear the sight of me,' said Catherine. 'Or

you wouldn't wander in and out as you do. It's my low origin you can't tolerate. As a matter of fact, I should put my case rather differently.' Her voice was like cream: smooth, rich and devoid of sweetness. 'I should tell them you were impotent,' she said.

'Tell them *what*?'

'I should say that you had tried but pitiably failed. They'd believe it. After all, you must want an heir.'

'You bitch!' The words came out in a near whisper.

Catherine put down the tweezers and watched him advance across the room. She had said it to provoke him but something in this prowling approach made her mouth go dry and her heart thunder not with excitement but with fear. As he reached her she could smell him, a mixture of heady masculine sweat and the spicy pomade he used on his hair. 'No one says that of me,' said Harry Buckingham softly. 'No one, do you hear, you low-born trollop?'

'One thing a virgin can't be is a trollop,' said Catherine. With an enormous effort she remained sitting steadily upright. She raised her chin. His eyes were not focused on her at all; they were a blank blue, transcendentally calm, and terrifying. 'What evidence have I,' she said in a shrill voice, 'that you are capable?'

His hands came out but not for any form of embrace or caress. 'Be silent,' said Harry Buckingham and closed his fingers on her throat.

She choked, kicked, fell from the stool to land on the floor with Harry on top. His grip did not ease. Her breath stopped and the blood pounded in her ears. Some ancient instinct, the same one that made frightened animals freeze in the hope of escaping notice, made her stop resisting. She went limp. His clutching hands shook her to and fro, as though she were a coney in a dog's mouth. Then they let go. She fell back, gagging, gasping, unable to speak for the pain in her throat, thankful only for the air now rushing into her lungs again and scarcely aware of what he was now doing until his weight descended on her and a new pain tore

361

her apart. He drove himself home, a human hammer pounding a human nail. It went on and on. 'I'll show you,' Harry said through his teeth. *'I'll show you!'*

But something else was happening, taking them both by surprise. What had begun as an assault melted into languor. The ache in Catherine's throat and the fury within Harry were swamped in the current which now swept them together towards some beckoning cataract. Clinging to each other, they crashed together over the falls. They rolled apart. Catherine sat up gasping, eyes wide and bright although one hand rose to caress her neck where the bruised muscles had at once reiterated their presence. Harry, as the ecstasy receded from his body, gazed at his wife appalled. Only a Woodville would loll sensually in the arms of the man who had just tried to strangle her. Only low-bred people had so little shame, so little pride. And he had yielded to her. Dear God, he had let her do that to him! Very well. She was now his wife in good earnest and there was no going back. He would wring from it what advantage he could. 'I meant to kill you for that insult,' he said. 'But you were right in one thing. I need an heir.'

Silently, Catherine stared at him. He rose, his face indifferent, and left the room. She watched him go, her hand still trying to soothe her windpipe. For an amazing, out-of-the-world moment just now, she had thought that perhaps, after all, they had broken through the barrier between them. But if instead he was going to give her only hatred, then so be it; she had her pride, too, although Harry might not know it. She would hate him back. She had better, since the only alternatives now were to live in terror of him or in vain desire for his love.

Matters marital were in the air that year, in one form or another. Anthony Woodville and George of Clarence might be unsuccessful suitors, but the Buckinghams had made their marriage indissoluble at last and weren't at all sure they were pleased about it. And Thomas Stanley (whose Neville wife, her health declining with the fortunes of her brothers, had slipped away through the lung-rot) had married again. In his own opinion he had also gone out of his mind, and he only wished he had realised the danger before the ceremony instead of halfway through the reception. To the day he died, that reception would remain one of his most embarrassing memories.

The Lady Margaret Beaufort had lost her second husband at the same time as Stanley had lost his wife. Both of them were wealthy and well-connected and it was not to be expected that two such valuable properties would long remain on the marriage market.

Margaret, however, had had enough of marriage as marriage. She was barren since she bore Henry Tudor at too young an age, anyway. She wished to be done with all that side of life. On the other hand, she did not actually want to retire to a nunnery. She enjoyed prestige and high society too much. And to retain them, she would need a husband, of sorts.

On his side, Stanley was interested in consolidating his wealth and his position and found Margaret, with her royal blood and her estates, an attractive proposition even if she wasn't prepared to companion him in bed. They had reached an agreement. They would marry, but as a business arrangement only, and not live as man and wife. Stanley had signed a marriage contract which said so.

But the wedding itself was conventional and after the vows were exchanged, the usual feast was held and Margaret consented to follow the pleasant custom of leading the first dance with her groom. So Thomas Stanley led her out into the midst of the hall in his London house, having instructed the musicians to play one of the statelier measures. The dance began. And then his stiff, serious bride, whose gown and headdress, except that they were blue and not black, might well have been a nun's habit, suddenly unhooded brilliant speedwell eyes and looked straight at him and there, enswathed in the touch-me-not robes, was Cleopatra.

Her hand was cool and unconcerned. She did not know at first what had happened to him. She had, quite simply, wished for a close look at the man she had just married on very slight acquaintance. But in so doing she had simultaneously overturned his cosmos and made him a butt for ribaldry. His brand new brown and yellow striped hose for getting married in was skin-tight and his russet velvet doublet was fashionably short. From his two eldest sons, watching the dance from the side of the hall, came a burst of adolescent hilarity.

He had dealt with his impertinent offspring later, privately, fetching the elder boy a clout which sent him sprawling. But he had never been able to deal with Margaret. At the sound of her stepsons' laughter, her face had become the face of a marble image on a tomb. To ensure that they stayed on simple conversational terms at their own wedding feast, he had been obliged to say (a bridegroom, aged no more than thirty-nine, had been obliged to say): 'I apologise.'

Since then, though they had shared a roof, Margaret had enforced the marriage contract rigidly. She dined with Stanley but otherwise kept her own apartments and he visited her by appointment, when she was able to fit him in between the six Masses which she insisted on hearing daily, and the various intellectual pursuits which were the other main interest of his erudite and pious wife. The visits were anguish but he couldn't stop making them. If Margaret entered a room, he knew who it was even if his back were turned. He had secret fantasies of the wildest erotic passages with Margaret Beaufort. If he had any self-respect left at all, it was because some of them included throttling her.

He now sat uncomfortably in her parlour, a visitor on sufferance who had interrupted her while she was busy translating a Latin devotional work into English. She had laid down her pen to talk to him but clearly considered his intrusion to be a nuisance. She was taking a mild revenge by choosing a subject of conversation which she knew wouldn't please him.

'The whole world has marriage on the brain these days,' he

said morosely in reply. 'And they're all impossible marriages.'

'Impossible?' said Margaret. And there, again, were the vivid blue eyes, shining out of the lean and scholarly little face. Margaret's lack of inches seemed actually to enhance her power. Stanley could hardly keep still.

'Naturally you want to further your son's interests,' he said. 'And I don't doubt that your Henry is all a young man should be, but,' said Stanley, some of its normal acidity returning to his tongue, 'he's also a young man with no money, no land and no prospects of either, living as a pensioner in the court of Brittany. If King Edward has been hinting at a marriage between your Henry and his eldest daughter, it's a trap. It means he wants Henry back on English soil. If he came, he'd find himself in the Tower, not in a bridal chamber. He is not a feasible husband for the King's eldest daughter or even for his youngest one.'

'I'm not a fool, Thomas. Certainly Henry must not come within the King's reach. I realise that. But what if there is some truth in these extraordinary rumours that Clarence has set flying?'

'If . . .? Margaret, I wouldn't advise you to suggest that in public.'

'I said, I'm not a fool. But in private, if there is any substance in these stories that the King, or the King's marriage – that's the latest one – are of questionable legitimacy, then one day all the old York versus Lancaster squabbles could break out again. In that case, a match to unite the two houses, in the persons of my Harry and the Princess Elizabeth, would be highly desirable for the peace of the realm. They would legitimise each other, as it were.'

'Margaret, what are you saying?' Stanley actually wiped his forehead. 'My dear woman, those rumours stem from Clarence and in my view, and that of a good many other people, Clarence is demented. It's been quite obvious ever since he started trying to make himself ruler of Burgundy, and when the King wouldn't countenance that, Clarence went clean over the edge. There was a time,' said Stanley grimly, 'when he wouldn't face the King across a battlefield but I fancy he'd do it now, if he could get an army behind him. It will be a good thing when he's dead.'

'Ah, you think that too?' Was her ruthless streak the source of her fascination? 'I mean,' said Margaret, 'do you believe, as I do, that very soon he will be?'

Compared to Margaret Beaufort, his Neville wife, for all her inborn ambition (being married to her had been like having a spurred rider in the saddle), had been as woolly-minded as a sheep. He had never really liked any of their children because they all took after her. If only he and Margaret could have had children! He wondered for the thousandth time what his present wife would look like naked and felt himself flush, growing hot and hard and longing.

'Edward's patience won't last much longer,' said Margaret. She sat there, serene, impregnable, face framed in a pleated gable headdress as though she were looking out of a church door. 'He can't afford it. Clarence has been in gentlemanly confinement for months now, since the Mistress Twynyhoe business, but he's still managed to do a remarkable amount of damage even from behind the Tower walls. I feel that very soon, I shouldn't care to be Clarence. Although,' she added thoughtfully, 'I should very much like to know all that Clarence knows. Wouldn't you? Because, mad or not, I have the feeling that he knows something.'

Astonishing, thought Stanley, that that clear, hard intellect did not extend to greater understanding of herself. She thought herself given to God and learning but he knew that she was only hiding behind these things. Give him a chance, and he would soon open her eyes.

Perhaps that was what she feared. Perhaps she did not want her loyalties divided, did not wish to be distracted from the one earthly being for whom she truly cared, the one whose image, Stanley suspected, even on occasion intruded between Margaret Beaufort and the Communion Host.

That studious, gingery-haired young man now in Brittany: Henry Tudor.

Chapter Twenty-Five

The Plantagenets: Death of a Brother

1478

'We must remember, my lords,' said Dr John Morton to the grim-faced councillors assembled in the Painted Room, 'that the man has been declared guilty of treason before a full sitting of Parliament. We cannot overturn such a verdict, we can only pass sentence. And that, unfortunately, is our duty.'

Bourchier, Hastings, Stanley, Stillington and then (lastly and reluctantly), Alcock, all nodded. But at the head of the table, Edward did not stir. His silence, however, permitted Morton to proceed.

'Three members of Clarence's household,' said Morton steadily, 'have gone to the block for treason.' More nods, from the midst of the furs and velvets which protected the councillors from the raw February cold. 'One charge,' Morton said, 'was that of putting it about that the next king's name would have the initial G. Others concerned the spreading of rumours which I will not here repeat, but we must bear in mind that even from within the Tower, Clarence has continued to slander the King's grace. There can be no doubt that he was and is manoeuvring to seize power and no doubt either that of all men in the world, he is the last who should be allowed to wield any.'

'Because he is afflicted in his mind!' said Gloucester with vigour. He had not nodded any more than the King. 'Illness isn't a crime.'

'He's also the brother of the King. Were he anyone less,' Morton said calmly, 'then mercy on the grounds of diminished mental powers might be possible. But in the circumstances . . .' His Gallic shrug was a mannerism picked up during his years of exile in France. 'It's a moot point anyway whether he is mad in truth or whether this is merely an extreme case of petulance. He isn't barking like a dog or plaiting straws into his hair. Are we, things being as they are, to urge my lord the King to ignore Parliament's recommendations? Rest assured, my lords, the King's grace knows very well what it means for brother to condemn brother. He does not need us to tell him that. What he does need is our help and not our hindrance, in performing a dreadful but a necessary act.'

Of them all, John Alcock thought, Morton was the one with the clearest grasp of the situation. He wished he had been clear-headed enough himself to speak first. He was hating every moment of this meeting, wishing himself with all his heart back again at Ludlow with Prince Edward. But a Council called to decide the fate of a king's brother who was guilty of treason could not be avoided on any excuse, and he, Alcock, should be facing facts. In fact, they were not here to settle Clarence's fate at all but to coerce Edward into signing the death warrant. He wanted them to coerce him. It must be done but he couldn't do it alone.

It *would* be Morton who had been the first to see. He often took the lead at Council meetings now, although he was not well liked by anyone except, apparently, Edward. Two years ago, when the King and Gloucester had led the army to France, it had been Bourchier and Alcock who had been left to run the country. But if the same expedition set out today, Morton might well replace Alcock. Despite his emotional preference for the life of a prince's tutor in Shropshire, Alcock could not help resenting his saturnine rival, while Thomas Stanley, citrus-tongued as ever, had been heard to mutter that Morton seeped everywhere these days, like a leaking oil flask.

But Stanley had given his nod. It was Richard of Gloucester who cleared his throat and said: 'I cannot

370

consent to this. I understand the gravity of the charge against my brother of Clarence but . . .'

Edward was visibly tired. He was only thirty-five but he was known to be spending too much time these days at the banqueting table and in the arms not only of Bess Woodville and Jane Shore but of others too. The marks of dissipation were becoming noticeable. This crisis would only drive him deeper into his excesses, Alcock thought anxiously.

Edward was thinking: for months past I have been stupefying myself night after night with drink and amorousness but before God I have had reason and Richard ought to know it. Does he think I'm enjoying this?

Richard's loyalty was without flaw and so was his competence. In the north country, men with grievances were apt to be told by their friends: 'go to Dick of Gloucester; he'll see you right.' Archers and men-at-arms sought his service in droves, because of the prestige it carried. But it had to be admitted that Richard could be unbelievably irritating.

Edward would never forget the flow of conscious virtue, the wrinkled nose and distastefully pursed mouth with which, two years before, Richard had prepared to sign the treaty which concluded their campaign in France.

The treaty had yielded much of England's hereditary claim to French territory but not for nothing. King Louis had been made to pay for that territory. Seventy five thousand crowns down to Edward and fifty thousand crowns a year thereafter, and an annuity for Dr Morton, which was fair enough, for he had worked himself day and night and lost weight negotiating the deal. But Richard had come near to bursting a blood vessel.

'I brought a thousand archers and a hundred men-at-arms and ten knights fully armed to France with me to fight for what belongs to England, not to . . .'

'I know, Richard, I know. And you poached half of them from Northumberland. He wanted to lodge a formal complaint, let me tell you. I talked him out of it but I warn you,

you're going to have trouble with the Percy family one of these days.'

'We're not discussing the Percys.' Richard was stamping round his brother's tent, trying to relieve his feelings by rapid movement. 'We're discussing this . . . this dishonourable peace!'

'Dishonourable? It's a valuable treaty. We need the money.'

'I know. You're in debt,' said Richard savagely. 'And next time you run into debt, how will you pay that off? Sell the Isle of Wight?'

'Richard –'

'Or Cornwall?'

'Listen –'

'I daresay that man Morton would get you a good price.'

'That's enough.' The King emerged from the brother and Richard recognised the warning. 'You will sign,' said Edward calmly. He did not put into words his power to break his brother but it was there. Richard had signed, but with an expression on his lean face as though he were the only person present who had washed properly that morning.

He had the same expression now. Edward passed a hand over his aching eyes. 'We cannot afford clemency, Richard. It would be gambling with the peace of this realm. Yes, he's my brother. Yes, I do still remember that once, he and you were my engaging little brothers whom I came to see every day when we were all in London, long ago. But you're both grown men now and George is a dangerous one. I dare not overlook what he has done and is still trying to do.'

'Who would draw a sword to put George on the throne?' demanded Richard with scorn.

'Some people would draw a sword to put the devil on it if he offered to pay them enough,' remarked Stanley. Dr Morton said: 'Is it in order to propose a formal vote?'

A few minutes later, in a silence which had a certain quality of support, since it told the King that those around him understood what this meant to him, Edward set his signature to the death warrant which been drawn up in readiness and was now placed before him. As he laid the pen down, his eyes met Richard's. 'Sometimes, Richard, even a king has to sign documents he would prefer to tear up,' he said.

'Can I see him?' Richard asked. 'To say goodbye? I haven't been allowed to see him since his imprisonment. Or must he die thinking that because we once quarrelled over my wife's inheritance, I have forgotten that we were ever brothers?'

Edward continued to gaze steadily at his youngest brother. A silent message, of the kind sometimes possible between close kin, was in them: 'I trust you, but don't fail me.'

'Yes, you can see him,' Edward said. 'If you will undertake it, I should like you to break the news to him. You will do it as kindly as you can. He should have someone of his own to help him at that moment. I cannot do it myself. It was my hand that . . .' He glanced down, at the pen. 'Only . . .'

'Yes?' said Richard impatiently. He had read Edward's wordless message but could not understand why it was there.

'I receive reports of him from his gaolers,' said Edward. 'He has – changed, so they say. Comfort him if you can, Richard, but don't let anything he says to you hurt you. He's liable, I gather, to say anything.'

Once again, the steady hazel eyes declared their trust and appealed for loyalty. Richard left the council chamber puzzled and subdued.

George of Clarence listened in silence to the halting speech which took away his hope. It came out stiffly, as though Richard's tongue hurt when moved. 'When?' asked Clarence.

The winter sun found its way through a narrow window

to gleam on his pale hair. Clarence's prison was well lit, and well furnished too. But it smelt nevertheless of staleness and old sweat, of breath laden with the day before yesterday's wine. The man who dwelt here had filled it with his desperation. He had paced this floor, pummelled that cushion, tossed on the bed, wrenched in fear and frustration at the tapestry, tearing a corner from its moorings.

'Tomorrow,' said Richard. 'By the axe. It will be private. George, you must have expected it, ever since you heard the verdict.'

I can see that you have. He did not know what to do with his pity. He could find no words for it.

Clarence sank into a chair, propped his elbow on a small table which also held a wine-jug and a used goblet, and tried to utter a cynical laugh. 'No doubt you did your best for me, Dickon. This is the way the dice falls, as Anthony Woodville would say. It comes to all of us, in bed or on the block . . .'

His defiance crumbled. He folded his arms on the table and put his head down. Standing like a stupid image, powerless to help, Richard watched and listened while his brother wailed out his terror of eternity. Then George sat up, looking about him in a frenzied way which Richard would have understood by instinct even if he never attended one of Edward's uninhibited banquets or seen his own son ailing. He caught up a washing basin from a shelf and handed it to George, who vomited into it, the remains of a meal in a red wine sludge. 'Have you seen a priest?' Richard asked.

Clarence shook his head. The hysteria had passed. He slumped shivering in the chair and raised wet, heavy eyes. 'I didn't think he'd do it. Not to his own brother. But I know too much. Only that's not my fault, it's Ned's. He shouldn't have done it, should he?'

'Done what?' Richard found an ewer of water and soaked a napkin. 'Here, wipe your face with this.'

'Fallen for that Woodville woman,' said Clarence. 'He

won't pay for what he's done. He expects me to.'

'See here, George, I don't know what you're talking about but though I don't care for Bess Woodville much, I keep my tongue off her. She is Ned's wife and if you speak of her like that how can you expect him to be merciful?'

'But,' said Clarence, passing the napkin across his mouth, 'she isn't his wife. Didn't you know?'

'Oh, for Christ's sake!' Pity became mixed with exasperation. 'How can you go on, even now, with these lies? What use are they to you?'

'It isn't a lie,' said Clarence, and despite the revolt of the stomach which Richard had just witnessed, poured himself a goblet of wine.

'Of course it's a lie!' Richard found himself marvelling at the speed with which pity could yield altogether to anger. 'Just one of many! Like saying that Ned had paid Ankaret Twynyhoe to murder Isabel and the baby.'

'My dear wife and my little baby. Why should they die if someone didn't poison them? And why should Ankaret poison them? She hated me but she wouldn't have gone that far just to spite me. So someone paid her and who would do that but Ned? No one has as much against me as Ned. He's afraid of me, you see,' said Clarence, with a travesty of smugness.

'He has changed,' Edward had said. Meaning this: that although Clarence wasn't plaiting straws in his hair, his mind nevertheless was limping like a horse which had cast a shoe. 'He's liable to say anything.' And to believe anything too, it seemed, to trace connections between things that were insanely far apart.

But Richard was in the habit of using reason and automatically he tried to pierce his brother's clouded mind with common sense. 'Your wife died of the childbed fever and your baby because it was born feeble, as children often are. Ned wished them no harm, and you know it!' Richard could not help himself. It came out as an accusation. 'Just as you know that our mother never played our father false and that Ned is truly his son. I saw that filthy pamphlet you put out! You know as well as I that when Father died, she as good as died too. How long is it since you've seen her? She still wears the habit and keeps the fasts and silences of the Benedictines in his memory. And it's sorrow, not guilt. I know.'

'Do you, little brother?'

'Yes, and so do you. My God, you've put that lying slander about to smear Ned's name and never cared that . . .'

'Going to punch me in the mouth, Dickon? At the very foot of the scaffold? Fie on you. I thought you had come here to comfort me. Who knows what's true and what isn't? I thought it would make a good softening-up tactic. You know, just to prepare people for the notion that all isn't what it ought to be in King Edward's household. Because it isn't. When Ned dies, which from the way he drinks and whores could well be soon, I ought to be the heir. Because Bess Woodville is not Ned's wife. Even if he's lawfully born his children aren't. Dickon, my dear innocent little brother, why do you think Ned kept me so strait while I've been here? Why have I been allowed no visitors of any importance? Because Ned was afraid of what I might say to them, of course. But I managed to slip out a few rumours through my servants. He didn't dare deny me an attendant or two. People might have wondered why. I'm surprised he let you come today.'

'I asked to come, to say goodbye. He knows I won't listen to slander.' He understood now the reason for that silent communication in Edward's eyes.

'It isn't slander. How many more times? I can prove it.' Clarence's expression was sly. He drained the goblet and poured another, imitating bravado now. 'Ask Robert Stillington,' said Clarence.

'Stillington? The Chancellor? The Bishop of Bath and Wells? What on earth has he to do with it?'

'Everything. Stillington,' said Clarence triumphantly,

'was the priest who married Ned to a woman called Eleanor Butler before Bess Woodville ever gladdened our brother's eyes. And Mistress Butler was still alive when Bess was crowned our queen.'

'You're mad,' said Richard. He believed what he said. If Clarence had not been insane already, then the fear of death had turned his brain. The room seemed impregnated with terror and madness, a smelly unkempt lair from which any horror might emerge. 'I've never heard of Eleanor Butler,' said Richard. 'And if Stillington had done such a thing, I can't see him telling you!'

'He didn't, he told God,' said Clarence simply. 'It was years ago. I knew him quite well then. I went to him for advice when I was trying to get the dispensation to marry Isabel. He's easy-going with his servants – they scamp their work and get away with it. The man who should have brought me to him just pointed the way and said: "He's there, through that door, at his prayers. Go in and wait." So I went in and there was Stillington at his prie-dieu with his back to me. He hadn't heard me. He was praying aloud, a most interesting petition. He wanted guidance and forgiveness because of the agonising secret on his conscience. It was quite a long time after the marriage, if you can call it that, of Ned and Bess, so I imagine that Stillington made a habit of that kind of prayer. I wouldn't be surprised if others haven't heard him at it too. I wonder if he still does it or if he's got used to his burden by now. I heard quite a bit of detail before I tiptoed away to come back more noisily. He never knew I'd listened. I made some enquiries about Eleanor Butler later. She's dead now, but she was in a convent then. She took the veil because she'd been disappointed in love, I was told. Disappointed of a crown, more likely. Oh, I had her name right. Stillington put names in his prayer, I assure you. Well, she's not the only one to be entitled to a crown and lose it. I shan't live to claim mine now. Ned's known that I know for a long time. He once threatened to have my head for it. But I never thought he meant it. After all, we're brothers.'

Clarence was growing hoarse, from the tears he had shed and the wine in his throat. Richard found himself withdrawing, a step at a time, repelled by the husky, suggestive whisper. With a great effort he kept the loathing out of his voice as he said: 'You're overwrought. I'll send you a priest. The . . . the execution isn't till midday. The priest will come early. I'll send in a barrel of malmsey wine as well. That's malmsey you're drinking, isn't it? When you've heard Mass, start to drink and drink deep. When the time comes, you won't know what's happening to you.'

He went out quickly, without the parting embrace he had come for, had imagined as he made his unhappy way to the Tower. His knees were trembling. Oh God, poor Clarence. But the filth, the muck, he was spewing in his madness. Ned had trusted him not to listen and he wouldn't. He'd never ask Stillington for the truth. He didn't want to know the truth. Let the beastly whispers cease, let the tale lie in the past where it belonged; let it die with Clarence. As for Stillington, he ought to be arrested for his blabbering tongue.

He had said that to himself before he realised that he was believing in the blabbering tongue. He jerked his mind back to order. His brother was to die tomorrow; this was no time for brooding over scandal.

He was used to the thought of death and he had seen it come for better men than Clarence. Neither gentleness nor piety had saved Henry of Lancaster; integrity had not saved John Neville. Richard had faced the spectre himself. On his forearm was the puckered scar from the wound he had taken at Barnet, and if that blow had landed where it was meant to land, he too would be dead now.

But this was worse. This was death establishing itself in the midst of his family like an evil demon, invoked by one brother to devour another. Well, Ned himself must break it to their mother. This, Richard said to himself, he could not, would not, do on Ned's behalf. Let the King defend his own decision to Cicely Neville. Though Richard could not now say that that decision was wrong.

He stepped out into the open where his escort was waiting and gratefully gulped the clean wind from the river. After all, what else could Ned have done? If Clarence were left alive to spread that story, it could bring down the whole house of York.

The worst of it was that Ned was capable of behaving as Clarence claimed. Perfectly capable. And hadn't Bess Woodville refused, even at dagger-point, to sleep with him outside marriage? Once, Richard would have liked nothing better than to learn that the marriage was false; now, seeing what might happen if it were proved to be false in this fashion, he shuddered at the thought. Had Eleanor Butler, he wondered, held Edward off in the same way, until he produced a priest? Oh Ned, Ned, you and your unruly passions.

His escort fell in behind him in sympathetic silence. He could hear them thinking: poor devil, he's had to break terrible news to a brother and to part from him forever. He wondered what they would say if they knew the rest.

Chapter Twenty-Six

Petronel: The Widening Crack

1477–8

When Isabel had been buried, I parted from Ankaret and went home to Eynesby, where I tried to keep my grief to myself as much as possible, for I noticed that my first outburst of it made Lionel impatient. My reunion with Perky Dick helped me. I found refuge in thinking about him, asking Chrissy to tell me all that he had said and done while I was away, playing with him, teaching him. But the grief was there, just the same. It was another secret to be hidden.

The news of Ankaret's death caught up with me in the spring. It arrived on a sunny morning brought by a courier from Middleham. He had come with letters from Richard of Gloucester to Lionel, giving instructions about the purchase of a new flock to occupy some grazing which Middleham had lately acquired. But there was a letter from Anne, too, addressed to me. It asked me to join her presently for a few weeks and it added: 'Has the news yet reached you concerning Ankaret Twynyhoe? I fear it will shock you.' And then it went on to brief but horrific details.

I had last seen Anne at Isabel's funeral. She and I and Ankaret had all wept together. Her anguish at this new tragedy came to me through the very plainness of her letter. 'She can't have believed what was happening to her,' Anne said. 'She was past the age for such things; her years ought to have been respected.' She could not have put it more simply or more forcibly. Saying that, I thought, she had said it all.

I read the letter standing in the hall. Lionel had already

scanned Gloucester's missive and gone outside; I had waited to see that the courier was being looked after. I went blindly outside. Lionel was standing in the courtyard, watching while Master Hardynge the secretary played with Perky Dick. This was not long before Hardynge died; he remained an enigma to me all the time I knew him but I had discovered one thing about him which was that he liked children. He was too stiff-jointed by this time to crouch or kneel, but he was sitting on a bench and leaning down so that he and Perky Dick could roll little wheeled knight-and-horse toys at each other. The toy knights had lances which could be adjusted a little. It was an instructive game for a child destined for knighthood. Lionel had already decided that by some means or other his son should achieve that position, and said he hoped to live to see it.

But this time I paid no heed to Perky Dick or his amusements. I stopped when I saw that the courtyard was not empty and Lionel, glancing round, saw my face and said: 'What is it, then? Bad news in your letter?'

I pushed it at him automatically and then gave him no chance to read it. Words tumbled out of me instead. I could see Ankaret in my mind as I spoke – elderly, dignified, accustomed to a certain standard of life and treatment. Ankaret, to be hustled from her home by soldiers, bundled roughly on to a horse and made to ride a hundred miles, thrust frightened and exhausted into a cell and – in imagination I experienced it with her – the exhaustion and the fear taking their toll of an ageing body, the trembling indignation of her attempts to defend herself, disbelief struggling with terror as she heard herself condemned. But imagination failed, backed away, from her last moments on earth, the rasp of the rope, the intoning priest and the choking jerk. I hoped that the fragility of age had stood her friend at the last, that death had come quickly. Before I had finished telling Lionel, I was weeping.

And Lionel, of course, was once more impatient. He had little imagination of his own. 'Aye, it's a bad business,' he

382

said. 'It's a shame but there's nowt to be done now.' I saw with anger that he wasn't even trying to imagine it, that his mind was somewhere else entirely. He turned back to the game Master Hardynge was playing with Perky Dick. 'T'lad's lefthanded,' he remarked.

I already knew that. I had noticed it some time before and had wondered how long it would be before Lionel noticed too. I had prepared my defence. With a huge effort I wrenched my thoughts away from Ankaret. I brushed the tears out of my eyes. 'Yes,' I said, 'I believe he is. I hope it won't make life difficult for him later on. Will you train him as a left-handed swordsman, as you did Geoffrey?'

I had thought it would be natural, when Perky Dick's peculiarity attracted comment, to mention Geoffrey as another example. It would be strange if I did not. But it was hard to do. It felt dangerous.

'It's queer,' Lionel was saying. 'There's no left-handedness in my family. Geoffrey gets his from his grandfather, Alison's dad.'

I shrugged. 'It doesn't necessarily run in families, does it? One of Chrissy's girls is left-handed but no one else is who's related to her.'

'Maybe,' said Lionel in a dissatisfied voice.

He now found that he was holding the letter I had given him. He glanced over it. 'Aye,' he said, returning momentarily to the subject of Ankaret. 'What a to-do. I mind on seeing her at Middleham. Poor old body.'

'I'd like to ask Father Chaplain to say a Mass for her.'

Lionel looked at me as though I had said I would like to ask the chaplain to stand on his head. 'He'd have to be paid. Her family will have ordered Masses for her. No need for you take that on too,' he said.

I went away, back to my room. I had never hated him so much – nor had I ever been so much afraid of him as I was now. And I was grieving doubly, for Ankaret as well as Isabel. I tried, after a time, to wash my face and command myself, to go about the house as usual. But by the next morning I had fallen ill with a savage headache and nausea.

I was ill for five days. I don't know what it was, but I think it was the sum total of all those violent, hidden feelings. They found their way out, in the end, through my body instead of through my mind. I was luckier than Sister Agnes, after all. Perhaps poor Ankaret was my saviour. She died at a time when my mind was still stronger than my flesh, and so brought on the crisis.

I recovered at last, perhaps a little more quickly than I admitted. While I was ill, I moved to the little attic room where Perky Dick had been conceived. I was glad to be there and not at all anxious to return to Lionel's chamber. Once I did so, life resumed and appeared to be as usual. Almost a year later, the news came that Clarence had been executed, and I could not pity him. Alive, he was a danger to innocent people.

But there were other dangers abroad as well.

Lionel had appeared to accept my casual comments about Perky Dick's lefthandedness. But that little incident was significant. My marriage had been flawed from the beginning but it was from that spring day in 1477 that I date the start of its actual destruction. I believe that it was on that day that, despite all my efforts, the cracks already there began irrevocably to widen and to run.

We had heavy snow the next winter and Eynesby was cut off for weeks, although we saved most of our sheep. The thaw came in March and the first news to arrive was from Middleham. It told us of Clarence's demise. The next came from Bouldershawe and Thornwood and was more mundane although serious enough. At both places, the snow had caused grave losses to the flocks. Lionel was angry and said there had been unpardonable carelessness. Thornwood, he said to me in a voice full of distaste, was mine and I could please myself, but the Grimsdales at Bouldershawe needn't think he would listen to any excuses about their rent. They must pay in full and bear their loss themselves. As it happened, Thornwood, which was prosperous (King Edward had rewarded me in open-handed fashion), did not ask for a remission. But the Grimsdales did and Lionel's refusal brought Master Grimsdale hurrying to Eynesby to plead. He was in the hall, trying to persuade Lionel to let him defer some of the payment at least until the following year, when hooves came trampling and splashing into our courtyard where the melting snow had left big puddles. A moment later John Steward came and told me that Master Nicholas Hawes was here, asking for my husband.

The name was familiar but I couldn't immediately put a face to it. 'Master Eynesby's busy,' I said. 'Bring the man to me.' When I saw him, I still couldn't recognise him, although I knew I had come across this small, red-faced man somewhere before. He had straight-staring eyes which scanned me from head to foot in a manner somehow disparaging. Whoever he was, he seemed to be someone who didn't like me. Civilly, I said: 'My husband is engaged at the moment but if you'll come to the hearth, you can wait in the warm and I'll send for some refreshments. Did you come alone?'

'Nay.' He had a strong Yorkshire accent. 'I hired two men to ride with me. When were t'roads ever safe for lone travellers? They're in t'kitchen already, takkin' their ease.'

'Then you must take yours,' I said, and led the way to the fire. Across the hall, Lionel glanced in our direction and then said: 'That's my final word, Grimsdale. You can keep back a quarter of t'rent this year but on Lady Day next year you'll pay it back, and a fee on top for the privilege. John Steward'll see you out. John! Master Grimsdale is leaving.'

'He hasn't changed, your husband,' said Hawes, taking a settle and stretching wet-booted feet to the fire. 'Still wants his money's worth, don't he?' Once more he looked me up and down, as though trying to estimate what I might be worth to Lionel and whether I had been good value. I felt uncomfortable. Lionel, coming up, said: 'Nicholas Hawes.

385

And what brings you back here after all these years? I take it you've a good reason or is it sheer impudence?'

'Nay, it isn't impudence,' said Hawes, and suddenly, seeing him side by side with Lionel, I knew him. I had last seen them together at the Smithfield tournament, more than ten years before. And before that, I had seen them here in this very hall when Lionel told Hawes to get out of York. Yes, Hawes disliked me. On both occasions he had thought I despised him. And then I heard what he was now saying.

'. . . I came by way of Silbeck; it was only right I went there first to tell his lady mother the news. It's to do with your nephew, Master Eynesby. I'm sorry I'm the bearer of bad news but someone mun do it. Sir Geoffrey is dead.'

I observed with detached interest that the hall looked exactly as it had looked a moment ago, before those words were uttered. No emotion moved in me. How strange. 'Oh, poor Alison!' I exclaimed, because this seemed to be the right thing to say.

'And how do you,' enquired Lionel acidly of Hawes, 'come to be the messenger? From whom? Where did he die and how?'

'He sent me hisself,' said Nicholas and I thought: he's pleased to be telling us. It's like scratching an itch for him, coming back to Eynesby and in a way that means we must treat him courteously. 'He was coming home,' Hawes said. 'He'd been in some noble household or other in Spain but his mother wrote asking him to come back, so he told me . . .'

'Aye, that's so,' said Lionel. I nodded. Alison's health had begun to fail after we heard that Geoffrey was settling in Spain, and last year she had written asking him to return. We had heard nothing and believed the letter had gone astray, but apparently not.

'I met him on board ship, coming back,' said Hawes. 'I knew him better than you think. I've had dealings of my own with him. I've been making my living, travelling backwards and forwards between London and the Holy Land,

386

guiding pilgrims. I was guide to Sir Geoffrey and the friends he had with him when they went out a few years back. So naturally, when I came across him on the ship last September, we talked. Just before we got into London, as we were coming up the Thames, he fell sick. He said the climate of England was too much of a shock to someone who'd got used to sunshine. It was a chilly September, if you recall. I took him to my lodgings because I couldn't think what else to do with him. He died there. He knew he was going and he charged me to bring the news home.'

'What was the illness?' Lionel asked.

'Lung disease,' said Hawes. 'I looked after him as best I could, which was pretty good, let me tell you. I've had some practice at it. Pilgrims get ill on the journey often enough. I've seen 'em through plague and typhus fever and food poisoning. I almost thought I'd save him too, at one point. I fetched a physician to him and my landlady, she's a decent woman, she sent up mulled wine and a feverfew brew of her own. But in the end . . .' He shrugged. 'He managed to say to me: take the news home, tell my mother, tell them at Eynesby. So here I am.'

'I'm obliged to you,' said Lionel. 'You'll stop overnight, I take it. There'll be a gratuity before you leave. Petronel, see that our guest is comfortable. I'm going to Silbeck. I may bring Alison back with me.'

I gave orders that food should be brought, told John to help Hawes out of his wet boots and went to find him a pair of slippers. When I came back with them, Lionel had already departed. 'I've just heard Master Eynesby ride away,' Hawes said. 'That's all fallen out very happily. I wanted to speak to thee alone but I thought maybe I'd have to fake a cold in t'head or a turned ankle to do it. I've a message from Sir Geoffrey for thy ears alone. And a gift. He sent thee this.'

I took the glove from him before I realised what it was. But as soon as my fingers touched it, I knew. They remembered its texture and the pattern of the beads on the back. It was the glove I had bought from a street trader long ago in London, and given to Geoffrey to carry at Smithfield tournament, as my favour. He had fought in my name and brought me his prize purse and then when he wanted to give it to Hawes, I had hesitated and Hawes had misconstrued. All this hurtled through my mind as I turned the glove over in my hands. I looked up, and into those unfriendly eyes. 'And the message?'

'He said to tell thee he was sorry; that he'd hurt you and that he'd acted unknightly and said what he should not. He said thee'd know what he meant. That's all. He was finding it hard to talk.'

I nodded. Had I not nursed Geoffrey through an attack myself? Hawes, however, had not finished. 'It's a funny thing,' he said. 'When he wanted to talk, he hardly could. But when the fever was up, he chatted away as though it were easy, not knowing he was doing it. Or what he was saying.'

I waited. The hall was empty but for us two, and it was very quiet. The fire settled with a homely rustle and a spatter of sparks as the flames seized on a piece of new wood. A draught stirred the rushes. A dog (there were always dogs about Eynesby) twitched as it dozed by the hearth. Below the domestic surface, danger, like a buried seed, was germinating.

'It wouldna have made much sense to most people,' Hawes said. 'Fever babble doesn't. But put together with that glove and his message . . . You look so prim and lady-like, mistress. Did tha really carry on like that in an ale cellar and a hayloft?'

I felt my face turn fiery. My breathing stopped as though it had been punched out of me. Then the outer door banged open and Perky Dick ran in with Matthew. Matthew had come to us when Geoffrey went away. He would be made a knight next year. For the moment, one of his duties was to instruct Perky Dick in riding. They had been out together that morning. Perky Dick was four years old, well grown and very well able to straddle a small pony. His hair was very fair and his face already had handsome lineaments although they were not markedly those of Geoffrey. In fact, they reminded me more of Geoffrey's august half-brother, the King. Perky Dick was going to have high flat cheekbones and long eyesockets. Although he would never be quite as handsome as the King, for his features were less symmetrical. Already one could see that the left eye was fractionally smaller than the right. Thank heaven, I sometimes thought, that he didn't inherit *that* from Geoffrey; it would have been far more telling evidence than left-handedness.

The two of them were laughing as they ran in, and they did not notice us standing by the fire. Matthew was chasing Dick in play and the little boy ran across the hall and up the stairs, presenting a small, strong back to us as he went. Both of them disappeared into the upper regions of the house.

'Back views are odd things, wouldn't you say, mistress?' said Hawes. 'They'll tell thee more at times than a face. That's thy son, I take it? I saw him in the paddock with his pony as I rode in. That's the son of t'house, I thought to mysen, from his looks and the pony's fine tackle. Seen from the back, he's uncommonly like his dad, it strikes me.'

Perky Dick might not have Geoffrey's features. But from behind, every line of his body was Geoffrey in miniature. I was sensitive to these things. I had watched for the tell-tale resemblances to appear. I had hoped that to others they were less evident. Hoped in vain, it seemed.

But at the sight of Perky Dick, as always, a jolt of sheer love had gone through me and it had aroused me. Dick was innocent. Whatever happened I must protect him, and therefore I must no longer stand dumb and stricken, but find a way to deal with this nasty little man.

Already, the heat had cooled from my face. I gazed at Nicholas Hawes with a calm which amazed me. 'Like his father? I wouldn't have said so,' I said offhandedly. 'Of course, they change as they grow up. But I fancy he will be a stockier man than Master Eynesby. In that respect I think he'll take after my side.'

I was gratified to observe what could have been a flash of appreciation in my enemy's eyes. They were gooseberry coloured, an unpleasing shade. 'I'm afraid I don't understand Sir Geoffrey's message,' I said. 'He never behaved in any unknightly fashion that I know of, and certainly owes me no apology for anything. If he was so very ill, he may have been confused.' Inspiration came to me and I seized upon it. 'The message was probably for his mother. She was much against his going abroad. Yes, of course. That must be it. I'll tell her.'

'He wasna delirious when he gave me the words for you,' said Hawes. 'I wonder if Master Eynesby's noticed owt about his son? He's a particular man, is Master Eynesby. And not an easy man when he's crossed. Might be best if he didn't hear about Sir Geoffrey's message to thee. Or about that glove. I've been mighty discreet over it all, don't tha think? Don't I merit a reward? Now what if I'd handed that glove straight to him?'

I raised my brows, wrinkling my forehead haughtily. 'What is all this about, Master Hawes? Is this glove supposed to be some evidence of impropriety? Your extraordinary remarks about my child seem to imply that . . . but really! The glove is nothing but a favour I once allowed Sir Geoffrey to carry for me at a tournament, with my husband's consent. I am of course grateful to you for bringing me the message which you supposed was for me, although I am quite sure it's for Mistress Silbeck. But my husband controls all our expenditure and I have no money. However, I'm sure he'll see that you receive adequate recognition of your trouble in riding so far to see us.'

'Adequate recognition,' said Hawes, smiling. 'Big words, mistress. Pity thee couldn't be a knight thysen – thee'd take a deal of unhorsing. But I think thee'd best think over all I've said, before Master Eynesby comes back. My, my! Who'd have thought it of thee! In an ale cellar!'

Behind my facade of calm and hauteur, exhaustion was setting in. My knees were trembling and there was an ache in my mind like the throb of a badly wrenched muscle. 'Really, Master Hawes. I've no doubt that Sir Geoffrey had his . . . his own private life. But it had nothing to do with me, I assure you. I find your insinuations both silly and offensive. I trust these slippers will fit. Ah, here comes Chrissy with your tray.'

Lionel returned in the afternoon, bringing a tear-stained Alison. I met them in the hall and saw to it that Nicholas Hawes was there.

'Alison!' I said, and took her red, bony hands in mine. 'This is such sad news. I'm so glad you've come to us. Though God knows, there's little comfort any of us can offer you. Poor Geoffrey . . .'

'He should have stayed in the sun, stopped where the climate was fit for him. It's all my fault!' Alison let me take her in my arms but her body was rigid. 'I shouldna have written begging him to come back. I only wanted to see him again, that's all it was. I only wanted to see him again!'

I guided her to a settle. 'Chrissy, mulled wine for Mistress Silbeck and quickly. Lionel, Alison, Master Hawes here has told me such an astonishing thing. Do you remember this?' I held out the glove towards Lionel. I had kept it in my girdle, waiting for this moment. 'It's the very one you let me give Geoffrey to carry for me at Smithfield. He still had it and at the end he asked Master Hawes to return it. Wasn't that a sweet, touching thing to do?'

'Oh yes, I recall.' Lionel took the glove. 'Kept it, did he? Well, well.'

Close by, I was aware of Nicholas Hawes holding his breath to see if my verbal dice-throwing would win or lose. But he did not speak. Alison, however, cried out: 'He remembered thee and not me at the end! Oh, Geoffrey, Geoffrey!'

'But he did remember you!' I said. I sat down beside her and once more took her cold hands in mine. 'He was on his

391

way home when he died. He was coming back because you wrote to him, because you wanted him. I think . . .' Warily, I skirted the matter of Geoffrey's message '. . . that he felt he'd displeased you by going to the Holy Land against your wishes. He wanted to make amends. Master Hawes thinks he felt that, from something he said in his fever. Carrying a favour,' I said, 'that's just a pretty compliment, a pretend game. But you're his mother. What he wanted to say to you couldn't be said with a trumpery glove. He was bringing you himself.'

The strange thing was, that my calculated words were worth their face value. Alison smiled weakly and said: 'Tha's kind. That's comforting me a little, Petra hinny.'

Lionel also smiled. Nicholas Hawes glowered.

I only caught a glimpse of the two men he had hired as escort but it did strike me that they were a villainous-looking pair. So it was no surprise to hear, through gossip that John Steward later brought back from York, that Hawes had been found murdered just outside the city, on the London road. We all agreed that his escort had done it, probably for the sake of the gratuity Lionel had given him, which had been quite generous.

The killers were not caught and I was glad. Hawes had been a danger not only to me but to Perky Dick. I felt that he, like the Duke of Clarence, was expendable.

PART FOUR
PLANTAGENET VERSUS WOODVILLE
1483

Chapter Twenty-Seven

The Plantagenets: Edward Quintus

April 1483

'Since you are not entering the church,' said Alcock to Prince Edward, 'you have no need to understand heresy in detail. You are to be a sovereign, not a prelate. King Henry the Sixth made the error of letting religion seduce him from kingship. As a king, your duty will be to set an example in observances, and to defend the faith. You may leave it to your servants in the church to tell you when it is threatened. However, since you've raised the matter, we'll discuss it. The heresy that God and the devil are powers of opposite but equal status is easily refuted. The devil is Lucifer and Lucifer is a fallen angel. Angels are beings created by God. Therefore Lucifer was created by God and cannot, accordingly, have equal status or power. What put this idea into your head, may I ask?'

'You've been telling me of my own family history, and the atrocities committed by my ancestor William the Conqueror when he put down the rebellion in the north.' The young prince's face was clear-skinned but a little too pale, Alcock thought. The boy was not as robust as one would like him to be. He caught cold too easily and had trouble with his teeth. But it had been a long winter; the summer sun might set him right.

'The victims,' said Edward earnestly, leaning his elbows on the table between them, resting his chin on his linked hands and regarding Alcock gravely, 'lost their homes and crops and stock. The men were slaughtered and the women left to starve with their children. They must have cried to

God for help. None was forthcoming. Evil prevailed.'

Alcock looked into the boy's hazel eyes, noted the unusual maturity of their expression, and discovered that he not only loved his charge but that he felt sorry for him.

It could not, he thought, be easy to be a boy born to be a king. The conditions of Edward's childhood were far different from those of his own. Alcock sometimes thought that the solidity of his burgher family in Hull must have been remarkable. Even though he was only five when his father died, his parents' united affection was impressed on his memory as was the way his mother and his uncles had closed ranks at once to protect the home and the business. But such things were not uncommon in that society. The people who comprised it all belonged to the same world, of trade, finance and shipping. They knew one another, had interests in common and therefore reason on the whole to trust one another. There were rivalries and feuds to some extent, yes, but for the most part the bonds – of business and marriage – were stronger than the divisions. Compared to the terrifying world of power and politics which Edward must inherit, and the quarrelling interests which it would be his task to reconcile, of great lords in competition over hereditary rights, of landowner versus yeoman, France versus Burgundy, opportunities of trade to be balanced against the risk of war, Alcock's home background was as cosy as a dovecot.

That couldn't be quite true, he told himself. There must have been difficult business decisions to take and far-reaching consequences to consider. But if so he had been too young to realise it and he had left home before he had time to find out more. To Alcock, the burgher society of Hull symbolised safety. He hoped that one day, Ludlow Castle, and the memory of such people as himself and Anthony Woodville, would be a similar haven in the mind for his pupil Edward. But it seemed that already, at the age of eleven, Edward was grappling with the solemn conflicts which would one day dominate his life.

And was clearly in some confusion about how to view them. 'Many men have asked the kind of question you have just asked, Edward,' he said. 'The only answer we can find is that God always triumphs in the end but it may take time. Human beings have free will. God Himself granted it to them. They therefore have power to pervert His plans – for a time. We have to believe that it can only be for a time. Edward, when I told you about the scouring of the north, this was not the aspect I wished you to address. I wish you to consider, and to discuss with me, the dilemma King William had to face. Whether, to ensure the peace and safety of an entire realm, he did right to sacrifice one group of people, many of whom were innocent. Now, I want you to think about this . . .'

The boy frowned, doing as he was bid, thinking. Kings had to be able to think. And in the world in which this particular prospective monarch was growing up, there was much to exercise the intellect. Ever since the Turks had seized Constantinople in 1453, manuscripts had been finding their way out into the world from its libraries, carrying with them ideas hitherto unknown to Europe on a vast selection of topics. Astronomy, medicine, mathematics, philosophy: all were being shaken up by new concepts. The new art of printing was making it easy for the knowledge to spread, too. A king must know how to judge wisely between one idea and another, must be able to comprehend new sciences.

In this task, Alcock thought, the boy's cultured uncle Anthony was an incomparable aide. His scientific learning far outstripped Alcock's. Alcock had been educated with a heavy bias towards Latin grammar. Other subjects had been covered, certainly, and he was interested in them, but he had never had time to pursue them as thoroughly as Anthony had done. He and Anthony, as mentors for Edward, made an ideal partnership, he thought, complementing each other without clashing.

'We could ask your uncle's opinion,' he said. 'Perhaps

we could have a little debate. I can hear his voice now. In fact, I think he's coming here.'

There had been, for some time past, a murmur of voices down in the adjacent hall. A visitor had come, or a messenger ridden in, Alcock thought. He did not encourage interruptions to his pupil's lessons, however, and had chosen a room which faced away from the courtyard for the boy's studies on purpose. He had taken no notice of the minor disturbance next door. But Anthony, apparently in talk with someone else, was indeed coming up the stairs. He came in. With him were the prince's elderly chamberlain Thomas Vaughan and a stranger, who wore the livery of a Tower of London courier. And at the sight of their faces, both Alcock and Edward stood up, the lesson instantly forgotten.

Oh no. No, no, no! said Alcock's heart, passionately and despairingly as first Anthony and then the others swept their caps from their heads. No, it's too soon, he's too young, he's not strong enough, not now, not yet, oh please God, please!

But the three men were kneeling, each on one knee, before Edward, who stood stiffly, a hand still on the back of his chair as he stared at them. There would be no time now to finish arming him for his life of struggle and responsibility. It had already begun.

'My lord,' said Anthony Woodville, looking up into his nephew's face, 'it is my duty and my sorrow to tell you that your august father, King Edward the Fourth, is dead. And to say to you, long live Edward Quintus, Edward the Fifth, King of England.'

'What?' they said disbelievingly, the housewives in the market, listening basket on arm to the proclamations; the landowners whose conferences with bailiff or tenant were interrupted by breathless messengers; the labourers who paused from digging ditches to hear the news from the parish priest on his way to his church to hold a requiem

Mass. 'King Edward, dead? From a chill caught fishing in damp weather? Too much high living, more likely,' some of them added. 'That Lord Hastings . . . but King Edward, dead? God preserve us all! Another minority king!'

The latter was a frequent comment. From end to end of the kingdom, mayors called their town councils to extraordinary meetings and nervously opened the proceedings with such remarks as 'Now, gentlemen, we are all agreed that we should take an oath of loyalty to the young King Edward the Fifth . . . er . . . we are all agreed, I take it?'

In London, Dr John Morton in mitred panoply (for he owed to King Edward an appointment to the bishopric of Ely, plus a bishop's London residence with which went the finest fruit and salad garden in the town), took his place in a hastily convened Council and thought he had never before seen a roomful of grown men behaving quite so much like ducks when a fox was on the prowl.

'We had no idea,' said Thomas Grey, the Queen's eldest son, his face quite blank with shock, 'that King Edward had made such provisions in his will. We always understood that should the King die before Prince Edward was of age, Sir Anthony Woodville would remain his guardian and that the Council would rule in the young King's name. But he has made Richard of Gloucester the boy's guardian! And made him Protector of the Realm, a proxy king. We've seen very little of Gloucester in the last few years,' said Thomas Grey querulously. 'He prefers to stay in the north. But . . .'

King Edward had been good to his stepsons. He had made Thomas Grey Marquess of Dorset. At the moment, however, Thomas did not sound in the least like a marquess. He was flustered and 'quacking,' Morton said to himself with disapproval.

But he knew why. The reason had hung unspoken in the air since that last horrified 'but'.

Gloucester did not like the Woodvilles. With the King's passing and Gloucester's assumption of power, they might reasonably assume that their day was done. By some means or other, he would surely move against them.

And in all probability, against Morton. He had never forgotten that French treaty. The trouble with Richard of Gloucester, Morton thought, was that he lacked a statesman's subtlety. John Doe could afford to see the world in black and white but princes couldn't. No one, though, had ever accused Morton of lacking subtlety. He sat quietly, taking the Council's temperature before venturing to commit himself to an opinion.

The Council, in distracted and unhappy fashion, had moved on to the question of the coronation date and the nature of the escort which should bring young Edward from Ludlow to be crowned.

'We mustn't overdo it. Too large or too well-armed an escort would look as though we were trying to snatch Gloucester's rights. He's not a man to trifle with.' That was Richard Grey. He normally lived in Ludlow and it was sheer chance that he was in London now. The irritated Thomas Grey of Dorset clearly considered it to be not so much a chance as a mischance.

'If we move fast enough,' he snapped, 'it won't matter what it looks like. It's vital to get the crown officially onto the boy's head while he's still in our care. What if Gloucester were to be tempted to seize power himself? It is our duty to the boy to see that he is crowned and anointed as soon as possible. Of course we don't want to usurp Gloucester's rights, but we must make sure that he doesn't exceed them. And what if he were to make the lad sign some edict to our hurt, as the price of being peacefully crowned?' What had at first been left unspoken was now forcing its way into words. 'Allowing for the journey and other preparations,' said Thomas, 'I estimate that the fourth of May is the earliest feasible date for the coronation . . .'

'The King only died on the ninth of April!' William Hastings was scandalised.

Thomas ignored him. '. . . and in my view, the journey to London ought to be well protected. Not less than five thousand men. Never mind about provoking Gloucester; we've already voted ourselves into control of the fleet and one can guess what he'll think of that.'

'This is intolerable!' said Hastings, heaving himself to his feet.

He had put on weight lately and loomed over the table like a well-dressed, angry bear. 'These proceedings are completely out of order! It is improper to set any date for the coronation before Gloucester arrives, and as for the escort, if it exceeds two thousand men, I shall walk out of this Council. Are we to behave as though the prince's legally appointed guardian intended to kidnap him?'

His fulminating gaze swept round the table and came to rest on Thomas Rotherham, who was currently the Chancellor and the Archbishop of York. He had held these posts for five years. He was conscientious and scholarly but some of the Council had doubts about him. In times of crisis he dithered, and he was too apt to look to Bourchier, the Archbishop of Canterbury, for a lead. At the moment, Bourchier had not yet arrived. He was still on his way from Canterbury. And Rotherham, who ought both as Chancellor and Archbishop to be speaking up for the King's will, seemed to be doing nothing but swallowing hard. As Hastings' eye transfixed him, he did it again.

'This is absurd!' shouted Thomas Grey. 'We are a properly constituted Council and we have standing enough to set a coronation date or choose a commander for the fleet or do anything else that is necessary!'

'My lord Archbishop!' said Hastings furiously to Rotherham.

Forced into speech, Rotherham did his best. 'I think that too big an escort would insult the Lord Protector, but an early coronation date might be advisable. I don't refer to danger from my lord of Gloucester, of course but . . . er . . . public uncertainty can breed unrest. A coronation would end uncertainty.' He managed to finish on a note of firmness.

'I propose a show of hands,' said Thomas Grey.

'Seconded.' Thomas Stanley spoke for the first time.

Morton, warily, voted with the majority on both counts and found himself therefore in favour of an early coronation date but also in favour of an escort from Ludlow of no more than two thousand. In public, he thought, it would be prudent to go with the crowd and avoid notice.

But in private, one might be more . . . candid. Across the room, he caught Thomas Grey's eye. Morton made a slight movement of his head. It meant: we'll talk later, together, alone.

'I want to send two confidential letters,' said Hastings to his secretary. 'One is a further letter to Richard of Gloucester at Middleham and the other is to Harry Buckingham. I shall need messengers immediately.'

The hawk-faced young knight lawyer, who had once been a page dressed in red and green but who looked much more at home in his dark lawyer's garb, said: 'I can arrange that, sir. Middleham and – did you say Buckingham? Would that be Brecknock?'

'It would. I don't greatly care for Buckingham,' said Hastings, correctly interpreting his secretary's tone of voice and the faint upward movement of his eyebrows. 'But I fancy that when he hears what's afoot, he'll support the right side.'

'It seems a pity that Gloucester hasn't arrived here yet.'

'It could be a great deal more than a pity! If he'd come south at once instead of tarrying to organise remembrance services, the infernal Woodvilles would have had no chance to move into the power gap after the King's death. And they are moving into it, Catesby. They have control of the fleet, and on the way here from the Council I passed Thomas Grey of Dorset in conversation with Dr Morton of Ely and I caught the word 'treasury'. Coming from those two, it sounded ominous. Now, these letters . . .'

'For the love of God,' said Hastings later, to his empty

room, after the letters had been written and Catesby gone to see to their despatch, 'stop doing everything so bloody correctly, Richard, and get here, can't you?'

Buckingham rarely entered his wife's solar and when he did he knew he wasn't welcome. They considered him an intruder, did Catherine and her ladies. They enjoyed sitting there in their cosy feminine semicircle, stitching away at the gleaming fabrics which would one day be splendid dresses and tunics and altar cloths, and gossiping. Very probably, they were gossiping about him. As far as possible he kept away. When obliged, as now, to invade their conclave, he did so with a noisy slamming back of the door and took pleasure in dismissing all except Catherine with a peremptory jerk of his head.

'And to what,' said Catherine, when they had all gone, 'do I owe the honour of this visit?'

'I have just learned, madam, that your angelic kindred are conspiring to overset King Edward's will and seize the person of the young prince. They want to take control of him and the power that goes with his signature. I intend to set out at once with three hundred men to give the lawful Protector Duke Richard all the help I can in outwitting this plot. What have you to say?'

Catherine gazed at him and thought how ironic it was that in a deadly conflict between her blood relations and her husband, her chief feeling should be relief because the quarrel would remove Buckingham from her side for an unspecified length of time.

The establishment of a physical link between them had produced children. It had also, despite its origins in near-murderous fury, given them both a considerable degree of bodily satisfaction. But Harry resented that satisfaction. He was like an addict unable to break a habit he despised. Once, they had lived together – and slept apart –on terms of chilly indifference. Now he came to her often but balanced it by continually gibing at her and at her family.

She retaliated as best she could, though she sometimes grew weary and when this happened, would catch herself trying to placate him. This time she made a muddled attempt to combine the two.

'I know nothing about any plots! I must say I'm surprised you want to become Gloucester's lackey, though. After all, you're a descendant of Edward the Third just as much as he is. You could even say you had a claim to the crown yourself. At least you'd be as fit a Protector of the Realm as Gloucester is.'

'Humph!' said Buckingham, for once not displeased by his wife's remarks, although he wouldn't give her the satisfaction of knowing it.

Edward Quintus opened his eyes and did not know where he was.

Memory came back slowly. He had left Ludlow, of course. He was riding to London and he was in a hostelry at a place called Stony Stratford, somewhere in Northamptonshire. He also remembered that he was unhappy because his father was dead.

And he, at twelve years old, was King of England.

Edward had not known his father well. His uncle Anthony, his brother Richard Grey, his dear tutor Dr Alcock and his elderly chamberlain Thomas Vaughan, had been his near companions. But King Edward had been there in spirit. 'Your father the King is pleased to hear of your progress in Latin.' 'Your royal father is concerned that you should improve your archery.' Or is sorry to hear of your illness, or was happy to have your letter. Your father this, the King that.

Now, the sense of that unseen yet powerful presence was withdrawn and he knew too that he was not the only one to feel bereft. The faces of the adults about him were anxious and he was aware that there was some sort of panic about getting him to London quickly.

True, they had not set out from Ludlow in any unseemly

haste. They had waited to hold the St George's Day celebrations on the twenty-third of April. But throughout all the rituals, the feast and the service in the Norman chapel on the eve of the twenty-third, and the ceremonial procession round the hall on the day itself, there had been an undercurrent of unease and impatience. The escort which had come to fetch him looked to him like an army, and his uncle Anthony had said that a larger escort still had been proposed at first. Furthermore, his dear tutor Dr Alcock, most uncharacteristically, had quarrelled with Uncle Anthony and with the chamberlain Vaughan. Sitting in his favourite window seat in his private chamber, he had heard their raised voices in the hall adjacent.

He didn't understand what was wrong and no one had offered to explain. Sooner or later, he must bring himself to ask. He would ask Uncle Anthony as soon as he came back. That had been the latest disquieting thing in this uncomfortable succession of them. Uncle Anthony had ridden off yesterday, just after they had reached this hostelry. It was something to do with his brother Richard Grey, who had gone with him. Richard had met them on the road and said he had come to greet them but his horse was exhausted and desperate tidings were what sprang to mind at the sight of him, not courtesy calls. And he had taken a fresh mount and been gone, with Uncle Anthony, in half an hour, to an unknown destination.

The curtains round his bed were swept back with a rattle of wooden rings and there were Dr Alcock and Thomas Vaughan, both fully dressed.

'Good, you're awake,' said Vaughan. 'It's time to move. We should get on our way to London.'

Edward could not remember Vaughan being anything but elderly but in the last few days his hair seemed to have grown visibly scantier and his mouth more sunken. His voice had a tremor as though he were afraid of something. Beside him, Alcock's large form and round face looked the same as usual, and yet gave off a different aura. Normally

Alcock seemed to combine boyishness with authority. Now the boyishness was gone and the authority was mingled instead with an unspoken anger. Edward did not think his tutor was angry with him, but he found the change alarming nonetheless.

'Should we not wait for my uncle?' he said nervously. 'Where has he gone?'

'Back to Northampton. He'll catch us up. Up you get, now. Let's have you into your clothes. Hot water and food are being brought.'

'But why did he go back to Northampton? We'd only just left it!'

'It's time he was told,' said Alcock, looking at Edward, but speaking to Vaughan. 'No, Vaughan! He is entitled to know what is being done in his name. Anthony warned me once not to over-protect him, and he was right. It would be no kindness. Edward, your uncle and your other relatives – and Thomas Vaughan here is in agreement with them – want to get you to London and crowned as soon as they can because you are very young to be a king. They reason that your youth makes you vulnerable to challenge from a rival claimant. The formality of crowning would confirm you in your position. I repeat, I do not accept that there is any other claimant and I have taken issue with your uncle and Vaughan over this . . .'

'I know. I heard you. It was in the hall at Ludlow. But I don't understand what you mean by another claimant. And why has Uncle Anthony gone back to Northampton?'

'To hold the other claimant off,' said Vaughan. 'If he is one, that is. Dr Alcock may well be right, but we must take no chances. Your Uncle Gloucester is said to be a formidable man.'

'Uncle Gloucester?'

'Get dressed!' said Thomas Vaughan, unusually emphatic. Edward, hearing the urgency in his voice, obeyed.

He was in the courtyard, mounting his pony, when the

mystery was dissipated at last. A squadron of black-clad horsemen swept through the gate and halted in the yard in a flurry of skidding hindquarters and tossing manes. Two men dismounted. One he knew for Harry Buckingham, who had visited him at Ludlow once. The other . . .

The other was a wiry man with dark brown hair swinging on either side of a thin face, and black velvet cap to top it. Both men came at once to where Edward sat on his pony. They knelt, baring their heads. The full blue eyes of Buckingham, the narrow hazel eyes of the stranger, looked up at him. It was the stranger who spoke.

'You have not seen me since you were a tiny child, but I am Richard Duke of Gloucester, your paternal uncle and by the terms of your father's Will, Protector and Defender of the Realm of England and of your royal person. Will you dismount and return with us to your lodgings? There are things, my lord, that you should know.'

'But it isn't true, it can't be! My uncle, my brother, would never . . .' Edward knew that his voice had a maddeningly un-adult treble and worse, a tremor. 'Why have you arrested them? You've even arrested Vaughan! What has my poor chamberlain done?' Alcock, who mercifully had not been arrested, placed a hand on his shoulder. The pressure of the hand said 'hush' but Edward could not hush. 'They haven't been plotting against you! They only wanted to protect me, to see that I was crowned. They felt responsible for me; I was in their care. If my father did indeed make you my guardian, sir, then I am sure they . . .'

'In London, you shall see the will for yourself.' Richard of Gloucester was clearly ill at ease in the presence of his distraught nephew. 'As for the rest – it's all true. I'm sorry. Your escort did indeed intend to get you crowned quickly. They wanted to establish themselves as regents and rule till you were of age. Their intention was to cut me, the lawful Protector of the Realm, out. They've already appropriated both fleet and treasury. The next step might well have been my removal. That is the usual pattern in these things. They have used their fear of me, the fact that you are young and that I am the King's only surviving brother and therefore a possible rival to you, as an excuse to sway the Council into consenting to their behaviour. I was not prepared to sit still and let myself be shuffled out of my proper responsibilities and possibly out of the world as well. Would you expect me to?'

'My lord, I know it isn't true! I'm sure they tried to behave wisely and honourably! I have every confidence in the men my father placed about me. And I love my Uncle Anthony, and my chamberlain is old . . .' He was losing the thread. 'My father would have wished those men and the Queen my mother, to rule on my behalf until . . .'

'Government is men's business,' said Buckingham roughly. To him, clearly, Edward was neither King nor nephew but a child who should do as other children did, which meant do as he was told.

'I want to see my Uncle Anthony,' said Edward mutinously. He shook off Alcock's hand. 'And my brother Richard Grey. If I'm King, I can insist. Where are they?'

'At Northampton, under strong guard,' said Gloucester gravely. 'They came there to meet and delay me if they could. Your brother Richard Grey had brought word from London that someone had been in touch with me and alerted me to the danger. Perhaps your relatives really did think they were acting for the best, Edward. Perhaps their distrust of me clouded their judgement. But I am concerned with what they did rather than with what they thought. I regret that your reign must begin with an order that cannot be obeyed, but one of a king's first duties is to recognise his enemies, even when he finds among them those who call themselves or believe themselves to be his friends, even if some of them are his kin.'

'Oh, I understand that,' said Edward Quintus grimly, with meaning, to his friend and kinsman, Uncle Richard of Gloucester.

'It was madness from the beginning. I said it was,' said Richard Grey to his uncle Anthony Woodville. He spoke low but no one could hear them anyway. They were shut in a room in a Northampton inn and the guards were all outside, though obtrusive enough, pacing the courtyard below with heavy feet. 'I was out-voted. I've been afraid of Gloucester from the first. He's never liked the Woodvilles but at least if we'd kept from moving openly against him, he'd have had no excuse to arrest us! My brother Dorset thinks that because we're the Queen's sons, nothing can happen to us, but I'm not so sure. Oh, why don't you say something?' Richard attempted unsuccessfully to laugh. 'What – not even a philosophical maxim about life being a game of chance, and the turns of Fortune's Wheel?'

He turned questioning eyes on Anthony Woodville and then saw to his horror that in his uncle's face was the same fear that he knew was in his own.

Anthony Woodville was thinking that Richard Grey looked very young for twenty-three. Very young and somehow, enduringly so. As though that frightened schoolboy's face would never grow any older.

Afterwards, though Dr Alcock tried hard to compensate for the absence of all the others, the loss of his half-brother and his chamberlain and his beloved Uncle Anthony was too overwhelming. Others attended him, respectfully enough, but they were strangers. Despising himself for it but unable to hide his grief, Edward broke down into tears at last, a child again.

'He'll get over it,' said Buckingham brusquely.

'He can't be allowed to arrive in London for his crowning like this,' said Gloucester rebukingly. 'We have to make friends with him. He is my nephew, after all, my brother's son. Our common blood and our common loss should make a bond between us. He needs to be *helped* to get over it. There's a wall of grief and hostility in him and it's absurd to dismiss it in that tone of voice.'

Buckingham stiffened. After all, that stupid woman to whom he had been forcibly married was right about one thing. He as much as Gloucester was descended from kings. He was entitled to be addressed with more respect than this.

But in the evening, he joined with Gloucester in suggesting to Edward that he might like to practise the signature with which he would in due course ratify his royal commands. The tutor, Dr Alcock of Worcester, helped them. 'Yes, let us see how *Edward Quintus* looks in your handwriting.'

So Edward sat at a table, dutifully tracing out his new signature. Gloucester and Buckingham wrote their own names under his, with their mottoes. *Think of me often*, wrote Buckingham, smiling at the boy and thinking that if this sulky, supercilious brat were his own son, he'd box his ears.

Loyalty binds me, wrote Gloucester, also smiling and wishing that Edward Quintus, just for once, would smile back. He wished Anne were here. She might know how to talk to this withdrawn and bitter child. 'I mean it,' he said, pointing to the motto.

But Edward Quintus, fretting for his companions and above all for his Uncle Anthony, did not hear the earnestness in Gloucester's voice. He did not respond.

Chapter Twenty-Eight

The Plantagenets: The Dice are Cast

1483

Reason had abandoned Bess Woodville.

She knew this but had no strength left for dragging common-sense home by the tail.

At one moment she had been a queen, loved and protected, mother of children and capable of bearing more. If her husband was not always faithful, at least while he lived her position was secure.

The next moment he was gone and she was alone with the foes she had always known were waiting for their chance to strike, and even the friendly female rhythms of her body had ceased. The only power she had ever had in her own right had been based on her femaleness. Without it, she was a soldier without weapons. She was terrified, and angry.

Most of the anger was for her son Thomas Grey and for William Hastings. Thomas had brought them all to this by bidding against Gloucester for the young King's person. 'Better powerless than headless. Why couldn't he see that?' she had wailed when the news came that Gloucester had intercepted the royal party and that her brother Anthony and Richard her younger son were under arrest.

As for Hastings and his busybody letters to Brecknock and Middleham, Hastings and his hedonistic passion for the best wine and the prettiest girls, and his notions of friendship, which had involved sharing these pleasures with the King to the ruin of her husband's constitution; she heartily wished William Hastings dead.

But what she felt for Richard of Gloucester was not

anger. Richard of Gloucester was the cause of the terror. She had feared him since she first met him, when he was no more than a boy, but a boy whose coolly appraising hazel eyes had told her that he despised her.

Now he was full grown and held her loved ones in his power and whenever she thought of him, what she saw in her mind was an ogre.

Tired out, grieving, torn between rage and dread, she sat on the floor of the Abbot of Westminster's house (hallowed ground and therefore qualified to be a sanctuary) and sobbed. Her mourning skirts were getting dirty on the rushes. Her children huddled close. Elizabeth, the eldest, sat nursing the sleepy, querulous youngest child, three-year-old Bridget. Small Richard dozed, leaning against them. The rush to sanctuary had been late at night and the children had been fetched from their beds. It was still the same night and the sun was still below the horizon.

On either side of Bess, exhorting her to take courage, were her host the Abbot of Westminster and Archbishop Rotherham, the Chancellor.

'Madam, the Duke of Gloucester has always been a loving brother to your royal husband. He won't harm you.' The Abbot's words were dignified although the circumstances in which he was uttering them were somewhat less so. Twice while he was speaking, the Abbot had to step quickly aside to avoid Bess Woodville's servants, bringing in her belongings. Bent double under a bulging sack or walking backwards with one end of a huge oak settle, a man was apt to expect right of way.

Some of the valuables being brought in weren't strictly Bess's to appropriate, either. Abbot and Chancellor watched, with some horror, the progress of a chest with an inlaid silver pattern on it, recognising it as part of the Tower treasury and therefore state property. Bess saw their faces and wondered why these stupid men did not know that threatened people needed insurance. At least Thomas had understood that much. He had had the chest brought to her.

Rotherham was saying patiently: 'We have had assurances direct from my lord of Gloucester that every courtesy will be shown to you.'

'I don't believe him! He'll try to take my baby's crown! Thomas said so. What will become of us all then? What will become of my little Edward? If he didn't mean us any harm to begin with, he'll surely mean it now he's been challenged. He only needed the excuse. He hates me and all my family!'

Abbot and Archbishop exchanged despairing glances. She was hysterical but there was a disagreeable amount of truth in what she said. At the beginning, most of the rumours about Gloucester's dubious intentions had been put about by Thomas Grey to frighten his family and the Council into following his lead. But there was no doubt that he had done all he could to make them come true. Gloucester had indeed been provoked, and it was a long-established fact that he didn't like Bess or any of the Woodvilles very much. It didn't follow that he would harm his beloved brother's widow or children, and there had been a time when he was on quite friendly terms with Anthony, but . . .

He had been wielding power in the north for years. He had grown. But into what? No one now knew him well enough to be sure.

They were both exhausted, having been up all night organising this flight into sanctuary in response to Bess's frantic appeals. 'Madam,' said the Abbot, 'in the past, Gloucester has been on the side of moderation. I believe that he protested openly against the death of his brother Clarence, and against that of Henry of Lancaster.'

'Anyone can say anything!' Bess almost snapped. 'It's what they do that matters. He may have had some kindness for Clarence. Clarence was his brother. But he took the warrant to the Tower to get Henry of Lancaster killed. Edward told me, five minutes after he'd put the warrant in Gloucester's hands.'

There was an uncomfortable silence. It was broken by

413

Elizabeth of York who suddenly tumbled Bridget into the arms of a neighbouring sister and shot to her feet. At sixteen, she was still slight of build and her mourning serge almost extinguished her physically. But she was angry and it couldn't extinguish that. 'It's all nonsense! Of course Uncle Richard won't hurt us. He's supposed to be the Protector. Father wanted him to look after Edward. And he wouldn't blame us for what Thomas did. We need not hide in here, we need not!'

'Be quiet, Elizabeth, you don't know what you're talking about!' shrieked Bess.

'Indeed, yes. Sit down, my child,' said Rotherham. He bit his lip, visibly uncertain what to do. Then he appeared to summon resolution. 'Madam, if it will make you feel safer, I suggest that you take charge of your late husband's Great Seal.' In these days of crisis, he as Chancellor had been carrying the Seal with him everywhere on a chain round his neck. Now he took it off. 'With this, any request you make to anyone for aid or money will have full authority as being made on behalf of your son the King. And if plans are made to crown anyone other than your son . . .'

'I can't believe that such a thing is possible!' interjected the Abbot in a shocked voice.

'. . . we have his brother Prince Richard here and he can be crowned in Edward's stead at once,' finished Rotherham. *I'm trying to reassure her*, said his sidelong glance at the Abbot.

From behind him came a series of deafening crashes. He and the Abbot spun round. 'What the devil are you doing?' shouted the Abbot at the men who were attacking the outer wall of his house with pickaxes. 'Bringing in the Queen's bedstead, sir.' The largest pickaxe-wielder paused. 'Won't go through the door, sir. We'll rebuild the wall, never fear.'

'Oh, dear God,' groaned the Abbot.

Secretly Rotherham echoed him. He had just realised that on impulse he had publicly countenanced the Woodville fears of Gloucester, on very little evidence, and that on top of that he had handed Bess the Great Seal of the Realm. The Council and Gloucester, who was after all the lawful Protector, were unlikely to take an understanding view of either.

Bess Woodville, who was now wrecking the Abbot of Westminster's property, had in all probability just wrecked his, Rotherham's, career as well. There was no doubt that without intending it, but simply by being defenceless and frightened, Bess Woodville was an extraordinarily destructive woman.

His quarters in the royal apartments at the Tower were comfortable and he had plenty of visitors. Delegations came to pay the City's respects, messengers arrived from all sorts of private people, with cakes, books, clothes, a longbow and a superbly tooled saddle, as gifts. Tailors came to measure him for his coronation robes. His tutor kept him company. Uncle Richard came and in stiff but kindly tones discussed the details of the coronation ceremony and told him that its date was now the twenty-fourth of June. Harry Buckingham came, dressed in turquoise satin and standing very tall. He had rendered valuable service by meeting Uncle Gloucester at Northampton, Richard gathered, and had been duly rewarded. He was virtually Viceroy of Wales, now.

Lord William Hastings, who had also rendered valuable service both to Buckingham and to Gloucester but was not yet Viceroy of anywhere, came one day just as Buckingham was leaving and cut him dead in the doorway, which was interesting.

All the visitors had tales to tell of events in the City and the world at large. But the things he wanted most to know, they could not or would not reveal. They did not know what was to happen to his Uncle Anthony or his half-brother Richard Grey or his chamberlain Vaughan. And when his mother and sisters and his younger brother would leave sanctuary and join him, they could not tell him either.

*　　*　　*

415

It was the evening of the seventh of June. In his City lodgings, Bishop Stillington of Bath and Wells had just gone to bed.

The lodgings were luxurious. He put out a wrinkled finger with a knobbly blue vein crossing it just above the knuckle and touched a similarly thick and knobbly vein of gold embroidery in the bedhangings. The candlestick by his bedside was gold, too. He was past the age of feeling ready to face even loss of comfort or status, let alone imprisonment or, heaven forfend, the block.

Well, no, he was a bishop. It wouldn't be the block, but a Tower cell would be bad enough.

At the Council tomorrow he must speak.

Suppose he didn't? But what if someone else had known all along and it came out later? Would his silence count as treason? But if he did talk, would that be considered treachery too? Had it been treachery to obey King Edward's orders in the first place?

He ought to ask Alcock. Alcock would know. Alcock was integrity personified. Alcock would say that he should have spoken up when King Edward first announced that he had married Bess Woodville. His silence then had been the treason.

'Oh, Christ have mercy,' moaned the Bishop of Bath and Wells, curling up into a ball and whispering his petition into his down pillow. 'I'm too old for all this responsibility. I can't do it. I can't tell them. I must. I can't. Oh God, let me die before the morning!'

Dynasties might topple and sudden death obliterate signatories but routine business must go on. Charters must continue to be granted, ambassadors welcomed, invitations accepted or declined, accounts scanned, marriages sanctioned, sheriffs appointed. Or replaced. 'I shall have to find some new men for quite a few positions,' said Richard to his secretary. 'There are complaints of bribery standing against

416

some of the existing ones. It will be a chance for some of my Yorkshire knights, perhaps.'

Other, odder tasks presented themselves. John Alcock, arriving in the Protector's presence at the end of a warm June day, found Richard and the secretary, Kendall, contemplating a table on which lay piled a remarkable assortment of keys, variously of iron, brass or – in a few cases – what looked like gold or silver, and ranging from the tiny and heavily ornamental to the enormous and clanking. His eyebrows rose.

'As requested, I've brought my key to Prince Edward's rooms. But I came with it in person because I want to ask if I can keep it. I need to come and go freely as far as my pupil is concerned. Are all of those Tower keys as well?'

'They are, and nearly all of them came with a plea to be allowed to retain them.' Richard sighed and sank into a chair. 'Do you know why I'm calling in the Tower keys? Bess Woodville had a set, a complete set, gates and treasury and all. And Thomas Grey asked her for them and that's how quantities of treasure came to be stolen from the Tower. He simply walked in and helped himself. What he purloined, we still haven't recovered. So I decided to investigate the matter of who has keys to what. And what do I find? Half London, apparently, can stroll in and out at will. The main gates of the Tower are ceremonially locked every evening and it's nothing but a farce. The gates are open all day – from dawn to sunset the place is as public as a market. And even when they're shut, at least a dozen people have keys to them. Those keys should be only in the hands of the Constable of the Tower and perhaps the King and one other designated official – the Constable of England, perhaps. The individual gatekeepers should use the Tower Constable's. And when it comes to keys for doors and gates inside the walls! The Tower Constable's butler has a complete set. I can't imagine why, as he only needs access to his master's rooms and to the stores. The Custodian of the Treasury for some unexplained reason has keys to the armoury as well, and the Armourer has the key to the outer Treasury. Cleaning maids have keys to the rooms in their charge and they lend them among themselves or have extra ones cut when it suits them. The City locksmiths must be making a fortune. The prisoners in the dungeons will be having keys next. ''Here you are, my friend, have a set of keys so that you can come in and go out as you like. Why not? Everyone else does.'' I'm making a fresh start. I'm appointing a new Constable for the Tower – Brackenbury, his name is – and I'm laying down clear rules as to who can have access to where. I'm keeping one complete set of keys, inner and outer, but mine is the only full set apart from Brackenbury's own. Buckingham can have a representative selection including keys for the outer gates. He's Constable of England and might have to act for me in my absence if the City were threatened, or Brackenbury turned traitor. Apart from that, people can have only what they absolutely must and there is to be a closer check kept on who comes in during the day. You can keep your key to the prince's apartments. Have you any keys to the outer gates, though?'

'Certainly not.'

'I'm glad to hear it.' Richard sighed again. 'I'm sorry I put you to the trouble of coming in person. All the same, I'm glad to see you. Will you sit down? I want your advice. All right, Kendall. We're finished for today. Off you go.'

Kendall and the clerks who in the background were tidying away the day's work, murmured their farewells and went.

'I wondered,' Alcock said. 'I thought perhaps you might be pleased if I called on you. If I can help, I will, gladly.'

Richard did not speak at once. While he waited, Alcock studied the Protector's face.

He had not seen Richard more than a handful of times in the five years between the deaths of Clarence and King Edward. He remembered that in 1478 when Clarence died, Gloucester, despite the responsibility he had successfully borne in the north, had still been very much the King's devoted brother, adult but subordinate. Even then traces of the boy Dickon were still discernible in Richard of Gloucester.

They were not discernible now. This man was fully grown, the last of the immature lines planed away from his face, authority visible even in the way he held himself.

And he was bitterly unhappy. When at last he spoke, Alcock heard it in his voice.

'I saw the faces of your fellow Council members, Alcock, this morning when I repeated to them what Stillington had told me. I had to tell them, you know. Stillington said that one of us must. Did Stillington consult you beforehand, by any chance, before he came to me?'

'No. If he had, I should have recommended him to keep quiet. The country needs peace and continuity and Eleanor Butler had no issue whose rights were being ignored. There's nothing to be gained by stirring such muddy waters.'

'Isn't there? I saw it in the faces of some of the Council, Alcock. If Stillington can attest that he married my brother King Edward to another woman before Edward married Bess Woodville, and that the first lady was still alive at the time of the so-called marriage to Bess, well – I gain, do I not? I gain the throne.'

'Do you want it?'

'I'd scarcely be a normal man, certainly not a normal Plantagenet, if the idea didn't attract me. Also, it could have advantages for the country. A king who is a minor is liable to be fought over by factions wanting to control him. That's happened already! We have had an attempted coup by the Woodvilles. And the boy himself is far from strong, by the look of him. That's a drawback to a king.'

'I see.'

Richard laughed. 'You don't approve, do you? Churchman though you are, you think that the past should be left quiet. That's the attraction of you, you know. That extraordinary trick you have of thinking in a way that's all

419

your own and owes nothing to any rules or laws. No one but you could have called an informal reception a political map of England! Do you remember that day? The dispassionate way you looked down at all my kinfolk and associates and wanted me to study them like a lesson! Oh, never mind. It's the here and now that we're discussing. Did today's revelations come as a shock to you?'

'Not altogether. There were Clarence's hints. Even at the time, all those years ago, I wondered if they were more than slanders. But I felt it best not to enquire. I have for years been in charge of King Edward's intelligencers, as you no doubt know. I must have a meeting with you about this at some point, when I will explain my organisation in detail. Edward Brampton, who assists me, would have to be present. I've built up our force of information-gatherers a good deal in the last few years. Apart from unobtrusive people like pardoners and peddlers, there are men – and a few women – in my pay in most big households. I had some such agents as long ago as 1477 and no doubt I could have found out more of the background to Clarence's rumours if we had wished to do so. But there are times, my lord, when sleeping dogs are best left snoring.'

'Clarence knew the secret,' said Richard. 'You were right, he wasn't just guessing or inventing. That was why he died. Stillington was imprisoned briefly some years ago, if you recall. That was because we found out that he'd let it slip to Clarence. He's lived in terror of being imprisoned again. Poor devil, he was almost wetting himself with fear when he came to me yesterday.'

'And you knew already?'

'Yes. And much as I dislike Bess Woodville and all her clan,' said Richard, 'at the time when I first heard the story, I considered, as you did, that it was best ignored. But now the matter is public, at Stillington's own insistence . . . and like it or not, the alternative to me now is a boy whose claim is suspect and who is himself too young and too frail in the eyes of many to make a strong king. According to the laws of England, Alcock, I ought to claim the throne. Bastard sons cannot inherit.'

Alcock was silent.

'Well, can they?' said Richard sharply. 'It would undermine the Church's whole stand on matrimony. Marriage is a sacrament, is it not, Alcock? An indissoluble union which cannot be replaced by another within the lifetimes of the parties unless they prove to be near relatives or something of the kind?'

'That is correct,' said Alcock, 'and perhaps I am not a good churchman. An unlawful child cannot be seen to inherit, but I tell you frankly that if I had had the chance, I would have dissuaded Stillington from repeating his tale. I too was watching the faces round the Council table today and – yes – some were shocked but some were frankly pleased. You will have support. Not unanimous, no, but adequate – perhaps adequate enough to carry the day. And I'm sorry for it.'

'You're very candid.'

The blue eyes which were so child-like, and yet so very shrewd, gazed at Richard across the table. 'I shall do nothing to harm this realm, my lord. Whoever is accepted as king by the Council, and crowned as king by the Archbishop of Canterbury, I will accept. But I claim the right to my private opinions, and the right also to express them at least in private, as we are now. I regard you, my lord, as a most able and admirable candidate, but I love the prince Edward and I have trained him for kingship.'

'He'll never forgive me, of course,' Richard said. 'When he's of age, he may well decide to insist that the Eleanor Butler story is my invention. One day I might have to fight him for the crown. Fight *them*. His brother will help him, no doubt.'

'Would help, conditional. We're not there yet. I am of the opinion that the Butler marriage should be further investigated. If it were proved invalid . . .'

'Did you know, Alcock, that when you are engaged in

421

anything one could call intrigue, your eyes actually shine?'

'I sincerely hope that isn't true, my lord. Stillington's intellect has . . . limitations. I should like the Butler marriage to be scrutinised by sharper minds. I don't personally care for Bishop Morton but he is highly gifted intellectually. So is young Catesby. It was a wise move, to put him on the Council. I admire that clear-cut, self-contained, legal mind of his. There may yet be a way out of this, and if there were would you be relieved or disappointed? And if the latter, my lord, why? I must ask you to consider that. Thwarted ambition? The pleasure of putting aside Bess Woodville whom you have always disliked? I don't ask you to tell me. I do ask you to be honest with yourself.'

'I don't know the answer,' said Richard candidly. 'The good of the realm and the state of the boy's health are involved beyond doubt. Ambition? I'm not sure. Bess Woodville? Oddly enough, I stopped positively hating her after the Desmond affair. It was such a stupid thing to do – it seemed clear that foolishness was at work rather than wickedness. Since then I've simply . . . held her in contempt. And just because of that, she isn't of sufficient account to weigh with me over this. No. Surprisingly, Alcock, you can disregard Bess.'

'I wonder if she knew,' said Alcock thoughtfully. 'Or guessed, or sensed, something fundamentally wrong with her marriage.'

'That never occurred to me.' Richard looked mildly interested for a moment, and then impatient. 'Well, I doubt if we'll ever know. I really don't want to discuss Bess. She's been a nuisance since the day my brother first set eyes on her and I sincerely regret that he ever did. Getting back to the present situation . . .'

'Sir William Catesby!' said the page, managing to get into the doorway and make the announcement just before Catesby himself rushed in.

He did not look in the least like a clear-cut and self-contained legal mind. His light-brown hair was as tangled as though he had come in out of a gale instead of from a calm summer evening, and he kept nervously brushing it out of his eyes. 'My lord . . . my lords . . .!'

'What is it?' Gloucester was on his feet, a hand going instinctively to his dagger hilt. Catesby took several deep breaths and forced himself to stand still with his hands clasped in front of him. Visibly, he pulled himself together to make a coherent report.

'My lord of Gloucester, this evening I was bidden to accompany my lord William Hastings to a meeting at the house of Thomas Stanley. I am employed by my lord Hastings to act as his secretary and legal adviser. So, although I had my suspicions about the nature of the meeting . . . my lord, you have asked me to join the Council and I owe loyalty both to you and to the Council accordingly. Also . . .' he broke off momentarily and then commanded himself again. '. . . there were five people there apart from myself. Lord Thomas Stanley was one, of course, since he was our host. Lord Hastings was another. There were also Archbishop Thomas Rotherham, Dr John Morton and Jane Shore who was formerly King Edward's . . . It's a conspiracy, my lord,' said Catesby. 'They think that the crown may be offered to you by the rest of the Council and if it is they intend to raise a rebellion. Jane Shore has been carrying messages to and from the Queen in sanctuary. The rising would be in conjunction with those of the Woodville family who remain free, and in the name of the Prince Edward. That's all.'

'Thank you, Catesby,' said Alcock. He smiled at Richard. 'I said it was a wise move to put him on the Council. In fact, as soon as he was appointed, I asked him to undertake a further task. Allow me to present to you, my lord of Gloucester, the latest recruit to my band of royal intelligencers.'

'It's hard to believe in one way,' said Richard to Alcock, after Catesby had gone. 'But in another they're the likeliest elements in a conspiracy. All for different reasons.'

'Even Hastings? But for him, the first Woodville coup

would have succeeded. This makes no sense. I believe Catesby implicitly – but still it makes no sense.' Alcock, for once, was out of his intellectual depth.

'Yes, it does. Hastings considers that he hasn't been treated well. I rewarded Buckingham, but not him, for services rendered after my brother's death. He's jealous.' Richard sighed. 'I didn't reward him, Alcock, because though I'm grateful to him, I can't forget how much he did to lead my brother into the excesses that weakened his health. In time, I would have come round to giving Hastings something, perhaps, but at the moment it seems to me that he was simply paying off a debt, and that I owe him nothing. As for the others . . .' Richard ticked them off grimly on his fingers. 'Morton knows I disapprove of him. He's the last person to want to see me on the throne. Rotherham can't hope for much under my administration, either. A man who would hand the Great Seal to Bess Woodville can't be trusted in authority. You were there, Alcock, when I stripped him of the Chancellorship. He's covered in emotional welts and I daresay could contemplate my demise with perfect equanimity. Jane Shore would do a favour for anybody, and I fancy she's gone back to Hastings' bed. He was her lover before Edward was. As for Stanley, he's married to Margaret Beaufort and her son is the last surviving Lancastrian sprig. She's said to be besotted with him. My brother once tried to get the boy into his hands. I wish he'd succeeded. I daresay Margaret Beaufort doesn't in the least want me, a grown man with a son of my own, taking control. It wouldn't leave a single chink through which her darling son could crawl to eminence, would it? She probably sees the present state of confusion as having all manner of possibilities and would like to prolong it.'

It was as shrewd an appraisal of the existing political situation as Alcock himself could have made. Long ago, in a minstrel's gallery in Westminster, Alcock the pedagogue had apparently made a major if accidental contribution to Dickon of Gloucester's education.

Richard paced restlessly across the room to stand looking out at the river. This Thames-side residence of Baynard's Castle was his mother's property. It had made a convenient base when he first arrived from Middleham, since it was staffed already while his own London house was not. He had had his own house opened and now that Anne had joined him, they had moved into it. But she had been ill when she reached London and he had continued to conduct daily business from other places, Baynard's Castle among them, to ensure peace and quiet for her.

Baynard's itself was a serene place. At the moment, the ebbing Thames lay calm as a mirror, reflecting a scatter of gold-tinted clouds. Richard looked at it as though wondering what such tranquillity felt like.

'Hastings is the one I feel most bitter about. He should have known I would give him his due in the end. I like him, essentially. I wonder whose was the initial impetus for this conspiracy, though?' He turned to look at Alcock. 'Stanley was the host. I wonder. Margaret Beaufort? But I'd like to know what she used as a lever.'

Chapter Twenty-Nine

The Plantagenets: The View from the Tower

1483

The Council, these days, met wherever was convenient according to the numbers to be present and the addresses of those attending. Baynard's Castle, the Painted Room at Westminster, and the Council Chamber of the Tower, were the three most frequent venues. This time, it was to be the Tower.

The Council Chamber was a pleasant place. In summer the hangings were removed, displaying the pale stone walls and rendering the place larger and brighter. Today the morning sun poured slantwise through open windows, shimmered off the walls and made sloping, attenuated arch-shapes on the polished walnut table. The knowing old raven, who over a long life had learned that signs of movement behind those windows meant that trays of refreshments would shortly appear with a chance of titbits, was already strategically perched on a sill.

Dr John Alcock, arriving early, looked at this agreeable meeting room and wished he was dead.

Well, no, not exactly that. He caught himself out in this improper and irreligious thought and checked it. But he did long to be somewhere else; saying Mass in his friendly, shadowy cathedral at Worcester, or studying with young Prince Edward in Ludlow Castle. Or, simply, in the Royal Apartments where Edward was now, for Edward was still his pupil and whatever was enacted here within the next few hours would be close to the boy in more ways than one.

The lad was not in good health, either. His gums were

427

badly inflamed and he was suffering from an outbreak of mouth ulcers. (It could well be best for him and for the country, said a cool and analytical part of Alcock's mind, if he didn't accede.) The physician was with him at present and Dr Argentine could be relied on. But I ought to be there, Alcock said to himself.

This was one of the times when his usual pure cerebral delight in running the royal intelligence service, picking good agents and providing them with cover stories and pretexts for going where he wished them to go and asking what he wished them to ask, was laced with disgust. Normally, when information was brought back to him, he was like a fisherman eagerly examining what had been caught in his net. But this time what had been caught had been ugly.

It was as well that it had been discovered. He hadn't suspected it in advance and had he done so, his investigations would have been all the more thorough. There were times for leaving mud alone and times for turning it over, and this could only ever have belonged to the latter category. He still loathed the outcome.

He was not the only one in Richard's confidence or as much of it as Richard had seen fit to offer anybody. Precisely what he meant to do today, no one knew. He would act, he had said ominously, and left it there. John Howard and Harry Buckingham, Cardinal Bourchier, Edward Brampton and William Catesby all, like Alcock, knew that much. They too arrived promptly. Most seemed just as usual except that Howard, who hated anything that smelt of treachery, had an air of menacing anticipation and Buckingham seemed fractionally too well dressed and pleased with himself. Brampton, tanned to a swashbuckling swarthiness by a maritime expedition to seize the fleet back from Thomas Grey, began a conversation, describing how Thomas had escaped to France and declaring that this was a pity. Alcock knew he was deliberately creating a natural atmosphere which would not frighten the prospective prey. Bourchier helped him, asking questions. Bourchier was very patrician and dignified in his red cardinal's robes and Alcock wished that the colour did not remind him so strongly of blood. Catesby was his usual calm, controlled self, listening to the talk with sage nods of the head. Could he really be as calm as he seemed? Alcock himself had recruited him, using the Council and the loyalty expected of its members, and gratitude to Gloucester who had put Catesby among them, as his persuasions. But it had been only a routine precaution. Ever since Warwick's final bout of scheming, he had been trying, on King Edward's instructions, and as he had explained to Richard, to provide an agent to keep eyes and ears open in each great household. He hadn't expected for a moment that Hastings would ever . . .

For God's sake, Catesby had been in Hastings' household since he was a boy! Belatedly, Alcock realised that between them, he and Hastings had put Catesby in an impossible position. The young man had done what was technically right but – didn't he *mind*? He ought to mind, thought Alcock indignantly and unreasonably, and sat with his profile turned away from him.

Hastings himself appeared, confident and jaunty, a little yellowed about the whites of the eyes from having been at the wine too late too often, and exchanging easy small-talk with Bishop Morton of Ely, who entered with him, on the good summer and its admirable effects on gardens and crops.

Two new Council members followed, a hard-featured Yorkshire knight called Richard Ratcliffe, and an amiable, round-faced viscount called Francis Lovell, who had been a boyhood friend of Gloucester's. Thomas Rotherham arrived, alone, looking drawn. Then Stanley came in with Stillington. They all sat or stood about, some listening to Brampton and some making desultory conversation among themselves. There was no sign of Gloucester. Despite Brampton's efforts, a tautness was developing. Alcock's stomach knotted itself unpleasantly.

Richard was late, and by the time he actually arrived Alcock had started a headache. The pulses of pain followed the hammer-beat of his heart. He noticed this phenomenon distractedly. Then Richard came in in a businesslike fashion and they all stood.

'My apologies for keeping you waiting. I overslept.' He looked, Alcock thought, more as though he hadn't slept at all. He had never expected Hastings' defection either, even though he understood the reason. 'It's warm,' he said, 'no need for formality.' He shed his doublet and rolled up his shirtsleeves and all round the tables, other doublets were loosened or discarded, to be hung on the backs of chairs. Cardinal Bourchier pronounced the customary prayer for God's guidance in the day's proceedings. They sat.

'The chief item this morning,' said Richard, 'is the matter of – for courtesy's sake I will continue to call her the Queen, my brother's widow – the matter of the Queen and her persistent clinging to sanctuary. It won't do. Whatever this Council ultimately decides concerning the succession, we cannot have even a courtesy dowager queen of England cringing under the skirts of the church with her children as though I were proposing to murder them all. We shall have foreign ambassadors asking why! Her proper place is with her sons, yes, but with both of them. At the very least, the younger boy should join his brother. I understand that the elder lad is ailing and has repeatedly asked to see his mother and brother. Regrettably, the Queen will not listen to reason. She won't even listen to Cardinal Bourchier here, who has tried to talk to her on my behalf, or to Bishop Alcock who has attempted it as well and whom she is said to trust. But something must be done.'

'She's terrified.' Alcock made himself attend. 'She is too afraid to believe any reassurances.'

'And the one thing that can't be done,' said Bourchier, 'is to remove her by force. That, the church will never allow.'

'Quite.' Brampton was impatient. 'But will you tell us, my lord, what instead we should do? My lord Protector has the right of it. This situation cannot drag on and what, in any case, of the poor Abbot of Westminster? He wants his house back or what is left of it. There has been damage, so I hear.'

Everyone laughed, including Richard. Alcock watched him wonderingly. A discussion about the best way to extract Bess from sanctuary began to bounce round the table. Richard, becoming serious again, appeared to be listening to it. Did he mean to take action this morning after all? Had he changed his mind?

'Can't we make it look as if we meant to use force, but not actually do so?' Hastings asked. Richard's eyes went to him once and then glanced away. A bleakness settled over the features which a short time ago had been laughing.

No, he hasn't changed his mind, thought Alcock. He's just unwilling to come to it. Poor devil. No, it won't be easy, accusing someone as attractive, to whom he owes so much, as Hastings.

'Well, yes, if she saw armed men in boats approaching, she would place her own interpretation on it.' Bourchier sounded doubtful.

'She's easy to intimidate. As Bishop Alcock says, she's already completely terrified,' said Stanley. 'She's no Margaret of Anjou.'

'And it is true,' Bourchier admitted, 'that her son Richard, being only a child, cannot be regarded as guilty of any crime and therefore has no claim on sanctuary. He at least might be lawfully fetched out, not by force, but by a show of it.'

'Yes, I agree.' Alcock massaged his forehead. 'And since I have no doubt that Prince Edward needs the companionship . . .'

'Dr Morton,' said Richard suddenly in a high voice.

They turned to him. Alcock, a desperate palm pressed to his left temple, which was now throbbing as though someone had hit it with a pick, then listened disbelievingly while Richard, as though a vital matter of state were not under

431

discussion, remarked that the strawberry garden in Morton's London residence was famous and that strawberries were in season: would my lord of Ely be kind enough to send out for some?

Rotherham was next to Alcock. 'What on earth is the matter with Gloucester?' he whispered.

'I wish I knew,' Alcock muttered back.

There was a bell with which to summon service. Morton, startled but polite, used it and requested the strawberries. Richard, who had been fidgeting, got to his feet. 'Excuse me for a while, gentlemen. Perhaps you could work through the next items on the agenda meanwhile. They don't require my presence. I won't be long.'

'Is he ill?' asked Stanley as Richard went out. 'Maybe he's eaten something that doesn't suit him. Is that why he wants to eat fruit now?'

If this waiting goes on much longer, Alcock thought, I shall withdraw on a plea of illness myself. Oh, my head! A clerk had followed Richard in at the start of the meeting and had the agenda. The next item was a straightforward matter concerning allocation of funds for new ships. They discussed it earnestly for some time. Alcock's headache eased a little. But it crashed back to life when the door was flung open and Richard strode back into the Council chamber.

Alcock, through a blinding haze of renewed pain, looked at his face and thought: this is it. He has had to work himself up to the point. Now he's ready.

Richard's face was frightening. He was quite white and his mouth was a straight, hard line. No one spoke. They all knew extreme anger when they saw it and this angry man was the Protector of England whose power to express fury was almost limitless. They waited, silent, to learn who was the target.

'Tell me, my lords,' said Richard, 'what in your opinion should be done to traitors?'

There were some stammered replies. There were also some petrified silences.

432

'Well? You, Hastings, what's your opinion? Stand up!'

'Traitors are to be condemned, of course.' Hastings, rising, spoke as if he meant it and perhaps he did, Alcock thought in agony. He had been loyal to King Edward and perhaps he conceived this conspiracy as loyalty to King Edward's seed. He knew the young prince. He had taken gifts to him. Perhaps it wasn't pique over lack of reward, but something more honourable than that.

Hastings was enlarging on his views of treachery. There were beads of sweat on his forehead for which the warm morning did not quite account, since he was one of those who had removed his doublet. Loyalty, he said, was a duty enjoined on everyone. Treachery must be utterly condemned. He looked straight into Richard's face as he said that and Alcock saw that he was reading terrible things there. His hand, resting on the table, shook a little. But he seemed to stop it by an act of will and his chin came up. 'Loyalty is required of a man,' he said, 'even if it means going down with a defeated lord, or standing by one who is weak by reason of infirmity or youth.'

It was a challenge. All round the table, indrawn breaths signalled comprehension. Richard comprehended, too. He stepped suddenly forward and shook his fist in Hastings' face. His shirt-sleeves were still rolled up and the long scar on his forearm, from the wound he had got at Barnet, was blazing red. 'You talk about the virtue of loyalty? I know what you and that . . . that witch Jane Shore have been about! I know about the new Woodville conspiracy, my fine, loyal friend!' The fist crashed down on to the table. 'I'll make good your condemnation of treachery, my friend, upon your body!'

In Richard's absence, Alcock had visualised him pacing a room somewhere, bracing himself for the hideous task ahead; Stanley had probably supposed him to be crouching in a privy. But he had spent some of the time, it now appeared, in conference with the Captain of the Guard, for at the sound of the descending fist a voice outside the door

433

shouted 'Treason!' and the door was once more flung open. Soldiers were in the room.

And with that, what had a moment ago been a dignified Council meeting holding a discussion on naval finances degenerated into something fantastic and lacking in any kind of dignity whatsoever.

Chairs scraped as people vacated them and backed to the wall in alarm. Richard was shouting names: *Hastings, Stanley, Rotherham, Morton*! Hastings made no resistance as he was seized. But Alcock was knocked from his seat as Stanley sprang up shouting and backed past him, hands outstretched as if to fend off the advancing soldiers. Flat on his back on the floor and entangled with his chair, Alcock saw a spear butt sweep by above and heard it crack against Stanley's head.

Stanley fell across him and rolled under the table. Rotherham was under it already, hiding, bony knees sticking up on either side of his ears, imparting an inappropriate air of farce to the proceedings. Alcock sat up, freeing himself from the chair, as Stanley, dazed but conscious, was dragged out swearing. The room was full of shouts, scuffling feet and protestations. Hastings seemed now to be requesting a hearing and the north-country knight Ratcliffe, apparently identifying himself with the Protector's cause, was bellowing insults at him in a broad Yorkshire accent. Catesby, watching from a safe corner, looked horrified, at last.

Alcock got to his feet and came face to face with Morton, who was complaining loudly and indignantly, trying to retain an air of authority and oddly enough almost managing it even with a burly man-at-arms gripping each elbow. Richard's voice rose above the uproar, dominating it. 'Take them away! Lock them up! Except for Hastings! I want his head off now!'

He meant it. There was a shaken moment in which even the outraged voices of Stanley and Morton were stilled, in which Hastings' mouth dropped open and *this-can't-be-*

happening appeared on his face as if printed there by William Caxton, to be replaced almost at once and just as legibly by *oh my God, it is*!

The first to move after that immobile instant, or aeon, was Alcock himself. Without asking permission or offering excuse, he made decisively for the door.

His pupil, the young Prince Edward, was in this building. The boy had known Hastings and regarded him as a friend; Hastings himself had very likely acted out of that friendship. Alcock hoped so. Alcock's place now was at young Edward's side. He should have been there from the start.

No one noticed him as he left. He in turn, hastening towards the Royal Apartments, did not notice that his headache had gone. Edward's quarters were empty. A basin on a side table held the mouthwash which Dr Argentine had prescribed. Had the boy felt ill enough to go to bed? Two at a time, Alcock sped up to the bedchamber, but this too was deserted except for a manservant who was smoothing the bedcovers. 'Will! Where is the prince?'

Will Slaughter was a blackbearded cockney whose alarming surname and thick facial hair belied his nature. He was actually a gentle soul whose salary mostly went to support a crowd of younger brothers and sisters, their father being dead. He shook his head. 'Ain't he down below, sir? He was there when I saw him last. He might have gone outside, perhaps. It's a lovely morning. I told him, earlier, the sunshine'd do him good. Poor little tyke,' added Will Slaughter in his rumbling voice, 'that there saltwater mouthwash the doctor give him made him feel that sick.'

'I must find him!' Alcock plunged away.

The gardens. The kitchens. The privy. The stables? The armoury? His head said that all this urgency was unreasonable but his heart wouldn't listen. He must find Edward. He should have cut that Council to be with him. It mattered; Alcock didn't know why, but it did. *Where was he?*

A maidservant carrying linen towards the laundry, whom

he stopped at random, finally provided the answer. 'Why, yes, I know where to find him, sir. I was fetching new sheets to his bed and he was looking that down in the mouth, so I said to him, there's a mastiff bitch over in one of the guardrooms, got some puppies. Why don't you go along and see, I said to him. They're old enough to climb out of their box now. I'm courting one of the men-at-arms,' she added hastily, eyeing Alcock's clerical garb with caution. 'We'll be married soon. So it was all right that he took me there once when no one else was there, to see the pups. I told Prince Edward where to find them and he . . .'

'Which guardroom? Quickly!' Alcock was not interested in the maidservant's morals. There were half a dozen guardrooms in the Tower, widely scattered. With luck, he was in one whose men were not involved in the scene in the Council Chamber. But if he had been there when Richard arrived to speak to the Captain . . .'

'It's the one that looks out on the grass in front of the chapel, sir.'

The nearest to the Council Chamber. Oh, it would be, it would be! He ran, bursting through doors, negotiating stairs and corners like a majestically proportioned whirlwind. A sentry at the guardroom door said: 'Yes, yes, the boy's here. It's all right, isn't it? I mean, he's the prince . . .'

'Was he here when the Lord Protector came? The Lord Protector did come, didn't he?'

'Yes, sir, but the boy wasn't here, no. He came just after the Lord Protector had called the guard out and they'd gone by then.'

'Good,' said Alcock. 'Let me by. I must get to him.'

The mastiff bitch had been given a small cupboard-like room to herself. She was lying in her box, serenely suckling her pups. Edward was there but he was not attending to the pups. He was staring out of the window. And Alcock, joining him, knew as soon as he too glanced out that his relief because the guard had not been called out in front of

the boy had been misplaced, that after all his sense of
urgency was right, that instinct and love in partnership
could recognise danger beyond the range of reason.
'Edward, come away.'

'No. I can't,' said the boy. 'I mustn't.'

The window overlooked a broad stretch of grass. On the
far side a pile of logs awaited use in some structural repairs.
One of them had been dragged from the heap and placed in
the midst of the greensward. And there were people.

At this distance there was no sound, but individuals
could be recognised. A number of Council members were
there, though not Richard of Gloucester himself. There was
a tall helmeted man, faceless behind a closed visor and
holding an axe. There were guards, and two of them held by
the arms a man identifiable as Hastings. One of the Tower
chaplains stood in front of him, speaking to him, holding a
book.

As Edward and Alcock watched, the chaplain made the
sign of the cross and stepped back. Hastings was shoved
forward on to his knees in front of the log. The man with
the axe stepped forward and the axe swung up. It all happened with unbelievable speed; could the journey from life
to death be so short? The blood went up in a red fountain an
instant before the thud of the axe travelled to the window.

Edward turned to his tutor. 'Was it because of me?
Everyone thinks I don't know that something's afoot but
I'm not a fool. I can read faces and I've sharp ears. I've
listened at the turn of the stairs and heard the talk among
the sentries and the maids. "If he ever gets to the throne,"
I've heard them say, talking about me. "King Edward or
King Richard?" I've heard them say that, too. Those very
words. But Hastings wouldn't have stood for it, he was my
friend. Did Hastings die because of me?'

Then his unnatural, unchildlike dignity broke and without waiting for an answer, he flung himself sobbing into
Alcock's arms.

'Oh, my boy, my dear boy,' said Alcock helplessly,

holding him, this surrogate son whom he loved but could not protect.

'Tell me the truth! Why won't even you tell me the truth? No one tells me anything!'

'The truth . . .' Gently, Alcock took the boy's elbows and moved him back so that they could see each other's faces. 'The truth is that Hastings was indeed involved in a conspiracy. I believe that, yes, he did it mainly out of loyalty to you. But it could have plunged this whole country into civil war. I am sorry, Edward, but it is better that you know that and understand it.'

Edward jerked away from him. 'You're being loyal to him, to that Protector, my uncle!'

'No, my loyalty as a Council member is to this realm and its security and peace; my loyalty as a bishop is to the Church and her laws. The other things – the whispers you've overheard – I can't tell you the truth about those yet because I don't know exactly what is to happen. I will come to you when I know what to tell you. I promise. Now come away.'

On the way out, after leaving Edward in his doctor's care, he encountered a puzzled young woman with a basket of strawberries. 'I was sent to bring these to the Lord Protector but I can't find out where he is and no one knows anything about it.'

'I'll take them to him,' Alcock said.

He was not entirely surprised when Richard had them thrown into the moat.

Three days later, he came reluctantly back into Edward's presence and gently drew him from the Latin verses he was trying to con. Edward's jaw was swollen on one side and he was pale. What is coming is for the best, Alcock thought compassionately. He will not have the strength to make a king. He may not even live to be a man. But I am glad that I will not be the one who has to tell him. What I have to say to him now is bad enough.

Admittedly, there was good news to leaven today's ration of disaster. 'I have two pieces of news for you, Edward. One will make you happy and the other will grieve you. I'm sorry. Let me arm you with the happy news first. Your younger brother Richard is on his way to join you. He was fetched from Westminster this morning and the barge bringing him here is already approaching.'

'He's coming to stay with me?' The effort of speaking was painful and Edward put a hand to his jaw, but his eyes brightened.

He's little more than a child, Alcock thought. He wants his mother, his brother and sisters, his studies, games to play and a safe world in which to grow up. As I had. Kingship is for men, the burdens and the perils. Yes, to my sorrow, I think the Council are right.

Edward's face was grave again. 'And the other news?'

'I'm sorry, Edward. I'm so very sorry.'

'What is it?'

It was even harder than he had expected. 'The recent conspiracy in which Lord Hastings lost his head . . . a revival of the plot through which your Woodville relatives tried to seize power just after your father's death . . . too much conspiracy, too many conspirators . . . examples, to discourage others and ensure the stability of the country . . .' He sounded to himself like someone reading a proclamation of which he didn't believe a single word, and Edward's hazel eyes, steady as those of a much older person, were unnerving.

'Please come to the point,' said the boy.

'It concerns your Uncle Anthony. He . . .'

Edward whitened. 'Is he dead too?'

'Not yet. But soon, yes, I'm afraid so. My dear boy, this is a cruel world. It isn't only your uncle . . .'

'My half-brother?' Edward whispered. 'Richard Grey?'

'And your chamberlain Vaughan. They're all to go together a week from now. The warrants are on the way north.'

439

'But they were nothing to do with Hastings! How could they be? They were already in prison!' shouted Edward. He put a hand to his jaw again. There were tears in his eyes.

'It is felt that . . . the original Woodville plot, and their survival after arrest, encouraged further conspiracy.'

'Did no one speak for them? Did no one try to save them?'

'Yes. A number of the Council, myself included, argued against these executions. But the Protector is adamant and his point of view not unreasonable. He regards the Woodville family . . .'

'I'm a Woodville!'

'You're a Plantagenet. Of royal blood. The Woodvilles are your mother's kin but they are also people who have tried to use you to gain power.' He must make Edward understand or the boy would harbour dreams of revenge which, however natural, could one day bring him into danger. 'The Protector wants to put a swift end to all these troubles and he feels that the Woodvilles are a source and inspiration of treachery. He is willing to show mercy to some of the other conspirators. Two of them are prelates anyway who cannot be executed, and Thomas Stanley has never been a friend as Hastings appeared to be. His behaviour is therefore less heinous. But the Woodvilles have shown themselves to be open enemies and . . .' He wished the boy would weep openly. How could one help him while he stayed so rigid? 'Edward, the Protector may be right. He is acting in defence of his own life and your father's will . . .'

'My uncle,' said Edward. 'My brother. Poor old Vaughan. He's not a Woodville, just one of their servants.'

'. . . and for the kingdom's sake,' said Alcock.

But he felt obliged to say 'the kingdom's sake' and not 'your kingdom's sake.' He had been expressly forbidden to speak of the succession yet to Edward. Those were the Council's orders before they sent him here today. But the boy already knew more than they realised and he was too intelligent to miss this nuance.

'Whose kingdom? His or mine? Don't tell me he's going to

kill my uncle and my brother and my old friend Vaughan for my sake!' A new, cold dignity had taken possession of him. The maturity of it was astonishing and the brittleness of it tore at the heart. 'I don't want to hear these things from you, Dr Alcock. I don't want to hear you defend the man who is going to murder the people I love best in the world. I can't accept you as my tutor any more. Please go away.'

He turned his back and walked to the table where the book he had been reading lay open. He sat down in front of it.

'Edward –'

'Please leave me alone, I shan't be alone for long. My brother will soon be here, won't he? I must compose myself before he comes.'

'When . . . when the time comes, I will arrange for Masses to be said for the souls of . . .'

The facade of dignity broke once more, as it had in the little room overlooking the green. But not this time into tears. Edward spun round on his chair. His face was contorted by pain; violent movement had sent agonising jolts through his aching jaw. But his anger was the greater force. It was the Plantagenet rage, which had on occasion, on the battlefield and in Council, turned his father from a genial lion to a dangerous one. He snatched up the book and hurled it at Alcock. 'Get out! Leave me alone! Never come back, do you hear me? Go away, go away, go away!'

Chapter Thirty

The Plantagenets: Decision

June 1483

Anne woke in the hot darkness of the curtained bed and knew that, once again, Richard was gone.

But she knew where he would be. She drew back the curtain a little and saw the gleam of candlelight from the window seat, and Richard's profile, bent over the open book in his hands.

The book was Anthony Woodville's printed translation of *The Sayings of the Philosophers*. Yesterday, Richard had left it lying open on the seat. And the day before, as well. She had looked at it both times, and both times it was open at the same place.

He must be exhausted. So was she, although she was more used to it. Over the last few years she had been exhausted so continually that the sensation was almost companionable, like an associate who eventually turns into a friend not because he is likeable but because he is simply, persistently, there.

Once, she had thought of herself as wiry, strong. But her first pregnancy had disabused her of that idea. Carrying little Ned had drained her vitality and bearing him had nearly killed her. It had been after his birth that her winter coughs began. She had found – just –the vigour to bring forth one more child, but her little daughter had ailed from birth and in due course died and since then there had been nothing but miscarriages, and after each beastly, joyless, painful letting of blood without the blessing of achievement, she had been left a little feebler.

There wouldn't be another baby now. For three years, she hadn't even conceived. The end of the miscarriages was a relief and she wouldn't have minded, except that the one child they had was so frail. Little Ned caught every illness that came within his reach and showed no sign of growing out of this. If . . .

If anything happened to him, she sometimes said to herself, she would have to be the strong one who said to Richard: we are cousins and we married without a dispensation. Break the marriage. Give me a home and an income and leave me to God. Find a wife who can give you healthy children, like the ones you got out of wedlock before we were married.

There were times when she thought she should say it to Richard now. The trouble was, she loved him.

In fact, for a few years after their marriage, she had loved him to desperation point, finding in him the stability her father had never had, and pathetically grateful – in clear-eyed moments she recognised the pathos – for the fact that he really seemed to think her well-being important.

Horrible pregnancies, agonising births, sickness, exhaustion and miscarriage had put an end to that, paid her debt as it were. There had even been a time when fear of pregnancy and its miseries had overcome all questions of love or duty and she had taken to retiring early and being very fast asleep all night.

But now that she seemed to be barren, she was glad of his love-making again, and her own affection had matured into something stout and deep-rooted, dependent neither on gratitude nor sex. Looking at him now, the bent head in the candlelight, she knew that there were other things he needed from her and she from him. In a fierce and dangerous world, she and Richard, being cousins, could offer each other the companionship of the kindred mind and the shared memories. Anne groped in the shadows for robe and slippers, and went to him.

'Richard?'

'You ought to be asleep. You're still not well.'

'You ought to be asleep too. How many nights is it now? Three? Four? You get up in the small hours night after night and sit here pretending to read that book of Anthony's. Are you worrying about him? Or Hastings? Because if so,' said Warwick's daughter staunchly, 'tell the ghosts to go away. Hastings plotted to start a rising against you and maybe to kill you. Anthony was just another Woodville in the end. He put his family before you or King Edward. You've probably stopped another civil war. I've seen civil war and I know what it means. You were right and the Council was wrong.'

'I know.' The candlelight, shining upwards into his face, showed her the deep new lines between his eyes and a hatching of small ones below them. 'But sometimes, at night . . . I dealt with Hastings quickly. He didn't have to live through his last night waiting in terror for the dawn. But the others did. I saw my brother Clarence the night before his death, Anne, so I know what they suffered. I can't help but wonder how I would bear such a night, myself.'

'Come to bed.'

'I'd rather talk. It's strange, I spared Hastings the worst of it but I was there to see his face when he realised what was going to happen. He condemned all treachery, Anne, he virtually sentenced himself out of his own mouth. And then he saw what he had done. I've seen men look like that on the field, when they realise that the blood pumping out of them on to the ground is their own. I liked Hastings, Anne. I disapproved of him in many ways and I couldn't bring myself to pile honours on to him so soon after Edward's death because I thought he was partly to blame for it. But I may have been wrong. Perhaps Edward would have gone on as he did anyway, having too much of a good time, too much to eat and drink and too many women. Maybe he led Hastings along, not the other way round. I'd have seen Hastings right in the end, but he didn't give me time.'

'Richard, you mustn't brood in this way!'

'If I don't think about it when I'm awake, I dream at night. Even keeping busy in the daytime doesn't distract me. The empty places at the Council table are reminder enough. And the wary looks from the Council. They were all shocked when I insisted that Hastings be executed at once, that I wouldn't eat my dinner until his head was off . . .'

'Did you say that?' asked Anne, startled.

'Yes. Not because I was impatient to see him dead but because I knew if I didn't have it done quickly, I'd weaken and reprieve him. It took me all morning to make myself challenge him in the first place. I couldn't have pushed a mouthful down until it was all over. I had to do it, Anne. I had to stop the plots and conspiracies. I remember quarrelling with Edward over Henry of Lancaster and Clarence but I know now why he had to get rid of them. It's like cutting off a gangrened limb. It's easy to criticise when one isn't the king, when one isn't the man responsible. I've the peace of the whole kingdom in my charge now and you're right, there's been too much civil war. But oh, God, to be the man who has to do such things . . . I remember going into that damned Council room and looking at him and thinking, there's Will Hastings, just as usual and if I don't kill him, he'll kill me. It hurt, Anne. I'd thought he was someone I could trust. I've tried to show some mercy to the others, to make up. Stanley and Rotherham I'm just keeping in custody while they think things over, and Morton . . .'

'He's the most dangerous,' said Anne. 'Lancastrian and very ambitious and I shouldn't think he sees much future for himself while you're Protector.'

'No, but I can't behead a bishop. I've put him in Buckingham's charge. He's been packed off to Buckingham's Brecknock estate, in Wales. That will keep him out of the way until things become calmer.'

'And when will that be? Richard,' she put her hands over his and looked up into his face, 'something else has been keeping you awake, hasn't it, apart from Anthony and Hastings. Have you decided yet?'

'Your hands are cold,' said Richard.

'And your flesh is like stone. So . . . separate. You have decided, haven't you? Are you going to tell me? Whatever you choose to do, I am here with you.'

'Are you, Anne? I'd be glad of it if so. Even my good friend Bishop Alcock . . . he walked out of the room when I had Hastings arrested, you know. And since then, well, he's gone on being the perfect Council member, loyal to the Lord Protector, putting the interests of the realm first, and looking at me all the time as though I were a student who had made a regrettable mess of an ablative absolute. The Council will offer the crown to me formally tomorrow, not because they approve of what I did to Hastings or Anthony Woodville or Richard Grey or Vaughan – in my place they'd have done the same themselves, to a man, but they don't know it any more than I knew it when I argued with Edward over Clarence – but because they think I'm likely to be a better choice than a sickly boy of uncertain legitimacy. And I shall accept it because . . . Oh Anne, you have a pretty husband!'

'Why do you say that?'

'In future years it may be said of me that I chopped men's heads like a gardener cutting nosegays, but lay awake at night in a sweat of terror over a boy of twelve.'

'A boy? You mean Prince Edward?'

'Yes.' In the candlelight, the smile which now curved Richard's mouth was decidedly bitter. 'The sickly boy of uncertain legitimacy. Dr Alcock, who is his tutor, is now in the depths of grief because when he tried to explain to Edward my reasons for executing Anthony Woodville and the rest, the young cub ordered Alcock out of his presence and won't have him back. Alcock refuses to press the matter; he says he will not force himself on the boy. But that's beside the point. What isn't beside the point is that the boy himself hates me. For him I shall never be anything but the man who killed his uncle and his half-brother and his chamberlain – and his friend Hastings whose death, it appears, he witnessed. The Council are setting him aside partly

447

because they fear he won't live long enough to come of age. I'm afraid of the opposite. If he survives for another five years, he'll be old enough to take his power to himself. The cub will get his teeth and for me they will be axe-shaped teeth. So I can't let Edward come to power, Anne. For me there is no longer any choice. I know all the arguments, for and against. Loyalty to my brother's will on one side; the Church's views on the sanctity of marriage and the dangers of a minority rule on the other. And none of them matter. I must take Edward's throne and keep him close, in self-defence. The matter will be made formally definite tomorrow but informally it has already been settled. So has the coronation day. It's the sixth of July. My coronation, Anne. Mine.'

He did not move, but she knew he wanted her to put her arms about him. She did so, and at the same moment faced a dreadful duty. 'The Council say King Edward's son is sickly, but the only heir I have given you is not strong, either.' She must get the words out somehow. It was time. Better she should say it than Richard himself, or some grave deputation of Council members. 'Richard, we had no dispensation. If it comes to it, if Ned grows worse or . . . Our marriage could be annulled. You could start again, with someone else. I shouldn't stand in your way.'

He drew back from her and then took hold of her shoulders. 'No, Anne. Who else would be a friend to me, close to me, as you have been and are? I can't do without you. Nothing will happen to Ned. I was a weakly child too. They hardly expected me to survive, but I did. I have Ned and I have you and I want no other child or wife. Do you hear?'

'You sent for me, my lord?'

'I did indeed, Buckingham.' Richard stared at Buckingham across the wide desk in what was now his regular business chamber at Baynard's Castle. 'It is regarding the sermon which you, on my behalf, arranged to be preached at St Paul's Cross this morning.'

Detecting anger in his lord's voice, Buckingham glanced pointedly to where Kendall, Richard's private secretary, and a number of clerks were busy at a side table, apparently sorting documents.

Richard took no notice of them. 'I gave you clear instructions, I think. The chosen orator, Dr Edmund Shaw, was to preach on the text Bastard Slips Shall Take No Root. He was to explain to the assembled citizens the facts of my brother Edward's previous contract of marriage with Lady Eleanor Butler, daughter of the Earl of Shrewsbury as we now learn that she was, and the implications for the succession.'

'Yes, my lord. And that was what Dr Shaw did,' Buckingham pointed out.

'He certainly did. Under instructions which you gave him and which purported to come from me. Tell me, Buckingham, when did I recommend that while he was about it he was to resurrect Clarence's slander that King Edward was illegitimate himself?'

'I feared that the secret marriage might not be enough.' Buckingham, to his own annoyance, quelled an inclination to stammer. Gloucester had become remarkably formidable during the last few weeks. On the way from the north, when Buckingham joined him at Northampton, he had been, at first, grateful for help. He had been changing for the worse ever since. 'Lawyers can be clever. They might find someone to say that the contract was no more than a betrothal and was repudiated by both parties before the marriage to the Queen. But if King Edward himself had no right to the throne . . .'

'No lawyer is likely to go to such trouble unless he is paid to and no one is proposing to make any such payments, I assure you, Buckingham. You don't appear to have thought this out very thoroughly.'

Buckingham, meeting his lord's cold eyes, found that they made him feel as if all his titles, and the satin and jewellery he wore, had suddenly become of no value, as though he himself were nothing but a schoolboy caught in a misdemeanour, such as squirting cherry stones out of an upstairs window at bare-headed passers by. Richard was inches the shorter of the two and sitting down anyway, and yet he seemed to tower above his erring henchman. The man Buckingham had taken for King Edward's worthy, overshadowed brother, a mere royal stand-in, had overnight become . . .

A king. Whether he was entitled to be a king or not was hardly to the point. He was one, like it or not.

'I thought it was necessary for your sake to make sure . . .'

'What you have managed to ensure, Buckingham, is that a large proportion of the citizens will now also feel that the doubt about the Woodville marriage isn't enough on its own. They'll be thinking that the Council and I are remarkably anxious to back it up with other arguments. Their good taste has also been offended. May I remind you that King Edward's mother, whom you have traduced in public, is also my mother? And this house where we now are, is her property?'

'I . . .'

'I have spoken to Dr Shaw,' said Richard. 'I told him how surprised I was that he, a learned doctor of divinity, brother of the Lord Mayor, should lend himself to such a shabby scheme. He is now so ashamed that I don't think he'll show his face in daylight for months. As for you, you are to make a speech of your own on my behalf tomorrow. You will be kind enough to keep your tongue off my mother.'

'I merely meant . . .'

'I know, Buckingham, I know. You only meant to put my claim beyond dispute. You can't. I shall have to spend my whole reign knowing that behind my back certain factions are whispering the word "usurper". I must keep my brother's sons out of sight, prisoners, for the whole of their lives and even at that they will be for ever a possible focus of

450

rebellion. In spite of the examples I have made, I'm afraid that their mother may attempt to intrigue on their behalf. Bess Woodville regards me as Beelzebub personified,' said Richard with sour amusement. 'She continues to cower in sanctuary, I think because she really believes that if she came out, I would have her beheaded. I really am not in the habit of beheading women – I only made Jane Shore do penance – and as for executing my brother's . . . let us continue to be polite and call her his widow . . . can you imagine it? But Bess apparently can imagine it and as the boys grow to manhood, the danger of conspiracy will become greater, not less. There are times when I wish from the bottom of my heart that they would simply die of plague. I shall never be free of having to guard my back. I may as well accept it and so had you. Tomorrow, my friend, be careful what you say.'

Buckingham went out. The heat of anger and embarrassment flamed in his face. He knew now where he stood with Richard. He was a subordinate, that was all, to be praised or rebuked at his master's will, in the hearing of others, if Richard so chose.

Who did Richard think he was? Buckingham was of royal blood, a descendant of Edward the Third, just as much as he, and Buckingham had served him well.

Deep in Harry Buckingham's mind an idea stirred and took shape, a tenuous shape as yet and a disturbing one, but decidedly interesting. That, surely, would make Richard value him as he should be valued. And if it didn't . . .

The idea solidified a little, lifted more of its outline into the light. It was a very serpent of an idea, a beautiful, wicked, sinuous viper of a scheme and when in his mind he touched it, it gave him the same shuddering pleasure that once he had experienced when he locked his hands round Catherine Woodville's throat and saw the terror in her eyes.

The new quarters which he and his younger brother had been given were well furnished, everything in them being either embroidered or inlaid with gold or silver or ivory. But for a princes' home it was small. The Garden Tower was like a modest house in size: bedchamber above, a room below in which to sit or study, and a twisting stair between. Outside, as the Tower's name suggested, there was a garden, with a herb patch and rosebushes, and an archery target at which they could practise shooting.

It was not exactly an unsuitable place for the young King of England to inhabit, but it was not quite right either, and it definitely wasn't the same thing as the Royal Apartments.

He had suspected from the first why they had been moved. And now he knew, for certain. And his previous suspicion, he discovered, did not cushion the shock.

Completely white, the blood gone even from his lips, Edward heard that he was Edward Quintus no longer. He stood stiffly facing his uncle Richard of Gloucester. His small brother watched them, not quite understanding. Uncle Gloucester's face was expressionless and his voice carefully formal as he explained the circumstances. When he had done, Edward forced his lips to move.

'It's all lies.'

'No. I am sorry, Edward.'

'My father and my mother were married. I am their lawful son. I am! Who will take my crown now?'

As if he didn't know.

'The Council has requested me as your father's only surviving brother – and also in view of the attainder of treason on the family of the Duke of Clarence – to accept this – this inheritance. I would say burden, but to you that would no doubt sound like hyprocrisy.'

'I'm a bastard, then. That's official?'

'You . . . yes.'

'So,' said Edward deliberately and giving the word another meaning, 'are you.'

The Duke of Buckingham had accompanied Gloucester. He was standing back, near the door. He made an angry exclamation. Gloucester turned to him. 'We must go.'

As they went out, Buckingham said: 'You are right, my

lord. That boy will be dangerous as he grows older. He will intrigue from behind the Tower walls, unless you chain him in the deepest dungeon.'

'He's ailing,' said Richard wistfully.

'The younger boy isn't. He'll learn from his brother.'

'I know. People are already saying that I intend to do away with them. Sometimes, Buckingham, I feel so tired I wish I had never been born.'

The Abbot of Westminster's house was well-appointed and – like the Garden Tower – had a pleasant plot of land attached. But Bess Woodville and her family, used to parks and palaces, found it constricted. All the same, thought her daughter, Elizabeth of York, the comforts might be more noticeable and the inconveniences less so, if only her mother would harp less persistently on how miserable they all were.

Elizabeth was not yet seventeen and life in an atmosphere of heavy mourning irked her. Had the mourning been solely for her dead father, she could have shared it, but her mother's thoughts did not seem to be with King Edward now.

The days were all alike. At dawn, the family rose for Mass. Her mother would awake sighing: 'Another wretched day to face.' She said it every morning and the constant repetition had rubbed a sore place in Elizabeth's mind. She had to clench her fists to keep from crying out: 'Stop saying that!' After Mass, her mother would indulge – there was really no other word for it – in half an hour or so of praying aloud, reciting her wrongs at the hands of her foolish relatives and the iniquitous Gloucester, and pleading for divine protection from the said Gloucester.

The domestic pursuits of the day would then begin, but it was Elizabeth who chivvied the servants into dusting the rooms and her sisters into conning their books or plying their needles. Bess Woodville spent most of the time staring hopelessly out of the window at the river. Elizabeth had to keep the younger children from disturbing her with noise. If they did, she might break her silence with angry demands for peace and quiet.

Meals were landmarks of a sort in the monotonous days. Elizabeth usually organised those as well. She was half angry with her mother and half afraid of her. Once or twice she said: 'Mother, I'm sure Uncle Richard means us no harm.' But the answer was always the same. 'He's made you a bastard. Don't you call that harming you?'

When the news came that her Uncle Anthony and her half-brother Richard Grey were dead, Bess said: 'There you are. I told you so.'

Elizabeth, who had scarcely known either of them, said: 'Well, they did try to upset Father's will,' and for that remark earned a most un-regal clout from Bess.

Bess herself did not know for sure what she feared. She was like a mariner adrift without sails in uncharted waters. On the sixth of July, the day when her brother-in-law was crowned, she sat all morning thinking about him. She could not understand him; he was so unlike Edward.

There had been nothing complicated about Edward. He had visited her father just after the battle of Towton that made him King. He had been engaged in post-battle relaxation, hunting deer instead of men. She had been staying with her father, asking his advice on a lawsuit connected with her late husband's estates. She had gone to waylay Edward as he rode in, thinking that he, with his new royal power, might be of more help still. She had waited under a tree with her two young sons and, as the royal party approached, she stepped forward. Edward drew rein. He had seen what she meant him to see: an enchanting vision of womanliness: downcast eyes which glanced up at him just once, as their owner rose from her curtsy, and in them a shy appreciation of his masculine beauty, while on either side of her stood a child, enhancing her female helplessness with their own, and guaranteeing her that most feminine of accomplishments, fertility.

What she had seen had been similarly enchanting. He was young and superlatively made, and he had about him already that gloss, that air of being more than life-size, which stamped a leader. Except for the minor hitch that he was looking for a mistress while she wished to be a wife, theirs had been a simple courtship.

But marriage had meant the position of queen, had meant the court and the Nevilles. And Richard of Gloucester.

Before she got the crown, she had craved it. Secretly, she admitted that now. The prospect had enthralled her. She couldn't even be sure that her virtue would have withstood Edward, but for the tantalising crown to encourage her. But once married and acknowledged . . .

Used to great physical beauty in their own family, the Nevilles were not much impressed by hers. What impressed a Neville were wealth and breeding and Bess had neither in the quantities they thought proper for a queen. They did not hide their opinions. As for Richard, she had known at once that he hated her influence over his brother. And worse, if the Nevilles had been unimpressed by her feminine aura, Richard was apparently entirely unconscious of it. Even in Neville eyes she just occasionally saw a glint of acknowledgement, but never in Richard's. He had at one time made what she understood to be an attempt to accept her, but the deaths of Desmond and his sons had ended that. Since then, she had never met his eyes without seeing his contempt in them, and he had never exchanged with her anything more than empty – or edged – civilities. She had no means to reach him, for her only strategies were those of womanliness. Dropped eyelids and a gently modulated voice, studied deference to the male, carefully displayed maternal devotion and exquisite dress apparently had no effect whatsoever on Richard.

What Richard liked was Anne Neville, that brown sparrow of a girl, whose childbearing record was pitiful and whose nature had something hard and rasping beneath the surface. Neville pride, perhaps. Anne had missed the effulgent Neville looks, just as Richard himself had. But yes, she had all their pride, Bess thought. She clearly did not consider herself to be in any way Bess's inferior, and in Richard's eyes she was not.

But it wasn't natural, Bess almost wailed to herself, for a man to be so indifferent to all the things that made a woman womanly. It was worse than the contempt, for that at least she could understand. The indifference was incomprehensible, and in her eyes rendered him both abnormal and inimical.

It had not surprised her when he turned into the frightening figure who had killed her brother and her son. It had not surprised her when, as if by magic, he had conjured up proof that she and Edward had never truly been married. Somewhere deep within her she had always had a fear that one day someone, somehow would undermine her marriage. Of course it had proved to be Richard. It would be.

She did not know whether she feared for herself at Gloucester's hands. He had killed Hastings too – Hastings who after all had shown himself her friend – and he must know that she had been in touch with Hastings. But Hastings' other fellow-conspirators were still alive. Visitors were allowed at the sanctuary and she had learned from them that Thomas Stanley was out of prison. Richard, indeed, appeared to be wooing the Stanleys. Thomas's wife Margaret Beaufort had a place of honour at today's coronation.

But she dared not find reassurance in that. In Bess's mind, her brother-in-law Gloucester, who today had been crowned King, remained and always would remain a dark spectre, the unknown. Who, being unknown, might do anything.

Towards the end of that coronation day a new visitor was announced.

The sanctuary was guarded. Give that Woodville woman a ghost of a chance, Buckingham had warned Richard, and she'd be over the Channel and hawking her sorrows, not to mention her daughters, round half Europe. 'It'll be: "give me men and arms to restore my little sons and you or any kinsman you name can marry their sister Elizabeth".'

The French would hardly need encouraging. 'Francis of Brittany is looking like an enemy these days. He's harbouring Thomas Grey,' was Brampton's contribution.

But although all who left the sanctuary were carefully scrutinised, few callers were denied and certainly not Reginald Bray, the steward of Lady Margaret Beaufort, not now that the Stanleys were once again respectable.

Bray was a quiet-spoken man with round brown eyes which never seemed to blink. He addressed Bess with careful deference and asked to speak with her privately.

'Take your sisters into the garden,' said Bess to Elizabeth.

But before they had been outside for long, clouds came up. Rain spattered on the grass, driving them all back indoors. Bray, however, was already taking his leave. It must have been only a brief call. Bess was giving him her hand to kiss, but Elizabeth, coming in, stopped short at the sight of her mother's face. She had never seen anyone's face look like that before. So calm and yet so anguished, as though Bess were suffering something that was beyond expression.

'I am sorry, madam,' Bray was saying gravely, 'to be the bearer of such distressing rumours. Let us hope they are not true. If that proves to be so, no one will be better pleased than my lady, or I. But if the worst has happened . . . My lady asks that you think where you would stand in this. She is willing to be your friend, if you will be hers and her son's.'

'What's happened?' Elizabeth asked her mother after Bray had gone. 'What is it? Why do you look like that?'

'It may not be true. I can't speak of it. Don't ask me to, Elizabeth.'

Her mother went away then into her private chamber. Later, Elizabeth heard her sobbing.

Chapter Thirty-One

The Plantagenets: The Snake Uncoils

July 1483

'You heard Dr Alcock's suggestion at this morning's Council,' said Richard to Buckingham. 'An excellent idea. If either or both those boys in the Tower could be induced to take priestly orders, we'd all sleep easier and I can stop praying for them to catch convenient diseases. Nor would I have to contemplate the prospect of one day being forced to execute them, when they're grown men. A sworn celibate can't found a dynasty. They wouldn't be half so attractive to potential plotters then. They ought to have a tutor and confessor anyway, and since Alcock is now unacceptable to them and refuses to try to change that, we need someone new. Someone discreet. I've given orders that they're to be kept from the public gaze, on the principle of out of sight, out of mind. Whoever teaches them must undertake not to carry messages or discuss his pupils with anybody else. My Progress starts tomorrow and therefore I can't deal with this myself. But as you're staying in London for a while to finish some private business, perhaps you'd see to this at the same time.'

That night, Harry Buckingham dreamed about a snake.

He had actually only seen one in his life, when out hawking in Brecknock. It had been basking on a flat rock and his horse had shied at it. But he had never forgotten it: the pattern of its scales and the gleam of its eyes. He had found it both alarming and attractive.

The snake in his dream was long and slim and silvery, its head raised from the midst of its coils and its ruby eyes watching him. He laid his palm against the cold, shining body and again he experienced that dreadful delight, the knowledge of being able to inspire terror, and to kill.

He did not fear this snake and it did not mind his touch. It was his. And if he asked it, it would do his killing.

When he woke, he knew the snake for what it was; his idea, ready for him at last, its fangs his to command and coil upon coil of delicious ramifications hidden beneath that sweet, evil, little head.

He had the opportunity now to carry it out but he would of course need help. There were things the Duke of Buckingham could hardly attend to in person, but that problem was easy enough to solve.

In every great household, among the soldiers who accompanied its master everywhere, among the servants and especially in that amorphous group of them whose duties were ill-defined, who were simply hands, feet and voices to be used for any task which presented itself, there were always a few men who were euphemistically known as 'reliable'.

The matter was not discussed. No steward, no Captain of the Guard, no bailiff or head groom was ever actually told that it was his duty to see that he had one or two such men among those he hired. But it happened. Buckingham, back in his London house, called his personal page and said he required two reliable men for a delicate and disagreeable task. The page transmitted this request to various household officials, and in due course candidates appeared.

The first to present themselves were not suitable. A cautious interview revealed that they might have, well, scruples. Buckingham shook his head, said that he needed someone with – he searched his mind for a sufficiently misleading attribute – more knowledge of the geography of northern England, and dismissed them.

The next two came in together. They were friends who had entered his employment together, they said, and they understood that he needed men who knew the north. They had both formerly been employed as hired escorts to travellers in that part of England and they thought they might do. Further probing revealed that they had no scruples whatsoever. It was a hard world, they said, and a man had to be hard to make his way in it. If the rate of pay were right, they did what they were hired to do and asked no questions.

'The rate of pay will be right,' said Buckingham. 'But if ever you speak of the task I shall set you, even in the confessional, be warned. I shall hear of it and then you will do the paying, and with your lives. The business in hand is not mine but the King's. It requires absolute, unquestioning loyalty and ruthlessness.' They were quiet, thick-shouldered men with steady, unsmiling, unrevealing eyes. Their faces did not change. 'And knowledge of the north is not, in fact, necessary,' said Buckingham. 'Now listen . . .'

Buckingham was Constable of England and in his possession was what Richard called a representative selection of the Tower keys. This didn't, as it chanced, include the key to the boys' new apartments. It was rather awkward, Buckingham thought, that they had now been moved from the Garden Tower back to the inner keep. He had keys for the Garden Tower all right. If only he had had the chance to act just a few days sooner. He approached the difficulty with caution, but it proved almost absurdly easy to resolve.

'Brackenbury, did Dr Alcock have a key to the young Lord Edward's quarters while he was still the boy's tutor?'

'Yes, sir.'

'In that case, the new tutor should have one. There's to be a new appointment shortly. He'll be teaching them both.'

'Good. Those boys need regular occupation.' Sir Robert Brackenbury was one of the cultured breed of knight, as Sir Anthony Woodville had been. He considered that a man should have knowledge in his head as well as muscles in his body, and that an appreciation of poetry and music were the mark of a gentleman. 'The elder boy, in particular,' he said. 'He's never quite well, it's true, but a steady routine of lessons might help him. Is it known yet who the tutor will be?'

'A learned priest but no final choice has so far been made. I propose to bring a possibility to see the boys tomorrow. Please have a key ready by then. I'll take charge of it personally and hand it over when an appointment is definite.'

'You're accompanying the candidate yourself?'

'Yes. The King has been good enough to place the appointment in my hands. And of course,' said Buckingham, 'I'm the boys' uncle.'

'Their uncle?' Brackenbury was momentarily puzzled.

'By marriage. My wife is their mother's sister.'

'Oh yes. Of course. Should you have a key of your own, my lord? I would have to obtain authorisation, of course, but in view of the relationship . . .'

'No, thank you,' said Buckingham virtuously. 'The King has wisely decided to limit the number of keys in circulation and I don't wish to interfere with that. The tutor's key, of course, is official. You may expect us at ten o'clock tomorrow morning. The King has signed a pass.'

The new quarters were the third set of rooms that the boys had occupied in the Tower of London. They were actually more spacious than the Garden Tower had been, but the furnishings this time were second-rate. The hangings and chairs were only of fair quality, clothes had to be stored in a scarred old arrow chest, and if their mattress was of down, the bed itself was decidedly ancient.

Moreover, they were hardly ever allowed into the open air now. 'The King's orders are that you're to be kept out of the public eye,' Brackenbury had told them. 'It's thought best for everyone, you included.' On the rare occasions when they did go outside, a Captain of Archers always came with them. They were allowed to practise archery or play with a ball perhaps for an hour and then they must come back inside. They had no visitors apart from Sir Robert Brackenbury himself and they had only one servant. True, it was Will Slaughter, who had looked after Edward when he first came to London, and certainly he took good care of them, even cooking for them in a small kitchen attached to their chambers, and worrying about Edward's sore gums. But he was a man of limited outlook, and worse, he had been forbidden to act as a channel of communication to anyone outside and refused to disobey orders.

'It 'ud be as much as my job's worth if I were to take messages, Lord Edward.' That was another thing. He was forbidden to address Edward by his proper title. 'Your lady mother's still in sanctuary, that much I know and can tell you, and the King's off on his first Progress round the country, showing hisself to the people. But more than that I can't say.'

Edward missed Dr Alcock.

Alcock had always taught him to respect the law and cultivate the virtue of obedience, but Edward had the oddest feeling that Alcock was capable of throwing any amount of laws and virtues out of the window if he felt that by doing so, he could serve some nobler cause. Alcock, he was sure, would have carried innocent messages at least, and he wouldn't have been caught at it, either.

But Alcock had defended that murderer, that usurper, Uncle Richard of Gloucester. Edward had sworn never to speak another word to him and he would keep his oath, though the sense of bereavement was great. He had lost enough people who were dear to him; it was hard to have to do without his tutor as well. His ulcerated gums pained him and refused to heal despite the mouthwashes recommended by Dr Argentine, whom Brackenbury had once or twice consulted on Edward's behalf, although the doctor, like everyone else, was forbidden to come in person. Edward was miserable and in bed at night he sometimes cried, although he tried not to as it upset his little brother.

Little Dickon was by nature light of heart and Edward did not want to dampen his spirits. Indeed, he almost fed on them. 'Oh no, Dickon,' he said once, when his own depression had made the smaller boy tearful, 'don't you take to crying too. If I didn't have you to laugh and make me play games sometimes, I couldn't bear it.'

But it was very difficult to keep up any kind of cheerful pretence for long at a time, for there was something else, too, something that he must on no account attempt to share with Dickon.

He could say to Dickon: 'I'm crying about my father, or Uncle Anthony, or losing my inheritance.' But from this other thing, he must guard his brother with all his might.

He had once, cautiously, tried to raise it with Brackenbury but Brackenbury had been so horrified that he hadn't tried again. 'Danger? Here? Most certainly not. I am charged with ensuring your safety as well as your privacy. Whatever put it into your head that you're in danger? From whom?'

'Uncle Richard. We'll be dangerous to him one day and he knows that.'

'Even the King of England can't order me to harm you or allow harm to come to you. This is nonsense, my boy, and a slur on my integrity,' said Brackenbury indignantly.

But it wasn't nonsense. Lying awake in the night, looking into the darkness, *feeling* the Tower all round him with the thick stone walls which had hidden so many cruel secrets since William the Conqueror built the first of them over five hundred years ago, he sensed the approach of menace. He had been isolated, hadn't he, cut off along with Dickon from visitors, from the right to communicate or even be seen? Things could happen to them and who would know? Brackenbury seemed trustworthy but other men had been bought, or threatened, or hoodwinked.

And then, at last, they had visitors.

The arrival of his Uncle Buckingham, with a pass from the King and a priest who was introduced as a possible replacement for Dr Alcock, was a surprise and at least a distraction, although he didn't like Uncle Buckingham very much and didn't like the prospective new tutor at all. His uncle's walk was too much like a swagger and always had been, and as for the priest, he was pasty of face and hardly spoke to Edward or Dickon direct but kept on talking about them to Buckingham instead, as if they were deaf. He and Dickon learned to their outrage that 'they would benefit from wholesome discipline and plain wholesome food' and that 'their tender minds should be nourished by wholesome books.' He kept on using the word wholesome and made it sound threatening.

Uncle Buckingham, of course, had not arrived unattended. Their very first visitor since they changed apartments was actually a cloud of visitors. Apart from the priest, Uncle Buckingham had two men with him. He addressed them as Master Dighton and Master Forrest. They were quiet, powerfully-made, neatly dressed, respectful but watchful. They peered about the room as though they were Uncle Buckingham's bodyguard, suspecting assassins behind the arras. Buckingham asked Will Slaughter to show him and the priest round the apartments and the two men came along as well. They stared at every detail, and at Edward and Dickon, with calm, expressionless eyes. It came into Edward's head that a mouse must feel much as he did now, when it knew itself observed by an owl or a cat. They had watchful eyes like these.

He tried very hard not to pursue this thought. It was something else he must not share with Dickon.

He had longed for more company but now understood that there are visitors and visitors. He was glad when these left. The day then relapsed into the pattern which was becoming familiar and which he had thought tedious. Perhaps it wasn't as bad as he had supposed. It would certainly be much worse under that tutor. Once more, he longed for Dr Alcock.

The day had turned wet. There was no chance of even a

little outdoor play and his mouth was in any case feeling sore again. He used the latest mouthwash, which was slightly less revolting than its predecessor, and tried to play with Dickon. But any kind of running about made his gums throb again and the game petered out. Dickon, disappointed, sat down to read, swinging his legs glumly from the edge of a settle. Edward looked out of the window but there was little to see beyond a patch of wet grass, a length of grey wall, and a staircase which was under repair. There was also a mound of timber and stone for the repairs, protected from the rain beneath roped-down oxhides, and unpleasant to behold because it was from that pile that the log had been dragged on which Hastings was beheaded.

He glanced away, towards the staircase, and saw that it led up to a chapel. He and Dickon hadn't even heard Mass since they had left the Garden Tower. Alcock would be horrified if he knew. The new tutor, he supposed, would take that over.

There was a meal, time for prayers with Will, and then they must go to bed, although it was still quite light, in the curtained four-poster. Will had a truckle bed beside them. Slowly, the evening faded into darkness.

The rain had ceased. Later in the night, the moon came out and a shaft of moonlight found its way through a gap in the curtains. Edward awoke. He put out a hand to close the curtains and then stopped, taut, heart drumming.

With cautious slowness, as though someone were trying to make as little noise as possible, the door which led out to their living chamber was opening.

Will had awakened too. His bed creaked and Edward saw his shadow as he sat up. 'Who's there?' Will's voice was low, but it sounded alarmed.

Then the door swung back and there were people in the room. Wide-eyed and shaking under his rugs, Edward saw two shadowy figures yank the struggling Will from his bed. His outcry faded, as if he had been gagged. Edward thought they were binding him.

Then they came towards the four-poster. He shouted for help, knowing that no one could hear him through the thick Tower walls. The faces of the intruders were horrifying in the moonlight: dark, masked blanks. Dickon woke and screamed as well, and equally in vain.

A mailed fist struck Edward's painful jaw and the agony of it exploded inside his head. Then the sheets and rugs were being flung around him, bundling him like a package. In the moonlight he saw the white pillow raised above his face.

He fought for his life. During the first few seconds, he was aware that beside him Dickon was fighting too. Then there was no more Dickon, only himself and his own torment of starved and straining lungs and drumming ears, his own wild battle for breath, for manhood, for life even as a poor unknown man, a servant, a slave, just to live. Oh God, let me live! Not the darkness, not yet, not yet, no no no . . .

And then the pain was over and he was sliding, sliding, and the darkness had received him.

The old arrow chest which had done duty for a clothes press now provided a coffin. And the hollow under the chapel staircase outside, which the workmen had excavated in order to reach the unsteady structure they had come to repair, made a convenient grave. The repairs were complete and the workmen had already begun filling in the cavity with rubble. It was only necessary to shift some of this to make room, and then pile it back to hide the chest from sight.

The staircase was in a small tower of its own which screened their activities from any overlooking window. It was safer than carrying the chest any distance in the moonlight. But rubble could not be moved in total silence and the lanterns they had brought cast misleading shadows so that now and then they tripped or set a stone down awry. Every time a piece of rubble grated, they stopped, tense, waiting to hear if anyone had been disturbed. They were sweating heavily before they had finished.

But no window creaked open, no indignant voice challenged them. They came out of the staircase tower and whispered to each other.

'The room. The servant.'

'Yes. I reckon.'

Back in the boys' apartments, Will Slaughter lay bound where they had left him. His terrified eyes looked up at them over the cloth that stopped his mouth, as they knelt beside him and one of them drew a knife. 'Don't worry,' said the latter soothingly, as he cut the rope which bound Will's hands. 'You won't be hurt. We'll leave you to cut your own feet free. Then you can raise the alarm. You're going to have to do the explaining, my friend. With just a little bit of luck, Brackenbury'll think you did it. He's bound to want to know where the boys are and you won't be able to tell him, will you? You may have to face a bit of questioning. Down in the dungeons as like as not. We'll leave you the knife, where you'll have to roll to reach it. We want just a little bit of a start.'

When they had gone, Will tore the gag from his face, lurched across the floor to the knife and feverishly sawed himself free. He was in a frenzy of grief and fear and urgency. The grief was for his murdered charges but the fear and urgency were for Will Slaughter. He would indeed be questioned and he knew all about the methods available for making such enquiries. He knew what the dungeons were like, too. He had been employed at the Tower since childhood. He was very well acquainted with it.

Well enough to know how to get out of the place, even in the dark, without keys. The assassins had apparently had keys to the doors they wanted. Will had not, but he knew where to lay his hands on a coil of rope in an unlocked lumber room, and where to find a poorly patrolled length of wall with a crenellation to which the rope could be attached. He was a young man and fairly athletic. He succeeded in letting himself down, thankful now for the darkness because it kept him from seeing the drop. He still had to cross the moat, but this could be done by a little swimming and a good deal of wading. Despite a dredging operation three years before, the moat still sank markedly when the tide was down and it was ebbtide now.

By morning, Will Slaughter had vanished into the crowded tenements of the City. He had loved his charges but he could not help them now. He could only save himself.

Chapter Thirty-Two

The Plantagenets: The Most Untrue Creature Living

1483

'When your Progress halts in Oxford,' Richard's old friend Francis Lovell had said, 'my home at Minster Lovell will be only a few miles off. Spend a day or two with me. We've the best stocked dovecot in the country. Mine's a peaceful sort of place. I don't remember our Middleham boyhood as nostalgically as you do. As I recall it, the place was always cold. The climate in Oxfordshire is better.'

'I'd welcome a day or two just listening to doves,' Richard said to Alcock and Brampton as the Progress, a mile-long serpent of horsemen, baggage animals and carts laden with bedding, plate, clothes chests and comestibles, clattered, jingled, rumbled and whinnied its way into Oxford. 'I shall accept. It will be a private visit. I shall take only a small household, but I wish both of you to be part of it. You're restful company.'

Richard needed rest, Alcock thought, examining the King's haggard face. He hadn't recovered from the horrors of the summer. Richard was not a man who could order the deaths of former friends and not suffer for it, nor was his crown precisely an unalloyed triumph. If Minster Lovell were all that Francis Lovell claimed, it might indeed be good for him.

They arrived on a sunny afternoon. The house was built of grey stone, standing round three sides of a broad, grassy square. On the fourth side was a landing stage and a smoothly flowing river. Recently, to add both to the security and the consequence of the house, Francis had had a new tower and guardroom built overlooking the water and these were imposingly battlemented. It made not the slightest difference. The essential character of Minster Lovell was drowsy, especially on warm July afternoons. The river curled by, swans sailed on it with their cygnets, dragonflies skimmed, the doves murmured.

'One of the reasons why I do not get homesick for Portugal,' said Edward Brampton, surveying the house as he sat on his horse in between Sir James Tyrell and Master Lionel Eynesby, who were also present as part of Richard's household, 'is because in England there are places like this. Nowhere is there a summer so green and kind as here.'

They were awaiting their turns to dismount and have their horses led away. The service was willing but very slightly casual. 'Aye,' said Lionel Eynesby, 'but too much of this sort of living would make a man soft, given time.'

But in that softness, and during the easy, informal feast later on, Richard's taut face began to relax. Francis's wife Nan, who had a reputation for ill-temper, was not at the Minster and nothing marred the merriment. The resident minstrel was tuneful and the food, if not elaborate, still good.

'I feel as if I would like to stay here for ever,' said Richard the following afternoon.

He leant his elbows on a first-floor window sill, looking down on to the grassy square. Down there, Francis Lovell and James Tyrell were attempting to defy the sleepiness of the afternoon by giving some not too serious instruction in swordplay to the boys of the household. Every now and then a vanquished swordsman would roll in the grass in histrionic death throes and not trouble to get up, but loll there instead, inhaling the scent of warm grass or watching ants. Alcock, sitting beside Richard with one hip perched on the window seat, watched with amusement. 'I think I should introduce some exercise hours into my school at Hull. They benefit health and good temper.' He had fulfilled his ambition to found a school, some years previously, choosing his home town of Hull for it. He was constantly thinking of improvements. Concentration on the curriculum of Hull Grammar School had been his refuge from the sorrow of it when young Edward rejected him.

'Who wants exercise on a day like this?' said Richard. 'Is saying that a first sign of middle age, Alcock?'

'Call it a sign of maturity, my lord. You are appreciating the value of a calm, ordered life, perhaps.'

Behind them, a door opened. 'My lord,' said one of Lovell's esquires, 'I have here a messenger from London, Master John Grene from the Tower. He desires to see King Richard personally. He says it's urgent.'

'Then bring him in,' said Richard. His face wore a look which Alcock knew, although one rarely saw it on adult faces. It was the expression of an obedient child called from play to a hated lesson; dutiful but reluctant.

The esquire looked over his shoulder and beckoned, and Master John Grene came in. He looked doubtfully at Alcock. 'My lord King, I am the personal courier of Sir Robert Brackenbury, Constable of the Tower of London. One of my duties, on occasion, is to memorise confidential messages, repeat them to the man to whom they are addressed and then forget them. My lord . . .'

'You may speak in Dr Alcock's presence,' said Richard. 'Whatever the message may be.'

'Very well, sir,' said John Grene, and then recited his message. When he had finished, there was silence in the room. Outside, doves still murmured and shouts and laughter still echoed from below, but neither Richard nor Alcock heard them.

'Let me be sure I understand,' said Richard at last. 'Your master, Sir Robert Brackenbury, when he made his rounds of the Tower yesterday morning, found that the apartments where the late King Edward's natural sons were housed were empty. Neither they nor their servant were there. The bedding was in disarray as though there had been a struggle of some kind. When a search of the Tower was made, again by Sir Robert personally, a rope was found dangling over an outside wall. But he raised no public alarm and will not do so until he hears from me, because he wishes to know . . . to know . . .'

'Yes, sir. He wishes to know whether . . .' John Grene met Richard's eyes and faltered, but at length went steadily on '. . . whether the boys' disappearance is known to you, sir, and was on your orders. My apologies, by the way, my lord, for having taken so long to reach you. I had to follow you from Oxford.'

'Never mind about that. My brother's sons have vanished out of the Tower and Sir Robert Brackenbury thinks I might have arranged it?'

John Grene said stonily: 'I have repeated the words of the message, sir.'

Outside, the swordsmen's voices had ceased. A horse neighed somewhere and there were shouts of greeting and command, and a clatter of hooves.

There was disturbance enough to penetrate Alcock's stunned brain. He looked out of the window. 'My lord, the Duke of Buckingham has just ridden in.'

'Buckingham!' said Richard. He seized a handbell from a table and rang it furiously for service. The esquire reappeared.

'My lord of Buckingham has just arrived,' said Richard. 'No doubt he will wish to be brought to us, and our wish is that he be summoned here at once. Take Master Grene and see that he has refreshment.'

As the two went out, Alcock turned questioning eyes to Richard.

'Wait,' said Richard, 'you'll soon see what is in my mind.'

Buckingham, despite the commanding nature of the summons, took his time. When at length he came, Alcock saw at once that whatever reasons Richard had for his obvious suspicions, they were assuredly good ones. Harry

Buckingham's fair, handsome face wore a look of ineffable content. 'He's like a cat that's eaten someone's pet popinjay,' thought Alcock in disgust.

'We left you in London, Harry,' said Richard shortly, 'with instructions to arrange a tutor for my brother's natural sons, and with a pass by which to obtain access to them. A courier from Sir Robert Brackenbury now informs us that they have vanished. Can you throw any light on the matter?'

Buckingham, who had just knelt before Richard, straightened himself quickly. His face became startled. But it was a look less of complete surprise than of surprise and wariness mingled. Again, Alcock was reminded of a cat. This time, one which has heard a dog snarl close at hand.

'Vanished, my lord?' said Buckingham politely.

Tersely, Richard explained the details. Buckingham's eyebrows rose. 'From the sound of it, the servant Will Slaughter was bribed or coerced to do whatever was done and has now escaped, no doubt down the rope that was mentioned.'

'Will Slaughter was personally selected by me,' said Alcock. 'He was also adequately paid. His life was not open to blackmail and I have no doubt at all of his affection for his charges. I refuse to believe that Will Slaughter was responsible.'

'But if the boys have indeed vanished . . .' began Buckingham smoothly.

'If? Unless Brackenbury has gone mad and is seeing things that aren't there, or not seeing things that are there,' said Richard, 'they have certainly vanished. I gave you a pass to visit them, Buckingham. Did anyone else use that pass, by any chance? Did you at any point have the key to the boys' apartments in your hands? If so, did you lend it?'

'I was going to say,' said Buckingham in a very gentle voice, 'that if the boys have indeed disappeared, my lord, might it not be for the best?'

There was silence.

My boy, Alcock was thinking. My dear boy, my Edward, my almost-son. The mind I fed and trained, the valiant, dignified lad with the ailing body which nonetheless had a king growing up inside it. The boy who trusted me. The lad I loved.

He looked at Buckingham and did not know how angry his own eyes were. *You*, Alcock was thinking, *was it you?* Buckingham caught his eye and flinched.

'Don't be afraid to tell me the truth,' Richard was saying, in tones of horrifying cynicism. 'There won't be any reprisals. I'd look a nice fool, wouldn't I, sending you to the block for murdering my little incubi? I can hear the tavern talk now! They'd say that not content with killing my nephews, I've taken to killing my servants too.' At the word 'servants', Buckingham stiffened but Richard paid no heed. 'Your head is quite safe. So are your damned honours and estates and the freedom of your person. But I want the truth. Did you see to my nephews, or not?'

'As a matter of fact, I came to tell you about it although I would have preferred to do so more privately. Yes, my lord, I did. It needed doing. In a few years if not sooner, they would have been the centre of a rebellion. I understood that you couldn't give me direct orders to attend to them. But you implied it. You have said, more than once, how much you wished an outbreak of plague would relieve you of their presence. No doubt you have said it in the hearing of others besides myself. Perhaps I was just the first to decide to act on your behalf.'

'Thank you, Buckingham. We are extremely grateful for your thoughtfulness. You may go. We said we'd take no reprisals, but we're not obliged to tolerate your company. Get out!'

'My lord –'

'Out!' Richard's voice rose. 'Take your horse and your men and go to London or Brecknock or Hades but take yourself out of my sight and stay out of it until I recall you, which may not be within either of our lifetimes. Go now! I don't care if you're tired, I don't care if you're thirsty. Rest and drink elsewhere. You are the most untrue creature living. What are you standing there for? Didn't you hear me? *Go!*'

Whitening, Buckingham spun on his heel and went. Richard brought a clenched fist down on the nearest window ledge. 'Oh God, Alcock, they're dead!'

'Yes,' said Alcock. Dead, my Edward and the little boy who was his brother. God send it was quick, without fear or suffering. He might never know. There were not even any graves to visit.

'I did say it, you know.' Richard turned his back and stared out of the window again. 'I said I wished they'd fall ill, and I was afraid of the future. They'd always be dangerous. The elder boy hated me. Buckingham isn't guilty by himself. I'm culpable too.'

Alcock said nothing.

'You loved them. Well, one of them. Say what you like to me, Alcock. But say something, for God's sake say *something*!'

'When Prince Edward was born in sanctuary, his mother was afraid for him,' Alcock said. 'I thought it was only guilt – she felt guilty, you know, because of Desmond's sons. But perhaps it was more than that. Perhaps it was a kind of foreseeing. Perhaps it's even partly why she seems to fear you so much. Tell me,' the priest in Alcock took over automatically, 'when you made those comments about plague, did you hope someone would take them as a covert order? Did you mean to imply that you would be grateful, in lieu of an obliging epidemic, for a dagger in the dark instead?'

'No! I swear it, Alcock! No!'

'Before God do you swear it? Turn round and face me. Do you swear it in the name of the Father, the Son and the Holy Ghost?'

'Yes, I do so swear.' Richard sank down on to the window seat. He met Alcock's eyes. His body, however, seemed to have shrunk. 'But . . .'

'But?' prompted Alcock.

477

'I am sick with outrage. And I am also relieved. In years to come I and my own son will be the safer for this. I'm no saint, Alcock. I'm not even a good man although I've tried to be. I was as loyal as I knew how to be to my brother Edward – even though there were times when I felt he'd failed me. I'm still trying to be loyal, to rule as he would have me rule, to learn from my memories of him. But there is scarcely anyone else that I dare be loyal to now except for Anne! All the others, all of those who have power in my life, appear now to be enemies. The Woodvilles, Hastings, the boys themselves. All I can do is survive. It doesn't make for virtue, when you're continually spinning round and round to counter an attack from first this direction and then that. You don't have time to wonder if you're doing right. You do whatever you think may succeed. I didn't order the boys' deaths, Alcock. When I talked about plague, I wasn't giving veiled commands. The oath I swore just now was genuine. But don't imagine I haven't lain awake at night playing with the idea of getting rid of them. I've even thought of ways. Don't absolve me too easily.'

In Alcock's stomach there was a shivering. Hate the sin but not the sinner; he knew the rules. But none of the elder priests who had taught him his calling had ever foreseen this. He had never understood before that to be able to love also meant being able to hate. If he had not loved young Edward so much, he would not now be prey to such an intensity of loathing. He shuddered back from the man before him as if from some horrible deformity. He made himself speak quietly. 'What do you intend to do about Buckingham?'

'What can I do? He must stay out of my sight, that's all. I don't know how long for. I can't see ahead. Nothing in the world will bring the boys back now and nothing will ever convince the world that I wasn't responsible, will it?'

'No,' said Alcock, with a degree of grim satisfaction. 'You will have to carry the odium to your grave.'

And if you have realised that much, I'm glad. Go on, my

lord, blame yourself. Lie open-eyed at night and wonder if in your deepest heart you did indeed mean your words to be acted on. Agonise over it! Enter Purgatory here on earth and give me the pleasure of watching you.

So many times in the confessional, Alcock had heard people say: 'I didn't mean that to happen, Father. I was angry, I slapped the child, I pushed him. I didn't mean to make him deaf, I didn't mean to knock him over on a stone floor and break his arm.'

I didn't mean to kill him.

'But it isn't murder, is it, if you didn't mean to kill?' He had heard that said, too. He had said no, that God knew the secrets of all hearts. It was easy enough to comfort the murderer when the victim meant nothing to you. Now he found himself wishing that one day Richard should know bereavement as he, Alcock, was knowing it at this moment. He jerked his thoughts up short. There were things that even the most bereaved had no right to wish. Even the boys' mother was not entitled to such a prayer . . .

'Their mother certainly won't believe I didn't order their deaths,' said Richard. The cynical note was there again, with a vicious edge.

'She may believe it, one day. She has faced that accusation herself.' He watched that sink home and then grabbed once more at the handrail of his vocation. 'My lord, do not now set out to become what report will make you. God knows the truth, if no one else does. Make your peace with Him and compound your sin no further. As a king, you have recommended yourself to your subjects already, making yourself available along the road to Oxford to poor men seeking justice. Don't go back on that. You must set out to be the good lord to us all that you swore to be on your coronation day.'

'And you, Alcock? Will you remain on my Council? Or retreat to your cathedral in Worcester on a plea of advancing age and infirmity – or private but irreconcilable differences with your King?'

'I shall remain on your Council. If I withdrew, in the kind of climate that will shortly develop, as rumours of the disappearances begin to circulate, men would ask why. Any talk of irreconcilable differences would certainly make them think they'd guessed the answer! I wish to see a stable government and I have believed what you have told me. I shall do nothing to harm you or your administration.'

'You're a good friend, Alcock.'

'The inner Council had better be informed, privately, of the facts,' said Alcock. 'And now, if you will excuse me, I will go to the chapel. Alone.'

The parish church lay close to the house but the Lovells had a private chapel in the house itself. There, kneeling with his hands to his eyes in the stone-cool dimness from which the sun was excluded, he could yield to his grief. There, in solitude, John Alcock hallowed with tears and prayer the unknown graves of Edward Quintus and his brother, Dickon.

Dr John Morton, Bishop of Ely, under technical house arrest at Brecknock, had found his captivity not too rigorous. Respect for the Church perhaps accounted for this. He was even able to receive a letter from Margaret Beaufort. It spoke of scandalous rumours, and said that her husband Thomas Stanley was too afraid of Richard to be of much support to her and she hoped that should the gossip prove true, the Bishop of Ely would stand her friend and that of Queen Bess Woodville.

Gladly, thought Morton, if, that was to say, he was ever in a position again to stand anyone's friend. He hoped that when Harry Buckingham came home, his conditions of imprisonment would not alter for the worse.

But when Buckingham rode in, he came very quickly to Morton and led him to a quiet room free of eavesdroppers, and his manner was not at all that of a gaoler. It was more like that of a conspirator.

'My lord?' said Morton enquiringly.

'I've quarrelled with King Richard. Irrevocably.'

'Indeed. May I ask why?'

'The rumours,' said Buckingham. 'The rumours that he has murdered his brother's sons. You'd heard that such tales were going about?'

'Yes.'

'They're true,' said Buckingham. 'I taxed him with it. And he has admitted it.'

In the Abbot of Westminster's still commandeered house, Elizabeth of York stabbed a needle upright into a piece of embroidery like someone pinning a challenge to the floor with a dagger and said: 'It's all absurd. I know Uncle Richard can't have murdered my brothers. I will not give my word to marry this Henry Tudor. Margaret Beaufort and Dr Morton and Buckingham may all think it's a good idea but I do not! Why should I? If he ever gets to the throne it will only be because he killed Uncle Richard to reach it!'

'Your uncle has killed enough people, hasn't he?' snapped her mother. 'You don't seem to mind that. You are a foolish girl with a head full of rubbish.' Bess Woodville's nerves felt as though someone had been scrubbing them briskly with a handful of scouring grit. 'You'll marry where you're bidden.'

'And when and if.' Elizabeth hurled the embroidery down on to a table. 'Oh, I am so tired of this narrow place. I want to go to banquets and balls again. I want to dance with Uncle Richard again! He's the best dancer I've ever known except for my father. But I don't suppose he'll ever speak to any of us again, not after the things you've said about him!'

'To listen to you,' said Bess acidly, 'anyone would think you'd fallen in love with your own uncle.'

Elizabeth said nothing. Surprised by the silence, Bess turned to stare at her daughter. Elizabeth was standing by the table, sticking the needle in and out of the crumpled cushion cover she had been making. Her eyes were lowered

481

and her naturally pale face had turned the colour of holly berries.

'Sweet Jesu!' breathed Bess, but not aloud. The child had only had occasional glimpses of Richard since he left for the north when she was six years old. Once in a while, he had come briefly to court, or met them all at some midland castle; on one isolated occasion, he had personally visited them here. That was all.

Put a half-formed passion into words, and it may complete itself. But this could be no more than a fantasy. Better let it die away, into silence.

Chapter Thirty-Three

Petronel: The Drowned Rebellion

Autumn 1483

In that dramatic year of 1483, two things of note happened at Eynesby.

The first was that Perky Dick, now nearly ten years old, was sent away to complete his education in another household.

The second was that at sixty-seven Lionel began to feel the first real twinges of age and decided to defy them. He had gone to London with Richard of Gloucester as one of three hundred gentlemen in deep mourning who set out for the south with Gloucester when the news came that King Edward was dead. He came back with the new King Richard's Progress after having spent that nerve-racking summer in London in Richard's household, and he was exhausted. And in spite of that, he still rode off to join Richard in the field that autumn against the rebellion raised by Buckingham and Henry Tudor.

I never found it hard to part with Lionel. I found it very hard indeed to part with Perky Dick, though I endured it with outward calm. It had a good side, and that I was so well aware of this shows all too plainly how uneasy the preceding years had been.

It is the custom, of course, for boys and often for girls to finish their growing-up away from their parents. Parents are apt to spoil their children, that's the theory. But if circumstances had been different, I would have tried to delay Dick's departure. In the years since Geoffrey had gone, as I had expected, my son had been the only sweetness in my life. If there had ever been any hope at all of things coming right between Lionel and me, it died finally and for ever during the quarrel that threw me into Geoffrey's arms. And if there had been a patching-up when Perky Dick was born, 'patching' was all it was. I could not forget that quarrel.

But a new kind of disharmony began after Nicholas Hawes's terrifying visitation, when we learned that Geoffrey was dead. Shortly after that, Lionel said to me bluntly that he had concluded that I was unlikely to have any more children and henceforth we might as well sleep apart.

At first I was glad – glad of privacy in which to remember Geoffrey (and find that after all, I mourned him) and glad to be relieved of Lionel's attentions, or rather, his increasingly vain attempts at them. I supposed at first that he was making an excuse because his abilities were finally waning altogether.

But as time went on, I wondered about this. Again and again I would wake in the night, chilled with dread, and ask myself: does he know?

The signs were small but they were there. I would look up and find him watching me or Perky Dick in a curious, calculating fashion. And he made remarks. 'You'd better ask Petronel about that, Alison. She knows Lady Scrope better than I do. I'm right amazed at times, how well she gets to know people without me noticing.' Or: 'Don't argue, Petronel. Dick will be brought up as I say. Happen I'm *supposed* to be his father.'

I once asked Alison if she had let anything out to Lionel but she denied it and I believed her. I tried to convince myself that I was imagining things, but although he offered me no violence, the undercurrent gradually became so marked that this was quite impossible. Since I dared not challenge him, I took the opposite course, of avoiding confrontation at all costs. I adopted more than ever a policy of preserving an amiable and helpful face at all times, keeping the household smooth beyond reproach, entertaining guests with grace and courtesy.

Alison's health failed anew after Geoffrey died and she never regained it. When she too died, I shared Lionel's grief. If only I tried hard enough, I used to say to myself, I might one day actually come to believe that mine was a normal if businesslike marriage, and more to the point, Lionel might come to believe it too.

But instead he grew increasingly resentful over my small attempts to take an interest in Thornwood, my manor. Although I knew he disapproved, I had tried to visit it occasionally and get to know its people. Lionel now commenced a campaign of finding reasons to prevent my visits and finally told me outright that there was no need for me to go at all. He also kept me away from Middleham where he knew I was welcome. And then he took to being harsh with Perky Dick.

This alarmed me, especially as Dick's resemblance to Geoffrey was becoming more noticeable every year. To me, with my guilty knowledge, it seemed to trumpet the truth. Lionel never actually spoke of it, but his harshness grew and grew. There was no question of him encouraging Perky Dick's left-handedness as he had encouraged Geoffrey's. He set to work in the conventional fashion to eradicate it. And the comments that Lionel did not make aloud, someone else did: Ralph, the cook.

Ralph had eventually stopped behaving as though I were a tiresome child but he had never liked me. We had finally reached a somewhat ridiculous compromise by which he respected me as lady of the house but I also respected him as king of the kitchen and we negotiated like a couple of princes of equal status, and frequently through ambassadors. As often as not, I sent John Steward to convey my instructions, and Ralph would send an underling to me if he wished to offer alternative menu suggestions for a dinner, request stores to be ordered or – very often – say that something or other couldn't be done.

Ralph now began a new form of veiled insolence, subtly implying that in Lionel's eyes, Dick was of small account, and commiserating with me over the left-handedness in a curiously suggestive way.

'I'm not sure I can do that, mistress. T'marchpane for t'master's got to come afore makkin' fancies for t'lad. Mind you, I can see you want to pamper t'lad. Cack-handed folk have a harder time in life than t'rest. Like being born wrong side o' t'blanket.'

The other servants of course knew of the dislike between us and there was some taking of sides. John and Chrissy were staunchly on mine, but the clerk who took over the secretary's post when Master Hardynge died took his example from his master and from Ralph and patronised me to the very verge of discourtesy.

There was nothing to be done. Perky Dick and I were as helpless in Lionel's hands as though we were his slaves. He had sequestered the proceeds of Thornwood, so that despite King Edward's good will, I was utterly without resources of my own. When Perky Dick wept because he had been made to write or practise with weapons with his right hand, and then hit because he performed so badly with it, I dried his tears but knew that to protest would only make things worse.

So I was glad for his sake to see him go. He was bound for my own home at Faldene. Lionel had said that his northern accent could do with tempering, so Faldene was a natural choice. My father had died by then and my brother Simon was in possession (Tom having taken over his own inheritance at Grinstead). Dick went south in the summer, riding with the wool train, which was escorted, in Lionel's absence, by John. I watched his small figure ride out of sight. He sat his pony well. Geoffrey, I thought, would have approved.

I rarely thought of Geoffrey these days. He had loved me, but only after he had used me to strike at his uncle. He had protected me from Lionel, but he had also stupidly sent

Nicholas Hawes to bring me his apology for his failings. Even for a sick man, that struck me as an amazingly inept thing to do. Geoffrey was nothing to me now.

And yet, in that case, why had I shed secret tears over his death? And sought not one, but half a dozen opportunities, to slip up to that little attic room where Perky Dick had his beginnings, so that I could stand there among the dust motes and look at the old truckle bed and remember? And how was it that every now and then, some chance thing (often a movement of Perky Dick's head) could bring back memories of Geoffrey so vividly, laughing down at me as we lay in the heather with the skylarks soaring and singing above, or catching me against him in some brief, stolen embrace behind a door? When these memories returned, his imperfections would be as nothing. Suddenly, unreasonably, I would be wild with longing for those days to come again and I would ache with emptiness because I knew that they could not.

Yes, perhaps it was as well for Perky Dick to be out of my sight.

He had of course gone for the foreseeable future, but Lionel came back in late summer, complaining of stiff joints, went off again in October to help King Richard put down the Buckingham rebellion, and reappeared once more in November. Eynesby was dealing with problems of its own by then. On the day of Lionel's return the moors were lost in drizzle, and beyond the fence the river was in spate with the rains which had washed away Buckingham's ill-planned insurrection. It had all but washed our sheep away as well and Lionel could not have forded it. He had foreseen that, and come back by another route, through Bouldershawe.

He had taken about thirty men with him when he went, raising them mainly from Eynesby and Silbeck (which Alison had left to him). I therefore had only a few men, mostly older ones, and some women and lads to help me when the cloudbursts started and we had to rescue the flock, which were on exposed pastures and at risk from flash floods, landslides and the simple effects of saturated wool.

Indeed, we had to rescue them twice, for there was a brief dry spell followed by further cloudbursts, as bad as the first ones. At his homecoming Lionel found four waterlogged ewes drying out in the hall and the house pervaded by a smell of wet fleece. I had to move the ewes so that Lionel and Matthew, who had journeyed with him, could sit by the fire and have their travelling clothes put to steam.

'It's all over,' Lionel said as the household gathered round. 'Buckingham's done for. Margaret Beaufort was in it,' he added to me, knowing that I would recognise the name easily. 'Well, she would be. It was all in aid of her son, Henry Tudor. She's under house arrest, but only in her husband's home. Richard always gives women the benefit of the doubt. I'd have had her head off,' said Lionel with a snort. 'Morton – Bishop of Ely – he was in it too but he got away. Across the Channel, very likely. But one of Buckingham's servants sold him to the King. He pleaded to see Richard,' said Lionel with grim enjoyment, 'but the King wouldn't have it. He had Buckingham's head instead. I was there.'

He was smiling his thinnest and most mirthless smile and I wondered if Buckingham had seen it from the scaffold. I had heard no good of Buckingham, but I could pity him. How terrible, at the moment of one's death, to see others rejoicing in it, to know oneself friendless even in such an extremity.

'God was with the King,' Lionel was saying. 'Everywhere Buckingham tried to go with his army he found a flooded river in the way. His men deserted and the Tudor fellow was caught in the storms when he was at sea, coming over from Brittany. We think he was cut off from his fleet. He turned up off Dorset with only two ships. We somehow fancied he'd have set off with more than that.'

'Well, he'd be a fool if he didn't,' I said.

'He was no fool,' Lionel said. 'I was with the detachment that was watching the south coast. I saw the two ships myself and I was there when Tudor sent a herald in a small boat to ask for news. They'd seen soldiers on the beach and wanted to know who we were. We tried to make them believe we were Buckingham's supporters come to conduct Henry to London in state but no, Tudor was no fool and nor was his herald. Not that it would have done him much good if we had been Buckingham's men,' Lionel chuckled drily. 'A few of them that were came over to us and they said some interesting things. One was that Buckingham intended using Tudor to help him knock out King Richard, and then meant to turn on him. Buckingham had an eye to the throne himself. He died crying, did I mention that? A fine sight it was, that execution.'

'What a lot of people seem to want King Richard's throne,' I said lightly, keeping up the facade again, pushing aside that sharp comment about the benefit of the doubt. 'I wonder what will happen when King Edward's sons grow up?'

Even as I said it, I knew that the light tone was ill-chosen. They would grow up, inevitably, to be the pretexts or leaders of risings and to end as Buckingham had, friendless on a scaffold. It wasn't pretty.

But what Lionel said next was less pretty still. 'So the news hasn't got here? They won't grow up, girl. They're dead.'

'What? But? King Richard wouldn't . . .'

'It's being said he has,' said Lionel, 'but as it happens, no, he didn't. By chance, I know it. The news found him in a private house and I was there in his suite, by virtue of being an old Middleham face. He's not bothering himself to publish a denial. Why waste his breath, he says. But it was Buckingham that did it, thinking to please. That was the root of the quarrel between them.'

I sat thinking it over, for once distracted from my own concerns. 'How horrified the King must have been,' I said.

'Aye, but the boys would have been a menace to him one day, that's right enough. I fancy that's the real reason why he won't deny it. He's not quite sure how horrified he is. He's honest, you know. He's got a conscience. It's always as well to be honest, Petra.'

'I'm sure it is.' I smiled into my husband's enigmatic eyes. 'Well, it's a tragedy, but I suppose the land will have peace now. We're not likely to hear of Henry Tudor again.'

But little Ned, the only son of King Richard and Queen Anne, died the next year, destroying the succession. Little more than one year after that, Henry Tudor sailed again.

PART FIVE
PLANTAGENET VERSUS TUDOR
1484–1485

Chapter Thirty-Four

The Plantagenets: Of Raising the Dead

March 1484

'I know the boy is dead. Strange to say, I received the messenger before you did, Margaret. This happens to be my house. You were hearing one of your everlasting Masses.'

'There's no need to be offensive, Thomas,' said Margaret Beaufort calmly. She sat tranquilly in the parlour of their London house, her long-fingered hands resting lightly in her lap. 'I wanted a sensible discussion with you. This new development could be of great importance to us. And to Henry.'

'Henry! On the subject of your son,' said Thomas, 'you're hardly sane. And he's not much better himself! I hear that even after the Buckingham debacle he still took an oath to come as a chivalrous rescuer to England to right the wrongs of the York family, capture the throne and marry Princess Elizabeth. I suppose you imagine that now, with the succession wide open, this is his chance?'

'Why not?'

'He can't do it without backing, that's why not. The Duke of Brittany helped him last time but he won't risk the expense again. And even though Henry is now in France with a crowd of hangers-on, the French don't appear to think he's more than a weapon to brandish at their old foe England. They aren't reported to have come across with anything really useful, such as money or arms.'

'Ah, but this development could change that. I have already written to Henry, pointing out that he can now bid for England without having to face the embarrassment of a dispossessed child heir. Richard found that such a problem,' said Margaret. 'Oh I know that you and the rest of the Council say that Buckingham was responsible, but not many people believe that. And even if he was, I fancy the idea was Richard's.'

'Fancy what you like, but don't talk about it in public. Richard wishes the matter simply to die away, largely because he knows that most people will think as you do. Did I hear you say you'd written to Henry?'

'Yes.'

'Thank you! So now I am to be involved in another treasonable conspiracy, am I? Emanating from my own house! Has it occurred to you that perhaps the Queen and the Princess Elizabeth may no longer wish to be parties to it, by the way? The Queen, after all, has left sanctuary.'

'She couldn't stay there for ever and the Abbot was making a great deal of fuss about getting his house back. She made Richard sign a guarantee of safety for herself and her daughters first.'

'She is also comfortably settled in the country and there's talk of bringing some of the daughters to court, I suppose in search of good marriages. I fancy,' said Stanley, 'that someone has had a quiet word with Bess Woodville.'

'Nevertheless, she has no reason to love Richard. If he didn't kill those two boys in the Tower, he still killed Richard Grey and Anthony Woodville, her son and her brother. She'll co-operate, and if she does, so will Elizabeth. Elizabeth would have a chance of becoming Queen! That would be a good marriage if you like.'

'And you'd be the King's mother. Very nice for you. You're even prepared to risk my head for it. Could I ask what you think is in it for me?'

Margaret smiled. 'Well, Thomas, there might be something.'

And by the blinding blue of his wife's eyes, once more, Thomas Stanley was enslaved.

* * *

In France, at the house of the Chancellor Pierre Landois, the bell was ringing which called the household to dine.

The slightly built, ginger-haired young man Henry Tudor, who was there as a guest, was slow to respond. He was sitting in his room with Thomas Grey of Dorset, who had recently joined him, and with his uncle Jasper Tudor, the brother of Henry's long-dead father. Jasper had been a Lancastrian exile throughout all the days of Yorkist rule. He had spent them in France, and made contacts which Henry was now finding useful. It was Jasper who had wangled them the invitation to stay with the Chancellor. He and Dorset were listening while Henry, in a slow and thoughtful voice, read a letter aloud.

'Even in this slippery court,' said Jasper when his nephew had finished, 'that ought to make a difference.' The years in France had not removed his Welsh intonation. 'It ought to, but will it?'

Henry said: 'I am sick of living as the pensioner of other men. Make a difference? It had better.' He looked at his companions with shrewd, light-coloured eyes. 'The predicament that Gloucester was in, with his brother's children as leftovers, cannot now be applied to me. In England there are men who wish to avenge those murdered boys but fear to see history repeat itself. Now that Richard's son is dead too, it can't. I think we should make a list of likely names and get in touch with them. When we have assembled enough promises of help, let us try the French government with that!' He smiled at Dorset. 'We already have money, thanks to you – enough at least to make a start. I shall be asking the French for a contribution but I am at least in a position to make a fair-sized one myself. The outlook, my friends, seems promising.'

The hall of Nottingham Castle had changed little since the day when King Edward stood there with a handful of companions and read the repulsive Warwick proclamation which sought to eradicate the power of the Woodvilles.

Warwick had failed but time and events had done it for him. They had all but eradicated the house of York as well. The solid Norman hall had far more permanence than the fragile flesh and blood creatures which had built and used it. Its massive stone was a grim comment on their transience and its gloom did nothing to offset this. It was no place, thought Alcock, as he hurried in, to learn of such bereavement as this.

There was a subdued bustle in the hall; preparations for dinner had begun but the servants were sombrely clad and they shook out cloths and laid platters too quietly. The men and women of the court stood about, talking in voices too low to carry more than a foot or two. Alcock paused, glancing round, and then saw Edward Brampton coming towards him. No, it was Sir Edward Brampton now, of course. He had become a personal friend to Richard as he had to King Edward, and Richard had knighted him.

The bandit face was worried. 'I'm so glad you're here!' said Brampton.

'I came as soon as I could. This is dreadful news. How is the King?'

'What would you expect? He is frantic, and the Queen is ill. She will not attend the funeral. Perhaps that is for the best. No woman should see her own child buried.'

'But what happened?'

Brampton made one of his un-English gestures, shoulders to ears and elbows in. 'Who knows? The child was at Middleham. He fell ill and within days he was dead. The messenger who brought the news, found the parents – my lord King and the Queen – here. That was three days ago now. Since then . . .'

'Alcock,' said Richard. 'You came.'

He had entered the hall, accompanied by James Tyrell and the northerner, Master Lionel Eynesby. They were both often in his household these days. No doubt Richard, just now, was glad to have their familiar presences near. He had sent for Alcock, perhaps, because Alcock's presence

496

would also be familiar, as well as bringing priestly comfort.

'. . . there is very little you can do,' Richard was saying. 'I've dragged you from your diocese pell-mell and now I'm wondering what for, but I'm very glad to see you.'

Alcock, looking at him, thought: If ever I wanted you to know the grief the death of a child can bring, I want it no longer. For after all, to do this to you, a child did have to die. You were guilty of nothing worse than a few careless words. It was Buckingham who conceived your nephews' deaths and he has paid. I wouldn't have anyone suffer as you are suffering now, just for a few words. I never saw a countenance so ravaged. You look as though you have been walking in hell.

'I will conduct a service presently,' he said, 'and hope it may lead God's comfort to you. It can only come from God. John Alcock the man cannot comfort you, that is true. But I can say to you that I grieve with you. The whole land is doing that, my lord.'

'Grieving with me and wondering how I propose to fill the gap,' said Richard. 'My responsibilities give me no respite. As a king I don't even have the right to concentrate on sorrow. Before my son's coffin is in its tomb, I'm supposed to be deciding who to name as heir in his place. If such a thing were possible,' he added savagely, 'I should be expected to set to work to get another. It's all been far too much for Anne. She's lost both her children now. We had a daughter who died when she was small, if you remember.'

'How is the Queen?' Brampton asked.

'Sleeping. The physician gave her something. She hasn't slept for the last two nights and now she's running a fever. The physician says I ought to take something tonight too. I suppose I must but I would rather not. All I want to do,' said Richard, 'is lie on the floor of a stone chapel and weep till the chill of the stone enters my bones and freezes my tears. Or take a horse and falcon and ride after the speck of the falcon in the sky till I've outridden myself or crashed over the edge of the world. I want my little Ned back again! We weren't even with him when . . .'

497

There was a mild stir nearby. Trumpeters were in position by the door, preparing to sound the fanfare for dinner. But since Richard was there, they required his permission.

'What?' Richard looked round. 'Oh yes, yes, sound away. I suppose other people must eat. I don't want anything.'

Alcock saw that the others, Brampton, Tyrell, Eynesby, were all looking at him hopefully. Clearly, there was nothing new in this scene. No doubt they had been trying for days to persuade Richard to eat, sleep and otherwise care for his health.

'I will see you to your chamber, sir. The physician shall be consulted on what you should eat and drink. I shall urge you to heed his advice. You are right, you have a duty to the realm. We cannot have you falling ill too. And what,' said Alcock, inspired, 'would the Queen do? She will depend on you, now.'

Poor Anne, she must carry the burden of this grief too. Edward Quintus and his brother were avenged but Alcock would rather, infinitely rather, they had been left to rest in peace.

Like a tutor with a pupil who had been sorely hurt and needed help, and surprised by the depth of his pity, he led Richard away.

Alcock watched the physician persuade Richard into taking food and drink and a soothing draught, bade him goodnight – an empty phrase in the circumstances – took his own dinner and climbed the precipitous stair to his guest chamber. It was neatly prepared, with pleasing tapestries, a good sealskin bedcover, and a prie-dieu opposite the bed. His own attendants had the adjoining chamber through which anyone who wished to speak to him must come. His room did have a direct door out of it, leading on to another stair, but this was bolted on the inside.

It was Alcock's preference to keep his attendants on the far side of a wall. Many men, even tough warriors and devout priests, detested sleeping in a room by themselves. For them, the night was peopled with ghosts and demons, and the shadows outside the lit circle of lantern or candle represented unknown dangers. But Alcock was not of this company. He enjoyed solitude. His valet wished him good sleep and withdrew and Alcock, having prayed for a while for Anne and Richard, found himself even then too restless for bed and sat down in a chair to compose his mind with a little reading.

Round him the castle settled and the silence deepened. His eyes were growing tired when, very softly, there came a scratching on the bolted outer door.

He went to the door with the book still in his hand. He stood listening. He might not fear the dark, but that sound had something very furtive about it and, besides, what kind of visitor was it who would not announce himself to the bishop's staff? The scratching was repeated. He threw the door open, stepping back from it as he did so. Sir Edward Brampton, Sir James Tyrell and Master Lionel Eynesby filed silently in.

Master Eynesby closed and bolted the door. Tyrell prowled round the room brushing the tapestries with his hands. Alcock, arms majestically akimbo, watched them without speaking. Tyrell nodded satisfaction and Brampton, with signs, indicated that he wished them all to sit on the bed and draw the curtains round them. He had a lantern, which he put in the middle of the bed on a pile of Alcock's books. They settled themselves round it, cross-legged except for Alcock, who was not of the build for it. He enthroned himself on pillows, with his back against the bedhead, and regarded his uninvited guests coldly. 'And now, perhaps,' he said in an annoyed whisper, 'you will be good enough to tell me what all this nonsense is about?'

Brampton grinned. In the dimly lit velvet cavern he looked like a robber chief holding council. 'It is a matter both confidential and delicate. Eavesdroppers we must not have. We apologise for our very peculiar behaviour but we wish, my lord bishop, to ask you a question.'

'I'm agog with curiosity. I can't imagine what kind of question merits all this. What is it?'

'There is something we need to be sure of,' said Tyrell. 'Two things, in fact. Are the two sons of King Edward indeed dead as they are said to be? And if so –'

' – Can you, my lord bishop, vouch for it that King Richard is indeed not responsible?' said Brampton. 'In the only statement which he made to the Council – and it was made to only a few of us and no clerk reported or even heard it – he said that they had been murdered by Buckingham, who had believed that it would please the King, and that he preferred to make no public statement but that you could confirm what he said. We are asking you to do so.'

'Certainly I can confirm it. I was present when Buckingham admitted what he had done and Richard ordered him away. I would have thought that I hardly needed to confirm it in words. I was the young prince's tutor. If I were not sure – I mean *sure* – that the King was innocent, do you imagine that any loyalty to the Council or the office of kingship or even to the realm would keep me by Richard's side? If I had had the slightest doubt, I should have gone back to Worcester, dismissed my surrogate permanently and settled to a life of confirmations, ordinations and the founding of schools and chantries. And before thus retiring, I should have told Richard why. I doubt that he would have argued. I repeat, I was Prince Edward's tutor. What do you take me for?'

'An entirely honest man and a respectable bishop,' said Brampton softly. 'Which is what we all thought, but we needed to hear you say it. Now we can go on to the real reason for this meeting. What we have really come to discuss is the resurrection of one or both of the late King Edward's sons.'

There was a flabbergasted pause.

'*Resurrection?*' said Alcock.

'Yes.'

500

Alcock was betrayed into something near to blasphemy. 'Do you imagine that you're Jesus Christ? Or that I am?' He remembered to keep his voice down but he nevertheless sounded outraged. 'The boys are dead. That's the end of it.'

'You take me too literally,' said Brampton. 'True, we cannot breathe back life into the bones of the departed. But we might appear to do so.'

'I wish I knew what you were talking about. I've known you for many years, Brampton, and I can't imagine what has come over you. This is ridiculous!' hissed Alcock. 'I am the Bishop of Worcester and shortly to be made Chancellor. And all three of you are grown men of position and dignity. And we are crouched here like schoolboys, holding a secret society meeting in a dortoir! I am aware that when confidential matters are being discussed, ensuring privacy can lead to absurdities. I can only say that where I used to find such absurdities amusing, my taste for them has dwindled!'

'Perhaps, but secrecy we need. Privacy we need too.' Brampton was evidently the chief spokesman. 'How else should we gather to talk?'

'The best place for confidential meetings is in the middle of a field or on a deserted beach, where you can see people coming before they can hear you talking!'

'Such meetings among ourselves we have already had. But we prefer not to be seen together too much, even out of other men's hearing. Listen,' said Brampton, 'is it not plain enough that now that the King has no heir, no natural replacement of his own getting, he is very vulnerable? There is something here to talk about, privately. Is it not all too likely that Henry Tudor will move again as soon as possible?'

'If he does, the fact will be reported,' said Alcock. He and Brampton, after all, would make sure that it was.

'Quite. And no doubt,' said Brampton, 'at the first Council after this sad funeral is over, plans will be put in

501

hand for strengthening the army and guarding the coast. That will be plain common sense. But is it not the case that, if a report got about that one or both of King Edward's sons was still alive, that rumour would form a strong bulwark against the Tudor? After all, he has justified his pretensions by vowing to marry the Princess Elizabeth and so restore the line of York. Her brothers would be decidedly in his way.'

'We think,' said Tyrell, 'that it would sound most convincing if only one of the boys were rumoured to be living, and that one the younger. The elder was not in good health, or so we understand.'

'And what do you want me for?' demanded Alcock.

'As one who knows the truth about the boys' deaths, you have a sort of right to know the truth about any apparent return to life,' said Brampton. 'Apart from that, your advice would be welcome. We have to set the rumour in motion, and make sure it reaches France. Now, how best to go about it?'

'I'd prefer not to go about it at all. What if there were a rebellion in the alleged survivor's name?'

'I doubt it,' said Brampton. 'The faction in favour of the boys is the Woodville faction. Sir Anthony and Richard Grey are dead and Dorset is reputed to be fraternising with Henry Tudor. There is a risk, yes, but it is a small one. So, I repeat, how would you proceed?'

That renegade part of Alcock which so immorally rejoiced in subtlety and could not bear to reject an opportunity of showing his gift for it, rose up. He opened his mouth to say, 'I haven't the slightest idea and I disapprove of this entire enterprise,' and said instead, 'Has Richard been consulted at all? I take it that he hasn't.'

'Hardly,' said Brampton. 'There has not been time and it will in any case need a great deal of time before I for one would care to speak to him about it. He does not like to hear the names of his nephews mentioned, and the death of his own son is a bad enough grief without all us officious people pointing out that it's a practical catastrophe as well. Yet the scheme will take some setting up. We cannot afford to wait, and therefore . . .'

'The first step,' said Alcock decisively, 'would be for someone, an informer, to arrive on Henry's doorstep in France saying that he had some interesting information and was it worth anything? It probably would be. Why shouldn't our tame informer make a little on the side? When induced to repeat his story, he would have a tale of a boy, fair-haired, the right age, on a boat or staying at an inn, who appeared to be not what he seemed. Whose adult companions mostly called him Dick but occasionally forgot themselves and said "my lord", and seemed alarmed at the sight of armed men riding by. But if I were Henry, I fancy I would try to get corroboration. Have you considered that?'

'I told you Alcock would be our man,' said Brampton to the others. They nodded without speaking. Lionel Eynesby had as yet spoken not at all and Alcock wondered why he was there.

'The first informer,' said Brampton thoughtfully, 'would have to steer the enquiry towards an apparently disinterested person, who would tell the same tale. More than one, if possible . . .'

'It would be better still,' Alcock agreed, 'if the disinterested witnesses were genuine and there really was, or had been, such a boy as they describe.'

'Ah,' said Brampton. 'It's odd that you should say that, because when this idea was first mooted, that was where it started.'

'Oh?'

'It began with a casual conversation,' said Tyrell, 'which chanced to be between us three.' His eyes took in Brampton and Eynesby. 'We were saying, if only the rumours could be silenced by the King producing the boys – or a boy – who would look convincingly genuine. Then we said, well, of course it couldn't be done. Imposters would soon be revealed. But a boy who is simply seen for a day or two here and there and then vanishes, who is never called upon to answer questions – that would be another matter. That was how this suggestion first arose. But making sure that the information was reported in the right place – to Henry Tudor, that is – was less easy. Sir Edward did have ideas to offer, which were very like yours, my lord bishop, but he wished to consult you. He said that you had resources, contacts, which would be useful.'

'We both have,' said Alcock. 'There seems little point now in concealing it. Both of us, but particularly myself, employ a few men whose business is to carry out delicate missions for the King. But I can't think offhand of anyone who could provide a fair-haired boy of the right age and status. An urchin off the streets couldn't do it. The boy must have something princely about him, so that when our informant leads enquirers to witnesses – a sea-captain or an innkeeper, say – who are not in the plot, they say the right things. No, the idea may not be feasible after all. The boy could be put in danger, too. I know very little about Henry Tudor's character, or those of his supporters but . . .'

For the first time, Lionel Eynesby spoke. 'What,' he said, 'if we told you we had a boy? The right age or near enough. Fair-haired, well-bred, and with Plantagenet blood?'

There was a pause. 'One of Richard's sons?' Alcock asked. 'But Richard keeps a paternal eye on both of them and has regular reports of their progress. One lives in his castle of Sheriff Hutton in Yorkshire, and the other is in a private household. In fact, I arranged for his upbringing. Neither the King nor I would tolerate for one moment any jiggery pokery with either of those boys.'

'Oh no,' said Brampton. 'We understand about that. It's neither of those. It's not a son of Richard we have in mind.'

'No, not at all,' said Eynesby. 'T'lad we're thinking of is his half-nephew.'

*　　*　　*

504

'Mind you,' said Brampton to James Tyrell and Lionel Eynesby the next morning, as they strolled casually together across the bailey, 'some of our ideas had best be kept from Alcock. He will go so far but no further. Besides, it lies far ahead. It may never come. If it does, it will be because not only my benefactor King Edward, but his brother King Richard are in their graves and there's a Lancaster upon the throne.'

'You see things differently from Alcock,' Tyrell said.

'I do. I think of myself as English but I will never be all-English. It is not to be thought of, among the peoples of the south, that one's benefactor and his house should be destroyed and supplanted and no vengeance be taken. And for this vengeance, plans must be made in advance.'

'I too, owe much to the house of York,' said Tyrell calmly. 'And it is not only the men of southern Europe who pay their debts.'

'Aye, even t'men of northern England do,' said Lionel Eynesby.

'Who is your creditor?' Brampton asked.

'That's private. But I'm with you,' said Eynesby, 'every step of t'way.'

Chapter Thirty-Five

The Plantagenets: Advice from King Herod

1485

'Are you all right?' said Richard quietly, in Anne's ear.

'Yes, quite all right. What a magnificent occasion this is. Everyone is here. I'm glad, Richard. It shows how much support you have in the realm.'

You will need it when I'm gone.

The words were not said but Richard nevertheless heard them. Because they were both dressed in full royal robes and crowns, and were sitting enthroned in the hall of Westminster for the Feast of Epiphany, symbols rather than human beings, he did not stretch out a hand to touch her. But in his mind he did so and Anne, sensing his thoughts just as he had sensed hers, drew a little, a very little, comfort from them.

It was something, a crumb. What she longed for most was to go to sleep in his arms at night, but this had been denied to her lately on the orders of Richard's doctors. The bouts of illness which had plagued her, the fever she had run after little Ned's death, had apparently been more than the limping of a physique weakened by bad pregnancies and by grief. She was diseased and contagious and her husband's doctors feared that she might contaminate him. They had forbidden him to share her bed.

The irony of it was that although she was far from 'quite all right', one or two people who had not heard the truth had unwisely remarked that the queen was in looks today. But none of them had seen her at close quarters. If they had, they would have seen that her colour was too hectic and her skin too transparent, that her arms were as thin as sparrows' legs. And if they had taken her hand, they would have felt the heat of the fever which was permanent now, and burning away her flesh.

The doctors said that the sickness had probably been in her for a long time, perhaps since before that journey from the north after King Edward died, and the shock of Ned's death had jolted the ailment into new voracity. She had realised quite soon after that what was wrong with her and tried to hide it from Richard. Later she understood that Richard, along with the physicians, had been trying to hide it from her. But the first flecks of blood coughed into her napkin had put a stop to that, for everyone knew what those signs portended, and it was no longer any use for the physicians to say they wished Richard to sleep apart from her for fear he should catch bronchitis.

'Well, there you are,' she had said, quite fiercely, to the doctor who came to examine the stained napkin. 'Please don't lie to me any more. Or you, Richard. I can see that it's no surprise to you. Well, it's no surprise to me either and I haven't the strength any more to pretend about it. I have the lung rot and I'm dying, aren't I?'

Richard turned to the doctor. 'Out!' When the man had gone, he knelt down by the bed and put his arms round her and she knew how thin and hot her body felt in his grasp. He said: 'Anne, don't leave me. Not you as well as Ned.'

'I wouldn't if I could choose. But I shan't have very much choice, shall I?' said Anne, and managed for just those few seconds to sound vigorous and common-sense about it. Then she gave way because, after all, putting it into words did make a difference. While the thing remained unmentionable she had been able, it seemed, to keep the knowledge of it away from some inmost citadel of her being. But once the words were said, those hidden walls went down and terror rushed in like a pillaging horde. She had collapsed, crying wildly, in Richard's arms, and Richard, putting his own grief away, had set his mind to steadying her.

But one got over that. Oddly enough, one did get over it. She had been granted the grace of time in which to prepare and the disease was intermittent. There were days when she felt a little better. She had succeeded so far in attending most of the occasions and ceremonies at which the Queen's presence was expected, such as this Epiphany Crown-Wearing. Surprisingly, the fact that it was the sixth of January and very cold made her feel better and not worse. Cold, snow-laden air went more easily into her diseased lungs than the mild air of summer. Because of that, she was able to bear the dragging weight of the velvet robes and the heavy crown of gem-studded gold. If only she could have gone north again, she sometimes thought, back to Middleham, she might have stood a chance – not of life, she knew that now, but of staving death off for just a little longer. As it was the summer would probably bring about the end.

But the thought of undertaking such a journey exhausted her, and one of the things which had helped her to get over the initial terror was that this illness had shown her that before she died, she would probably feel so extremely unwell that dying would come as a relief.

Nothing, however, healed the grief. She must leave Richard behind, leave him alone, and this, she knew, would matter to him. He would be left free to remarry and get his much-needed heir but he would have no one truly close to him, who shared his memories as she did.

Well, in time he would forget her, she supposed. Given time, he would acquire memories to share with someone else. Dying wouldn't be quite the same as taking leave of him, as she had once thought of doing, by divorce, retiring to a separate house or a nunnery so that he could provide himself with another queen, and with a succession. There would be no packing of luggage, no ghastly moment of deciding, well, let us get the parting over, and stepping towards him for the last embrace, the last kiss, before making the huge and unimaginable effort of walking away from him, over the threshold and out of his life.

Dying required no such effort. She would only have to lie back and close her eyes.

Death, Anne thought, was the journey you undertook without actually having to go anywhere at all.

She wondered who her successor as Richard's queen would be. And then, despite her weakness and malaise, was hit and overwhelmed by a surge of purest anger. There was one person who would very much like to be that successor. God send that Richard would never be such a fool!

Out in the splendidly hung and decorated hall, the feast was proceeding amid a wealth of ceremony which turned the business of serving food and wine into a kind of dance. When main dishes were served, the pages knelt on one knee to present them to their lords, all at the same moment, so that a repeating pattern of crimson velvet slashed with gold made a decorative frieze all along both sides of each upper table. The pages had been similarly dressed at Christmas. The feast had been held in this self-same hall and now, vividly, the memory returned. Last Christmas had been a glittering festivity, at least for some.

Between Anne's ailing health and the loss of their son, no occasion had meant very much either to her or to Richard. But for Elizabeth of York, not yet eighteen and only recently arrived at court, with the confinement of sanctuary not far behind her, it had quite obviously meant enchantment. Richard had said as much, with avuncular amusement.

Winkling Bess Woodville out of sanctuary had proved possible in the end but very, very difficult. It had taken hours of patient persuasion on the part of Bourchier, and even then the public oath which Richard had had to take, guaranteeing the personal safety of Bess and her daughters, was embarrassingly comprehensive. But it had included a promise to see the girls suitably married to gentlemen who would be instructed to love them and to treat them well. And although Sir James Tyrell had found a house in East

Anglia to which Bess could retire with the younger girls, the older ones had had to come to court to be seen.

Elizabeth, as ethereal as her mother to look at but her father's child in the openness of her manners, had come gaily back from the dance on the arm of a young gallant. She curtsied herself gracefully out of her partner's company and stepped on to the dais where Anne and Richard were sitting. She was especially exquisite today in one of the dresses which Anne had given her when she left sanctuary, for she had grown out of all her old dresses, and fashions in any case had changed. The dress was of turquoise and silver brocade, made of the same material as Anne's own. But Elizabeth looked much better in it than Anne did. No amount of cosmetics, or the attempts Anne had made to improve her appearance by lightening her hair, could conceal the marks of ill-health. She could not do justice to any brocade, however beautiful. She was conscious of it and Elizabeth's words stung when she said: 'Dear Aunt Anne, why are you not dancing? It's such fun!'

'I might begin coughing again,' said Anne. 'But I want to see you enjoying yourself. You are, I hope?'

'Oh yes! It was so dull and cramped in sanctuary and not very exciting in the country, either! This is like coming back to life!' She smiled at them both, a heart-stopping smile, an incredible amalgam of Woodville enigma and bold Neville charm. When she married she would only have to smile once at her husband, with that beautifully moulded rosebud mouth, to make him her servant for life, Anne thought. 'Aunt Anne,' she said, 'Uncle Richard – may I dance with you? Dear Aunt Anne, would you mind?'

'Of course not,' said Anne graciously and also, to her own annoyance, a little coldly. It was undignified to be envious of a frivolous chit like this. Richard smiled back, assenting, and rose to give his hand to his niece, who folded small, trusting fingers into his and went off with him to join the set.

Since then, they had learned from Sir James Tyrell that

Bess Woodville had been very reluctant indeed to let Elizabeth come to court. Was it, Anne wondered, because Bess had some inkling of the real state of affairs?

Richard apparently had none. Returning after the set, resigning Elizabeth to another partner, he had said indulgently: 'What a child Elizabeth still is. But what a beautiful child, and did you ever see such a delightful smile? She doesn't yet know what it's for, but wait till she finds out!'

He must have been blind, thought Anne crossly now. Elizabeth had known. A man might be deceived about that; a woman, never. Elizabeth had inherited that taut pink rosebud mouth from her mother and, with it, an inborn knowledge of sex. She had known that by wearing a dress of the same material as Anne's she cast Anne into the shadow; she had known of the barb in her sweet surprise that Anne wasn't dancing; and she had perfectly understood the devastation of her smile.

That Christmas feast had set a pattern. Elizabeth had joined them more than once since, always dressed, one way or another, to challenge Anne, always seeking to dance with Richard and to charm him. She was here tonight, seated not far off, frustrated no doubt because she wasn't close enough to talk to Richard. Good, thought Anne, splendid!

And then she wondered at herself. What did it matter to her who Richard married when she was dead and gone? And in any case, it was most improbable that he would scandalise the country by marrying his own niece. The York versus Lancaster squabble couldn't be resolved that way. It would create more problems than it solved.

But of course, it was not possessiveness of Richard that was really gnawing at her.

In fact, Anne admitted to herself, it was raging jealousy of Elizabeth because she was young and strong and lovely and admired, because life stretched shining before her, with a husband's warm arms, with love and marriage and children, all still to be enjoyed. And because Elizabeth would see next Epiphany and she, Anne, wouldn't.

After all, it seemed, one did have to pack luggage for the journey into the dark. You packed the memories, the feelings you wanted to preserve throughout eternity. She must beware. She didn't want to spend forever consumed by bitter recollections of looking like an expensively draped skeleton and sitting out of the dance, while Elizabeth disported herself like an incandescent angel with Anne's husband.

She must not think of Elizabeth too much. There were other things, better things, to take instead. Richard rescuing her from Master Taberner's attic. Richard cuddling her against him on their wedding night, leading her so kindly through the rituals of love. Ned squeaking in his cradle, astonishingly tiny and astonishingly perfect, an achievement she could hardly believe was hers. Middleham, home alike of her childhood and her marriage, its candles alight to guide the late-arriving traveller home from the moors . . .

She must have moved, or swayed, without knowing it. 'Are you certain you're all right?' Richard whispered again. 'If you need to withdraw . . .'

'No, I'm quite well, I promise.'

It mattered. She had risen from her bed today, put on these terrible robes and the crown which was making her neck muscles ache with strain, because they were to be worn at the Feast of Epiphany, which commemorated the dream in which the Magi had been warned not to reveal the whereabouts of the infant Jesus to King Herod.

At Epiphany, neither Richard nor his wife must appear anything but well and normal. Both must be present. Anne must not faint nor Richard frown, and neither must leave early.

There must not be the least suggestion, whatever it might cost them, that they knew that it had been whispered that King Richard was King Herod come again.

* * *

There was a stir at the door. A messenger had arrived and was in agitated conference with the ushers. Richard raised his voice. 'If that man wants to see me, bring him here.'

The man came to the dais and knelt. 'My lord, I am sent to you from France and I bring vital news. I am sorry to intrude upon this Feast but . . .'

'What is your news?'

'My lord, I bring confirmation that Henry Tudor is preparing to invade.'

The Council of War in progress in Paris meant business.

Where Henry Tudor had once had to confer with his friends informally in his chamber, now he had a small council room in one of the palaces, and it could not be mistaken for anything but a battle headquarters. The lidded settle on which Henry sat contained much of the treasure filched by Thomas Grey of Dorset from the Tower of London and presented by Dorset to Henry's cause. Dorset himself was at this moment out placing orders for arms on the strength of it. Within the council room, the tapestries had been removed and a map of England now adorned one wall. Large-scale charts of sections of coastline adorned another, with rocks and shoals marked, together with ports and towns near the sea and roads leading inland, their destinations written beside them.

Two hired clerks sat side by side, each with a pile of letters and memoranda, and made careful additions to a list of lords, some exiled and some still in England, who had offered help, and what resources each could provide: how many knights, archers and pikemen and how much cash. The lords still in England were a mixed collection. Some were domiciled in Wales and had an emotional attachment to the Welsh name of Tudor. Some were traditionally Lancastrian. Some, Henry had earlier remarked drily, were 'southerners who don't care for all these north-country sheriffs in their midst'. He was a young man in years but he had the crackly voice and some of the mannerisms of a lawyer twice his age, and an acerbic sense of humour not unlike that of his stepfather Thomas Stanley.

Stanley's name did not feature on the list of those who could be counted on. According to Henry's mother, who sent regular letters (and one or two agents whose messages were outspoken on subjects which Margaret Beaufort preferred not to mention), Stanley was teetering like a tightrope walker between fear of Richard and lust for Margaret and might topple either way. He featured instead on a separate list of doubtfuls.

Henry himself was at this moment in talk with his Uncle Jasper. Jasper, it seemed to his nephew, was unnecessarily worried.

'I can't see any cause for such anxiety. What does this tale amount to? A fair-haired boy, travelling from England to the Low Countries, whose attendants absent-mindedly call him "my lord" and are then shushed by other attendants? Uncle Jasper, it happens all the time. A childless lord breeds up a young nephew or cousin to think himself the heir – then the barren wife dies, the lord marries again and gets an heir after all, and the first boy is out in the cold and has to learn to take a lower status. This one was probably being exported to Bruges or somewhere to learn how to make a career as a merchantman. The fair hair means nothing. He was sailing from the east coast and fair-haired lads are as common as ants along there. Forget about it, Uncle. If any pretenders turn up in days to come, I'll deal with them. Even if the child really was Richard of York,' said Henry coolly, 'he's still only twelve. It will be years before he's old enough to be a nuisance. By then, it should be very difficult for him to prove his identity. He'll have lived under another name too long. If I am King of England by then, I shall patronise him as an amusing imposter. Which he will be, of course. The child Richard of York is dead, or King Richard would have paraded him at the time of my first invasion. Now, Uncle, give me the benefit of your experience on this vexed question of stores. How much do we carry with us and to what extent do we live off the land in England? On the whole, I'd rather not acquire a reputation for pillage and ravaging the moment I step ashore . . .'

'I can only say,' said Alcock, 'that I'm sorry to pester you with more work at present. But these are all appeals I have received from people within my diocese of Worcester, who feel they have been the victims of injustice . . .'

'Sit down and we'll deal with them.' Richard's voice had in it the patience of beasts of burden down the ages. Alcock, setting down the documents he carried, regarded him anxiously. Richard gave him a lopsided smile. 'It will be a break from preparations for the war.'

'How are we placed for repelling an invasion?'

'I wish I could be more certain of a few key men. Stanley and Northumberland, to be more precise. I've had an excellent report from John Howard on the number of well-armed men Norfolk can raise in an emergency. Kendall's just about to send off a letter of thanks and acknowledgement to him.' He nodded to where the secretary sat writing. 'If all my lords were as trusty as Howard,' said Richard wearily, 'I could go hawking all day. Unfortunately . . . Do you know, Alcock, I can't even get myself worked into a fury about Stanley and Northumberland. I try, but I can't *care*. It was all right when the news first came. I was relieved then, glad that the thing was coming to a head, like a boil about to burst. But now . . .'

'Now?'

'Anne was still alive then,' said Richard slowly.

Alcock nodded. 'And now you want to concentrate on grieving, and events won't let you. Is it any help if I tell you that having work one is forced to do can speed the process of healing perhaps more than anything else?'

'No,' said Richard. 'Though I'm sure you mean well.'

Alcock, tactfully, did not reply. Richard picked up the bundle of documents which the bishop had put before him and then laid them irresolutely down again. 'I wish I could explain to someone how I feel. I used to be able to explain things to Anne. She always knew what I meant however badly I put it. It's as if the simplest, most common-place things – the shimmer of light on new leaves in the wind, or just the act of sneezing – they're privileges all of a sudden, Alcock, because I'm here to see the leaves or catch a cold, and Ned and Anne are not. But at the same time, they mean nothing at all. Nothing means anything. Not even Henry Tudor and his damned army in France.'

Alcock was out of his depth despite a long experience of counselling the bereaved, and glad to hear the voice of the page announcing Francis Lovell.

Lovell had the air of a one-man delegation: formal fur-trimmed long gown, velvet cap placed at a precise angle.

'My lord, I did have an appointment.' He glanced doubt-fully at Alcock and Kendall. 'And this is a somewhat pri-vate matter.'

'Appointment?' Richard rubbed his forehead. 'Yes, I believe you did. Nothing has to be private from the bishop here, though, or from my secretary. You can tell the door-keeper to keep everyone else out. Then come and sit down and tell me about whatever it is. You sit down, too, Alcock. I thought I'd already told you to.'

'I'm here alone,' said Lovell, when the doorkeeper had been instructed, 'but I represent a number of other people. No, perhaps privacy isn't so vital.' He rattled off a string of names. 'I'm here on their behalf. It's such a difficult matter to broach, however. They chose me to put it to you because of the length of time I have known you but . . .'

'We used to roll about in the courtyard at Middleham, wrestling, as lads. And they feel that because of that I'm not likely to have you instantly beheaded if you irritate me?' said Richard. 'Out with it, Frank.'

'We wish to ask, sire,' said Francis Lovell, visibly bracing himself, 'if you intend to publish a denial of the rumours.'

'Rumours? About my nephews' alleged deaths? That would be difficult. After all, however unfortunate it may be, they actually are dead. As I've said before, I think it better to let speculation die away for lack of fuel.'

'Not those rumours, sire, I mean the stories that are circulating about the Lady Elizabeth of York.'

'Elizabeth? No one's saying that I've done away with her as well, are they? She's here at court.'

'No, sire. They're saying you intend to marry her.'

Richard opened his mouth but nothing came out of it.

'We know there's nothing in it,' said Lovell. 'But some people think otherwise.'

Richard regained control of his larynx. 'There's most certainly nothing in it, by God there isn't! Where did you hear this?'

An expression of distaste crossed Lovell's round, tough features. 'It's everywhere. Inside the court and out. Women gossiping in street markets, grooms chatting in the stables. I first heard John Howard's men bandying it about.'

'Catesby has made a report to me on it,' said Alcock, 'but he said it was only a casual sentence he overheard: I did not consider it worthwhile to trouble either you or the Council with it, sire. But, yes, it was one of John Howard's men who said it.'

'Howard wasn't among the people you said you represent, Lovell. There'll be a denial all right. But more than that, there'll be an explanation. Howard is in Westminster. Have him sent for, Kendall.'

'I am extremely sorry,' said Alcock while they waited, 'but it was a single phrase which might have been misheard. I noted it but I genuinely thought it too trivial to report. Catesby himself thought the speaker might have been joking.'

'It's all right, Alcock.' Richard gave him a grin which, if wry, was also understanding. 'It was a reasonable mistake. The idea is so absurd that it's very hard to imagine that the remark was meant seriously.'

'But according to Lovell here it is being meant seriously.

And I,' said Alcock with annoyance, 'missed it.'

'Caught out in something on which you've always prided yourself, eh, Alcock? None of us are perfect. Ah, Howard.'

John Howard entered the room in a manner which suggested reluctance. Alcock glanced at his craggy face and then at Richard's thin, tense one, from which all trace of amusement had abruptly vanished, and knew what Richard was thinking. If Howard, one of his oldest and most dependable associates, were somehow a source of malicious rumours, was any safety left anywhere? Alcock and Lovell would themselves become suspect if Howard were false. And then Richard would be alone as he had not been even on the day of the sixteenth of March, when Anne slipped out of life, and in the sky the sun went into eclipse as though to join in the mourning.

'I have to raise a most unpleasant matter,' said Richard to Howard, and elaborated.

Howard listened in silence. 'Yes, I've heard the talk,' he said simply, 'but I'd hoped you never would. I regret the big mouths among my men.'

'What I want to know is how the rumour started.'

'I'll have to tell you now, I see. The girl herself, I mean the Lady Elizabeth, began it.'

'The Lady Elizabeth?'

'Yes. She's a pretty thing. I suppose I've been fatherly towards her, I think I wished I had such a daughter. No doubt that's why she wrote to me.'

'What did she write to you about?' said Richard evenly.

'She wanted me to put her case to you.' Howard looked uncomfortable. Richard had not invited him to sit and he stood there awkwardly in their midst, the only one obliged to stay on his feet. 'I refused,' he said. 'Naturally, I hoped that would be the end of such nonsense but . . .'

'*What case, John?*'

Howard hesitated and Richard's mouth compressed. 'That she wanted to marry you,' said John Howard at last, baldly.

'That *she* wanted to marry *me*? Not the other way about?'

'No, no. The story's been twisted by scandalmongers. She wanted me to act as her intermediary and when I said no, she apparently relieved her feelings, which for a young and carefully-reared girl seem remarkably forceful,' said Howard disapprovingly, 'by complaining to members of my household about my hardness of heart. That's what happened.'

'What precisely did her letter to you say?'

'My lord,' said John Howard, visibly appalled, 'must I?'

'Yes, you must. We must know it all. All.' Howard had put an unwilling hand into his belt pouch. 'I see you came prepared,' said Richard. 'Despite your scruples. And you've kept the letter.'

'If it came to the point, I would rather you read it yourself than that I should have to repeat its gist.'

Richard held out his hand for the missive and Howard, drawing it from the pouch, surrendered it. He turned dark red as he watched the King read but Richard's own face did not change. When he had finished, he handed the letter, with an air of contempt, to Alcock.

'When one becomes King, Alcock, things happen which generally speaking one does not discuss with representatives of the Church. Women,' said Richard distastefully, 'make signals. But this girl is my niece and my ward, and she knew my wife, and Anne is not two months dead. I am ashamed of Elizabeth. Go on, Alcock, read the thing. Then pass it to the others. I want all of you in this room to know the truth about this, for I don't want doubts in any of your minds.'

Silently and disbelievingly, Alcock took in the words penned in Elizabeth of York's educated Italian script. Before he had got to the end of the first sentence, he too was ashamed of her.

I beseech you, the letter implored, *to mediate with my lord Richard in this matter of a marriage between him and*

*myself. Such a marriage would set at rest the feud between
my mother's family and his . . . In the past I was once
promised to Henry Tudor but it was never with my consent;
my will is to my lord King Richard only . . . He is my only
joy and I am his in heart and thought. If you will help me
. . .*

'Adolescent moonshine,' said Alcock. 'Mixed with a little political cleverness. I suppose one can take heart from
the fact that Elizabeth of York evidently doesn't suppose
you murdered her brothers, my lord.'

'Well, you did your best on my behalf to explain to her
and her mother and sisters, Alcock,' Richard said. 'You
and Bourchier between you. Elizabeth at least seems to
have believed you.'

'Yes, I think she did. Bess Woodville didn't. I am sorry
for Bess,' Alcock said. 'She's been so badly frightened now
that she only dares to believe the worst. I understand that,
although I fear it made me impatient with her. But
Elizabeth was willing to believe, from the start. Now I wish
she hadn't!'

'So do I. When did you receive this letter, Howard? It
isn't dated.'

Howard hesitated again. Then: 'February, my lord.'

'February? But in February, my wife was still . . .' Stark
outrage appeared in Richard's eyes, the real Plantagenet
fury which was always there under the surface, which had
shown itself even in Edward Quintus the day he ordered
Alcock from his presence. 'You have my leave to go, all of
you. Oh, except for Alcock. I wish for one witness and the
Church will do admirably. Kendall, another errand for
you. Fetch me the Lady Elizabeth of York. Instantly!'

Instantly, of course, meant as soon as she could be
found. While they waited, Richard unburdened himself to
Alcock.

'I realise that the Council has been worrying, ever since
the last year, over my lack of a direct heir. I believe that you
were not aware, Alcock, that one faction sent me a deputation

after Anne's death, petitioning me to consider a new marriage. But they at least had the decency to wait until my wife was actually dead, and they did have the welfare of the kingdom at heart. And when I told them to go away, they went. In fact, I had to call them back myself and admit that they did right to raise the matter even though I couldn't then see my way to doing anything about it. They accepted my wish to grieve. Which is more than Elizabeth does, apparently!'

'What will you say to her?'

'I don't know, but I shall think of something,' said Richard ominously.

He did. When she came, and sank into the usual curtsy, the words burst out of him like water from a ruptured conduit. He had been seated. He shot to his feet, came round the desk and stood over her.

'How dare you?' he shouted at the bent head with its maidenly lawn cap. 'How dare you intrude on my loss with the obscene suggestion that I should marry you?' He flourished the letter at her as she looked up. 'I'm your uncle, you stupid, foul-minded girl! Ask the bishop here what the Church thinks of that! And above all, how dare you harbour such indecent lusts while my wife was still alive!'

He stopped, breathless. Elizabeth came gracefully upright and raised limpid eyes to him. Alcock saw that the King's anger had frightened her and also that she was enjoying her own alarm. He remembered the story that once, in a fit of rage at Bess Woodville's obdurate chastity, her father had held a dagger to Bess's throat. Bess had remained 'unperturbed'. Had got a thrill out of it, most likely. She might be timid in other ways, but not when it came to dealing with male desires.

Once he had very nearly desired her himself. Now the thought of that distant and respectful worship revolted him. The object of it had not been worthy.

'I'm waiting,' said Richard to Elizabeth, 'for you to explain yourself.'

She gave him the infuriating, shattering smile which he had once thought so innocent. Alcock saw him recoil from it.

'Dear Uncle,' said Elizabeth gently, 'I ask pardon if I have offended. I did all these things because I love you.'

She seemed to think that this was a justification. Richard retreated to his chair once more. There was a pause and then Richard turned to Alcock. 'You were right. The matter is – trivial. It isn't worth being angry. She doesn't understand what she's talking about or what harm her behaviour could do. Go to your chamber, Elizabeth. Remain there until you're sent for. When you are, it will be to start a journey north to my castle of Sheriff Hutton. I have a natural son and daughter there, along with my brother Clarence's children. You can join them.'

'My lord, I'm not a child!' She had gone pale. With hurt, Alcock thought.

'Oh yes, you are,' said Richard. 'When you talk of love in that puling way, you are a baby. The daughter of a king – the *eldest* daughter of a king – recognises her responsibilities. She does not abandon them, not if she's grown up, that is, for love. Any more than kings' sons do, or kings.'

Elizabeth's slim, fair-skinned hands clenched on a fold of the dark gown she wore, in mourning or a pretence of it, for Anne. 'My lord,' she said, 'that is a criticism of my father.'

'So you understand that much?' Richard considered her with mild surprise. 'Good, then perhaps you are starting to mature after all. Before you withdraw to your room, then, I have something to say to you. You may sit. Now listen. Any love you bear to me must be only the kind of love which exists between near relations. I would not dream of applying for a dispensation for a marriage between an uncle and a niece. Even if Rome were willing, I would not be, and the Church here would strenuously oppose it as a most undesirable precedent. Alcock?'

'The King is correct,' said Alcock.

'Quite. It would cause nothing but scandal. Pay attention, Elizabeth. I shall make a public denial of the rumours you have so irresponsibly started. You will go to Sheriff Hutton. And in due course you will marry. You will not marry for love and you will certainly not marry me. I pray that God in His mercy will grant love to you in your wedded life but your purpose will be to marry for the safety and peace of the realm of which your father was king. Crowns are not made of roses. Do you understand?'

Elizabeth paled still more. 'Am I only a pawn, then? Are women always that?'

'Very often, yes. Your Aunt Anne once complained of much the same thing. I made it up to her as best I could. I hope your husband will make it up to you. But it's the way of the world. Get used to it.'

'And who,' said Elizabeth, 'will my husband be?'

'That remains to be seen. It is a question which must wait until after I have fought Henry Tudor and decided the issue between us. If I prevail, I will find you a trustworthy English lord. Meanwhile, I now accept that I must secure my own dynasty lawfully. Sir Edward Brampton leaves for Portugal next week, taking with him my formal offer for the hand of a Portuguese princess. The marriage will take place after I have dealt with Tudor. The negotiations are at a delicate stage and not yet to be announced. You will speak of them to no one. I tell you only to put an end, once and for all, to your nonsensical daydreaming.'

'But,' Elizabeth was trembling, 'have you no feeling for me at all, then, my lord?'

'For the love of God! It would not be of the slightest importance if I had. Have you not been listening? But the answer, as it happens, is no.' He let that sink home, seeing her shrink into herself. 'I have an uncle's affection for a niece, albeit a naughty, childish niece.' Again he paused, while she absorbed the blow. 'It was my wife,' he said, 'Queen Anne, my Anne, for whom I had that kind of love, and it is that love which I am about to violate for the sake of the kingdom. You are not concerned in that; you have another destiny. If it chances that Tudor deals with me

524

instead of I with him, then you will become his queen. Have you not wondered why, since he took that oath to marry you, I haven't put you beyond his reach by marrying you elsewhere? If it comes to the point, I don't want you beyond his reach. I want you free to become the means by which your father's blood, the Plantagenet blood, can be passed on to the next generation to give us a line of kings with Plantagenet blood, whatever their name may be. And the means by which, at last, York and Lancaster are finally reconciled. In a sense,' Richard smiled wryly, 'if you ever wear a crown, Elizabeth, it *will* be made of roses. Red and white, mixed together.'

In a trembling voice, Elizabeth said: 'May I ask a question?'

'Naturally.'

'I know that you explained things to myself and my mother, but there are so many rumours. Are my brothers really dead? You see, I have heard a story that one of them has been seen, alive, travelling to Bruges. So . . .'

'Mystery always breeds rumours, Elizabeth.' Richard spoke quite kindly. 'Something of that kind was bound to happen. No, they are dead. If you ever become Henry's queen, and any pretenders arise, rest assured that they will be false. You will not have to face the choice between a brother of yours on the one hand, and your husband and son and your own throne on the other.'

Elizabeth's eyes widened. It seemed that for a moment she had even forgotten her infatuation and her hurt. 'I never thought of that.'

'Think of it now,' said Richard.

Chapter Thirty-Six

Petronel: News of an Innocent

Summer 1485

I rose on that incredible morning, not to an ordinary day – my ageing husband was once more preparing to ride off to war and in the circumstances the household was anything but ordinary – but to what I thought was a predictable one.

I knew what I expected to happen in the course of it. Lionel, still determined to defy his years and to answer King Richard's second call to help fight off Henry Tudor, would practise for an hour or two with his horse and arms. He had had new armour made, lighter in weight than before. Under it he would bandage his wrists and knees to support them. Given these concessions, he believed he could convince his body that it wasn't almost seventy years of age, but still no more than fifty. 'It's not as if I'll need to engage in hand to hand work,' he told me when we heard that men were being mustered at Nottingham in readiness for the imminent invasion. 'But I want to lead our men there and give what service I can.' He would leave within the week and every able-bodied man from Eynesby, Silbeck, Bouldershawe and Thornwood would go with him. He had told me to send orders to Thornwood. My tenants there hardly knew me, but they acknowledged me and had sent me four men, well-armed, strong and willing. Lionel was proud of the force he had been able to raise.

When he had finished his own practice, he would assemble the men to drill them, and he would make Matthew exercise the white stallion that the Abbot of Jervaulx was sending to the King, through Lionel, to use as a charger. Lionel had the wisdom, at least, not to try riding White Surrey himself. The horse needed strong young hands on the reins.

I meanwhile would be busy, as I had been for a month, doing what Lionel had no time to do – overseeing the mid-summer shearing and supervising as the fleeces were baled and making sure they were properly marked before they went to London. For part of the way the wool train would have the protection of Lionel and the men. After Nottingham, he had said he would send a small escort on with it, provided that the invasion had not then begun. There was no knowing what conditions on the roads, or in trade, would be like by the time our wool set out; war was a disruptive thing. We could only hope for the best. Lionel's sharp young clerk, who was in orders and therefore not supposed to fight, would go with the wool to arrange its sale.

I came down early, therefore, to break my fast in the hall. I remember regretting that Ralph the cook was over military age and, unlike Lionel, prepared to admit it. What a shame, I thought, that he wasn't going to the war too. But I was glad that John Steward was also past the age to go. I recall that as I ate I also thought that although it was unlikely that the war when it came would reach as far north as Eynesby, we should nevertheless be ready in case it did, and what a good thing that the place had been built as a fortified manorhouse.

It was a sweet June morning. All the doors were open so that the fresh summer air could blow in. The moors were green and bronze in the sun and the sky was full of larksong. There were a few small, harmless clouds about, like tufts of white wool. I had finished eating, and was just about to go in search of the head shepherd, when Lionel came half-way down the stairs, and called to me. 'Petronel, come up here.'

'Is it to do with the shearing?' I asked as I followed him

up to his chamber. 'Simeon Shepherd was asking . . .'

'No, this has nowt to do wi' sheep.' We reached Lionel's room and he closed the door behind us. 'Come, we'd best sit down,' he said. So I sat on the bed beside him, half-turned to face him. 'What is it?' I asked.

'I've something to tell you, something I've been putting off. First I thought to savour it, choosing my moment. But now – Tudor'll sail all right, the war will come and what if I don't come back? It seems that the time is now and it's a surprise to me, but I'm sorry for you, lass.'

'I don't understand,' I said. The soft June breeze whispered in at the window. My heart had for some reason begun to pound.

'A few days back,' said Lionel, 'I told you you couldn't go south with the wool train. I didna want you going near Faldene. You'd have gone there for sure, to see your son. I couldn't let you do that.'

I waited.

'But if I don't come back,' said Lionel, 'likely as not you'd be off to Faldene straight away, to see him. So I must tell you now, he's not there. He left Faldene a year and more ago. You'll not be seeing Perky Dick again.'

'What do you mean? Has something happened to him? Is he dead?'

He couldn't be dead, not my little lively Perky Dick. Lionel's colourless eyes were watching me. I evaded them, looking round the room instead. It seemed just as usual, a little untidy, perhaps, because some of the gear Lionel was to take to Nottingham was strewn about. If Perky Dick were dead, the roof would crash in, the sun go out, the world dissolve in weeping . . .

Children did die. It happened. How many times had it happened to Chrissy? Why should Perky Dick be immune from plague or I, Petronel, be immune from bereavement? I turned back to Lionel. 'I asked you, is he dead?'

'I've sent word to tell Faldene so,' said Lionel. 'I even toyed with the notion of letting you think the same. But I reckon I'm entitled to tell you the truth.'

'What truth?' Hideous thoughts reeled through my imagination. If Perky Dick were not dead, then what? Maimed in an accident? Struck blind? A leper?

'As far as the Faldene folk are concerned,' said Lionel, 'last summer I took him away from them and sent him to Calais to learn the wool trade from the other end. That's where most of our wool goes to be graded and taxed on its way to Burgundy, where the bulk of it ends up. It struck them as reasonable enough to send him there. They'll shortly learn that he fell sick of some childish disease while he was there, and died of it.'

'But he hasn't.' I said it as a statement, not a question.

'No. As far as I know, he's in excellent health. But he's not in Calais. He's – well, across the Channel, never mind exactly where. He's engaged,' said Lionel, 'upon the business of the King. It's a great honour for one so young. There are a few attendant dangers, maybe, but when did a king's business not have those? The honour outweighs the danger, as you know. You've been to Calais on a king's errand yourself.'

'You're hinting,' I said. 'But at what? What kind of royal business can a child of Perky Dick's age carry out? Please be plain with me!'

'I mean to be. Last summer, after the word came that the King's own son was dead, an idea was mooted, to spread a rumour that one of King Edward's boys was still living.'

Again, I waited. I could not see what this had to do with me or Perky Dick. Indeed, it was hard for me now to believe that I had ever been part of the Gloucesters' household. I had seen little of the former Middleham people since they went away, for I had not the rank for a queen's attendant. Lionel, who had once tried to keep me from Isabel and had successfully kept me from Anne at Middleham, would never have held me back from going to the Queen. Sometimes I derived a sour amusement from thinking how perverse this turn of Fortune's famous Wheel must seem to him. For Anne never summoned me after she became Queen and for the last two years I had been uninterruptedly at Eynesby, my life as remote from the affairs of the court as that of any farmer's wife.

'The idea of starting the rumour,' Lionel said, 'was to discourage Henry Tudor, and to discourage men from joining him. I lent Perky Dick . . .'

'You lent him? As if he were a . . . a horse? Lent him for what, pray?'

'For the purpose of laying a trail across the Channel. He made a journey, on a ship carefully picked for the character of her captain. Certain of the King's friends,' said Lionel with a bleak grin, 'spent a lot of time last summer hanging round Dover, talking to ships' captains in taverns to find a suitably garrulous one that Henry's agents wouldn't find hard to pump if they felt like it. Perky Dick crossed in that ship, with a party of attendants who were a bit more respectful to him than people in charge of a young lad rightly ought to be, and now and again addressed him as "sir" or "my lord", apparently in error.'

'I see. But Henry Tudor is going to invade after all.' I pointed to a bundle of Lionel's spare clothes, lying on top of a chest. 'That's why you're wanting all these things packed. The plot didn't work. So why can't Perky Dick come home and be himself again? Why go on pretending he's dead?'

So he told me.

I listened numbly, disbelief slowly turning to the realisation that he meant it. 'He'll refuse you!' I said, grabbing at hope. 'He'll grow into a man and he'll refuse you!'

'He will have had years of moulding by then. And he may not care to find himself on the street without a name to call his own or a roof over his head.'

'But of course he'll have a roof! His home is here, at Eynesby! He's . . .' I stopped, knowing what the next words ought to be and suddenly unable to speak them. *I thought to savour it* said Lionel's voice in my head.

Lionel smiled, that thin smile I knew so very well. 'Were you going to say he's my son? Petronel, Petronel, he's my great-nephew, isn't he? Geoffrey was his father. And since Geoffrey in turn was the son of the old Duke of York, Perky Dick is, by blood, a Plantagenet.'

'How did you find out?' I asked. 'And when?' I did not trouble to defend myself. I had sensed long ago that he knew. I had not dared to confirm it, that was all. This new certainty was almost a relief.

'Nicholas Hawes,' said Lionel. 'Did he want you to pay him to stop his mouth, by the way? He didn't say he had, not to me, but it's a fair guess. He surely tried you first. You were the likelier victim.'

I didn't answer. Lionel smiled again. 'He nursed Geoffrey in his final illness. Perhaps he told you? What with the fever and the weakness, Geoffrey talked. I know it all. How you shared baths with him. How you coupled in the ale cellar and out on the moors. Nicholas,' he said, 'suggested that I should pay him to avoid the ignominy of being known as a cuckold.'

'And did you?' I asked. I felt cold. How could he have known, for certain, all these years, and never charged me with it? I was realising it, slowly. He had gone on, living with me if not sleeping with me, housing, clothing, feeding me, eating at the same table, making conversation. It was because he had done all that that I had sometimes said to myself that no, it was impossible, he couldn't know. But he had been watching me without comment and acknowledging Perky Dick, waiting his time – for what? For this?

'Did I pay him?' said Lionel. 'Oh yes. I gave him some money. But he'd hired two men to ride with him in case of footpads. I had a word with them. They were a type, you know. Reliable for anything as long as they're paid. I paid them more than I did him. I paid them to silence him in some lonely place and told them to reimburse themselves further from the silver in his saddlebag. I gave them good characters afterwards and no doubt they found themselves employment in some good household. John Dighton and Miles Forrest, those were their names.'

'All these years,' I said. 'And you never spoke.'

'God save me,' said Lionel unexpectedly, 'I didn't know what to do. At the start I'd been proud of the lad, boasted about him. Was I to throw him out, put you away, let the whole world see me as a deceived old greybeard whose young wife had palmed off another man's bastard on him? Story-tellers use that theme too often and the laugh's on the greybeard, always. By the time Hawes came, I'd countenanced the boy for too long. And besides . . .'

'Yes?' I said.

'You'll not believe this,' he said violently, 'but I tried to forgive you. I lay awake of a night, telling myself, she's young and I'm ageing. Geoffrey was dead and gone, it was all over anyhow. If I couldn't pretend to myself that the boy was mine, at least I could lie to the world. I could keep my pride. That meant keeping you, but I'd lie there and try to think of you as an erring child. But you're my wife and the anger wouldn't die. It grew.' I knew, at once, what he meant, how it had swelled inside him like ice swelling in a water pipe until the pipe breaks. 'And then,' he said, 'when the talk of laying a false trail about the young prince began, I saw how I could serve both my anger and my king.'

I am cold, I thought, because I am close to him and he is ice to his bone marrow. Only a cold, cold man could have lived so long with such anger and been silent.

'You're gambling,' I whispered. 'Gambling with Perky Dick's life.'

'Or preparing a glittering future for him,' said Lionel. 'If the King falls in this war, that is. If King Richard prevails, Perky Dick will be safe enough, in obscurity.'

'Used,' I said bitterly. 'He and I, both of us, have been used, as if we were animals or things. Even by Geoffrey.'

'By Geoffrey?'

'He started his pursuit of me to even the score with you. Because of Eynesby. He resented being cut out of it.'

I watched his face as I said that. Except for a slight rise of his brows, there was little to see. 'I sometimes wondered about that,' he said reflectively. 'Geoffrey was very like me in some ways. He always wanted debts paid, his own and other people's. You haven't surprised me. Tell me something. I agree that I am using Perky Dick, and clearly you know that your lover – for all his no doubt romantic talk – did the same to you. But in what way have I done so?'

I almost laughed. 'You all but said it yourself, just now, when you said I was young and you were ageing. I was fourteen to your fifty.'

'What of it? I made you mistress of a fine house. It wasn't such a bad bargain.'

'Wasn't it? You blamed me for not having children!' Suddenly I was shouting. 'How could I help it if the babies didn't come? You drove me into Geoffrey's arms! Bargain, indeed! You never think of anything but bargains! I was handed to you to settle a dispute, like a sheep or a heifer. And then you blamed me for the barrenness which was your fault, not mine, yours!'

'Barrenness is never the man's fault.'

'Then how do you explain it that no woman ever had a child from you, that I never had one in years and years and yet I managed it with Geoffrey?'

His ears, predictably, had gone red. 'I've been unlucky with women all my life!'

'God in heaven, you're still blaming me!'

'Did you never think how it was for me? Year after year and no son to follow me. And then, at last, Perky Dick. I was proud of him, Petronel. He was the assurance of my manhood. The first doubt came in when I saw he was left-handed. Just as well I cured him of that. The little prince Richard of York was right-handed, so Perky Dick has to be too. It was that that started me thinking. I remembered little things, times when your eyes shone when Geoffrey came into the house, the way your gaze would sometimes follow him. I remembered the day I learned that Alison had been seen at the Michaelmas Fair in Eynesby and not in your company, on a day when you'd gone to visit her or so you said. But I didn't want to believe it. Every day Perky Dick grew more like Geoffrey, and I'd say to myself, well, they're cousins. And then,' said Lionel, 'Hawes came. Oh God, it was like being trapped in a pit. I had nothing, had I? No wife, no son! No self-respect. Did you never think of that, my girl? It was worse than if Perky Dick had never been born at all!'

'And did you ever think what it would have been like for me, how you'd have made it for me, if he hadn't?' I asked, and then I saw that, incredibly, he was crying. I had never imagined that Lionel could cry. He sat there, pressing his long bony fingers into his eyes. 'Thee hurt me, lass,' he said, his accent thickening. 'Thee hurt me, going to another man like that.'

'And you hurt me,' I said, 'when you struck me for failing to conceive. A woman can't conceive to order.' My voice was harsh. There was a small worm of pity deep within me but deep within me it must stay. The hurt he had inflicted on me had done too much damage. He thought his own wounds past healing, did he? Well, so were mine.

'What happens now?' I said.

'For Perky Dick? As far as you and I and Faldene are concerned, he is dead. If King Richard wins the war, Perky Dick remains abroad, being fostered. If Tudor wins – I have told you what lies ahead for him. Either way, he is disinherited. As for you, I'm putting you away. I can do it now. I shall let it be known that our child is dead and that you wish to withdraw to a nunnery. I shall find you a suitably strict one, my dear. Of course you are disinherited too. There was a time when, in default of children, you might have come in after my death for all my three manors. But since you'll be taking the veil, I shall will them, appropriately, to the Church. As for Thornwood . . .'

'Thornwood is mine,' I said.

535

'Thornwood,' he said, 'will buy your way into the nunnery. They all want dowry of some sort. You'll give me no trouble, I hope. I've no mind to see you live soft anyway. You'll go to a place that keeps its rule to the letter. But unless you go quietly, I'll hand you to the abbess as a faithless wife who wants extra watching. Then you'll find yourself shut away in a community where every eye will be on you in distrust and disapproval. Be wise, go quietly, and I'll spare you that.'

'Very well,' I said. 'You've not yet chosen the place, you say?'

'No, that I've still to consider.'

He left me presently. I stayed all day in my own chamber, praying, trying to soothe myself by remembering that Perky Dick was, as yet, still safe. I might never see him again, but he lived and was well.

That night, as so often before in the course of my life, I resorted to deception, the weapon of the helpless so much frowned upon by the strong, who never understand that it is they themselves who drive us to it.

The room where I slept was next to Lionel's. I waited until the house was quiet and the night deepening, and then I began to cry out as if in nightmare, and finally I screamed. A moment later, Lionel was beside me, shaking me. I appeared to wake and I said I had had a bad dream but I would not tell him what it was.

Two nights later I did it again. And this time, sobbing, I said I had dreamed that I was back in Withysham. 'It was such a horrible place!' I cried. 'It was always so cold and the abbess was so cruel!'

My mother had told me not to talk to Lionel about Withysham. She had given me questionable advice in some respects but not about that. My very reticence on the subject, all these years, inclined him to believe me.

When he set out for Nottingham, accompanied by the wool train bound for the south, I went too. Ten days from the day when I learned what had befallen Perky Dick, I was again in Withysham, in my beloved Aunt Abbess Eleanor's arms.

Chapter Thirty-Seven

The Plantagenets: The End or The Beginning

August 1485

The night had begun warm and velvety, but as the dark hours passed the air cooled. Wisps of ground mist drifted on to the slope below the camp. It had been the twenty-second of August 1485 for three hours now. Autumn was not far off, and the scent of the night air proclaimed it.

The sky was clear. Stars were moving across it towards their dawn stations and below them, like earthbound equivalents, twinkled the crimson campfires: those of Richard and his close supporters nearby, and, further off, those of Northumberland and Stanley, both equivocally placed. Those in the distance, on lower ground towards the west, were Henry Tudor's. The calm eyes of heaven; the burning eyes of war.

Richard wondered if Tudor were also awake. His own head was heavy with sleeplessness, yet he called himself experienced in the business of war. Tudor was not a war leader at all. He would never have acquired an over-developed right shoulder from practising with a sword too big for him, trying to match an elder brother's prowess. So the agents who had seen him said in their reports.

He stood at his tent flap, looking out. The world was still, but not entirely silent. From the horse lines came a whinny, surely the voice of his new stallion White Surrey. Sentries exchanged passwords; a fire crackled as it burned low; blanket-wrapped forms on the ground muttered and stirred. But no one was speaking to him or pressing on him now. He had as much privacy now as a king ever had.

His eye lit on those questionably placed campfires of Stanley and Northumberland. Northumberland was too far to the rear and Stanley too neatly placed between Richard's forces and those of Henry Tudor. The message in both cases was as plain as if a courier had brought it. 'I have not yet decided whether or not to fight, nor upon whose side.'

Northumberland had never liked him, ever since Richard came to the north and challenged his supremacy, and Stanley, undoubtedly, was under the control of Margaret Beaufort and the tempting promises of his stepson Henry. No doubt Henry would reward him well for his support, if he gave it and Henry became king.

In his own camp he had one of Stanley's sons as hostage, but Stanley was known not to like his sons very much. Oh well, if Stanley failed him, but both of them survived tomorrow, then Stanley would go to the block but not his hapless offspring.

He shouldn't be so careless with his son's life, though. He was lucky to have him. He, Richard, had done what he could to protect his own natural children. He had warned the boy in Sheriff Hutton to eschew ambition if the crown went to Tudor. The existence of the other, his own namesake, in the care of Alcock's cousin, was known to very few. With luck he would remain out of public knowledge and live out his life in peace. 'If I die,' Richard had said to Alcock, 'see that he's put to a good trade. Masonry, perhaps.'

The night was now very cool indeed. Misty cloud was drifting over the stars. He shivered and turned back into his tent. There he threw himself face down on his pallet. He had tried. Oh God, how he had tried. Veering from one challenge to the next, containing every danger as best he could before another threat rose up to distract him. Anthony Woodville. Hastings, Morton, Buckingham, Tudor. No end to the diabolical procession.

He had done his very best with the impossible situation bequeathed to him by Edward. I loved you all my life, Ned, and you rewarded me by leaving your sons with the Wood-villes and yet making me Lord Protector. If I leave this world tomorrow and we meet in heaven or hell, I shall have some bitter things to say to you.

If he did leave the world tomorrow, he thought, turning restlessly and longing to gather Anne's small-boned, beloved shape against him, he would hardly care. If he lived it would only be to face an arid future. He would have to force his reluctant body to breed sons on some unfortunate Portuguese princess. She would be lost and homesick and probably without a word of English, so that he would be unable even to talk to her, and he would be grieving all the time for little Ned and Anne.

I did the best I could, trying to be the kind of king you were, my brother. I tried to imagine what you would do, when this and that happened, and then I tried to do it. Tomorrow I shall go on trying. I will direct my armies; if need be, I shall fight. If it comes to the point, I shall try to reach Henry Tudor himself and kill him personally. If I am cut down on the way, at least men will say I made a good end.

It was difficult to imagine fighting. His skin, his eyes, his very brain, were parched with sleeplessness. At least half the men out there didn't expect him to conquer. They too had read the significance of Northumberland's and Stanley's choice of camping sites. There had been warning messages pinned on the tents of his best supporter, John Howard of Norfolk.

He was so tired. Had Anne felt like this before she let go of life and slid away from him, he had thought at the time, so very easily?

Somewhere across the dark, dew-drenched midland fields, a cock began to crow.

Bosworth morning had come.

Chapter Thirty-Eight

Petronel: The Proud Ending

Summer 1485

Withysham Abbey stands in a vale on the northern edge of the Sussex downs. Southwards, the smooth high backs of the downs march across the sky, and the rainclouds from the sea blow inland over them. Northwards there are woodlands, the remains of a greater forest, now interspersed with farmland. Some of it belongs to the abbey, which over the centuries has grown.

The abbey buildings vary in age. The guest parlour, which one enters by ducking under a low lintel and stepping down to a sunken floor, was built in Saxon times. But the church was built and paid for only a hundred years ago by my great-great-grandfather at Faldene. Its proportions are lofty and its pale stone reflects the light from the tall windows. Even in dull weather, the church of Withysham always seems bright inside.

I had kept all these things in my memory through my nineteen years away. To my joy, when I saw Withysham again, it did not seem much changed. Nor did my Aunt Eleanor. She was a little smaller than I remembered her and a little more lined, but that was all. The essential Aunt Eleanor, the way she stood with calm folded hands as I came to greet her, her eyes and her smile, were as they had always been. As I knelt to her, my abbess now, all the intervening years and experiences might not have been. They were squeezed out into an irrelevant dangling loop, like a girdle if you hold it in your hands and bring the two ends together.

She did not ask about those years and I did not tell her a great deal. She gave me her condolences for the death of my son. Lionel had sent her a letter, which arrived ahead of me, in which he gave that as my reason for wishing to come to Withysham. I had, with some artistry, shown anguish and distress at the prospect, but not resisted, and he had kept his word. I suspected that he was glad to, that he did not wish to admit even to an abbess he had never met, that he was a cuckold.

When she had finished with the condolences, she did say: 'I think you were not happy in your marriage, Petronel. Or you would not want to leave your husband now. The child belonged to both of you, after all.'

'You are right. I wasn't happy. Nor was he. He's as pleased for me to come here as I am, Mother Abbess.'

And that was all. I turned the conversation, asking for news of Withysham, and whether or not the abbey had yet been able to found the daughter house which had been Aunt Eleanor's ambition in days gone past. It still was her ambition, she said, and was still unrealised.

Then I took my place in Withysham, serving a novitiate before I took my vows. Nuns don't probe into each other's pasts. We think of ourselves as beginning life the moment we step across the abbey threshold.

Naturally, I wondered sometimes what was happening out in the world. News reached Aunt Eleanor from time to time and she would tell us at Chapter anything that she thought we should know. We heard that Henry Tudor had landed at Milford Haven and Aunt Eleanor ordered us to begin a chain of prayer, day and night, not for either side to win but for an outcome according to God's will and for the souls of those who would die. Every day and night thereafter, between the offices, at least two or three of the nuns stayed in the church to pray.

I joined several of these night vigils although I did not spend them all in silent petitions connected with the war. Nor did I pray for Lionel. My prayers were for Perky Dick, wherever he might be, and I welcomed the chance to put my mind to it so intensely.

I preferred the night vigils to those in the daytime. In those dark, solemn hours, with only the whisper of the candles within the church, and the murmur of the wind outside, with oneself and maybe two companions the only wakeful human beings in the abbey and perhaps for miles, it was easier to believe that one's prayers had power. They went out into air which was not already strewn with a thousand million seeds of speech and thought. They might have room to grow.

We heard that Tudor had struck inland, gathering men as he went. And we heard, at length, that the Battle of Bosworth had been fought on the twenty-second of August and that Henry was victorious. After that there was silence for three weeks. Then Matthew came.

He did not come alone, but with my brother Simon from Faldene and my half-brother Tom Grinstead. They had not been at Bosworth; they had not set out until Tudor had actually landed, and then not managed to get there in time. Later, when we heard that Tudor was sequestering the lands of everyone who could be identified as having been at Bosworth, we all felt that this was just as well, though at the time both Simon and Tom felt badly about it.

Matthew had sought shelter at Faldene on his way to me, and thus made contact with them. He had been delayed in getting there because he had been wounded in the thigh at Bosworth and had had to rest for ten days, hidden in the hayloft at a friendly Yorkist farmhouse, before he could travel. Simon and Tom had been home before him and when my family heard the news he brought, my brothers came with him to the abbey.

Matthew knew nothing of the final quarrel between me and Lionel. Though there had been tattle in the household about Perky Dick's paternity, only Lionel and I actually knew the truth. Lionel's desire not to be laughed at, and my attempts to keep the surface of life smooth, had amounted

543

to an unintentional partnership. They all thought I had really come here out of sorrow for the death of my son.

Matthew therefore thought he was bringing me tragic news. He stood in the middle of the guest parlour, holding his cap in his hands – just like Walter long ago – and couched it in terms that were as plain and as kind as he could make them.

Lionel had been killed at Bosworth. But he had made a good end and died quickly. At the very last, with Stanley and Northumberland still holding off and John Howard already dead, King Richard had gambled everything – his kingdom and his life – upon one last effort to destroy his enemy personally.

He had turned White Surrey's head towards the place where Henry Tudor had been pointed out to him, close to the Red Dragon banner of Wales. He had set spurs to the stallion and drawn his sword, and made for his adversary at full gallop.

His friends had ridden after him: Robert Brackenbury, John Kendall, Richard Ratcliffe, Francis Lovell – who was taken by surprise and trailed slightly behind – and other, less well-known men, one of them Lionel Eynesby.

'And me,' said Matthew simply. 'I rode after Master Eynesby. But something brought my horse down – an arrow, I think – and so I fell and was set upon. I'd have been killed except that a shout went up and the two men who'd jumped on me suddenly rushed off to join in . . . well . . . what was happening further up the slope. There'd been a dip between the two main armies, you understand, with long grassy slopes on either side and a boggy patch and a stream at the bottom of the dip. We'd just charged across that when my horse collapsed. I'd been hurt – I was just about able to stand, leaning on my sword. I couldn't get up there to help, or do anything. Stanley's men had come into the fight at last. They have red jerkins and they were easy to recognise. But they'd come in on Tudor's side and the Tudor forces and Stanley's were all clustered round hacking at something I couldn't see, but I knew what it was. I could see blood splashing up. They were like hounds worrying a quarry. Then, all of a sudden, Francis Lovell was there. He just appeared on his horse, pulled up suddenly, and said: 'You're Eynesby's lad, aren't you? By Christ, I'll rescue somebody yet!' and with that he hauled me up behind him and got us both off the field. He'd been left behind in the gallop, I think, and decided to save himself. I don't blame him, there was nothing anyone could have done, nothing. Master Lionel was in that scrimmage, Mistress, along with the King. They're both dead. But it was a splendid end; the sort of charge that minstrels make lays about. You can be very proud of your husband, Mistress Eynesby. I hope I've not distressed you too much.'

Surprisingly he had distressed me a good deal. I had hated Lionel and with good reason. He had bullied and frightened me, driven me to do desperate things and blamed me for doing them, and where was Perky Dick now? What kind of future must he face and how long a future would it be?

But I could not deny the gallantry of Lionel's passing. With King Richard, at least, he had kept faith. If I couldn't call what I felt by the name of grief, nevertheless I felt something. Admiration, perhaps, for that one aspect of Lionel, the valour and fidelity he had given his lord. And a shuddering horror for what he must have experienced in his last moments. It had been quick, Matthew had said, but there must be a gap between the moment when the axe first bites into you and the moment when you die. Terrible things must happen in that gap: mortal pain; the knowledge of being past the point of no return, as good as dead while still living.

All this, I suppose, was reflected in my face. I saw the compassion in those of Matthew and my brothers. I had wanted to talk to my brothers, to ask them how they did, renew my acquaintance with them after so many years, but I could not, not now. I wanted to be alone.

545

Aunt Eleanor, who had come with me to the guest parlour, saw my expression and stepped forward. 'Come, my daughter,' she said. 'I will take you to the church. You need to pray.'

Some weeks later my brothers returned to visit me, without Matthew, and then we did renew our acquaintance. I got them to talk to me of Perky Dick, as he was before Lionel took him away (though for his safety, I knew I dared not reveal that he was still alive). And it was then that they told me how relieved they were that after all they had not reached Bosworth in time, for it was being bruited abroad that Tudor meant to confiscate the property of those who had, and might not limit his depredations to the big land-owners either.

'Who did Master Eynesby leave his lands to, Petronel?' Tom asked. 'By rights, according to your marriage contract, Bouldershawe ought to have come to you – though taking the veil would make a difference. But whoever it is will most likely lose the inheritance now.'

'He left everything to the Church,' I said. 'I doubt if King Henry will want to start his reign by squabbling with the Church over a matter of land and money. I imagine that the bequest will be honoured.'

Later the same day, I asked to see Aunt Eleanor and was admitted to her study.

'Mother Abbess,' I said, 'my husband made a will bequeathing his lands – three manors – to the Church. In effect, I suppose that will mean the diocese of York. But Withysham has a claim to them through me, especially to the one named Bouldershawe. Under my marriage contract, as one of my brothers has just pointed out, Bouldershawe should have been left to me – which now means it should go to my nunnery. Dear Mother Abbess, if Withysham makes a claim and it is allowed, then I shall have the pleasure of bringing you not just Thornwood, but Bouldershawe as well, and maybe Silbeck and Eynesby.

The Abbey of Withysham would then be more than wealthy enough to found its daughter house, and will even have a place to put it. I should be so glad and happy, dear Aunt, if I could do this for you.'

Chapter Thirty-Nine

The Plantagenets: Richard Liveth Yet

1486 onwards

'But you gave me your word!' said Thomas Stanley, outraged.

'And you gave me yours and failed to keep it,' Margaret Beaufort replied, coldly.

'I did not!' He couldn't endure it, to be refused now. His body had thrummed, his heart sung for Margaret ever since that triumph at Bosworth. At last she would lie in his arms. 'My men struck Richard down. *My* men!'

'Yes, and you sent him word in the morning that you hadn't made up your mind.' Margaret's tone remained as icily blistering as a north-east wind. 'You waited to see who would win. You swore to support my son, not perch on the fence till it was clear that supporting him was safe. You failed me, I say. Our marriage contract stands as it always has. I shall devote myself henceforth to the support and furtherance of my son King Henry and my future daughter-in-law Elizabeth of York and their children. I expect to find them more worthy of trust than I have found you.'

'You and your son! I had a son to consider as well!'

'I'm sure he's grateful. You were as ready to betray him as to betray Henry, were you not? I hear he threatened to take his own life when he learned what his father had said in that message to King Richard: "I have other sons!" I have no time, Thomas, for those who use faith to God or loved ones as a flag of convenience when their real interest lies only in their own safety. If you wanted to protect your son, you should have protected him and done with it. I would respect that more.'

His bodily disappointment was so intense that he knew when he was alone, he would pound walls with clenched fists, tear things, kick things, probably end by cooling his fever with a purchased harlot. But this inhuman imitation abbess need not know it.

'I kept my word,' he said with dignity. 'Yes, I sent that message, "I have other sons." Do you think I enjoyed it? God forgive me for it; I did it for you, you with your saintly airs, your broken faith, your disdain of all that is most real in me and all that I devotedly offer you. Keep your inviolate bed and your unnatural chastity. I have no wish to lose my manhood through frostbite.'

He left without waiting to see the effect of his remarks. He hoped that just for once Margaret Beaufort had seen herself as something less than a pattern of perfect right-eousness.

But he had a strong feeling that the hope was quite forlorn.

'So you're here to bid me farewell, Dr Alcock? But you will still be on the Council, surely? You will come to court from time to time?' asked Elizabeth of York, Queen of England.

'Yes, indeed,' said Alcock. 'But I have been appointed to a new diocese, that of Ely, and I wish to get to know it. When Archbishop Morton had the bishopric of Ely he did much for the district in draining fenland and reclaiming land. I hope to match him in my own way. I propose to donate ecclesiastical buildings and perhaps found a univer-sity college, and to take a personal interest in both.'

'You are still interested in education, then,' said Elizabeth politely. She was not, he thought, herself much interested in this conversation but she might not be feeling well. The businesslike Tudor had been as efficient in bed as anywhere else. The child Elizabeth now carried had been conceived at once. Perhaps, now that the weather was so warm, it was wearying her. He wondered if she were happy. He doubted it.

He did not precisely pity her. Every parish had its share of the poor and ailing, folk who could not earn enough to feed or house or clothe themselves or their families. Elizabeth of York had palaces to live in, enough fine clothes to fill an average cottage and enough of the choicest food on the table at one sitting to satisfy one of those needy souls for a week or more. She wasn't ill-used either. Henry Tudor was almost certainly as meticulously well-mannered in private as in public.

But the coronation to which Elizabeth was entitled, as consort, had not yet been held and there was no doubt that Henry kept her out of the public eye. She gave audiences only for private or charitable purposes and no audience room was hers to use. She was giving this one enthroned amid embroidered cushions upon her canopied bed. Nor was she giving it alone. Her mother Bess Woodville and her mother-in-law Margaret Beaufort were both here, stitching as they sat together in a corner of the wide chamber. They were said – by a sentimental public – to be the best of friends. Alcock, who knew them rather better, had reason to think that beneath their queenly manners there was incomprehension, distrust and rivalry. It would be interesting to see which of them finally gained ascendancy over the other.

Or over Elizabeth, which was probably what they both wanted. No, behind the royal trappings, Elizabeth was no more than a vessel carrying the York blood through which Henry ruled (whatever he might say about right of conquest) and hoped to pass on to an heir who would unite York and Lancaster in one body. And very probably she knew it.

And he was sorry about that. Her mother Bess Woodville had enchanted him once and Elizabeth, until lately, had possessed a good measure of that same power of bewitchment. Alcock was immune to it now. He could glance across the room to where Bess was making conversation in her cool, unemphatic voice about embroidery stitches, and see only a well-preserved, middle-aged, very ordinary woman, who would have made an excellent chatelaine for a manor but had never had either the courage or the intelligence to be a genuinely good queen. He could look at Elizabeth and see in this young matron not even a shadow of the seductive young girl she had once been. But he still hadn't forgotten what it was like to be bewitched. He would have liked to see Bess and her daughter ripen more joyously than this.

He had been thinking, while he talked to Elizabeth about buildings and colleges. He finished speaking and realised that Elizabeth had not only been uninterested; she had hardly taken in anything he said at all. She was looking away from him, tracing out the embroidered pattern on a cushion with a forefinger. 'Dr Alcock . . .'

'Yes?'

'I want to ask you something,' said Elizabeth in a low voice.

'By all means.' Alcock dropped his own voice to match hers. 'What is it?'

'You know things,' said Elizabeth. 'My father always said that you made it your business to know things, you and Edward Brampton. Brampton's in Portugal, I know. He went there before Bosworth. But you're here. There's a rumour, there has been for some time, about my brothers, or one of them. That one of them is still alive. Do you know anything about it?'

Very carefully, Alcock said: 'I have heard the rumour, yes. It refers to your youngest brother, little Richard.'

'Could there be any truth in it?'

He hesitated. Then, still cautiously, he said: 'I should think it most unlikely.'

'But it could be true, couldn't it? No one ever saw them dead, that you know of, did they?'

'No, I can't say that they did. Why?' He looked at her kindly. 'Do you very much want it to be true? You must have grieved for your brothers.'

552

'I did. And I know that Buckingham claimed he had had them killed. I know that Uncle Richard believed that. But even Buckingham wasn't actually there when it was done, was he? I don't mean that I want it to be true. I'm afraid in case it is, that's all.'

'Afraid?'

'Yes, of course. I'm afraid I may one day be confronted with my brother and . . . have to deny him.'

'Oh,' said Alcock. 'Yes, I see.'

Elizabeth looked at him. 'You understand, don't you? If my brother Richard walked through that door now, alive, I would have to say to him, go away, you're dead, stay safe in your grave. If you insist on coming out of it, I can't protect you. What else could I say? I'm the Queen. To marry me, King Henry legitimised me by Act of Parliament. If one of my brothers were still alive, the same Act would legitimise him too. And where would my husband be then? Or any son of ours?'

She put a hand on her distended stomach as she spoke. Then she smiled. It was partly a maternal smile but it was also proud. 'This may be England's prince,' she said. 'Here, under my palm. If I stood face to face with my brothers now, I should say that they were not my brothers, that they were strangers, imposters. But I don't want to have to do that.' The smile faded. 'When I think of that, I become afraid.'

'At the present time it's unwise for you to brood on such things. Have you told King Henry of your fears?'

'No.'

'I think you should. He will be able to guard you from them. If . . . if anyone ever comes forward, claiming to be your brother, the King can see that you are not confronted with him. Ask him to do that, he'll appreciate your loyalty. It impresses me, I must say. You have an excellent understanding of your duty. Your father taught you wisely. Don't think I don't realise how torn you must feel.'

'It wasn't my father,' said Elizabeth surprisingly. 'It was King Richard who told me what to do.'

He was half-way to Ely before a dreadful misgiving slid curved steel talons into his guts.

He, together with Brampton, Tyrell and Lionel Eynesby, had laid a false trail in an attempt to discourage Tudor and deprive him of support. They had used a real boy, a real Plantagenet, a natural descendant of the Duke of York, for the purpose.

The ploy had failed, but what had happened to that boy? Alcock remembered he had been Eynesby's – well, stepson. Alcock had been sorry to hear it. He had met Mistress Eynesby, been instrumental in sending her to Calais, and excellently well pleased with her efforts there on the King's behalf. It had been very saddening to learn how she had deceived her husband. He remembered thinking: oh well, they all prove imperfect in the end. First Bess Woodville, now Petronel Eynesby.

But Lionel Eynesby had apparently acknowledged the boy. Yet now, although Eynesby was dead, his stepson was not master of his lands. Mistress Petronel was in a Sussex abbey called Withysham and there was an acrimonious lawsuit in progress over whether Withysham or the diocese of York should have the Eynesby estate. The Archbishop of York was annoyed about it and all the prelates on the Council knew the details, because he kept on indignantly telling them.

Brampton and Tyrell were both alive and overseas. Was it possible . . .?

It was all too possible. There always had been something ruthless about the quiet Tyrell, and Brampton, who was so loyal to the house of York, had southern European notions of loyalty. He was capable of going to extremes, believing that his honour demanded it.

They and Eynesby might even have had something of the sort in mind from the start. Or why had it mattered that the boy was a Plantagenet? Any lad with fair hair and a reasonable accent would have done for a mere decoy.

They all prove imperfect in the end. Bess Woodville. Petronel Eynesby. John Alcock.

He had taken such pride in his ability to be subtle, had so regrettably enjoyed intrigue. He had enjoyed it so much that again and again he had ignored the warnings from that other side of his nature, which had told him that he was engaged in a questionable business and would have been better off staying in York or Hull as a dominie.

He looked back and was filled with aversion, hating the John Alcock he had allowed himself to be. It seemed to him now that all his life he had been nothing but a mischievous dabbler in the lives and affairs of others, a spider-creature, using gold to tempt the incautious into his perilous web. But Peter the Pardoner and others, who like him had been casualties, had at least been adult, had had some say in their own fate.

No more of that, John Alcock, he said to himself. From now on he would devote himself to his diocese, to building churches, founding a college, taking an interest in the school he had already launched at Hull to replace the struggling establishment which had had to pass him on to St Mary's. He would cease to resent the fact that Henry had taken the Chancellorship from him and given it to Morton. And if anything happened, he would keep his mouth shut. His old master Stillington had shown what trouble could come from revealing knowledge of long-dead scandals. If this Plantagenet boy reappeared, alleging that he was Richard of York, matters must take their course without comment from John Alcock.

After all, he didn't actually *know* anything. He hadn't seen the bodies of the princes. Elizabeth was right there: no one had. He hadn't even known the younger boy well, he wouldn't be able to tell if a pretender were genuine or not.

He wouldn't give much for a pretender's chances of survival, though, not against Tudor.

He rode on, trying not to think about it, trying to ignore the clutch of a terrible foreknowledge.

He strove instead to concentrate on his school at Hull, and the college he hoped to found, and the wide horizons of opportunity he hoped that they would open over the years for hundreds of young men. Perhaps that would make up for the innocent he had so abominably betrayed, the boy he had helped to send to be distorted – without any choice in the matter – into an identity not his own, and to die in the end upon the scaffold.

It was Abbess Eleanor's desire to found a daughter house which finally led the Ecclesiastical Commissioners to their decision. Not only Bouldershawe, but Eynesby too should go to Withysham. Silbeck alone was granted to the diocese of York and even then, Withysham was to have the option of leasing it back. The abbey could now afford that with ease and took the option up. With the three properties which had been in dispute, together with Thornwood which had been in its hands already, Withysham became possessed of a very respectable parcel of land in the county of Yorkshire.

The Priory of Eynesby came into being three years later. John, the former steward of Eynesby house, and his wife Chrissy had already taken over Silbeck as rent-paying tenants, and the former Eynesby servants had been gradually dispersed, most of them to the other houses. The only exception was Ralph the cook, who was summarily dismissed.

The house at Eynesby was easily adapted as a small priory. Even the chapel, to begin with, sufficed for worship. Later, a bigger church and a new wing for the house might be added, but there was no immediate haste.

Under the management of Prioress Petronella, as she was known in religion, having taken the name of Saint Petronella, the Eynesby lands and sheep flocks flourished. Of course, she was well equipped for her task. She had been Mistress Petronel of Eynesby and she knew as much about rearing sheep and selling wool as any shepherd or wool merchant. She knew the local people too. Indeed, as prioress she soon came to know the tenants of Thornwood far better than when she had been their landlord in her own right.

It must seem strange to her, people said, to come back to her former home and live there in a fashion so altered. Indeed, she admitted to Mistress Chrissy that at first she hadn't wanted to come and would rather have stayed in Sussex, with Abbess Eleanor. But, she added then, the appointment was an honour, and now that she was here she found the work of establishing the priory a great joy to her. 'There are compensations, you know,' she said, 'in living in a place with memories, even if not all the memories are happy. The unhappy ones begin to slip away after a time. In the end, I think I shall be left with only the good ones.'

This remark was very much in character, for although she was so efficient, she was tender of heart and humble. As prioress she could have laid claim to a sizeable room for herself, and furnished it well. Instead she chose a tiny room high up under the roof and slept there on an old truckle bed which had been there already when she and her six nuns arrived from Withysham.

When she had lived in the world as Mistress Eynesby she had known some of the great families of the land, and she would sometimes admit that she had never quite been able to set aside her interest in public affairs. In the 1490s, when a young pretender called Perkin Warbeck appeared and claimed to be Richard of York, the younger son of Edward the Fourth, she followed his fortunes closely. Indeed, she exhibited anxiety about the risk he ran, saying that he was very young to be in such danger of death. When he was executed in 1499, it was thought to be on his account that she ordered a Mass to be said for the soul of an unnamed young man who had died untimely. This was considered to be another example of her tender-heartedness.

She fell seriously ill shortly after that, but even then refused to be moved from her bare little room under the roof.

She recovered, although it was noticeable that from then

557

on she seemed markedly older. The following year the building of a new church and an extension to the house was put in hand. When the extension was finished, her nuns urged her to use one of the rooms in it, saying that her upstairs cell was too chilly a place for her.

But she would not. She slept there every night, for another twenty years, until her death.

Author's Note

John Alcock has been curiously neglected by the historians concerned with Richard the Third and the Princes in the Tower. Even Audrey Williamson, who has pointed out the remarkable respectability of those who remained steadily loyal to Richard, regardless of the rumours about his nephews' fate, and who listed a number of them, did not include Alcock's name.

But John Alcock, as well as being a bishop, a highly regarded civil servant and a man whose integrity was never questioned either during his lifetime or after it, was also the tutor of the elder prince, Edward. In all probability he carried out much of this task in person. He was deeply interested in education as a subject, and the instruction of a Prince of Wales was at once a great responsibility and a great challenge. It was not a matter for delegation to subordinates – certainly not as the boy grew older.

What little is known of the young prince suggests that his education was a success and this in turn points to a good relationship between pupil and teacher. What little is known about Alcock suggests a warm-hearted man who would be likely to develop an affection for his young charge. At the very least, a strong personal interest in the boy would seem natural.

I find it inconceivable that when the rumours that Richard had murdered his nephews reached Alcock's ears (and in spite of Josephine Tey, there *were* rumours), he did not try to discover the truth. If so, he must have arrived at some conclusion. Even if his enquiries were merely stonewalled, that would have amounted to evidence of Richard's guilt.

Granted, there was little he could actually have done. A fifteenth-century king could not be brought to book for such a crime unless those who wished to do so led an uprising. Alcock was a responsible civil servant of a country which had already, in his lifetime, seen far too much of civil war, and might well have considered such a course unthinkable. (Although Alcock was in the party which Richard intercepted at Stony Stratford, he was not arrested as being concerned in the attempted coup; it looks as though those who knew him simply took it for granted that he was law-abiding.) But it is very hard to imagine how, under the circumstances, he could have borne close association with Richard and he did have open to him the private sanction which businessmen and politicians have used down the ages. On finding themselves on a board of directors or in an administration whose behaviour they can't condone, they resign.

Alcock could have done this. He had a brilliant and satisfying career behind him, and he was Bishop of Worcester. He could have withdrawn from the Council and devoted himself to his diocese, while retaining a large part of his status and authority as well as his own integrity.

What he actually did was continue to work serenely beside Richard and in due course become his Chancellor. There is no sign that Alcock (or indeed any of his respectable fellow-bishops on the Council) even quarrelled privately with Richard. So what really happened? We do not know, but the indications are that Richard's Council did – and were satisfied with what they knew. It looks, in fact, as though they knew that Richard was not guilty but for some reason found the whole matter too embarrassing for a public statement.

My book is fiction. I have romanced shamelessly about the origins of Perkin Warbeck (who was probably a natural son of Edward IV) and I have similarly romanced about

560

Alcock's connection with espionage. There is no evidence that he was ever involved with such a thing, but the responsible positions he held must have brought him into a degree of contact with it. Although Henry the Seventh is generally credited with inventing the secret service, Edward the Fourth did possess an intelligence service of sorts and perhaps my imaginative flights here can be justified.

But I am certainly sure that Alcock knew more than he ever told to anyone. When I picture him, I see a dignified bishop in robes and mitre. He has an intelligent, kindly face and the well-kept hands of a man who prefers intellectual to manual toil. And one carefully scrubbed forefinger is resting alongside his nose.

A selection of bestsellers from Headline

FICTION

SUCCESSION	Andrew MacAllan	£4.50 ☐
DECLARED DEAD	John Francome &	
	James MacGregor	£3.50 ☐
WINNERS	Penelope Karageorge	£3.99 ☐
BRIDIE	Christine Thomas	£3.50 ☐
THE BROTHERS OF		
GWYNEDD QUARTET	Edith Pargeter	£6.95 ☐
DAUGHTER OF LIR	Diana Norman	£3.99 ☐

NON-FICTION

IT'S ONLY A MOVIE, INGRID	Alexander Walker	£4.99 ☐
THE NEW MURDERERS'	J H H Gaute &	
WHO'S WHO	Robin Odell	£4.99 ☐

SCIENCE FICTION AND FANTASY

SLAVES OF THE VOLCANO		
GOD		
Cineverse Cycle Book 1	Craig Shaw Gardner	£2.99 ☐
THE ARGONAUT AFFAIR		
Time Wars VII	Simon Hawke	£2.99 ☐
THE CRYSTAL SWORD	Adrienne	
	Martine-Barnes	£3.99 ☐
DRUID'S BLOOD	Esther Friesner	£3.50 ☐

All Headline books are available at your local bookshop or newsagent, or can be ordered direct from the publisher. Just tick the titles you want and fill in the form below. Prices and availability subject to change without notice.

Headline Book Publishing PLC, Cash Sales Department, PO Box 11, Falmouth, Cornwall, TR10 9EN, England.

Please enclose a cheque or postal order to the value of the cover price and allow the following for postage and packing:
UK: 60p for the first book, 25p for the second book and 15p for each additional book ordered up to a maximum charge of £1.90
BFPO: 60p for the first book, 25p for the second book and 15p per copy for the next seven books, thereafter 9p per book
OVERSEAS & EIRE: £1.25 for the first book, 75p for the second book and 28p for each subsequent book.

Name ....

Address ....

....

....